The Arrow Chest

The Arrow Chest

By Robert Parry

To Ruby

Copyright © Robert Parry 2011
ISBN-10: 1452801142
ISBN-13: 978-1452801148

All rights reserved. Except for the quotation of short passages for the purposes of commentary or review, no part of this publication may be reproduced, stored in a retrieval system or transmitted in any form, electronic, mechanical or otherwise without the prior permission of the author and publisher.

Cover illustration: 'Daphne' by Amos Roselli

- Contents -

1	Tower Green, London 1876	1
2	Maid of All Work	13
3	A Story Told in a Garden	29
4	Rivals in a Brightly Lit Room	47
5	Séance	60
6	Entry in a Journal	77
7	Solent Crossing	83
8	Portrait and a Conversation	95
9	A Secret Caress	109
10	Dreams and an Invitation	124
11	Motif of Roses	133
12	The Gable Hood	150
13	A Thing of Beauty	168
14	A Crescent of Green Lawn	182
15	Laurel and a Cuirass	203
16	Cigars and Brandy	220
17	A Mysterious Book of Verse	234
18	Now Cease, my Lute	252
19	The Magician	273
20	Window onto a Fabled World	295
21	Restoration	314
22	Wild Garlic	322

'I know only this, that our earliest love is an experience that must shape us in a way which is quite unique. It has become clear to me now, that in my blind ambition and greed I have made a terrible mistake. I should be the most happy of creatures, and yet have become the most wretched - the key to my heart, the means to my salvation, clasped within the hand of a tyrant. I have done everything possible, tried so hard not to love you, but have failed. It is useless pretending otherwise. And now I must face the consequences. I know now that I shall love you, and only you for the rest of my life and neither age, nor time nor the vagaries of fortune shall make wanton with my determination never to forget you.'

From an inscription written in the margins of a book of verse, once owned by Lady Bowlend, and in response to which, over a number of years, the painter Amos Roselli, compiled the following extravagant and implausible story:

Chapter One

Tower Green, London, 1876

'Mister Roselli?'

The lantern held aloft with its meagre glow hardly cuts the fog that makes it seem like night upon the river, as along the cobbled pavements of the Inner Ward the gentleman approaches. He is dressed formally in top hat and tailcoat. 'So good of you to come!' he adds.

'You must be Doctor Murry?' Amos responds by way of greeting, aware that his voice is trembling. Will he really be able to go through with this?

'Correct,' the older man states in a crisp, officious tone and, after the briefest of handshakes, turns to lead his guest along the narrow lane of flint and limestone walls towards the hallowed building - merely glancing back over his shoulder from time to time as he goes and adding, with the typical black humour of the medical profession, 'A rather special lady awaits you, if you care to step this way.'

'Indeed, if what you suggested in your letter can be verified,' Amos begins again.

'Oh it's her all right,' Doctor Murry interrupts, still walking with brisk and echoing steps towards the Chapel doorway. 'The wood of the arrow chest that served as the coffin has long since decayed, of course, but the skeleton remains – or most of it.'

'Most of it?'

'The skull is separated by some distance and rather

fragmented, as you will see, though I have distinguished it from the others.'

'The others?'

This was getting worse and worse.

'Oh yes – the workmen have unearthed dozens of them. All victims of summary justice in former times.'

With his large leather portfolio containing his sketchpad and artist's materials clutched to his side, Amos Roselli turns up the collar of his topcoat, not entirely sure whether it is the cold or his own inner chill of terror that urges him to do so. He has been the recipient of some bizarre commissions in his time – but never anything quite like this.

The Chapel of Saint Peter ad Vincula with its great Tudor windows that seem to occupy almost every available inch of its south-facing wall is familiar to him as a tourist visiting The Tower, though he has never ventured inside until now as, together, the two men enter through its surprisingly small doorway - the all-invasive, penetrating fog of the city seeming to accompany them. Inside, all is silent, pungent with incense and the smell of mould and damp – but also with the distinct, musty odour of freshly dug earth.

'I did consider asking you to bring along one of those newfangled *camera* things,' Doctor Murry says, availing himself of a pair of pince-nez spectacles and fixing them to the bridge of his nose with a nervous little wriggling movement, 'but given the brief time available I concluded that a good artist's eye, pencil and paper would prove to be the most practical. Would you agree? The light is very poor. Not easy to find your way in, let alone get around.'

'To be entirely truthful with you, Doctor Murry, I think at this moment I am more concerned with being able to find my way *out*, if need be,' Amos states, setting aside his top hat and feeling that the scarlet of his own cravat might be the only remaining trace of colour left in the entire world - and even that becoming drained of its pigmentation in the all-pervasive gloom. He is aware of an echo to his own voice in the empty building.

'Over here you will discover the positioning of the bones, and their condition,' the doctor continues, and not responding much to the younger man's attempt at levity as he hands him the lantern and with steadying hand motions him towards an area close to the aisle of the chapel where all across the floor leading up and into the chancel a considerable number of ancient flagstones have been lifted to reveal the yellowish-brown London clay beneath. It is clearly an extensive and major renovation of the entire chapel area that is being undertaken. All the wooden pews that would normally have been ranged in the centre of the nave have been stacked against the north wall, leaving just one abandoned haphazardly in the centre for use by the workmen, and upon which the Doctor himself takes a seat as Amos, lantern in hand, crouches above the bare earth at the foot of the chancel and looks down.

'You will notice some decayed fragments of elm wood interspersed with the bones,' the doctor continues pointing in the general direction with his cane. 'As you can see, the skeleton is perfectly consolidated and symmetrical, well formed. The bones of the skull would indicate a well-proportioned oval face, a high intellectual forehead – oh yes, and a large orbital ridge and socket. She would have had large eyes, probably quite remarkable eyes. Well shaped hands and feet, too, with long, tapering fingers. A fine young woman.'

'Any evidence of that notorious sixth finger?' Amos inquires, still holding the lantern over the earth and its scattering of white bones.

'Ha! Ruddy nonsense! Do you imagine for one moment that Henry the Eighth would have settled for a wife with six fingers? Propaganda, my boy – spread by her enemies, of which the unfortunate Boleyn woman had quite a few.'

'Really? I don't know an awful lot about it, to be perfectly honest.'

'No matter. All we require from you, young man, is a record of the find,' the doctor states while getting to his feet to fetch some candles from the altar and which he brings over to assist in the task. 'The workmen insist that all these *rotten old bones*, as they call them, must be moved away by tomorrow and placed somewhere else. A few sketches will have to suffice. And now, alas, I must be off to meet the wife. A social engagement at the Mercer's Hall, you understand ...'

'What, you don't mean you're going to leave me here - alone?' Amos demands feeling a sense of panic.

'Why you're not afraid of the dead are you, my boy?' the distinguished doctor teases him. 'Tell you what, I'll ask one of the Yeoman Warders if he could come over to keep you company. How's that?'

'That would be most welcome,' Amos responds. 'And a further lantern of some sort would also be convenient, if he could bring one.'

The doctor nods his understanding – for the already gloomy afternoon is fast turning to the early dusk of an Autumnal evening.

Once alone, Amos unpacks the contents of the slim leather case containing the tools of his trade, including sketchpad, pencils and a small canvas campstool with metal frame, which he unfurls and sets down by the exposed soil. Then with the large pad of cartridge paper perched on his knee, he sets to work with a fine pencil - drawing and recording as intricately as he can in the poor light the remarkable discoveries that have been unearthed just these last few days. According to the newspapers, the bodies of three females have been found in this particular area, two belonging to young women whose ages were less than twenty years and therefore, in the view of the historians, most likely those of Katherine Howard and Lady Jane Grey. The body that has commanded the most interest, however, is undoubtedly this one: the three-hundred year-old skeleton of an older woman, probably in her early thirties, and almost certainly, therefore, that of the second and by far the most notorious and maligned of all of Henry VIII's unfortunate wives: Anne Boleyn.

Staring down at the eerie collection of scattered remains, he tries to imagine the person they would have once belonged to. The famous painting in the National Portrait Gallery is familiar, of course. As a student visiting he has looked upon it many times in passing – and has even been fortunate enough to have seen the magnificent Holbein sketch purported to be the only genuine likeness made of her in her lifetime. A longish face, the high forehead framed by the dark hair, and those large black eyes with the slightly amused, slightly mocking look, shrewd, educated – and in truth probably far too clever for her own good in an age where women were not supposed to be too clever at anything at all. Yet, surely no one deserved a fate such as hers! With a macabre interest he searches for the vertebrae of the neck. But these are hard to detect. Only the rib cage, thoracic spine and scapulae are obvious – and then, some distance away, the skull bones. How many pieces would it be in now, that neck? he wonders, becoming lost in concentration.

Just then, however, his attentions are diverted. Footsteps are heard outside, approaching – marching towards the Chapel in heavy boots, and leading Amos to the happy conclusion that this would surely be the Yeoman Warder sent to keep him company. Thank God! And yet he seems to be taking an inordinate length of time to arrive! The loud, robust footsteps approach, then stop, then come on a bit more, only to pause again, shuffling about: and still always remaining outside.

'What the hell is going on out there?' He mutters to himself and, unable to contain his curiosity any longer, and with his sketchpad under-arm, walks to the doorway.

Indeed, a Yeoman Warder in his dark blue uniform with its distinctive scarlet trimmings is there outside, a lantern that he has brought with him set down on the ground at his feet. He is not exactly on guard, however, but is instead leaning up against the wall and smoking a pipe – an object that he deftly and swiftly conceals with an artful swivel of the palm the moment he catches sight of Amos at the door, his other hand waving away any traces of smoke – an instinctive movement of one skilled in hiding his little vices from public view, Amos reflects, as he shares a smile with the good gentleman and thereby disarms the situation somewhat.

'Don't worry, your secret is safe with me,' Amos jests. 'But please do come in, Sir. Anyone with the breath of the living would be most agreeable companionship in this place.'

And so it is, with a slightly awkward grin and a nod of gratitude, that the old fellow – and whose name, Amos learns, is Ted – removes his characteristic narrow-brimmed hat and steps inside. More lanterns are discovered and lit, and soon Amos has taken up his pencil and pad again and returned to his bones, much more clearly visible now with the additional light, while Ted himself takes a seat on the solitary pew nearby – though he will not smoke his pipe he states with firm resolve, a mark of respect - since the Chapel has always been, and still remains, a place of worship for all the inhabitants of the Tower, himself included.

'Can't be sure if these are the neck bones,' Amos remarks at one stage, prompting the gentleman to come over and glance down for a moment with a shrug of the shoulders before returning to his seat, which he is anxious to do, it seems, for he is clearly no anatomist.

'I suppose the axe would have crushed them at the moment of her execution,' Amos continues, speaking almost to himself.

'Oh no, there was no axe, Sir,' the Yeoman Warder states quite categorically, confident within himself. 'Queen Anne was beheaded by a swordsman sent over from France. A special act of mercy from the King.'

'Oh, really? Had she wanted it that way?'

'Oh yes, and the King duly obliged. Very good of him, that, don't you think?'

'Very generous!' Amos observes sharing in the old boy's irony as the later continues to make himself comfortable on the solitary pew by putting his feet up on a nearby toolbox.

'Bit of an artist are you, Sir?' he inquires, somewhat irreverently, Amos thinks.

'Yes, that's right. This is not my usual subject matter, of course. But, to be frank, one simply has to take the work as it comes.'

Amos is aware of the other man's eyes upon him, scrutinising his relatively flamboyant appearance. He would be looking at Amos's long curly hair touching his shoulders, aware of his meticulously trimmed half-beard with its pointed tip, he would have noted his unusually colourful cravat and waistcoat and chequered trousers - all conspiring against him and all serving to advertise his eccentricity – *a bit of an artist*, to be sure, conspicuous in this age of dull uniformity, of almost permanent mourning in sympathy with the widowed Queen. For it was a sad fact that ever since the death of Prince Albert the entire nation has been plunged into a continuous state of grieving. Victoria herself wears nothing but black these days and will probably continue to do so from here until eternity - her preferred jewellery all of *jet* or fine black glass - and to some extent everyone is expected, almost by royal decree, to follow suit.

'Not one of them kids, then, with all the money - what do they call themselves, the Raffle-lights or something?'

'The Pre-Raphaelites, you mean? No. I'm not, unfortunately numbered among them,' Amos replies with a smile, thinking of the long-disbanded brotherhood and beginning to warm to the old fellow despite his direct manner. 'But I am hoping to become an Academician shortly.'

The old fellow's face is an interesting one, Amos reflects as he pauses in his work and glances over his shoulder at the man, still seated there on the solitary pew behind him - quite an old-fashioned countenance, as well, with his turned-up handlebar moustache and bushy sideburns, and it betrays what is no doubt a genuine sorrow for the disruption to the Chapel and all its noble inhabitants - a fine old fellow, and Amos would far rather be doing a sketch of him this evening than what he has to render at present. Yes, he would be a military man, like all the Beefeaters here, someone of long service, familiar with The Tower, its ways of governance, past and present, and would probably view an intruder such as himself with more than a little suspicion; a rebel of sorts. *A bit of an artist.*

'You are aware of the illustrious lady and her story, I take it?' the Warder inquires, and when Amos replies that no, not really, that he does not know too much about Tudor times at all, the old fellow begins to put him right and to lay open its mysteries.

'One of the worst miscarriages of justice ever to have occurred within these walls,' he begins with a rueful shaking of the head as Amos turns back to his work. 'Oh yes, there were many poor souls dispatched by that cruel tyrant, Henry. Folks say he was a great king. But that's rubbish. At the start he might have been, but power corrupts, see. And Queen Anne - well she was just tossed aside when she couldn't produce the necessary male heir. They accused her of all kinds of things to get rid of her – treason, witchcraft, adultery, even incest with her own brother. Not a shred of evidence for any of it that would stand up in a court of law today – not any that has survived, at any rate. Trumped up charges! Why, they say that King Henry ordered up the executioner to be bought over from France even before the trial had begun! Disgraceful!'

'How long was she married to the King?' Amos inquires, now genuinely engrossed in his drawing and not bothering much to turn to the other man any longer – content, in fact, to let him chunter on and get whatever he wanted to say off his chest. It was comforting, moreover, having that other voice in the room. He wanted him to go on talking.

'Married little more than three short years,' he grumbles, 'though Henry was courting her for over twice that length of time, they reckon. But she wasn't interested. She had seen the corrupting ways of court life in France where she had been sent for much of her education, and when she came back as a handsome young woman, studied and clever, her sister had already become the mistress of the King – and that, by all accounts, had shocked and appalled her. Though don't get me wrong, Anne was no candidate for the nunnery. No, she'd have had her sweethearts – several gallant young noblemen there were who vied for her hand, but the King warned them off, see. Thomas Wyatt the poet – he and Anne, they were childhood sweethearts - known each other all their lives. She was his inspiration, they say. But the King soon put a stop to all that. And Henry was not the kind of man you argued with, see. He'd have you pulled to pieces on the rack for your trouble – or hung in chains above the river yonder 'til you rotted. No Anne was in his sights, like a creature hunted with arrows, and there was not much she or anyone else could do to put a stop to it. Oh, she tried to stay away from court, tried to avoid the king's attentions, but it was of no use. In the end it was all too tempting for the family. Imagine the pride, the advantages, the wealth that a catch like that would bring with it. Anne's fate was sealed.

'She made a brave end, though. One of the shortest and yet most excellent speeches from the scaffold ever made by man or woman, they say. The Frenchman took off her head with a single stroke. And what then? How do you reckon she was treated, her poor body thereafter – the woman for whom a king had once given his blessing to a whole new Faith in our land, a Reformation that defied the Pope himself? Why, they put her in an old arrow chest - that is a large box used for bow staves as well as for arrows - not of great length, in fact, though long enough, I suppose, for one who has no head. Meanwhile, the poor head itself, upon which a king of England had once lavished his kisses, was placed alongside her in the same box. They put it beneath the floor here and forgot about her. Terrible. Though if you reckon that was the end of the matter, or of the lady Anne, you would be mistaken. No, not at all for those of us who have served and worked here over the centuries. Her unquiet spirit has always continued to walk within The Tower precincts and is experienced often by reliable witnesses. Sometimes it's just a sound that you get, a rapping noise, or a cry. Sometimes it's a definite shape that you see, like the figure of a woman - as plain to behold as you are to me sitting there drawing her bones.

'Listen, I'll tell you a story, and it's as true a tale as you'll ever hear. It was not that long ago when one of our number was on sentry duty one evening close to the Queen's Lodgings yonder. It was late, and the place was more or less deserted, apart from him, the guardsman, poor soul – because then out of nowhere she came – softly, an apparition, a kind of white mist, he said - shaped like a woman in an old-fashioned gown and as she came close he could see she was wearing a queer-looking bonnet, too - not like the ladies have these days - and that there was nothing inside the bonnet, either, no face at all.'

Amos feels the hair standing up on the back of his neck as the story is related.

'*Who goes there!*' the old man shouts suddenly very loudly by way of continuation, and at which Amos almost jumps out of his chair. A long, unruly pencil mark shoots up across a good proportion of his paper, prompting him – once his heart has calmed down – to reach for his eraser with a rueful glance back at the Warder who is, nonetheless, smiling broadly at his reaction.

'Who goes there – being the appropriate challenge, you

understand, under such circumstances.' he continues. 'But it made no difference. And as the apparition continued towards him he thrust out his bayonet. Straight into it he went – only to have something like a bolt of lightning shoot right through him, to which the poor fellow passed out on the spot. Well, being slumped up against a wall at any time is no position to be found in when you're supposed to be on guard duty. He was accused of sleeping on the job, see, or worse of being drunk in charge, a very serious offence – and was only saved from the ultimate punishment of the court-martial by the eyewitness account of another officer who upon hearing the challenge that night had rushed to a window in the Bloody Tower yonder and had seen it all take place. He said that the faceless spectre walked right through the bayonet and that the sentry, poor fellow, then collapsed. It was a terrible shock to this gentleman, by the way – and he never really recovered. Died shortly after from a heart condition.'

'God, that's astonishing, isn't it!' Amos says, shaking his head as if in amazement, though continuing to ensue any lengthy conversation – for he was still hoping to complete his labours here this evening as quickly as possible and return to the normal world.

'A most unfortunate young lady,' the old fellow mutters to himself, sounding almost tearful now, his voice. 'The flower of England, the rose of sweet youth plucked down, plucked down … ah, yes …'

Amos works on, but after a few more moments he suddenly realises that it has gone very quiet. He turns once more to search out the old fellow, but he is gone – no longer on the pew – nowhere to be seen! Amos gets to his feet and searches around the nave and aisle, but there is no sign of him. Out for a crafty smoke, eh! Amos concludes ruefully. So he goes to the door to check, but there is no sign of the old fellow outside either, no smell of tobacco as before – and not a sound in the entire empty precinct apart from the distant noises from the docks along the river and a single, penetrating screech from an owl somewhere over at Tower Hill.

Alone, Amos returns inside to his work, and quickly has the whole drawing finished. With a sense of relief, he packs up his equipment and is almost ready to depart when footsteps are heard approaching the Chapel again – two people this time – and to his surprise in comes Doctor Murry once again, this time arm-in-arm with an elderly woman in a long overcoat, with an elegant broad-rimmed hat sporting ostrich feathers and whom he introduces as his wife. They have come from the Mercer's Hall on their way home to inspect Amos's handiwork, he says. And, setting his lamp down, he takes up the sketchpad itself to examine the work more closely. Meanwhile, a little hesitantly, with caution in her high heels and lifting the train of her skirt as she goes, his wife steps over to the exposed earth and looks down, determined to examine the remains for herself – out of a certain macabre curiosity, perhaps. Her perfume brings a welcome fragrance to the background of church incense.

'Fine work, my boy,' Doctor Murry declares holding the sketchpad at arms length for a moment before handing it back to the artist with a nod of approval. 'I should think you could jolly well go home now, don't you!'

'Indeed, I shall,' Amos laughs. 'And gladly!'

Mrs Murry also comes over to take a look at the drawing herself. With a little glance of admiration in his direction, she, too, seems impressed.

'And you have been here all this time on your own! How awful!' she says with a note of sympathy.

'Oh no, Madam,' Amos responds, 'your husband was kind enough to send one of the warders to keep me entertained? I must say, I'm glad …'

'Warder? What warder?' the doctor asks, looking puzzled.

'The old fellow – the Beefeater who was here.'

'Oh there was no one available,' doctor Murry replies. 'Sorry about that, young man. We did make enquiries at the barracks. But there were only three on duty and they said they couldn't spare a soul.'

'But he was here … for at least an hour, while I worked,' Amos protests, though speaking gently still. 'He sat over there – on this very pew, here, look!'

But the good doctor, glancing unproductively towards the empty bench, merely shrugs his shoulders. It is a mystery –

and so all three, Doctor Murry, his wife and Amos, wander out and along to the nearby barracks to make enquiries, to ask among the Warders there whether anybody had, indeed, come over to the Chapel earlier this evening. No, they reply, they have all been here, at their duties the whole time. There has been no one else. Could Amos perhaps describe the man in question? - to which he does, and with the utmost urgency, feeling suddenly most disturbed. He even does a quick thumbnail sketch on the margin of their duty roster to indicate the gentleman's distinctive appearance.

'He said his name was Ted, around your age, a grey beard - upturned moustache.'

At which the three warders exchange meaningful glances among themselves, and appear to be not at all pleased.

'We – er – do know the gentleman to whom you are referring, one of them states rather awkwardly. 'Ted … he is sadly no longer with us.'

'But he came in and …'

'No no, Sir, I'm afraid what you are describing is the unfortunate colleague of ours who saw the ghost of Lady Anne Boleyn one evening some years ago. He, it was, who was seen to thrust his bayonet into her apparition and fainted. He passed away quite some time ago.'

Chapter Two

Maid of all Work

'I can only say I wish you the very best of luck, young lady. You will certainly need it!' These, she recalls, were the parting words of Mrs Edwards that day as the woman packed her belongings into her portmanteau ready to leave. 'Your new employer here is a most unusual gentleman, to be sure, as you will shortly discover.'

Beth and Mrs Edwards had been alone in the sparsely furnished attic space that served as servants quarters where the newcomer had been brought following her guided tour of the home, including a resume of the numerous tasks and responsibilities that she was about to take on and which - as a 'maid of all work' - would involve the combined skills of housemaid, parlour maid, cook and chambermaid all in one: typical of what was required in homes of modest means and which, by all appearances, this particular home undoubtedly was. She had been wondering if it would all prove too much for her.

'And is there no lady wife or mistress of the house?' Beth had inquired, even then a little uneasy about the new post she had agreed to fill: the second only in her young career and straight into the home of a single and, by all accounts, rather eccentric young gentleman!

'There was a lady ... once,' Mrs Edwards had stated, 'but she left - as I am about to do and over which I shall make no further comment, accept to say, that she is by all accounts thriving and possible well out of it.'

'Really?' are they divorced, then?' Beth had inquired, feeling more and more that she might not be suitable for the work required here and that, even now, Mrs Edwards – a tall, formidable woman in a high buttoned, starched collar – might find fault with her youth and inexperience and send her away.

'They were never married,' the older woman had replied with a barely discernible shudder of disapproval rippling through her tightly laced body – and then, placing a firm hand upon Beth's shoulder, adding in a whisper: 'Young lady, you will be made painfully aware of the truth of all I have told you as you take up this position which I give to you with my blessing. This is no ordinary household. Mister Roselli has very little income, and even less in terms of prospects. He is a good man – but an artist. There are all sorts of strange young women that come and go. And heaven only knows where his brains are most of the time!'

'Emm!' Beth sighs in a quite involuntary manner as she sits here this afternoon in her apron, her mop cap and her dull, somewhat tattered working clothes, alone in the house one whole year later, and still with the portentous words of Mrs Edwards ringing in her ears, recalling all those dire warnings of the departing predecessor. That last statement about the whereabouts of Mr Roselli's brains, is something with which she can certainly concur, she thinks, as she takes a well-earned break for five minutes upon one of the more comfortable chairs in the parlour – though why all this should come to mind at just this moment, she cannot explain. Perhaps, she fancies, it would be something to do with the anniversary, or so she regards it, that fateful day a year ago when she had first come into service here at the narrow, cramped little terrace house in Mornington Terrace and into the home of the not-so-famous painter, and not-so-successful man about town Amos Roselli. One whole year ago! Where has all that time gone!

With still so many chores to attend to this afternoon, with so many arduous duties still to perform, she knows she must rouse herself to action. But it's no good. Feeling suddenly quite exhausted and also somewhat faint from hunger, she takes herself downstairs to the pantry, instead. But there is not much here in the dingy little rooms below street level that might revive her other than a little hard cheese and a stale end of a loaf that has certainly seen better days – none of which, she reflects, would probably be missed if it were to disappear. So she eats it – and, taking a seat once again, this time in the adjacent kitchen, even puts her feet up on a stool, not caring one bit about ever being discovered in such an idle state because that, in any case, would be extremely unlikely in this desolate and lonely place. Any other position in any other household in London, she knows from conversing with other girls in service, and there would always be company, always some other human being to talk to or with whom she might occasionally share a grumble or a joke; there would always be perks to the job, too - always ample food and leftovers from grand meals. But here Mister Roselli would rarely if ever take a meal at home or even ask for one to be prepared, but would instead invariably dine out at his club or somewhere in the West End. Apart from his artist's studio on the first floor, his home was a place that he merely visited from time to time rather than a place to be lived in or appreciated in any domestic sense, and heaven only knows what time of night he would return sometimes! Often, she would rise at six-thirty in the morning as her duties demanded, to light the fires, fetch water from the yard – and then in he would come, only just returning home, all dishevelled and clearly the worse for a night out with all his rowdy artist friends. He would stagger past her at such times straight into the nearest armchair and pass out. The other night he even came home with his sketchpad under his arm looking as if he had seen a ghost, all pale and trembling. What on earth would he have been up to? she asks herself - and at which thought, the harsh voice of Mrs Edwards comes into her head yet again with another of her dire warnings: 'He will return home at all hours, and expect you to be there for his breakfast when he wakes up – usually sometime in the afternoon. The effect this will have upon your daily routine and commitments you can only hazard to guess at this stage. You will need the patience of a saint.'

Yes ... prophetic words, to be sure, Beth thinks to herself

again as she urges herself back to her labours for the afternoon, and in preparation for which she removes her old round-rimmed spectacles, without which she can hardly distinguish a face at more than a few paces, and attempts to clean them as best she can. But they are so ancient and badly scratched that they are really becoming next to useless. Nor do they much improve her appearance when she wears them. She realises this all to well, as she stands on tip-toe to examine her young but disappointingly plain and undistinguished features in the hall mirror as she passes: the reddish hair, clipped into place beneath her white mop cap, the snub nose and those rather fulsome lips that she so hates about herself. Will she ever grow out of it, she wonders? People say you do, that as you approach seventeen or eighteen years your features develop and you lose that typical, chubby-faced look of childhood. But even though her body is lean and thin there are no signs of this metamorphosis occurring just yet. Sometimes it all seems so hopeless – the prospect of anyone ever taking a shine to her, as had happened to Mrs Edwards, of course, now a married woman with a home and servants of her own, they say. And what, she wonders, would she ever do if those spectacles were to break? She could never in a thousand years be able to save enough on her current meagre salary to buy new ones.

For the next hour, and fighting back the occasional tear, she attends to the laundry and does some ironing of sheets, and then busies herself with the bringing in of coals and the making up of the main fire again: hard, back-breaking work as ever. She is not tall, in fact quite diminutive of figure still and – again - can only hope that she has a few years more of growing ahead of her, because the worst of it here is the sheer size of the range that she must work on, so high above the ground that when she brings a large saucepan of any kind to the boil she needs to employ a wooden platform to stand upon in order to look down safely over the brim. Meanwhile, stepladders must be used to reach all but the lowest of the shelves or to dust or fetch plates from the tops of cupboards. The whole place appears sometimes to have been designed and constructed by a race of giants – leaving her with a daily routine which would be considered too much for an army of servants, let alone just one tiny, hungry young girl, so that not for the first time this afternoon is she compelled to contemplate her future. The entire situation is in every respect dire and it is, she suspects, surely time now to hand in her notice and seek pastures new - a suspicion confirmed a moment later as with a loud slam of the front door Master Roselli himself returns home, hurrying up the newly scrubbed tiles of the hallway in his muddy boots, discarding his wet top hat on the table and rushing past her like a whirlwind, the tails of his coat and wayward tresses of black curly hair flying out in all directions as he goes, and with little by way of acknowledgement of her presence or of the warm welcome she has prepared for him. Instead, he hastens straight up to the first floor and to his studio merely calling over his shoulder for some strong tea as he goes. That clinches it for her. She will confront him now, tell him. She is going to leave.

'Ah Beth, you're an angel. Thank you,' he declares as she enters a few minutes later with the pot of tea, milk and sugar all neatly presented on a silver tray. 'Look, what do you think of her?'

Amos is pointing to a canvas he has been working on for several weeks now. She has seen it before, of course – often when dusting the studio or cleaning up various empty wine bottles or absinthe glasses. An elaborate scene from some ancient mythology, it shows one particularly beautiful female in the foreground accompanied by several half-naked young women in various poses of seductive engagement – typical of what he was always producing - and usually, as now, with a single fortunate young man dressed in chain mail or armour of some sort placed in their midst. All very meaningful and symbolic of something or other, she thinks as, wholly overawed by the prospect of having to voice an opinion (he has never asked her before about any of his paintings) she wipes her hands upon her apron and walks over to the precious object itself, which is clamped still within the tall uprights of its easel.

'It is - er - very modern, I should say, Sir,' Beth answers tactfully, aware that her employer tends like many young men of his social set to idolise the current fashions in art which she has heard described as being somewhat melodramatic and serious.

'Rather *Burne-Jones-like*, the colouring, don't you think?' he suggests, evoking the name of one of the more popular painters of the day. 'And what about the seductive young nymph located here to the right? Rather like Leighton's, eh? - or a touch of the *Holman Hunts?*'

'Why yes Sir, if you say so, Beth answers meekly. 'I don't really know ...'

'Of course, I'm sorry, Beth. I suppose you wouldn't have had too much opportunity to visit galleries, would you? But you are aware of the reproductions, the posters and the magazines with paintings in them?'

'Oh yes Sir ... and your work does remind me of those - truly. They *are* all the rage now, aren't they, these kinds of paintings?'

'Yes, and that's the trouble, Beth,' he agrees with a note of untypical despondency to his voice. 'They are all the rage. It has all been done before, in other words. Everything I do has been done before, and miles better than ever I could aspire too. I am beginning to realise that now. The train has left the station, Beth, figuratively speaking, and I have not been aboard. And I cannot mitigate my failure as an artist anymore with so much as a shred of genuine originality. There is no hope for me, Beth. No hope at all. Anyway, is there anything to eat in the house, I'm starving!'

'No Sir,' Beth replies firmly, 'there is nothing. And, as a matter of fact, without any allowance to buy provisions there is also little to be gained by my going to the market with an empty purse.'

'But can't you get credit? I mean, most of the shopkeepers round here will give you credit. Just mention my name ...'

'I do indeed, Sir, mention you name - but this of late only serves to make it less likely that we shall ever receive credit. I don't know why, but ...'

'Yes, well, all right,' Amos interrupts swiftly. 'There would be good reason, no doubt, for that,' he adds waving the embarrassing matter aside - and upon which he takes out his wallet and searches within its numerous vacant folds and partitions before announcing, 'Ah, look Beth! Here is a ten shillings note. I knew I had one in here somewhere. Go and fetch some food - because I will be eating here at home this evening, and you shall cook something on the lines of - er - shall we say lamb chops and potatoes, how's that? And a little glass of spring water, too, will do nicely. No wine. I have to be sober - I mean, *at my most lucid and alert* in the morning because I have received an important commission. Yes, that's right - I'll be going to an estate in the country, tomorrow, for the whole weekend, in fact, to paint the portrait of one of the landed gentry. What do you reckon on that! Not exactly the most profound or spiritually uplifting of work, I suppose, painting some overbearing toff in a frock coat, but one commission of this kind soon leads to another, and then another. Soon I shall be successful - not perhaps exactly in the way I would have wanted, but at least it should pay the bills. Why, we might even be able to employ another girl to help you, a scullery maid or something.'

This is excellent news, of course - particularly the part about bringing in some help. Beth nods and smiles. She has never seen him so enthusiastic about his prospects. And with a little giggle of merriment and unfamiliar happiness, a feeling that she cannot rightly explain, she puts on her bonnet, grabs a shawl to wrap around her shoulders and hurries off to the market with the ten shilling note - and quickly, before he can call her back or change his mind.

In the high street where the busy stalls of fishmongers and grocers line the curbs outside of the fashionable shops and arcades and where already the profusion of gas lights fill the foggy air with their own distinctive, nebulous glow, she encounters none other than Mrs Edwards again, the very same lady she had been thinking of today, she who had handed over the house keys to her one whole year ago and who had warned her in such harsh tones about her future under the employ of Mr Roselli.

'Young Beth - well, well!' the older woman exclaims, quite pleased to see her. How nice!

Having already bought those items that she needs, Beth walks with her for a while, exchanging gossip - pausing, too, from time to time outside the various shop windows to admire the view - the dressmakers especially where several of the very latest fashions are proudly on display, fashions that proclaim the most radical shift in the silhouette of the female figure in a good many years, namely the transformation from the cumbersome bustles and gathered skirts of old, to sleek, sensuous tight-bodiced waistlines, with narrow sleeves and sheer, clinging fabrics wrapping the hips and thighs before finally bubbling out just above the knees in glorious ankle-length folds and flounces. The ubiquitous bustle, in other words, has died – or if not exactly died then has at least gone into a state of exile for the time being, giving way to fabulous one-piece dresses without any waist seam at all and thus showing the entire curvaceous female form in all its glory.

'Outrageous!' Mrs Edwards declares, her own prominent, heavily padded bustle thrust almost up into the sky behind her and suddenly appearing to Beth to be from some bygone age of formality and stuffiness. 'Who on earth would ever buy such things? And where would anyone ever wear them!'

'They are quite interesting, though, Ma'am – for formal occasions,' Beth ventures to argue, wrapping her shawl even further about her shoulders as if to conceal her own poor cambric dress with its patched sleeves.

She loves the latest fashions. But this is not the full extent of the delights on view, for alongside the sheath dresses, as they are sometimes called, are to be seen those of the even more radical *anti-fashion*, the fabulous gowns inspired by the various arts and crafts movements of the day – loose, uncorseted, free-flowing lines that Beth adores perhaps more than anything else – the gorgeous hand-dyed fabrics, the intricate embroidery and exotic brocades all of nature's own beautiful colours and textures; like something magical from bygone times.

'Oh, how wonderful!' she sighs. 'I do so wish that I was tall and comely and that someone would lend me such a garment if only for an hour!'

'Well, that's not going to happen!' Mrs Edwards says as with an urgent and insistent tug of the arm she steers Beth away from the unrealistic temptations set before her – almost as if from a dream and back into the harsh reality of her noisy surroundings. 'They're not for the likes of us!' she adds as they begin walking again, the great vista of elegance and beauty that Beth had glimpsed a moment ago suddenly vanished, all contracted once again into the dull, grubby streets in which she finds herself with all their foul smells, coarseness and squalor. 'Anyway, tell me now - how is your life with Mr Roselli these days?' Mrs Edwards asks abruptly. 'Are you contented?'

'Oh well, as contented as one might be in such circumstances, yes Ma'am,' Beth answers with diffidence as they continue to negotiate the crowded pavements, and aware with a sense of surprise that this was not at all how she had been feeling a little earlier - this afternoon, when she had been so desperate and tearful. What ever could have happened to change things, she wonders?

'Really!' Mrs Edwards responds with perhaps just a trace of disappointment to her voice. '*I see,*' she adds with special emphasis.

What on earth did she mean by that?' Beth asks herself, anxious. Mrs Edwards has been fortunate, of course; she has found a respectable husband - a man who has taken her out of service, rescued her at a young age before her vitality and usefulness, and therefore her wages, would have started to decline. She has a child now, Beth has heard, and staff of her own: an admirable lady. And then, as they continue their walk, she turns to Beth and makes her an astonishing offer, namely a position working in her own household if she would like to consider it.

'Oh, Mrs Edwards, that is very kind!' Beth exclaims, not quite knowing whether she feels flattered or apprehensive.

'How much is Mister Roselli paying you?' she inquires, perhaps sensing the younger woman's ambivalence.

'If it please you, Ma'am eight pounds per annum, living in.'

'Eight pounds! Disgraceful! That's even less than I was earning over a year ago. He doesn't even have the goodness to pay you a decent wage, that's plain to see.'

'I believe his circumstances might be about to alter, though' Beth argues. 'His poor father is unwell, I understand,

and when he passes away, Mr Roselli will inherit a considerable sum, and also property.'

'Nonsense! Who told you that?' Mrs Edwards demands.

'If it please you, Ma'am, Mr Roselli did himself. Though I think he had been drinking at the time and perhaps ...'

'Balderdash and piffle!' Mrs Edwards interrupts. 'He has no prospects of that kind – none at all. A keen imagination, yes – I'll grant you that. He has imagination in abundance. But imagination does not put food on the table, or clothes on your back. I'll pay you eleven pounds and ten shillings per annum, young lady, plus all your lodgings and food.'

Beth confesses that she is very flattered and will certainly bear it in mind, she says. But she also reminds the older woman that she is settled for now. She tells her, too, that Mister Roselli has often honoured her with conversation, and even asked her for an opinion today on something to do with his work.

'Conversation! Opinion!' Mrs Edwards exclaims, halting on the spot in the street and looking poor Beth up and down in a most critical and sensorial way. She seems particularly tall at just that moment, Beth thinks as she stares up into her large, somewhat bovine face. 'You watch your step, young lady!' she adds waving a menacing finger in Beth's direction. 'In my experience there's only one reason why a gentleman employer would become interested in conversation with a menial – and that is for a reason that will land you in trouble, and tarnish your reputation soon enough. Why else do you think a man like that would be interested in you - plain little thing that you are? Or do you see yourself on the arm of the handsome young artist? Do not be deceived. They're all rogues, all of them. Your loyalty is misplaced, Beth, and will be betrayed soon enough.'

Beth is appalled that she should speak to her like this. So upsetting, too, being reminded of her plainness.

'Ma'am, there will surely always be those who will betray our loyalty. Only I don't suppose we should stop being loyal just because of that, do you?'

'Oh, fine words, young lady! But make no mistake: no matter how virtuous you strive to be, you will be sucked in; bit by bit, you will be drawn into his dissolute life, and then you will be lost. You'll finish up on the streets with a starving baby to feed. Is that what you want?'

Beth shakes her head vigorously by way of denial. She knows, too, that Mister Roselli is an honourable man. And feeling quite tearful by now at all these constant reprimands, she longs to find an excuses now to get away. But that is not to be, not just yet.

'Remember, young lady,' Mrs Edwards continues, turning to face Beth once more, 'there are rules by which those in service must be governed – and they are there for a good purpose. Never forget them. Familiarity of the kind you have just mentioned, or familiarity of *any* kind is not something you should ever encourage. Why, a servant of your rank should not even make an observation on the weather, let alone offer her opinion on anything of importance! Carry out your duties in silence, young lady. And if you should ever encounter your employer accidentally as you go about your work - on the stairs or in the parlour, for example - always turn your face away or avert your eyes. Same goes when visitors come to call. Unless it's to deliver a message or to ask a necessary question, you should refrain from talking to any lady or gentleman of quality – and then to confine your comments to as few words as possible. And whatever you do, don't go responding to salutations - a *Good Morning*, for example – unless it is with the briefest of nods. Especially never respond to a *Good Night*! Goodness only knows where that might lead! Never use your hands when speaking. Never argue or dispute anything that is told to you - and never, *never*, converse with your employer about his business affairs. Finally, if you are obliged to accompany your employer out of doors at any time, remember to always walk some distance behind. In other words you should exercise temperance at all times. The rest is simply a matter of working hard and getting on in life, as I have done. You would do well to remember what I have told you, young lady. And so good day to you!'

'Thank you, good day Ma'am,' Beth responds, picking up her shopping bags to set off home – and which she does at quite a pace.

Upon her return, much later than intended as a

consequence of Mrs Edwards's homily, Beth quickly dons her apron and cap and prepares the meal Mr Roselli has asked for, the lamb chops with some potatoes; she even finds some sprigs of rosemary from the yard for flavouring, and all this she places in the oven before hurrying upstairs to determine whether there might be anything further wanted of her. Her employer is still in his studio – a place that has suddenly become very untidy, with a considerable number of sketches laid out on the tables and several unframed canvases propped up against every available chair or table leg and taking up almost every available inch of floor space as a consequence. They are all studies of what appears, even to her untrained eye, to be the same subject: a slim, dark and stunningly beautiful female similar to the one that he showed her earlier.

'Oh good! I'm glad you're back, Beth. Look – what do you think of some of these?' he asks, standing in the midst of it all, hands on hips. 'Just give me you honest, uneducated opinion – just as it comes to you. I'm sick and tired of listening to all the pompous art critics and the so-called experts. You tell me what *you* think …'

'Of the lady, Sir, or of the work.'

'Well … both, *both*.'

'She is very lovely, Sir.'

'Yes … and?'

'Anyone you know, Sir?'

'Well yes, as a matter of fact, I do know her – or used to at any rate. I might even be bumping into her this weekend. You see, this young woman has been a friend of mine ever since childhood. I have painted her and drawn her likeness a thousand times. She has been my muse.'

Beth nods and keeps silent, not quite certain in her mind regarding what 'a muse' might be, and also recalling the words of Mrs Edwards: that it would not be her place to engage the Master of the house in conversation. He seems to be somewhat peeved at this obvious reticence on her part, however, and bids her take a seat, which she does a little reluctantly, sitting very upright and tense on the end of the chaise longue, the only available spot not covered by some painting or drawing of his beloved lady.

'We grew up together in the country, you see,' he continues somewhat wistfully threading his way over to the window and then back again where he picks out one of the sketches and holds it in his hand. 'Our families owned land so close to one another and so near to the local rivers that it was a regular thing for us just to take a row boat and visit each other. Our schools were some distance apart, unfortunately, and both were boarding establishments, so there were big gaps in the calendar when we would be parted. But in the summer we would both be home and then ... why we would be inseparable. We would spend our time on the river in that old row-boat, or in the orchards in springtime, strolling together for hours amid all the butterflies and the bluebells and all the cherry blossom, or sometimes in late summer with the ripe apples from the trees which would crunch beneath our feet as we walked - always arm in arm like the closest of lovers – only we were *never* lovers. No - not at all. Hard to believe, as I look back on it, and that anybody could resist my charms, but it's true. My friends used to tease me something rotten about it – that I would have this stunner of a girl on my arm most every day, and yet never became anything more, never a fiancé, never a wife. I suppose it's difficult to have known someone as a child and then to think of them in anything other than in a sisterly sort of way, don't you think? Anyway, almost always when we met I would make sure I had something to record her likeness - always a sketch pad, a stick of charcoal or a box of coloured chalks for drawing. And then sometimes she would sit for me at her home while I worked in oils. Up until last year she was a regular visitor here to my studios. She has featured in almost every successful painting I have ever finished or sold. What you see here, everything, is all drawn from her likeness, from girlhood to womanhood – from the tender age of ten or eleven right through to her late twenties when I last saw her.'

Beth remains silent, unsure of how to respond - until he prompts her with a little nod of the head and to which she inquires, 'And where exactly might the lady be now, Sir?'

'Now? Oh well, she's moved on to better things, Beth. No need to model for an artist, these days. She's become a married lady, as a matter of fact, and done rather well for herself.'

'And are you pleased, then, that she has found happiness at last, with someone who can be a lover?' Beth inquires with amazing boldness, realising with pleasure that she is defying Mrs Edwards with every breath, and also sensing that her spectacles are beginning to steam up somewhat.

'Why ... yes, of course. And even if I wasn't, I would only have myself to blame – because the gentleman in question first encountered my lovely muse here one morning in this very room - a certain Lord Oliver Ramsey of Bowlend who arrived to discuss a commission for a portrait for himself and was so smitten with my Daphne that it marked the start of a whirlwind relationship that culminated in the noble Lord divorcing his wife – they were already separated - and, in a very short space of time tying the knot with Daphne herself. Ha! I seem to recall we were working on a mythological theme at the time ... yes, let me see, this one here: a painting in which I represented her as the sorceress Circe, poisoning the waters. Well, the waters were certainly poisoned for me that day, when Lord Bowlend snatched her up.'

'You must have been very uncertain about what to do, Sir, when that happened.'

'Oh, well, he's a very powerful man, you understand, a millionaire several times over. Not the kind of person you stand in the way of. I do miss her, though. She was my most cherished source of inspiration. But then, let's be honest, what did I have to offer her by comparison! Look at me, Beth – look at where I live! This kind of life. It's humble - you realise that - very humble in comparison to what he could provide. Anyway, this, I'll have you know, is the very fellow I am due to visit this weekend - to embark upon his portrait, at last – the very one that he came here to organise all that time ago. And even though it could prove painful if I encounter my lovely Daphne and see her on his arm ... well, it really is an opportunity too good to pass up, don't you think.'

'Do you mean the opportunity of the portrait, Sir, or that of meeting your dear friend again?' Beth inquires, by this time completely oblivious to the consequences.

He looks into her face for a moment as if surprised. How perceptive of her, he thinks! But there is no time to dwell on such wonders – for just then, almost simultaneously, they both catch the smell, the unmistakable and altogether dreadful aroma of burning food emanating from the kitchen downstairs.

'*The chops!*' Beth screams, and in a second is up and out of the door, her little feet clattering down the wooden stairs towards the kitchen, and he in hot pursuit. Here, amid Beth's cries and occasional curses, he drags the burnt offerings from the oven and hurls them into the sink where, encountering a little puddle of water therein, they let off a gigantic hiss and cloud of steam that quickly fills the entire room. Clambering up onto her stool, meanwhile, Beth opens the window, and soon all is clear – apart from her eyes, which are, he is distressed to see, full of tears and self-recrimination.

'Oh well … not to worry, Beth. My fault, you know,' he states, his hands thrust into his pockets and keeping his distance from her, not quite knowing what to do. 'Perhaps I'd better dine out this evening after all, eh? Set out clothes for me for tomorrow – something for the country, and my best accessories, cravat and cufflinks and so on – you know the kind of thing. I will return shortly because I must catch the train from Waterloo at nine.'

And with that, Amos puts on his overcoat and hat and is gone, leaving her alone amid the carnage.

The lamb chops appear, on inspection, not too bad – burnt, yes, but only on the exterior. And so with a little artful trimming with a sharp knife they become quite edible – or edible enough for one who is so hungry. He is not to know, anyway, she tells herself. He does not see her, and will be none the wiser; so she even cooks up a few more potatoes as well – and very nice they are too! Of course, he also does not see how a little later that evening, still hard at work, and after scouring the oven and cleaning the sink, she goes up to his rooms and prepares his clothes for the journey tomorrow. He does not see how she carefully folds his shirts and places them into a suit case, or how she almost tenderly takes a selection of his finest embroidered waistcoats in her hands and sets them out upon the table in his bedroom, ready for him to choose one tomorrow. He does not see how she takes an iron to his collars and handkerchiefs, and places them lovingly into his wardrobe, each to their appointed compartment labelled with a little silver plaque set into the wood. He does not see any of this, but she does not care. He has told her his story and asked her what she thought of his work. And she knows now that she is not going to be leaving him after all, not now, not ever.

Chapter Three

A Story told in a Garden

The men are marching back from the shoot, their dogs at heel, their guns under-arm, glancing with silent disdain at Amos who has at just that moment alighted from his carriage close to the portico and is supervising the unloading of his luggage. The group of tweed-coated gentlemen accompanied by their loaders and beaters regard the flamboyant newcomer in his top hat, his long, cutaway morning coat, his portable artist's easel, folded and placed on the ground nearby, with a blend of suspicion and silent amusement as they walk past, slightly threatening in their studied indifference before dispersing to go their separate ways – the estate workers off down the drive to their own homes, the gentlemen themselves – all affluent guests for a shooting weekend it would seem by their appearance - vanishing somewhere into a side wing of the mighty building.

This is the country estate of Bowlend Court and is to be Amos's temporary residence for the next few days - a vast and sprawling edifice set amid the wooded hills of the Kent-Sussex border, a building so theatrical in its design, so perpendicular and towering in its lines that it would have been constructed, Amos surmises with his critical eye, not in some bygone age of knights and ladies – as it pretends to suggest - but in fact quite recently in the extravagant and overblown Revived Gothic style so popular these days. Tall, mullioned windows with pointed arches and turrets soar above him, capped with steep gables or improbable crennelations like some extraordinary throw-back to vanished times, yet with everything exaggerated, everything larger than life: whimsical and totally bizarre.

'Now don't forget,' Amos whispers to James his borrowed valet for the weekend and who has accompanied him on his journey from London, 'do not under any circumstances let it be known that you are not my full-time employee. You and I both know that I'm as poor as a church mouse, but these good people here must not suspect anything of the kind, understand?'

'I do understand, Sir, perfectly,' James replies, his large, drooping eyes – which always remind Amos of a not very animated basset hound – looking out at him, worldly-wise as he delivers a barely discernible though possibly slightly contemptuous bow by way of compliance.

James is not his real name, of course. But it remains a worthy enough appellation for the good gentleman who has been purloined from one of Amos's better-off artist friends expressly for the purpose of impressing his hosts on this his brief but hopefully profitable sojourn into the countryside among all the good and the great of the English aristocracy. How will he fare, he wonders? Would he be found out? Would they discover that he is really an impostor, that he is nowhere near as successful an artist as he has led them to believe? Would Daphne, Lady Bowlend be here? He feels a peculiar tremble of excitement in his stomach and also – paradoxically – a sense of dread that he might encounter her. How much would she have altered? Would she even bother one jot about his presence now she has become such a celebrated fixture of high society?

He wanders back again towards the portico with its balustraded stairs, it tall arches framed by rose hips of eglantine and crimson virginia creeper – and then suddenly there she is, standing in the great doorway, leaning against the porch in a lovely high-waisted gown – and surely striking a pose of some affectation expressly for his benefit, as if modelling for him already. It makes him smile at first, and then it makes him laugh – because she is teasing him just like she always did, and suddenly all his cares and misgivings have vanished.

'You are as lovely as ever!' he says, removing his hat and bounding up the steps. 'And just as mad!'

'Careful Amos, you must not embrace me this time!' she warns him as her eyes widen in that typically vivacious way of hers, black, penetrating eyes. No, she hasn't changed a bit, he thinks. Beautiful, haughty and yet somehow playful all at the same time. Resisting the intimate kiss that they would normally share, he accepts her ungloved hand and places this to his lips instead.

'Gerald and Mopsy are to join us this weekend,' she announces softly, almost a whisper, referring to her brother and his wife – and so putting him at ease straight away. 'So you'll have people around that you know,' she adds - while at the same time reaching behind with a lovely twisting movement of her slender waist to seek out a remnant of a flower - for in the past they would invariably exchange tokens of flowers upon meeting - though in this instance locating only a bright scarlet rose hip for his lapel. Her gesture, however, does serve the purpose of bringing her lovely face close to his as she weaves the stem into his coat. Feeling exceptionally happy to be with her again, after so long, he waits, therefore, without need for words, allowing her time to adjust to the emotion of being together once again, her hands upon his chest, lightly touching as she attaches the token.

'It must be at least a year,' she murmurs, referring to the hiatus in their friendship that has occurred since her engagement and subsequent marriage.

'At least – no, probably longer!' he says, also speaking softly.

'It seems much more, yes,' she agrees. 'Too great a time, at any rate. I am so excited that you have been asked.'

The opulence of that hand as it attends to his lapel almost bowls him over for a moment. Apart from her substantial wedding band, she has a large emerald ring on her middle finger, set in an exquisitely worked scroll. There is a bracelet of gold upon her wrist, and a twist of gold in her hair, as well - all bound up into an elegant chignon. And then he notices a tiny speck of blood upon her finger, pierced by a thorn from the rose, perhaps. 'Your finger,' he says, touching her hand for a moment, at which she raises her finger to her lips and, with hardly a movement of her mouth, sips the scarlet drop away - looking into his eyes all the while. The subtle language of the flower, the message of the eglantine is conveyed, therefore: 'I wound to heal.' And he has never seen her look so lovely, their faces so close together, her other hand still upon his lapel.

But then suddenly the magic is broken. A harsh male voice cuts the silence:

'Ah, ha! Our young Adonis has arrived, I see!'

The commanding figure of Lord Bowlend has appeared, almost from nowhere it seems - and with firm, deliberate strides now mounts the steps towards them.

'Eager to be at it?' he adds, clasping the younger man's hand in his and shaking it with tremendous vigour as he casts a disapproving sideways glance at his wife - by way of commentary on her frivolous greeting, no doubt. Having clearly just returned from an afternoon's shooting, he is dressed in woollen breeches and a hunting jacket, the coarse, tweedy fabric redolent of the woods and smelling of game - and on one of his sleeves are to be seen the distinctive stains of some kind of dried gore.

'Good afternoon, Lord Bowlend,' Amos declares. 'So good to see you again.'

'Oliver - call me Oliver,' he says.

Tall, well-met, verging on portly, with sturdy limbs, a rather square face and fleshy jowls, it is still just possible, Amos thinks, to detect the fine figure of a man who was once a royal guardsman. But he has certainly increased in girth since the last time he encountered him, and his appearance is a little untidy today, moreover, disappointingly so in terms of personal grooming - a shadow of a beard forming at this late hour on his large, double chin, his brown reddish hair, greying at the temples and slightly too long for its lack of volume, so that it all looks somewhat thin, with traces of baldness showing through.

Signalling to one of his men to assist Amos with his luggage he places a firm hand on the younger man's shoulder and says, 'I will show you to your room, Amos. I'll be shooting all day tomorrow, trying to beat my own record – need to bag at least seventy-four birds - and I'll be buggered by the end of that, y'know. So you and I need to mull over tactics straight away, if you don't mind - what kind of backdrop you envisage for the picture and so on. Myself, I favour a pastoral setting – but, I suppose, you might have other plans.'

'No, not at all. Whatever you say, Sir – I mean, er, Oliver,' Amos replies as, realising with regret that they are leaving Daphne behind, and catching for just one fleeting moment a look of concern and anxiety in her eyes as she watches him go, he allows his host to conduct him at a fast pace through and into the vast gothic-style atrium with its tall vaulted ceiling. He has just the briefest of opportunities to look around and admire the sheer size and opulence of it all – the whole place built on proceeds from the ever-lucrative armaments industry - before they ascend the broad iron staircase, cast in iron but painted to look like carved oak, then upwards past the many portraits of ancestors real or imagined that grace the walls – to eventually reach the guest room allotted for him down a long, well-lit corridor on the first floor. It is a comfortable chamber, well-appointed with a four poster bed and all modern facilities, gas lighting and water closet included and which, he is reliably informed by his host, is named 'the Cupid room' - due no doubt to various murals and paintings depicting the little rascal himself that line the walls, all of which are rather badly painted, Amos reflects, along with several lavish but equally tasteless renderings in marble or Minton china.

'By the way,' Ramsey begins again, once the footman has deposited Amos's case and left the room, speaking loudly in the same resonant booming voice as before, 'you will forgive me that we were unable to invite you to the marriage ceremony last summer. As we chose to put the whole campaign into operation in Scotland, I felt – I mean, we felt that the journey would inconvenience many of our friends. You do understand?'

Amos nods graciously. He is, of course, fully aware of why he was not invited to the wedding. He was simply not the right sort, not of the right class. The marriage in Scotland was also an excuse for yet another hunting trip, apparently, or so he had heard – deer shooting in the Highlands. Nice way to spend your honeymoon!

'Seventy-four birds – is that possible?' Amos inquires, feigning interest and endeavouring to revive the previous topic of conversation.

'Oh yes, I'll have a man loading for me – handing me the guns each time. Just hope this old shoulder of mine holds out. Could be nasty otherwise.'

To which Ramsey pulls back his right shoulder so suddenly and so violently by way of demonstrating the recoil of a gun, that it makes Amos jump with surprise, his feet not quiet leaving the ground, but almost – and upon which the noble lord takes out a monocle from his waistcoat pocket and places into position with a curious little screwing motion before remarking: 'Why, you're a sensitive little chappy, aren't you, Amos! Perhaps you should join us on the shoot tomorrow? Toughen you up a bit, eh?' he concludes, his pinched, monocled eye set in its large expanse of face regarding the highly-strung artistic temperament there before him with an obvious suspicion and distaste.

'Oh, no thank you, Sir,' Amos replies, aware that he will need to tread lightly here and not let his feelings show. 'In the time available, I feel I should rather acquaint myself with the items to include in your portrait: whatever formal robes or medals you suggest, and perhaps take photographs or run off some charcoal studies. Shooting or hunting – to be frank, it's all a bit alien to me.'

But his reticence is clearly not to the liking of his bumptious and overbearing host.

'More interested in hunting the ladies, eh?' the noble lord suggests, almost demands – having cast Amos in the role of the young dilettante already, it seems – like a dramatist who writes the script for everyone else in his life.

'*Chasing* perhaps, but never hunting,' Amos responds with modesty and an attempt at manly camaraderie and wondering just where all this might be leading. But abruptly Lord Bowlend appears to lose all interest in him. With the briefest of glances of acknowledgement towards James who is waiting patiently at the doorway with more of Amos's belongings, he turns and walks quickly from the room, merely turning for one brief moment to announce over his shoulder: 'Dinner, by the way, is generally at seven on a Friday evening. White tie.'

Discovering a decanter of sherry and glasses on the sideboard, Amos imbibes straight away – anything to steady his nerves. Yes, of course - why hadn't he seen it before! A bully and a braggart of the first rank, Ramsey would be suspicious of any sensitivity, any vestige of creative or poetic temperament in others – something he would probably regard as a sign of weakness: unmanly. And Amos catches himself wondering whether he will be able to stomach being in his company for a whole weekend, let alone painting his likeness in oils. James, meanwhile, hovering in silence nearby, is observing him with some impatience, his big sorrowful basset eyes raised in a gesture of enquiry.

'Will that be all, Sir?' he finally asks, clearly wishing to be gone - no doubt below-stairs to dine with the resident servants.

'Return to me in precisely one hour and thirty minutes prior to dinner, will you my man,' Amos replies as if his newly acquired valet were the perfect slave - only to receive a withering look from the slave himself. 'And remember, *mums the word*,' he adds, one finger raised to his lips, and to which the other man responds, though not altogether with a smile then at least with a nod of reassuring complicity as he goes.

'Welcome to Bowlend Court!' Amos breathes quietly to himself once assured of being completely alone - and drains the glass.

It is morning, and the whole estate is resonant with the calling of jackdaws and ravens, heady with the cloying fragrance of over-ripe fruit and the smoke from the bonfires of old leaves recently swept by the army of gardeners forever busy about the grounds. The sun is not yet all that high in the sky as Amos and Daphne, alone for perhaps the first time since his arrival yesterday, stroll together to take in the atmosphere of what promises to be the perfect autumnal day, un-stirring, the radiant air - and ideal, therefore, for the business of shooting, as Lord Bowlend and his chums were heard to utter upon their departure this morning within a large open wagon drawn by a pair of lugubrious horses – an enormous array of gun barrels, beaters' sticks and various other paraphernalia belonging to the men bristling out from it as if it were going into the teeth of some fearsome battle instead of their way to shoot a few over-fed birds.

'What did you think of our guests at dinner yesterday?' Daphne asks him once she has shown him around the stables and her own horses – her pride and joy.

He ponders very carefully before replying, hoping too that here at last might be an opportunity to make his feelings for her known. She is looking very lovely this morning, he thinks. Adhering once more to the arts-inspired fashion for day-wear with its arcane, almost medieval style of detail and texture, she wears a velvet cape about her shoulders rather than a cumbersome shawl, a style that allows her to walk briskly at his side, her hands free - as together, in the company of two handsome and lively Springer spaniels, they stride out along a wide avenue of box and yew that leads downwards from the house towards a long, winding lake, flanked on two sides by woods of purple and golden beech. Magnificent.

As for her question: yesterday's dinner - well, it was a remarkable experience, he has to admit as he tries to picture it in his mind again - the sumptuous dining room in the soft glow of the candles and gaslight, the immaculate tables heaving under the strain of enormous china bowls, of silver plate and Waterford crystal, the seemingly endless procession of courses transported in terrines from the kitchens by an indefatigable team of waiters, the astonishing variety of tastes augmented by an endless supply of Bordeaux wines or vintage Champagne, their bottles cradled in napkins and still covered with the dust of the cellars. He pictures Daphne herself, confident and flirtatious in a black silk taffeta gown with a long train that swept the ground - her lush dark hair arranged in a nest of carefully woven braids piled high. He could also picture all too clearly the contrasting and grotesque image of Oliver Ramsey, looking more like an emperor rather than a mere peer of the realm, seated at the head of the table as if on a throne, the sturdy arms of his vast, lavishly carved oak chair, scarcely able to embrace his circumference. And then there were the other guests, a curious mixture: Daphne's brother Gerald and his absurdly named wife, Mopsy, both as out of their depth as Amos himself had felt – with Gerald being as painfully aware of the fact as the light-headed Mopsy was clearly oblivious to it. And then there were Ramsey's own guests, including two other powerful men from the armaments industry – 'cannon salesmen,' as Gerald had contemptuously described them during a moment's whispered conversation: scoundrels who swore and smoked cigars constantly and who could never really be mistaken for gentlemen. How very formal and stiff they had all appeared, trying just a little too hard to be urbane in their white scooped waistcoats and tails, their starched, upright collars – and alongside them in contrast their loquacious wives, clad in diamonds, laughing constantly and overflowing with bland society conversation. Very little in common he had with any of them; he had drunk too heavily as a consequence, and in truth could not remember very much at all about anything else.

'Yes, it was – er – all very interesting,' Amos replies with a wry smile but, mercifully does not need to elaborate further because at just that moment, not too far away and with an abrupt and incongruous dissonance, the crackle and roar of a dozen guns breaks the peaceful atmosphere of the morning – echoing off the stone walls of the house behind them and causing any number of startled birds, mostly pigeon, to take to wing from some nearby bushes. The intended quarry, meanwhile, the partridge themselves in flight, are to be seen in the distance hurtling through the sky above the tree line of beech and elm, disturbed and flushed out by the tapping and whistling of a regiment of beaters and heading towards almost certain death as volley after volley of gunfire fills the skies. The first drive of the day has commenced, the ritual that will, she tells him with a little grimace of distaste turning down the corners of her mouth, continue almost unabated for the next several hours as the men move through the woods from one stand to the next. A frenzy of killing.

'This is my world now, Amos. You realise that, don't you?' she says, throwing a stick, rather irritably he thinks, for the dogs. 'And it's not real quality you will meet with in the people here. Just *new money*. My husband is a member of the Peerage, yes – but only by virtue of services rendered, as they say – along with all the other self-made men, the railway engineers and brewers they've packed into the Lords these days. The real toffs have only contempt for them and call them *the Beerage*. The old order has crumbled, I'm afraid. All the chivalry, all the gallantry of the past will have vanished soon, even within a generation, perhaps. Ours may be the best, but it will also be the last.'

To hear Daphne speak in such an engaged and political voice is totally new to him, and he regards her for a moment in thoughtful silence before walking on, allowing her to take his arm in her old familiar way – until soon they have reached a part of the grounds that affords a spectacular view back up to the house, a position from which Amos unfolds his little artist's camp-stool and sits himself down to work – she observing him from a wooden bench nearby as he begins to sketch some scenic material that might serve as a background to the portrait of her husband. The sun is gaining strength now and it feels pleasantly warm as he becomes completely engrossed in his self-appointed task, pleased to be here, pleased with himself and his own dapper appearance, his best morning suit with its braided trim, his scarlet cravat. Most important of all, he is pleased to be with Daphne – completely at one with her as always when in her presence.

Feeling that a photograph or two later might be more in order for recording the background, he is quickly finished with his sketch, and so transfers his attention to his beloved former model instead, bringing his seat closer to her so he may capture her likeness in quick, accomplished sweeps of his charcoal upon the pad as he has surely done countless times before but which has been a pleasure so cruelly denied to him of late.

How elegant she looks, the shapes and textures of her sumptuous attire amid the gold and crimson foliage of the garden! Her gloved hands, her silk hat with its broad rim, its plumes and feathers, and from which wayward strands of hair spill forth, framing her high cheekbones and the graceful, unbroken curve of her jaw. So familiar, that long and slender neck, those dark, perfectly arched eyebrows - the eyes themselves with their long lashes almost jet black even out here in the daylight - and exceptionally large, too, for the size of her face with its narrow, slightly pointed chin. Beautiful! He simply adores drawing her.

'Ah, this is just like old times, isn't it!' he remarks, smiling, full of simple enjoyment in the work.

'Oh, well not quite - because you are not telling me a story yet,' she argues, thrusting her chin skywards to best display her profile for him, knowing instinctively what type of pose he wants from her.

'A story?'

'Yes, don't you remember? Whenever we used to work together, you would always tell me all about whoever I was meant to be - all those wonderful and improbable mythologies from olden times. At one stage, I would be Circe, the next I would become Ophelia. I used to so delight in those stories, even though they were sometimes frightfully gruesome.'

'Well, I am sketching you as yourself today. So perhaps it is *you* who must organise the story this time.'

'Me!' She exclaims with an all too obvious mock modesty. She has a tendency to purse her lips and dilate her eyes when amused or expressing approval, something which can, and often is, misconstrued as being slightly flirtatious. Women find it disconcerting. The men, of course, love it.

'Yes, that's right,' he insists, endeavouring to remain unimpressed. 'Tell me the tale of the newly made-up Lady Bowlend.'

'Heavens, dear one, I should say you know it already well enough!' she protests, a little more hesitant now.

'Yes - but it will be different now. You will view it all in a new light now you are married, don't you think?'

'Oh yes, I suppose so. Would you really like that, dear one? Would it amuse you?'

He nods his encouragement, all the while scarcely looking down to his work but instead observing her all the time, creating the image of her as if by magic beneath his hand as it hovers in rapid little movements across the surface of the paper.

'I'm afraid Lady Bowlend's story does not have a terribly spectacular start,' Daphne begins at length as if referring to someone else. 'Her childhood was spent in quite an ordinary way, with two siblings, a suitably strict but caring father and a perfectly loving mother. Father was *something in the city*, and mother had been a singer prior to her marriage. They were comfortably off without being well-to-do, and they owned a small farm. Their family home was beautiful, therefore, and full of music and song. It was surrounded by gardens and orchards, and close enough to the lovely market town of Maidstone that she and her sister could walk to it and back again in an afternoon. There was an old pony named Gertrude which she would ride at astonishingly slow speed up and down the lane, and there were chickens in a little coup behind the barn where a enormous saddle-back pig was invariably also to be found in residence, being fattened up and over which the children were not encouraged to become too sentimental – for it would always be destined to provide bacon for most of the following year. Oh, and one day the goat devoured all the washing. Items were removed bit by bit from the line by the shameless creature and eaten on the spot – upon which the poor animal was chased down the road by mother brandishing a large garden implement of some description.'

Amos smiles as he works. It is perfectly lovely listening to her story.

'School was a terrible jolt for the young Daphne,' she goes on. 'To be sent away from such an idyllic world to a place with so many harsh regulations and unfamiliar customs. But she adapted, I am pleased to report, and became a celebrated model student.'

She breaks off at that point, catching a look of some scepticism in Amos's eye. 'Oh well, perhaps that's not entirely accurate,' she adds. 'In fact, she did achieve some notoriety at one stage, I suppose, for leading a rebellion of girls who insisted on staying up far later than they should in order to read outrageously slushy novelettes to one another by candlelight in the dormitory. And, having developed a somewhat infamous and displeasing ability to mimic the voice and accent of just about anybody she took a disliking to, she got into serious trouble one morning while taking off the teacher in front of the class, only to discover that same teacher had entered the room and had over-heard everything. Expulsion was on the cards, and only narrowly averted by some timely parental intervention.'

'Just a minute,' Amos interrupts at last. 'What about that good looking and talented young boy who used to live in the big house nearby? You haven't mentioned him at all yet.'

Daphne raises a palm as if to silence him and continues with, 'Wait, I am coming to that, because as you so rightly say, and for as long as she can remember, the young man you speak of has been a part of her life. Oh look – he is sitting there in front of her now - with a pencil or crayon or some such object in his hand, which is how she sometimes believes he lives almost every hour of every day. Holidays at home from boarding school were spent largely in his company. And even when she grew up, and as the age at which she must be chaperoned came upon her, still she would sneak away to be with him, and would find herself in mighty deep trouble with her parents as a consequence – until it was forbad that she should ever see him again. But no matter. For it was then that all her foreign adventures began, in any case – adventures that took her even further afield, to Switzerland this time and to the finishing school for young ladies at the foot of the mountains they call the Alps. The weather was cold, and the sun seemed to be constantly shining somewhere else, beyond the mountains that cast their shadow over the village almost from dawn until dusk in the winter, and not much more than that during the summer. Deportment and conversation were studied with some success while the ministrations of ever-tighter corsetry reduced her waist one inch at a time until at the end of the first year it was a breathtaking, *literally breathtaking* eighteen inches in girth - with most of her abdominal organs forced upwards to a place somewhere just beneath the level of her chin. Literature, poetry and painting in watercolours remained unperfected, meanwhile, as did the craft of dressmaking – while, in truth, she and the other girls really applied themselves to learning the art of flirtation as much as anything else – most of it wishful thinking because there was little by way of opportunity to put any of it into practice. Oh, and she also became proficient in the arcane and mysterious art of reading the Tarot cards - since she and her companions were forever looking into the future to discover what tall handsome stranger might be lying in wait. After this, there came several months in residence with a delightful family nearby, learning languages, growing up, becoming a lady, in fact, so that consequently young Daphne became quite fluent in French and German at one stage - though she admits to having probably forgotten the greater part of it all by now. Soon she was brought back to England for the purpose of finding a suitable husband, but things did not quite go according to plan because I'm afraid she became a bit of a rebel and begun associating with all the wrong sorts of people, including artists and poets. She became an artist's model at one stage, and is now immortalised in countless drawings and paintings by none other than yourself. You and she were inseparable at one time, I believe. Oh, but of course all that ended one fateful day when a certain gentleman recently elevated to the peerage came to the artist's studio to discuss a commission. He discovered the young Daphne - and thereafter pursued her relentlessly with invitations to the theatre and gifts of flowers and beautiful jewels. She was horrified at first, since there was an obvious age difference between them, and the gentleman in question was also not terribly subtle in his wooing. But eventually she succumbed, tempted by the obvious inducements of a life of utter luxury and merriment. Eventually young Daphne did get her man, therefore, and a catch far greater than her dear parents could ever have imagined in their wildest of dreams. She has become Lady Bowlend, and married to her dearest Polly, as she calls him – Oliver Ramsey, to most people - and one of the most powerful men in the land. In case you have not noticed, she lives here, my dear, with another beautiful home on the Isle of Wight where she expects shortly to be hobnobbing with royalty at Osborne. And you should count yourself very fortunate, I should say, to have her all to yourself this morning, and for so long.'

He laughs, delighted with her story. 'Indeed, I am,' he concurs, putting the finishing flourishes to his sketch. 'And I hope it is an experience that might be repeated now that ...'

'Oh, don't be so confident, dear one,' she sighs, and for a moment she appears uncommonly serious, her brows furrowed and her eyes downcast. 'I am a busy lady, I'll have you know. Oh yes, I am much in demand and occupied with all manner of important and stimulating duties.'

'Really?' he murmurs, not really discouraged, for he knows her when she is being ironic.

'Oh yes. I must attend to all manner of vitally important duties. I must open church bazaars and garden fetes, must organise the staff at home – to tell the head butler when to speak with the head gardener, and then tell the head gardener when he should visit the head cook. I must ensure that there are always sufficient scones and jam for tea whenever a visiting cricket team comes to our local ground and where I am to engage in endless prattle with women of such intelligence that they regard even the slightest reference to anything remotely aesthetic with a horrified blend of confusion and panic. I am almost exclusively occupied with important duties of this nature, Amos, so that all the art and science and all the exalted ideas of all the philosophers and dreamers over which you and I once discoursed are now as foreign and remote to me as good clean air in a London fog. Oh yes, you are surprised, dear one. But let me correct any misconceptions you might have regarding my existence in this paradise. My sole aim and ambition in life now is simply one of survival, to retain my sanity. And that is all.'

With astonishment, his hand no longer sketching but frozen in abeyance, Amos endeavours through his silence to bring her attention back to him so he can look into her eyes, only to discover, as she turns her face towards him, a new and unfamiliar pain, almost a startled look and then a tiny tear lingering there which she quickly dabs away with her sleeve.

'I had no idea,' he murmurs.

'No,' she says and smiles rather grimly. 'No one has any idea. And I'm afraid I have not yet told you the half of it, dear one. It is worse, far worse even than that. Being with you again like this, after so long, has made me realise that all too vividly – how very unpleasant it has all become compared to my former life.'

He is shocked. What could she mean?

'But then why go through with the marriage?' he asks, still gently. 'You must have known ...'

But she merely shakes her head, smiling as if to herself in a very untypical, self-pitying kind of way, not wanting to speak any further.

With an overcast sky that has come upon them now, its approach hardly noticed by either of them - and so chilly all of a sudden compared to when they had first set out, it is time, she suggests, to return to the house. And gladly he agrees.

Taking a different route back through a formal parterre and then alongside the red-brick walls of the estate's kitchen garden, each walking a little estranged from the other in the silence following her confession, his attention is arrested by a most peculiar piece of rock, a sculpture of some kind it seems. Well-weathered and damaged by neglect, half-buried amid tangled briars, its plinth long-since decayed or else removed to serve a better purpose elsewhere, it shows the head and upper body of a woman - her face obscured by a raised arm clutching at the folds of a cloak or shroud of some kind. Very dramatic, in fact a bit 'over the top,' he thinks, like something from a cemetery.

'What on earth's that?' he asks, and a little guffaw of laughter escapes his lips. 'It's pretty awful, isn't it.'

'Oh, that's been there for ages apparently. It's meant to be something to do with the Boleyns. At least that's what one of the gardeners told me the other day. What's the matter, dear one? You look surprised.'

Recalling his evening at The Tower not too long ago, Amos feels suddenly a sense of panic descend upon him. 'Nothing, nothing at all,' he answers. 'The Boleyns, you say?'

'Yes. Don't forget, Hever castle - it's only just down the road. They say the Lady Anne visited here, the old house before this one was built - hundreds of years ago, of course. Amos, you really do look queer. What's wrong with you?'

He feels the vitality draining from him and realises that

his skin has probably gone white judging by the look of apprehension on her face.

'Oh, nothing ... just that I had to do a drawing of her remains the other day - or *somebody's* remains anyway. Didn't you notice the story in the press?'

'Why yes, they found her bones in the Tower didn't they?'

'That's right, in the Chapel. I was called in to ... well, just a job. I don't want to talk about it, actually.'

'Heavens, why not?' she asks him, clearly amused. 'That sounds really exciting. What's wrong?'

'No - really, I don't want to talk about it. Something strange happened while I was there.'

They walk on until, bit by bit, she manages to extract the story from him of the ghostly Yeoman Warder, which he dismisses at first as a practical joke that someone must have been playing on him. It certainly seems to amuse her - bringing forth that incongruously girlish giggle of hers that she often produces when entertained or excited - almost a kind of squeal of delight and which he normally finds quite infectious. This time, though, he remains stubbornly reluctant to share in her levity, determined not to elaborate any further on his experience - at which Daphne begins to look at him with suspicion, and her eyes narrow.

'Amos, you weren't taking anything, were you? I know your crowd - what you all get up to. You all live on chloral and laudanum half the time.'

'What do you mean?' he demands, and this time it is his turn to laugh. 'Are you suggesting I'm the kind to suffer from hallucinations?'

To which Daphne merely raises an ironic eyebrow.

'Well, all right, ' he admits, we might have had a little loddy the night before, some of us, but that was well worn off by the time I got to The Tower. I had a glass of wine that afternoon, I suppose - or two - but I was in full command of my faculties. That Warder was as real to me as you are now. And I was as close to him as I am to you now.'

'Did you touch him. Ugh! It makes me shiver to think of that. Did you?'

'No - why should I touch him, for heaven's sake! He was

sitting behind me on one of the pews. Anyway, don't you take loddy sometimes? Come on, everyone does!'

The remark produces a look of some disparagement. 'Only at a certain time of the month, Amos – and that, dear one, is none of your business. It soothes the pain, that's all. And I never over-indulge – not like certain people I could mention who don't know when to stop.' But then she suddenly lets forth a little cry of consternation, as if startled; alert to something she has seen. 'Amos, keep walking,' she says, deadly serious now, 'and don't touch me in any way – there's somebody over there in the trees watching us through field glasses. Don't look, they've gone now anyway.'

Obeying, Amos keeps his eyes cast down. Someone spying on them! It is a chilling thought. And as they continue on their path back to the building – the spaniels by this time having raced on way ahead – he keeps his distance from her, trying to recall exactly what they would have done together this morning and whether any of it could possibly have been misconstrued by prying eyes. Aside from that, there is little else by way of further conversation between them until they reach the house and fall to debating with the staff there the more pressing requirements of the menu for an early luncheon which, alas must be shared with the returning party of gunmen.

Chapter Four

Rivals in a brightly lit Room

'It stinks – pah!' are the only words Oliver Ramsey can manage by way of response to Amos's attempt at photographing firstly the clothes the noble lord would be wearing for his portrait and secondly his head and shoulders at close range. This is not going to be easy, Amos concludes. He is here this afternoon in the upstairs study of Bowlend Court where for a moment both he and Ramsey succumb to a brief coughing fit as the cloud of sulphurous mist from the flash bulb disperses to reveal the man himself standing there, posing very imperiously in his finest frock coat and top hat, his face just a little speckled by soot. With an attempt at professional decorum, Amos merely arches his eyebrows with perfect indifference as he approaches and with a little wet flannel dabs the noble lord's cheeks, ignoring his protestations entirely and instead busying himself a moment later with the task of removing the glass plate with its delicate coating of chemicals from the camera and replacing it with another. But Ramsey is in no mood for further attempts at photography.

'What not another one, surely!' he exclaims. 'Aren't you supposed to be a painter, Roselli? Enough with all this hocus-pocus. Paint me, man – paint me! That's what you're here for.'

So with a little petulant shrug of the shoulder, Amos, dressed still very prestigiously in his best morning suit, his mustard-coloured waistcoat and crisp white shirt, moves his camera and tripod to one side and instead assembles in its place his small portable easel, upon which he secures a board so that he might do a preliminary sketch in coloured chalks of Ramsey's face, all in preparation for the finished masterpiece itself which will be executed in oils later on at his London studio. He works swiftly, with expert eye, sketching the fleshy jowls, the thick neck - around which it seems the man's bat-wing collar is scarcely able to stretch. Nothing really appears to hang well or to fit him, Amos observes, his clothes probably becoming too small for him with each few passing weeks as opulence feeds his appetite and results in more and more bulk – a process occurring evidently much faster than his tailors can accommodate. It is also not an easy room, here, in which to work because there is so much clutter, so many distractions in the décor to tempt the eye. In what can only be described as a kind of Scottish Baronial style, there is such a quantity of furniture present, so many rugs and carpets of various different combinations of tartan, all clashing in colour, that one can hardly move about. Ever since the Great Exhibition in London every home has to be like this, Amos reflects with dismay, every room resembling some monstrous emporium full of pictures, ornaments, curios and assorted bric-a-brac from all over the world. The walls, are festooned with hunting trophies in the form of various animal heads or antlers from unfortunate deer, while all the various alcoves and shelves bristle with specimens of taxidermy, stuffed owls, pine martins and foxes – anything and everything that has ever once moved and drawn the breath of life and could therefore be trapped or shot. Even worse: there in the corner of the room, resting against a cupboard, can be seen one of the very weapons responsible for this cold and dusty exhibition of slaughter: the double barrels of Bowlend's best and most-treasured twelve-bore shotgun. He had been cleaning the weapon lovingly when Amos had entered earlier and had only relinquished it with great reluctance so that he might sit still for once and give his undivided attention to the camera.

'So, remind me, Amos,' the noble lord begins again a little more kindly now and back on first-name terms with the troublesome artist, 'you intend that I should be represented full figure, face-on and positioned outside of the house, near the portico – is that correct?'

'Yes, if you are in agreement. It would present you as a man of property, of industry, too. Solid, powerful.'

'Emm ... I understand. And that I am also to be rendered as I am at the moment, in a formal coat, with cane – *n'est-ce pas?'*

'What's that, French?' Amos questions him, raising his eyes from his work and irritated by the needless digression into a foreign language while he is trying to concentrate.

'Yes, that's right! Ramsey replies somewhat gruffly – and to which Amos nods by way of confirmation, still busy working all the while with his chalks, several clasped in the palm of his left hand while he sketches with his right, constantly changing the colours and working rapidly as he examines the visage set before him. As agreed, Ramsey is looking directly towards the viewer, full face; a confident, haughty appearance; a direct challenge to the world and all that he surveys. But it is not an attractive visage, far from it.

Although Amos remembers him, even as little over a year ago, as being quite presentable, he is really no longer handsome at all. Where once his eyes would have been jovial and energetic with the sap of youth, they have already, in such a quick time, become small and suspicious. The eyes, in fact, remind Amos of pig's eyes: narrow, tiny in proportion to his face, alive only with an unpleasant animal magnetism, and with merely a crude, single-minded intelligence given over to the pursuit of bodily appetites – primitive and gross. It is disappointing, and perhaps Ramsey is even aware of this coarseness himself, because it is something which he attempts constantly to mitigate in conversation through the interjection of phrases of French – *excusez-moi* or *merci beaucoup* – mannerisms which he probably supposes lends him an air of sophistication but which, by its over-application, really only succeeds in making him both sound and look ridiculous.

'It will require at least one additional lengthy sitting,' Amos explains. 'This to be done at a later date – to put the finishing touches to the canvas. Hence the use of the camera, you see, which means that everything else can be compiled in my studio without you needing to be present.'

'When will it be ready?'

'For finishing – probably sometime in April.'

'April! That's bloody months away. Leighton does it in weeks.'

'Ah but Lord Leighton would certainly not be available at such short notice,' Amos argues. 'He would have a waiting list somewhat longer than mine.'

'Yes, that's true. I did approach him – and Watts - but they both said it would be bloody years before they could get around to me. I need something quick - so you'll just have to do. Anyway my good Lady recommends you ... quite *passionately* recommends your services, and I have agreed to it on those grounds alone.'

Amos bows a little gesture of gratitude, though feeling he would really like to punch the pompous ass on the nose. He doesn't even want him talking about Daphne, let alone using her as some kind of justification for having to settle for second best by employing him for the job. The pairing of his lovely muse with this man, the very thought of him touching and mauling the object of his devotion, continues to fill Amos with revulsion. He can hardly believe it. *'It is much worse,'* she had told him yesterday, referring to her life with Ramsey. What could she have meant? How would those chubby, animalistic hands of his with their hairy knuckles caress her in the privacy of their bedroom? How would he manoeuvre his fat bulk upon her? And how long would she have to endure it before it was all over? Such bitter conjecture makes Amos feel sick to his stomach.

With an abrupt snap between his finger and thumb, the chalk stick he is holding breaks in half. Too tight a grasp, he thinks; he is allowing himself to become tense, and that will not do. Oliver Ramsey, meanwhile, is smiling at him, surveying him as if he is aware of what might be going through the other man's mind: a shrewd, calculating kind of look which even includes an examination of Amos's tie pin and cufflinks, he notices, as if estimating his worth and value as a human being by the quality of the little diamond studs on his wrists.

'You and Lady Daphne were childhood sweethearts once, isn't that so?' he suddenly asks in a slow, deliberate kind of voice, probing, slightly ironic. And Amos wonders just how much she would have disclosed to him.

'I suppose one could say that, yes.' Amos replies, with restraint still, keeping his guard up.

'Well, I certainly have a lot to thank you for, Amos. After all, it was you who brought us together - remember, that afternoon in your studio, at work on your beautiful *femme fatale* in the typically obsessive manner of so many of your contemporaries – all that naked flesh.'

'You make me sound like a procurer, Oliver, like some kind of pimp!' Amos declares, endeavouring still to employ first-name informality as he was urged to do upon his arrival, yet scarcely able to repress his sense of irritation at this man's increasingly blatant and intimate tone.

'Well you wouldn't be the first of your fraternity to arrange certain – how shall we put it – liaisons between your models and gentlemen clients. Come on, you know that sort of thing goes on.'

'I can't imagine what you are referring to,' Amos replies with genuine puzzlement. 'It certainly isn't anything that would occur at my studio.'

For a while, Amos succeeds in working on in silence, without further interruption. But any semblance of calm that he has been able to summon up is soon dispelled as Ramsey suddenly remarks:

'You're a bit of a loose cannon, Amos. I don't know if I should encourage you quite as much as I do. I was surprised when you arrived here on your own – with only your valet in tow. Don't you have a wife, a sweetheart of any kind.'

'I have, until quite recently, come very close to marriage, if you must know. But it - er - didn't quite come to pass.'

'Cold feet?'

'By mutual consent, we each resolved that it would not be to our best advantage. That's all I am willing to tell you, if you don't mind.'

'Emm. Only you will, I take it, not be tempted to renew any former relations with my good lady – by way of consolation, that is?'

Amos remains silent. How should he respond to this

audacity!

'We have always been friends. I hope we shall remain so,' he eventually replies with composure.

'Friends? Why you're a rum sort of fellow, Amos. *Extraordinaire!* Daphne is not the kind of woman one desires as a friend, surely! What a waste that would be! Though you and I can be friends, Amos, can't we? Yes. And one must be able to speak openly with friends, do not you agree – man to man?'

Amos nods a grudging acquiescence. 'All right, Oliver. So tell me – man-to-man – what is it about Daphne that *you* value? Now that you have her, what comes next? Or are you just one of those fellows *to prize the thing ungained?'*

'What's that – Shakespeare?' he asks, echoing Amos's earlier irritation over his use of French.

'Yes, that's right?' Amos snaps back.

'Oh you can spare me all your poetic twaddle, Amos! And don't go getting your hopes up, either. I'm not tired of Daphne, if that's what you're trying to imply. I need an heir – a son preferably – and I enjoy a bit of sport in the making of it. And Daphne is the perfect quarry in that respect. She's a woman, yes, with the figure of one, by Jove – but she is also exceptionally beautiful, as you well know. And, after all, isn't it in the heart of every red-blooded man to want to desecrate beauty every once in a while? Joining the battle, hunting the fox, blasting a bird from the sky or ravaging a beautiful woman – you don't get tired of those sort of things. Daphne doesn't need to be put on some ruddy pedestal and worshiped. She is to be pursued, man! – chased and captured, night after night – her beautiful throat bared and then ...'

Realising that Ramsey is really trying all the while to make him angry, to contend with him or to test him in some bizarre sense, Amos merely responds by raising his eyebrows in a mild, questioning kind of way at the unfinished statement. 'Well? What?' he demands.

'Why, to be devoured, of course!' Bowlend answers in a voice that is chilling in its sense of crude anticipation.

Amos, meanwhile, attempts to return to the work in hand and to focus his concentration on the sketch – and for a moment he does succeed in establishing some measure of equanimity. But abruptly there comes the sound of footsteps, stumbling along rather than walking the length of the corridor outside their door - and then, scarcely preceded by any kind of rap or knock of courtesy upon it, the door itself flies open and in races Tommy Newman - Ramsey's business associate. Amos recognises him as a fellow guest at dinner, yesterday, though they had not spoken.

'Oops! What-ho, artist at work, eh!' he declares, coming over to stand at Amos's shoulder where there suddenly arises the distinct smell of alcohol. The man seems completely drunk.

A brash, scruffy, rodent-like creature, he has the look about him of one of the elder sons of the landed gentry, someone with too much time and too much money on his hands, thin and restless, and with a voice that sounds ten times louder than it probably really is in the atmosphere of concentration that Amos has been endeavouring to foster here abouts for his work.

'Ah, Tommy, m'boy. Welcome!' Ramsey states. 'Now, now! You just leave our sensitive young artist alone. He is in the throws of inspiration, don't you know.'

'Oh, inspiration, eh!' Newman echoes - if anything even more loudly before and launching into a tirade of jests and innuendo about the challenge of painting such a prodigious specimen as his good friend. 'Got room on that paper of yours, have you! Such a statuesque figure!' and so on.

Amos lowers his hand and merely stares in silence at the intruder, examining with revulsion his leering countenance, his repellent silvery grey hair too heavily oiled and shiny, his red blotchy skin and neck, hoping he might simply go away. But that is clearly not to be. Ramsey, on the other hand, appears to be glad and relieved at having a bit of noise and commotion about him again, and encourages the man to stay.

It is then that Amos notices once more - for he had seen it yesterday in various encounters with the man - how Ramsey's entire aspect would alter with the arrival of another male on the scene - a singular mannerism of his that causes him to stare in a most odd way, his head slightly lowered, his eyes looking upwards and outwards, big and round and intimidating as if about to charge. With women he was rather timid, and in a roomful of them he would become tongue-tied and coy. But put one male into the mix and the whole demeanour would become transformed into one of silent, simmering belligerence – as of now, and reminding Amos of some great stag in the rutting season, challenging all comers, anybody at all who just happened to smell wrong. Worse, Tommy himself, as if feeding off the chemistry of it all, and apparently delivered of a moment's inspiration, next rolls up a sleeve, rushes across and places his elbow down on a marble table top next to Ramsey for the express purpose, Amos is horrified to learn, of engaging him to a bout of arm wrestling. Unbelievable! Even more extraordinary, Ramsey obliges straight away, rolling up his sleeve too and placing his own elbow down next to his friend's, side by side, both men crouching over the table as they lock palms.

'All right you bastard, let's see what you can do!' Ramsey growls in a voice that is already offensive and threatening and yet which seems to be perfectly acceptable to Newman – who probably realises that being called a 'bastard' is about as close anybody gets to receiving a compliment from the noble lord. It is his version of a note of endearment. And thus the childish contest begins. Forward and backward their forearms go, each man grunting, sweating, for a good minute before Ramsey – with a snarl, a curse and a loud huffing sound – compels the other man's wrist flat down, onto the table, thereby occasioning Newman's body to twist and for him to actually fall to his knees in a drunken stupor – and from which he gets to his feet only gradually, rubbing his arm as if in pain.

'Bloody animal!' he cries, half mocking, half in bitterness at losing the bout, while Amos can only continue to look on, astonished, disgusted and realising with irritation that he is not likely to be able to return to his work for quite some time - a conclusion confirmed a moment later as Tommy, discovering Ramsey's shotgun in the corner of the room, staggers over to it and, with a flurry of excitement, takes it up for inspection.

'Oh, I say: behold the mighty weapon, what!' he declares opening the breach and then inspecting the barrel with a one-eyed squint along its length as he endeavours to demonstrate some form of non-existent expertise in such matters. There is a large window embrasure on the north side of the room, and Tommy next strides across and opens one of the casements to peer out. All seems well for a moment, but then, to Amos's horror and Ramsey's obvious amusement, Newman takes out two cartridges from a box nearby and loads them into the breach. Poking the gun out of the window, on unsteady feet, swaying this way and that he seems for a moment to aim at something, then swiftly lets off a double salvo, at which the entire room seems to quake. Vases on tables and mirrors on walls all shudder in unison as an acrid puff of black smoke blackens the air. 'Got 'im!' Newman cries. 'Got 'im!'

'What?'

'One of those … what do you call 'em, bloody magpie things. Right up the arse!'

'Good shot, Tommy!' Ramsey roars. 'You bastard, you! Good shot.'

The two of them continue to roar like schoolboys for a moment. But then suddenly, as if their eyes are drawn by a common magnetism towards him, they both turn and fix their gaze on Amos, their faces transformed abruptly, becoming long and grave as they observe his impassive features, registering with disapproval his silence and obvious distaste for the whole episode.

'Oh, I say! We haven't offended you, old boy, have we?' Newman inquires, his voice abruptly and menacingly low - though it is Ramsey who answers for him.

'Our friend Amos here doesn't approve of bloodshed. Isn't that so, Amos?' he demands with virulence, almost as if he were angry.

'Each to his own,' Amos responds, smiling as best he can through gritted teeth and hoping his disgust is not visible.

'Let's have a drink,' the noble lord suggests with a surprising change of tone, completely at variance with his raucous behaviour a moment ago as he locates a nearby crystal decanter and pours sherry for his himself and his two guests.

Realising that *any* kind of activity at all would be an improvement on what has just taken place, Amos decides to accept - humouring them for a while, though already wondering how he might excuse himself as quickly as possible and leave these two reprobates to stew in their own depravity. But it is not to be. They sip at their sherry, all three men, but no one relaxes; no one takes a seat. Ramsey wants to stand, and so Amos and Newman stand also, though the latter a little unsteadily. Amos notices that his shirt buttons are done up irregularly – clumsy fool! And he has several red marks on his throat - cuts from the razor while shaving. Obviously he can't even do *that* right! The silence is almost unbearable.

'I know! Let's talk about something cultural instead - for the benefit of our friend here, eh?' Ramsey suggests eventually and with an elbow of complicity digging into Newman's ribs – 'Why don't you tell us about your Germany trip, Tommy – what was it, some kind of music festival?'

'Oh, rather!' Tommy responds instantly. 'Yes, we got invited to the opening of this – er - opera thingy in Germany. Place called Bayreuth, it was. Somebody called Wagner in charge. The King there - friend of my old Dad, actually - is partial to his music. So he's built a theatre for it all. Bloody awful stuff. Goes on and on for hours without a trace of melody anywhere in the whole ruddy thing. Fell asleep, I did. Oh, but an interesting plot-line. Fascinating story, the bit I saw, anyway.'

'Oh really!' Ramsey chimes in, his eyes still fixed on Amos however, who can only cringe inside. His distinguished host has him where he wants him now, and seems intent on humiliating him in some sense.

'Yes. Norse legend, don't you know,' Newman goes on. 'Something about a wife, stuck in an arranged marriage. Lives in a big hut in the forest, with a dirty great big tree in the middle of the room. Bloody rubbish. Anyway, she's on her own one day and in comes this chap, on the run. Siegmund's his name. And they start making eyes at each other. In fact, they're really brother and sister, see, though they don't know it. All very nice and lovey-dovey, what? But then, of course, in comes the husband. Well, as it happens, this chap who's on the run is the sworn enemy of the husband's family! And so he, the husband, tells this bounder that he will have to fight him to the death the next day, only unarmed. Well there's a load of silly nonsense goes on with a sword stuck in the bloody tree and a spear and all that – all very allegorical, I'm sure, but the upshot of it is that this young intruder, this interloper who would have his way with the mistress of the house, is slain. Dies horrible on stage at the end of Act Two. Blood-curdling stuff.'

'Really!' declares Oliver Ramsey observing Amos's face throughout the story. 'Got his just desserts, I'd say, wouldn't you Amos?'

'Oh rather! Got what was coming to him,' Tommy echoes, making a curious stabbing motion as if thrusting a spear down into someone on the floor while also watching Amos closely for some kind of reaction, his eyes never leaving his face.

But Amos, determined to remain unimpressed, merely turns away and busies himself with the dismantling of his camera and tripod. 'I really ought to be taking this away now, Oliver, if you don't mind. The light has gone now, in any case. I can do no more this afternoon.'

'Oh well,' Ramsey declares straight away, 'time for a spot more arm wresting, then, eh! Come on Amos, let's see what *you* can do, this time. Come on! Here let me take you glass. Over here!'

And taking him by the sleeve, Ramsey almost hauls Amos across the room towards the table where he and Newman had enjoyed their bout a while earlier. "

'No Sir – really, I have no skill or strength for such things,' Amos protests.

'Oh but surely, Amos, you're a lad who fancies your chances, aren't you! You have the advantage of youth over me, moreover. Come on – I'd like that. In fact *I insist!*'

'If you don't mind, I really would prefer not to,' Amos repeats, and this time disengages himself from Ramsey's grasp with a rather petulant movement of the arm.

But just then he notices Tommy loading the gun again. He is standing in the embrasure of the window once more where he had left it leaning against the wall, though this time not looking out, but instead with eyes occupied with the goings on in front of him in the room.

'Now, now, careful Tommy!' Ramsey calls over to his friend, again an obvious note of complicity to his voice. 'Accidents do happen, y'know! Remember our friend, old

What's-his-name, playing about with a loaded gun indoors the other day. Got a couple of his toes shot off by accident. Now we wouldn't want anything like that to happen, would we!'

It is clear to Amos now that they would have arranged this ridiculous charade in advance. He has fallen into their trap. And Ramsey is already at the table, his sleeve rolled up, his thick, savage forearm eagerly bared, crouching in readiness. 'Come on Master Roselli, roll up your sleeve. Let's have a look at those muscles of yours!' he says, almost snarling now, his face all red and flushed with determination.

With the utmost reluctance, therefore, Amos removes one of his cufflinks and roles up his sleeve, placing his elbow on the hard cold surface of the table as they lock palms. The power of the other man is astonishing, and it will be all he can do, Amos realises, to prolong the contest for more than a few seconds let alone have any aspiration of winning it. This is, he tells himself, utterly, unbelievably ridiculous, like some terrible nightmare he has become embroiled in - the delicate tendons and ligaments of his painting arm in danger of very real, if not permanent damage; and he is defeated almost instantly.

But just as Amos assumes that the charade must be over and that he can get away, Oliver presents his sweaty palm towards him again.

'Best of three?' he suggests, in fact demands again, a stupid boyish look on his fat face, which does not sit at all well there on a man of his years, as Amos – suddenly feeling a little more competitive and angry - is compelled to take up the ridiculous contest once more.

But just then, footsteps are heard outside running up the staircase, which causes them to pause for a moment. And then a moment later when the door opens it is to reveal Daphne and her brother Gerald standing there – both open mouthed, agape with astonishment, a look of bewilderment in their eyes at the scene before them: the extraordinary sight of two grown men arm-wrestling at a table and a third nearby brandishing a shotgun.

'Did anyone of you fire a weapon from this window a moment ago?' Daphne inquires clearly none too happy. She is already dressed for dinner and looking gorgeous, her hair piled high, her lovely shoulders bared. 'I had thought I was mistaken, hearing things – but now I can see it is true. There shall be no weapons fired here. My home is a place of peace.'

At which, gathering the folds of her train in her hands she strides up towards Newman, leaning forward towards him as she goes.

'You?' she asks, looking into his face, her voice uncommonly resonate and commanding, a voice that Amos is not at all familiar with as he and Ramsey merely stare in stunned silence, their palms still interlocked but passive, as Tommy nods meekly at his accuser and attempts a childish kind of grin by way of apology.

'Get out,' Daphne whispers to him, a slow threatening sibilance, angered even more by his idiotic response.

Tommy trembles, and looks around as if searching for somewhere to place the weapon – eventually finding a convenient nook in the window recess. He lodges it there, upright against the panelled wall - though still only with some hesitation, as if his sense of co-ordination has deserted him. Not appearing to quite know what to do next, he stares back at her again, though this time in terror.

'*Get out!*' She screams now at the top of her voice. At which Newman simply runs from the room, while simultaneously Amos slams the unsuspecting knuckles of Lord Bowlend down so hard into the marble table and with such a roar of pain from his distinguished opponent that he suspects he might well have broken his arm.

Chapter Five

Séance

The pianist completes another charming piece, a nocturne from Chopin, and then as the gentlemen wander in from the billiard room, replete with brandy and cigars, it is the turn of some of the guests to sing. Few there are among them that have much ability in this department aside from Daphne – who, as Amos discovers, has been taking lessons from a German mezzo-soprano of some renown. This evening, in the drawing room of Bowlend Court, accompanied on piano, her performance is impressive: a rendition of something very lyrical from Schubert, sung in a warm, sensuous voice that features ample sprinklings of *'herzen and schmerzen'* and which Amos in particular finds utterly gorgeous - though he does notice that Daphne's sister-in-law, the blond and rather frivolous Mopsy, has resolved to put on a display of being bored, peering at the other woman through the lenses of a lorgnette from time to time, an object which she opens and closes like a weapon of some kind with irritable little snapping movements, before rolling her eyes and looking up to heaven in exasperation. Her little tantrums are not taken much notice of, however, and it is to considerable applause from the dozen or so other listeners that Daphne concludes her recital and returns to her chair once again - a natural pause in proceedings during which tea is served.

It is a delightful scene, beneath the sparkling chandeliers and gilded mirrors, upon exotic carpets from far-flung corners of the Empire, surrounded by lavish drapes of velvet and silk where every seam and every edge of every available surface appears to be brocaded or embroidered to the customs of some rare or expensive extravagance of good taste; it is quite simply intoxicating and also, he cannot help thinking, extraordinarily civilised when compared to the foolishness of the afternoon spent with Oliver Ramsey and his unsavoury friend in the cluttered little study upstairs. Yet still Amos cannot feel entirely at one. The six course dinner, amounting almost to a banquet, that they had endured earlier should have rendered everyone satisfied, and yet there remains a certain tension in the air, almost palpable, as though something untoward is about to happen - though what this could possibly be, still he cannot determine. The dreadful Tommy Newman has long-since departed, together with his indignant wife after being ordered not only from the room in which Daphne had discovered him, but also from the estate itself, despite protestations from Oliver, who sits now disconsolately in an armchair, his right hand bandaged as a result of Amos sudden and unexpected victory over him at their bout of arm wrestling. To Amos's surprise and relief, however, he appears settled at present - almost certainly no bones broken, the doctor who called assured him; just some 'bad bruising' - the bandage being more a precautionary measure.

Daphne's young brother, Gerald is nearby, and he and Amos greet each other heartily.

'Good to see you Amos! How are you?' he asks, taking his hand. Aside from attending his wedding a couple of years ago, Amos has not seen much of his childhood friend in recent times. A clever amateur poet and clarinet player, he has grown and matured into a good-looking, though perhaps slightly frail young man - for where the combination of height and slender build has produced beauty and elegance in Daphne, the same qualities have resulted in a relatively ungainly, awkward figure in the male version that was Gerald. Like all the men present, he is attired in the conventional white-tie formality expected of dinner guests - the kind of clothing that does suit him, however, Amos is surprised to discover, and he looks quite presentable.

'Good to see you too, my friend' Amos replies. 'I'm well – very well. And how is your good lady wife, may I inquire?'

'Mopsy – oh, she is fine and as gorgeous as ever. Trouble is, she does rather know it! Ha! Anyway, we have been married almost two years now, I just managed to pip Daphne to the post, didn't I'

'And a seat on the board, too, I hear - Lord Bowlend's right hand man, no?' Amos continues, recalling with amazement the rapid transformation of one who was once such a rebel, such an advocate of humanist ideals and rights for the socially disadvantaged - and yet who has already become a hard-nosed businessman, a major shareholder in a firm manufacturing ordnance and artillery carriages. Strange, and perhaps just a little disappointing.

'Well, I wouldn't quite put it that way,' he replies with a modesty that Amos knows is genuine enough. 'To be entirely truthful with you Amos, the business of making weapons to kill my fellow man still does not quite chime with my principles, and never shall. I really haven't shifted that much inside, y'know. But there you are! It was an honour, a fabulous opportunity and, at the end of the day, it does pay the bills and keeps Mopsy in the manner she is very quickly becoming accustomed to.'

Amos shares a moment of laughter with his old friend, though concerning his last observation there is also a degree of resignation apparent in his voice, almost as if he were slightly ashamed of himself and the choices he has made. He seems trapped, and Amos can only feel pity for him. The delectable Mopsy herself, meanwhile, in her figure-hugging gown and triple strand of peals proudly on display, can be seen conversing with great animation with some of the other ladies, discussing the merits of the latest fashions, no doubt, which have become off-the-shoulder and very sleek of late: tight-fitting lines that encase the waist and hips, only to flare out at the knees, a style unflatteringly referred to by the men as the 'trumpet shape' but which suits her well with her feminine curves. Though if this is a look and a style that sits tolerably well on Mopsy it is also one that finds its perfection in Daphne, who has the height and the elegance to carry it off without any trace of vulgarity. And Amos notices more than a casual glance of envy from Mopsy in her direction as Lady Bowlend herself walks with poise and dignity amid her guests, dressed in a lovely black gown of alternative taffeta and satin panels, sparkling with little tokens of opulence, earrings and brooches, rings and combs - smiling, laughing, speaking with each guest in turn, twisting all the men around her little finger as always and controlling everything with the unique look that only she can bring to her eyes. The paper fan, meanwhile, that she holds in her hand together with the complex code of signals that has grown up around the object over the years, becomes an expression of unending subtly and sophistication in her hands: to open it invitingly as her eyes meet his across the room; to draw it shut a moment later as she is distracted elsewhere; to raise it to her right cheek to express interest in a conversation nearby; or to beat it waspishly against her palm when irritated by another. It all happens so effortlessly, mirroring her emotions like another kind of musical instrument, and she the accomplished mistress of all its tones and complexities - held there so delicately between finger and thumb - and in comparison to which all efforts on the part of the other ladies in the room appear dull, crude or simply futile. Yes, he thinks - and Gerald is probably thinking it, too – Daphne really is breathtakingly beautiful as opposed to Mopsy's simple comeliness, making the younger, more ordinary woman look rather a tart by comparison – a shortcoming that Mopsy appears acutely aware of herself, and none too pleased about.

'Have you had a word with her yet, Mopsy I mean?' Gerald inquires, perhaps noticing Amos's eyes following her.

'Er – no, not yet. I expect we'll have a natter together, later on,' Amos replies, knowing, however, that it would most likely be only a very brief 'natter' - if anything at all. For the sad reality is that Mopsy tends to ignore men that do not have lots of money. Were Amos a painter of celebrity status with a world tour of his work taking place, he would no doubt fare better with her. But for now, he rarely receives, nor expects to receive much more than a nod of her blond head in his direction or the occasional vapid smile of greeting from her fulsome scarlet lips whenever she happens to pass by.

Meanwhile, the pianist has returned, and most people take their seats once more. The music, this time by Mendelssohn, is a delight and he becomes enchanted again, thrilled by the privilege of hearing it performed in such an intimate setting, the kind of surroundings for which it was surely intended. At moments like this it is as if another soul were calling to him from across some vast remove of space and time. He almost hears the heart beating, hears every sigh and breath of his fellow artist, and it touches him with a profound mixture of longing and seductive pleasure. It is, however, a lonely experience – for when he glances around the room at his fellow listeners he perceives only indifference at the best; apathy at the worst. There is a man fidgeting in his seat, scratching his nose for no particular reason. Another is looking discretely at his fob watch though the hour is not late. Elsewhere a woman is fluttering a fan beneath her chin, though the air is not warm. What are they thinking? What are they hearing, if not merely the sounds of a mechanical instrument, the tinkle of tiny hammers upon strings within a wooden box? How far away, how remote is the suffering and passion of a Mendelssohn or a Schubert for them? And then he catches sight of Daphne, and it is all so very different, her features so refined, so full of attentiveness, so very engaged, following every nuance with the ear of the trained musician. He has, to be sure, enjoyed the company of numerous lovely and clever women in his time, but he will never admire another quite as much or with quite the same passionate intensity as Daphne. This evening, he sees in her eyes the very resonance of his own listening heart and knows that he loves her still every bit as much as he has ever loved her; and he curses his misfortune and foolish indifference that he had ever let her slip from his grasp.

It is almost midnight, and the servants have departed to their quarters, far away into furnished attic spaces of remote wings, or down into basements and kitchens below stairs, so that only a handful of guests remain in the drawing room when Daphne announces that they are to begin the séance.

'What's this?' Amos inquires discretely of Ramsey - the two having just at that instant encountered each other at the drinks table and where, acknowledging his host's temporary disability and the part his own actions have played in it, Amos has kindly poured some fine old claret into his glass. The injury inflicted on the noble lord earlier should have resulted in a withdrawal of his favour, but if anything it appears to have had the reverse effect as, accompanied by a somewhat ironic raising of the eyebrows at Amos's tender ministrations, he replies:

'She sometimes likes to conclude the evening with a brief foray into the spiritualist world - you know, contact with the other side. It's either this, or else the tarot cards have to come out, or there is astrology - all that kind of thing. What can one do!'

'Do you have views - one way or the other - religious views, I mean,' Amos inquires casually.

'Never you mind!' Ramsey replies with a sudden and untypical turn of seriousness. 'Myself, I rather share in the opinion of the redoubtable Mr Darwin, if you must know. Brutality. Survival of the fittest. That's what orders our lives - nothing else. And seeing as we have done away with God as a result of that good man's discoveries, I suppose we must now seek our spiritual needs in follies of this kind. It is entertaining enough, though - as you'll see. And Lady Daphne is a sorceress at summoning the dead.'

Daphne herself, meanwhile, has been up and about and very diligent, at the centre of attention now and clearly very much the mistress of ceremonies as she prepares the séance table - a round, highly polished oak pedestal carried aloft into the room by her brother Gerald and upon which she places a number of round wooden counters, pieces from a draughts set probably, but each with a letter of the alphabet painted upon its surface. These are arranged in a circle, towards the circumference of the table. A brandy glass is then procured, wiped with a napkin and positioned, upturned, in the centre - while everyone draws up a chair and places their index fingers onto the glass itself. The gas lights are dimmed each to a tiny yellow ember; candles are extinguished, leaving only a solitary standard lamp with a red shade, burning oil, to cast any serviceable visibility on proceedings, as everyone - Gerald, his wife Mopsy, the cannon salesmen and their wives - all surrender to a most untypical seriousness, a look of concentration on their faces bordering on reverence for what is about to take place. It also becomes uncommonly silent, therefore - apart, that is, from a strange chant or ritual prayer of some kind, uttered by Daphne under her breath, scarcely audible and merely punctuated from time to time by the odd grunt of suitably masculine cynicism from her husband trying not to appear too accommodating or impressed by any of it. These important preliminary measures accomplished, the calling out for spirits in earnest can now commence.

'Is there anyone from the world of spirit here with us this evening?' Daphne asks in a special kind of voice - one that is firm, slow and very deliberate in tone. It is all exceedingly theatrical, Amos concludes, but gradually a strange and genuinely eerie atmosphere descends upon the scene. It remains uncommonly quiet but also quite chilly now, he feels, as everyone continues to stare - either at Daphne herself or towards the glass, upon which all fingers are still patiently and determinedly set. Gerald, meanwhile, availing himself of a little note-pad of the kind used by journalists, has taken up a pencil in his free hand - as if ready to take down any communications that might be forthcoming.

'Is there any spirit here?' Daphne repeats, if anything even more solemnly than the first time.

To Amos's astonishment the glass then begins to vibrate and almost straight-away to move - sliding slowly and, with everybody's fingers still pressed upon it, in a curious sideways trajectory out towards the perimeter of the table and towards one of the letters - an 'F.'

'I hope this is not going to be anything rude, is it?' remarks one of the cannon salesmen with an attempt at levity.

'Sssh!' Mopsy hisses through her bright scarlet lips, putting him in his place instantly and to which he looks more than a little chastened and embarrassed.

The glass moves to an 'O' next, and then returns quickly to delineate another 'O' before sliding rapidly to the right and to the letter 'L.'

'FOOL,' states Gerald by way of conclusion. 'Very nice, I'm sure!'

'What is your name?' Daphne asks in that same, slow, deliberate tone that she has adopted for the purpose – and, curiously, reminding Amos of the voice in which she had sung earlier. 'Tell us your name, please.'

After a short pause, the glass gradually slides into life again and moves straight towards the letter 'N' quickly followed by an 'A' and then another 'N.'

'NAN,' Daphne confirms. 'Welcome, Nan. Are you my Nan? What is your message?'

The glass shudders and, now gaining strength it seems, as if drawing upon the very energies of everyone present, it continues to move so swiftly that those who seek to adhere to it have considerable difficulty in doing so - their arms extending and flexing to keep contact with it – and which, after an emphatic 'NO' to Daphne's first question, swiftly goes on to spell out the equally grave but still unhelpful 'NONE.'

'How did you die?' Daphne inquires, undeterred.

But the glass becomes static now. Whoever or whatever is controlling its motion has ceased communicating, at least for the time being.

'How did you die?' Daphne repeats with patience, but firmly, too, as if speaking to a slightly disobedient animal.

'BEHED,' spells the glass, and for the moment returning to its former more-sluggish perambulations.

The word 'beheaded' is whispered in tones of awe by several of those present by way of interpretation.

'Poor Nan!' Mopsy says, almost as if personally addressing the spirit who has come to the table - but then, a little more frivolously, continues by asking: 'What is like having your head chopped off?'

'EASY,' spells the glass.

A little chorus of diffident laughter circulates around the table - though everyone is quickly silenced as the glass next sets out once again with astonishing speed upon a long unhesitating string of letters that looks to be spelling out something quite substantial – moving with such rapidity, in fact, that nobody can follow its drift at all. Gerald, however, does manage to take it down, and at the conclusion he runs through the letters and quickly interprets them, reading aloud in a tremulous voice the words:

'With a sharp sword. Clean. Like a paper-cut, only a thousand times stronger.'

Amos begins to shiver, a chill that permeates his entire being. He can feel the hairs on the back of his neck creeping.

'Why, Amos, my friend, are you cold?' Ramsey inquires, always keen to draw attention to any visible weakness or irregularity in the other man.

Daphne, however, and though she says nothing, regards her friend with a genuine concern and sympathy, a steady, penetrating gaze - for she would not have forgotten what he had told her yesterday concerning his visit to The Tower. It is, therefore, much to the disappointment of many of those present, that she draws the whole séance to a premature close. The lamps are turned up, the candles are re-lit, the buzz of conversation and conviviality returns to the room, and everybody with mixed feelings of excitement and relief heads for the drinks table once again.

'Somebody's Nan who had her head cut off. Ruddy gobbledegook, isn't it!' one of the cannon-salesmen declares urbanely and much to Ramsey's amusement. But Amos does not smile. He cannot get warm, and no amount of brandy or blithe conversation will remedy it.

It is early morning, overcast and raining, when Amos sets off on his return journey to London. He had not slept well after the séance. And this morning, as he closes his eyes in the railway carriage and listens to the hypnotic rhythm from the tracks, he allows a welcome drowsiness to wash over him, recalling the events of the previous few hours with more than a little unease – for the séance had been only the start of the unpleasantness. Unable to settle, he had got up in the night to stretch his legs and had wandered out through to the corridor and along to the stair-well to admire again the vast atrium with its neo-gothic arches and vaulted ceiling, its tall, elongated windows with their intricate tracery of stone and leaded glass through which the moonlight was shining, illuminating with an opalescent glow the grey walls, their pilasters and the great interior of the roof which even at the level of the first floor landing seemed to tower so very high above him. The only noise in the building was from the trickle of an indoor fountain set below in the atrium itself – everywhere at peace - until, that is, quite close to what he understood were his hosts' chambers, he heard a single clear and most unsettling sound. One poignant note, that's all it was: the sound of Daphne's voice – he was almost certain it was hers – and the one solitary word *'no'* murmured in the darkness - followed by an almost imperceptible retching sound, like someone being sick and then the groaning of a man's voice: Oliver Ramsey's.

The sounds had troubled him, and he was unable to settle at all after returning to his room. So he put on his dressing gown and sat for a while, this time gazing out through the latticework of his bedroom window.

Below could be seen the top of the portico and the late, withered leaves of the eglantine rose from which Daphne, upon his arrival Friday afternoon, had plucked the token of greeting for his lapel. It was still in his jacket, that small scarlet rosehip that she had placed there so lovingly. The rose itself, he could see clearly now, was growing from a large urn at the base of the portico instead of being rooted in the ground – typical of what would occur outside of a new building of this kind, of course. In keeping with Amos's own rich and romantic imagination, the sweet briar that she had touched and which she had allowed to pierce her finger should have been from a far more ancient bough, a scion of a root planted by some returning crusader of a bygone age. But not here. Here it was just something that had been carried in on a wagon from a garden nursery. What was Daphne doing in a place like this, he asked himself - married to a man like Ramsey? It just didn't make sense.

Troubled still in thought, he continued thus to peer into the darkness to where, beyond the lawns, in a wooded area, a badger could be seen roaming on the edge of a Rhododendron walk - its distinctive white-striped muzzle discernible from time to time, though not any of the black fur of the body, which was blended entirely into the darkness. There would surely be others, he thought, so he waited. Then another shape, much larger, began to emerge, this time looking like that of a human figure - for he could discern the outline of what appeared to be a thin cloak or drape of some kind that was wrapped about it. It also seemed to be terribly bent up and confused, lacking purpose or direction in its perambulations, like a frail elderly person or someone kneeling in pain or distress. What would anybody in their right mind be doing lurking outside in the grounds at this time of night, he wondered, and so scantily clothed? For a moment he recalled the odd piece of sculpture they had discovered abandoned in the grounds during their walk. Had that not also been of a cloaked figure, a woman concealing her face? And looking out now, straining his eyes in the darkness at the figure in the garden, it seemed to him then – and he hardly wished to acknowledge it – that there was no head to it at all. And then within a moment it had gone - having merged into the thicket of the trees and bushes, leaving him in doubt as to whether he had really seen it at all, or perhaps simply only imagined it. But he felt deeply disturbed.

With daylight, came the final gathering of the clan, an intimate circle including Lord and Lady Bowlend and Daphne's brother and sister-in-law, Gerald and Mopsy, all meeting early around the breakfast table - early because many, like him, were already preparing to leave for the city or back to their own estates. Everyone seemed weary and irritable – yet still reluctant to go their separate ways as though there were still things to discuss, differences to be aired: an uncomfortable and slightly brooding atmosphere.

It was an honour, of course, to be seated in such distinguished company, the informal family atmosphere in which all the intimate and cosy diminutives of address would be bandied about - where Gerald became *'Gerry'* and Oliver became *'Polly'* and Mopsy, of course, irreducible, remained just *'Mopsy.'* He should have felt elated, too, at all the many commendations in the offing - introductions to any number of Lord Bowlend's well-connected friends. There was even the possibility, regarded with mixed feelings by Amos, of becoming the next war artist for a prominent paper when 'The Big One,' as his well-informed host had put it 'comes along' - for Ramsey assured him there was something significant brewing up in the Transvaal again that would this time involve much more than just a few skirmishes. That would be a fine opportunity, of course, he said – and then promptly set forth on his own immediate mission to help himself to vast quantities of porridge and scrambled eggs before retreating behind the towering edifice of his morning newspaper, evidently his habit at that time of the day. Yes, all very flattering. But Amos found it hard to demonstrate the expected level of enthusiasm. Another war? The idea sickened him after the carnage and waste of human life in the Crimea just a few years ago.

'War is a terrible thing,' Daphne observed, pouring coffee for herself and the others, as if echoing his thoughts, and much to her husband's obvious irritation, flicking and flapping the pages of his paper from time to time as she spoke. 'Surely we should strive to live in peace with other nations. There must be something wrong when we have to lay waste so many young lives – and for what!'

'Politics behind it as always,' Gerald chimed in, equally glum-faced – for even though he was on the board, he still disapproved of many aspects of the firm's armaments business. Amos was fond of Gerald. No longer in the smart white-tie formality of yesterday evening, he had now reverted to his old scruffy self – rather as Amos remembered him from his younger days – those thick, old-fashioned jackets with their sloping shoulders that always left too much space around the neck – his collars rarely fitting snugly either. Dear Gerald!

'It's a deterrent!' roared Oliver Ramsey all of a sudden, peering out from behind his paper to regard all present with a look of exasperation. 'A strong nation with weapons is able to maintain equilibrium by deterring others who would otherwise make mischief.' he concluded in a voice that seemed to brook no argument before returning to the solace of his broadsheet.

'Oh yes, that's true, a well-armed nation does help keep

the peace,' Gerald agreed, 'which is laudable. But power and greed for its own sake, which is what warfare is about most of the time – well, it's a bad show, if you want my opinion. Perhaps we should consider doing something different with the firm. Expanding into more peaceful areas.'

Oliver Ramsey did not respond this time, however, and Amos could sense that he had already elected to ignore the rest of the conversation entirely, treating the whole feeble exercise in misguided squeamishness with the contempt it deserved – so that Gerald, after delivering his verdict, was left staring merely at an impenetrable and silent wall of newsprint. His wife, meanwhile, was clearly becoming more than a little impatient with all this soul-searching over breakfast. Having restricted herself to the nourishment of a mere grapefruit, in the interests of slimming, no doubt, and with the look of someone who would much prefer to be talking about the latest trends in fashion or coiffure, Mopsy tossed a wayward curl of blond hair from her eyes and with a rather affected gesture of despair, looking up to heaven, declared:

'Yes, war is so very dreary, of course. And nobody wants to see our boys coming home without arms or legs. But I mean who are we to judge such things! How can any of us possibly know what is right or wrong!'

'Don't be ridiculous!' Daphne suddenly exclaimed – and loudly, moreover, much to everyone's surprise. 'Of course we can judge perfectly well what is right and wrong. It's because of people like you, silly girl, that we are all in such a mess – not having any strength of our convictions any longer,' and upon which she slipped into a astonishingly accurate mimic of Mopsy's own lilting voice, clutching a hand to her forehead and continuing with: *'Oh how do we know, how do we know! It's all so terribly dreary having to think about it! My poor little brain is hurting so!'*

Mopsy – for once dressed plainly in cotton fabrics and woollens, and divested, therefore, of much of her usual silky veneer of glamour – looked mortified for a moment, because it really was an excellent imitation, and everybody laughed, with Gerald in particular seeming to be unable to control himself or to stop giggling, which annoyed her even more. Leaning across towards Daphne as if she would devour her she cried: 'Oh so I suppose you know best, do you. Who do you think you are, then, God?'

'No,' Daphne replied instantly, 'but I know the word of God. And it is *Thou Shalt Not Kill*. Or have all you clever, bright young things forgotten that?'

Mopsy, who was neither clever nor particularly bright, as everyone well knew, was clearly incandescent at this stage, furious over her sister-in-law's utter demolition of her personality. 'I never said I thought I was clever,' she insisted angrily, though also slightly tearful by then. 'I leave all that kind of elevated stuff to you, darling.'

'Then listen to me now, because you might just learn something!' Daphne responded instantly and clearly not done with the other woman yet, like a dog shaking a rabbit in its jaws. '*Right* is remarkably easy to understand, my dear, as opposed to *wrong*. Right is that which creates beauty and protects the innocent. Right is that which does not offend or degrade, that is selfless and steadfast and which keeps a place for us in this world where kindness can be protected. Right is right, in other words - and little fools like you who keep on questioning the patently bloody obvious will destroy us all in time.'

Mopsy, utterly beside herself by then, got to her feet and, hurling her napkin down onto the table, stormed from the room. And Amos caught a look of utter hatred in her eyes for a moment as she passed. Whether it was a long-standing feud between the two women or something that had just that moment flared up, he could not tell, but it certainly appeared a serious breach of friendship existed between them, almost a state of enmity. Gerald, meanwhile, simply shrugged his long, droopy shoulders and tried to make light of it. But the meal broke up quickly after that, with Oliver Ramsey himself looking particularly displeased. And thus the incredible and turbulent weekend at Bowlend Court drew to a hurried and timely close.

A hackney carriage, led by the white misty breath of its horse in the cold air, takes him from London's Victoria station to his home in Mornington Terrace. How pleased he feels to be surrounded by it all again, this familiar urban landscape of the city so orderly and civilised with its York stone pavements, its tidy privet hedges and rows of plane trees with their distinctive patchwork of peeling bark and tumbling leaves, all russets and golds at this time of the year against the grey skies of the afternoon. He loves the elegant brick houses, the narrow well-tended gardens that front them – with their iron railings and lamp-posts all black and shiny in the rain. It feels wonderful to open his own front door again, as well, and to step inside where all is warm and dry and so very peaceful. It smells so good, too! – that familiar combination of coal from the scuttle, beeswax polish on the furniture and freshly baked bread from the oven – a most alluring combination that indicates that Beth has surely been busy and has everything prepared for him. And she has. There is a warm fire in his bedroom; all his belongings have been tidied and neatly ordered; hot water appears within moments of his return – brought up by her in a jug and placed on the washstand next to the big china bowl – itself, flanked by two clean white linen face-towels. And there is even a little blue delft vase in the corner by the window containing flowers. How very kind!

'What news, Beth?' he inquires as she comes in again and hands him the mail, not generally a pleasant prospect even at the best of times – as the batch of letters usually contain only bills. 'Has anything happened during my absence? I bet all the chaps have missed me, haven't they?' he inquires, picking up the latest copy of the bohemian-inspired Belgravia Magazine instead, and flicking eagerly through its pages for any news of a more agreeable kind.

'Only one visitor Sir,' she replies. 'A lovely young lady called early on Saturday afternoon.'

'Oh, really?' says Amos, gaining interest suddenly and putting his magazine to one side.

'Yes. She it was who left the flowers – though not her name or even a card, I'm sorry to say, which, as a matter of fact, I thought was a little irregular. She told me I should put the flowers in water straight away and place them in your chambers ready for your return.'

At which Beth points - quite brusquely, he feels - towards the vase and the red and white roses therein. He goes over to examine them and to take in any fragrance that they might still contain. They look very bright and cheerful, he thinks with approval - the popular message of 'love and beauty' proclaimed therein, and all set against the window and the grey-slate rooftops of London outside in the rain. Roses. Where on earth could they have come from at this time of year! How kind!

'What did she look like,' he asks. 'You - er - said she was lovely?'

'Very dark brown hair, Sir, and very unusual eyes - quiet large and black. Though I know well-enough who it was, anyway. It was her, Sir - your lady that you have painted so often.'

And as if to give support to her observation, Beth steps across the room to one of the very few portraits of Daphne that is framed and properly hung on the wall and nods approvingly in its direction.

But Amos merely laughs in response.

'The young woman in this portrait? No, Beth. I was in Lady Bowlend's company all day Saturday, in Sussex.'

'Well, it was her double, then, that's all I can say,' is Beth's only response. 'The spitting image of her. And she said she would not come in, and before I could say another word she was away, within a blink of an eye. Are you all right, Sir? You look very pale all of a sudden.'

Amos stares at his maid for a few moments in disbelief.

'Saturday afternoon? Are you certain?'

'Yes, around two o'clock.'

Amos waves the matter aside, smiles and shrugs his shoulders. He waits until Beth has left the room, and then tries to take stock of what she has told him. He, washes at the dressing table and then, donning his warm, cashmere smoking jacket and cap, all nicely aired and comfy, of course, elects to take an afternoon nap on the bed. Yes - so good to be home! So good to be back to normality. Yet the usual pleasant slumber that he would award himself after a busy weekend of travelling will not come. Instead, he remains awake on his bed and stares at the ceiling. He knows there is nobody who could be remotely mistaken for Daphne – not even her elder sister, who was nothing like her in appearance or manner in any case. There was simply no one, not anyone living at any rate that could imitate her – and a fearful anxiety begins to bear down on him, to tear at his entrails, because as he turns his attention back to the little array of roses again he notices for the first time a rather disturbing component languishing there among them, one he had not registered a moment ago – for there, entwined within the little bouquet itself with its bland and innocuous stems of florist's greenery, is the addition of several mulberry leaves - their symbolism clear to anyone familiar with the more secretive and subtle language of flowers. *'I love you, but shall not survive you,'* it says. It is a chilling message – one of tenderness mixed with despair – and so very disturbing after all he has experienced already these past few days. Tired and exhausted as he might well be, therefore, still he cannot rest – and finds himself wondering, in fact, whether he might ever be vouched a decent bit of sleep ever again? What on earth was happening in this peculiar life of his, and where could it all possibly be leading?

Chapter Six

Entry in a Journal

My observations from the Island. How wonderful - all of us here together: myself and Polly, our Steward David and so many of our loyal staff who have accompanied us from Bowlend Court and who still tend to our every wish and whim – and with such efficiency! We have been here one whole week at our villa, our summer retreat which goes by the somewhat grandiose name of 'Parnassus.' We are only just becoming accustomed to the change of pace, which even on what the locals term 'a busy day' is more like a quarter of the pace of London during the quietest of Sundays. The house itself, however, is a jewel which would grace any street in Mayfair or Bath - well aired and spacious – and every window is draped with the most beautiful mauve and lilac velvet curtains, so it is as warm as toast at night. The furniture is all modern, with delightful Jappaning and lacquer work everywhere, and there is a croquet lawn outside which is being mowed and rolled at present and should be serviceable, they say, as early as tomorrow. The grounds are landscaped in a classical way with parterres of clipped box and yew but with wilder stretches that border onto meadows that run down to the sea, full of primroses and violets and nodding daffodils that are beginning to fade.

I am expected to become pregnant. The whole world is constantly gazing at my belly looking for some indication of swelling, but it remains stubbornly as flat as a washboard and my courses remain as painful as ever. We have been 'trying,' as the polite euphemism has it, and no doubt will continue to do so. We have established quite a routine because Polly is most enthusiastic that an heir should be produced as soon as possible. This is what life is like now - married life. I am not certain it suits me at all, but I will do what is best. I will not disgrace or disappoint my family, and I will not become an embarrassment to Polly, who continues to be so good to me in his way. I long to be able to let my cares vanish here, to become uninhibited and free. Perhaps it will happen.

Over the next several weeks things should become more stimulating. We are to have visitors - my parents, firstly - so proud of their daughter, bless them - and perhaps later on also my dear brother Gerald and his wife, who still seems to envy me so much. I do so wish she would not; for my life is surely no happier than hers. I must try to be good to her and not to tease. Contentment and fulfilment - these are the things by which we should judge a person's achievements, not just wealth. Even she must realise that!

Still, I must say, wealth does have its attractions. I am slowly becoming used to it, and this is a locality that does not fail to oblige in terms of feeding my newly found vice of extravagance. There are some gorgeous little shops and emporiums in the high streets and the squares of the towns, and I am permitted to bring home as many hats and gloves, as many books and jewel cases as I please to keep me amused. We also have a grand piano here in the drawing room, and thus I am able to continue with my studies, though singing to my own accompaniment I still find impossible.

Also, perhaps every bit as exciting because it is imminent, is the news that my dear friend, the painter Amos Roselli is to visit shortly. He is to complete Polly's portrait here and because the house he has leased nearby (I have been to inspect it this morning) is so cold and wretched, he should - I am going to suggest - do well to move his belongings here and stay with us, at least until his valet and his maid join him, which I understand shall be after the weekend. Only then shall we release him. A more accomplished and talented artist I have yet to encounter. A more tender and gentle spirit I have yet to meet with in this life. But I must say no more in these pages, lest it ever be misconstrued. Let us hope that his portrait for Polly will lead to even better things for him. Already I have permission, wrung by slow degrees from my husband, that his next work shall be a portrait of me. It will be the first since my marriage and it will be done here, as well. So I am very excited.

And now let me tell you about the locals, about all the Good and the Great that come here for the summer months or else, in some cases, have chosen to make the Island their permanent home ever since Victoria and her much-lamented Prince Consort Albert built their Italianate palace at Osborne. The Royal Yacht Squadron at Cowes has always attracted the world's most opulent and successful yachtsmen (and their wives and mistresses), but once the Queen and Albert set up their home here - not to mention the Poet Laureate Alfred Tennyson, as well - it was, they say, as if a gold rush had begun. Villas and summer homes popped up like mole-hills everywhere around the coast of this unique, diamond-shaped isle which measures not much more than twenty miles from the eastern tip to where we are, here in the West and where the chalk stacks towering above the waters of the English Channel rival, I would say, even those of the cliffs of Dover – for they are every bit as dramatic. The magnificent grass downland that caps them, and which begins its ascent not a stones-throw from our front door, rises to a height of five hundred feet, they say, and then the downs themselves become more and more narrow as you walk them to the West until they finish in a thin wafer of chalk and the unique and justifiably famous outcrop of tall, spectacular pinnacles they call the Needles, immortalised in oils some years ago by none other than Joseph Turner himself.

I am beginning to suspect that there is so much more to be discovered about what is to be my home for the next few months – for this enchanted island has, they tell me, hosted an astonishing and varied menagerie of creative genius - from Keats and Wordsworth, Dickens and Swinburne, Rossetti, Holman Hunt and Lewis Carroll in the recent past, right up to Watts, Ruskin, Millais, Longfellow, Princep and Anne Thackeray today. Is that not amazing! I feel quite done-up already just sitting here thinking about it - while Lord Tennyson himself is actually a neighbour! He really does live just down the road, as does the painter George Fredrick Watts - though we have yet to meet either of these fine old gentlemen in person. In fact, Tennyson has become, they say, rather reclusive in recent years and spends much of his time endeavouring to be invisible and to cheat the tourists who linger around his estate and the paths on which he is wont to walk in his long black cloak and broad-rimmed hat – reluctant in the extreme that anyone should obtain so much as a glimpse of him. He calls them his 'cockney invaders,' and looks really blue on anyone who bears even a remote resemblance to a sightseer. Poor man, I hear he is driven to abandon the Island entirely during the summer months sometimes because of them. I hope he does not leave us too quickly this year, as I would so like the opportunity to meet him before he departs.

But how? That is the question. He does entertain, but it is a highly cultured and intimate circle of famous names such as Ellen Terry, George Watts or the Princeps, luminaries from the stage or the arts that cluster around him – though sometimes eminent statesmen, as well: the Queen's beloved Albert when he was alive, the Duke and Duchess of Argyle, the fabulously exotic revolutionary Garibaldi or even Prince Alamayou of Abyssinia, no less, who will turn up at his home – a gorgeous, long-fronted house called Farringford, all covered in ivy and virginia creeper – and very grand inside, by all accounts. I have so far only had a view of it from the road. Perhaps when Amos is among us we might fare better since he knows Watts – and it would surely be more his hunting ground, anyway, because half the island population is, I swear, engaged in writing poetry or painting, or else taking laudanum or some other such opiate so that they all seem to exist in a permanent haze of inspiration and passionate debate over every latest turn in architecture or epic poem or passing trend in painting. Everyone knows everyone, all intimately involved with one another or else obsessed with the presence of any number of bizarre classical deities, legendary Arthurian knights or mythical creatures from classical literature whose presence seem as real to them as the coalman or the vintner might be to us when they call - that is, all the good, common people who have to remain sober in order to look after the rest of us (otherwise nothing would ever get done). It is an island of cultivated minds. Their hold on reality is but a tenuous one and ideal, therefore, for someone like Amos. As for my dear husband, he is not, I fear, sufficiently up to the job in that respect and would be as out of his depth as a goldfish in an ocean were he to be set among them for more than a moment - and Tennyson would no doubt run a mile in double-quick time were Polly to ever encounter him on the downs and engage him on the topic of precision engineering and armaments.

Nearby to Farringford is the broad, elegant tower of Dimbola overlooking the bay, the former home of the pioneering photographer, Mrs Cameron who with her depictions of pale women in flowing robes, her winged angels and her knights of the grail, has left such vivid memories behind among those who knew her - and is still regarded, quite rightly, as the 'Pre-Raphaelite of the lens.' Amos, I understand from his last letter, is longing to go there on a little pilgrimage to see what he can learn, though I suspect he is unaware that she has recently departed for Ceylon, complete with her own coffin, and that the present owners are not in residence either so he may well be disappointed. We shall have to make amends with our celebrated Russian psychic Madam Alenushka who is due to host a reading for us next week. She is quite fabulous, by all accounts, and visiting the island this summer to do the rounds of all the best houses. They say she charges handsomely for her services, being also quite outrageous and self-opinionated in her ways. But we shall have her of course. Polly is quite agreeable to it if it keeps me amused, so we shall see if she is any better or worse than my own modest efforts to contact the 'other side.'

I wonder if having a celebrity such as Madam Alenushka visiting us might render the 'occult' more acceptable to Polly, instead of having to endure the indignity of his wife trying to read the tarot cards or to hold séances? There is little room for the spiritual dimension in his life as yet, I fear. He remains terribly cynical. If it cannot be seen, heard or smelt, and especially if it cannot be tasted or touched, I am afraid he is not at all impressed – not yet. I would love to convert him, to show him that there is more to this world than just what can be seen in front of our noses. I would love him to mellow, and for his heart to become more open and gentle. Anyway, she is to stay with us overnight, the mysterious Madam Alenushka, so we are hoping for great things from her. Perhaps a kindly spirit or angel will visit us (or else one of the other sort).

Polly is away this afternoon, and I am charged with supervising the trimming of the laurel hedges. Not too drastic, he says, as they do afford us some privacy from the road. I do enjoy working in the garden where I can be alone, or take a book with me to sit in the little arbour or summerhouse there and pretend to be the perfect hermit, surrounded by the fragrance of wild garlic at this time of the year, such a very special kind of plant. Is it true, I wonder, that it was once used to ward off evil spirits or vampires? That could prove quite useful shortly.

The bluebells, too, are a delight.

Chapter Seven

Solent Crossing

The loud rhythmic pulse of the mighty paddle wheels as they cut through the water is mesmerising and slightly disturbing. It is becoming rough – and, not being the best of seafarers, Amos is seriously wondering whether the pitching of the boat will be at all to the liking of his delicate stomach and that he might not end up making a complete fool of himself before the little ship reaches its destination. It is, however, a fine afternoon - the glorious sunshine of spring breaking through the skies of showery rain sweeping in from the West – the little wedges of cloud skimming so close to the surface of the water that they leave long, silvery filaments of light upon the sea that dance and shimmer from place to place upon the waves as they go. It is beautiful, and yet he cannot help asking himself still whether he is doing the right thing, and whether the romantic allure of his island destination might ultimately prove to be his undoing? Away from London, away from the Academy, away from all his friends, his clients and the work that provides his modest income, away from the predictable life he knows so well: it is all such a gigantic gamble.

The overnight train from London's Waterloo has taken him on the South-Western down to Portsmouth and the newly opened terminal adjacent to the harbour. His luggage, consisting of several cases and one large elm chest containing his easel, paints and canvases all closely packed together, have been placed safely on board by the porters, and now here he sits with tangled hair, on the windy deck of the paddle steamer, his reefer coat straining at the button as he gazes out to the turbulent waters and the English coastline receding into the distance as the modest sized vessel, a side-wheeler with two passenger decks, ploughs its way across the narrow band of water called the Solent towards the famous Isle of Wight and to where within the next few days he is hoping to put the finishing touches to Lord Bowlend's portrait and, of course, incidentally, to see Daphne again - a prospect which also fills him with a curious blend of excitement and foreboding.

Meanwhile, here on board, he has struck up a conversation with an elderly couple seated opposite him outside on the main deck - the woman glancing with alert observation at everyone around her; the gentleman for the most part seeming to prefer the contents of his newspaper with which he struggles valiantly to bring under control in the stiff, squally breeze. Apparently, they are residents of the Island and are, they assure him, acquainted with just about every living soul of merit who dwells there. So Amos asks if they are at all familiar with the pioneering photographer Mrs Cameron.

'Mrs Cameron? No, sadly, you are couple of years too late, young man,' the woman replies.

She has her shawl wrapped up around the sides of her face to protect her from the breeze, and upon the occasional piercing shaft of sunlight she is forced to shield her eyes, too, with one raised hand as she speaks - such a unique combination of gestures that it makes Amos want to put pencil to paper, and luckily he has a tiny sketchpad in his jacket pocket. So he sets to work straight away, much to the couple's amusement. It is a strange feeling: oddly liberating, sketching out here. And it is not just he who is behaving differently. Everyone, he suspects, is beginning to alter in a subtle kind of way: becoming a little more noisy, a little more jaunty and carefree than would normally be the case. He has been told of this, forewarned: a manifestation of the liberal and somewhat risqué seaside culture that has grown up in recent years among the resorts of the English coast. And nowhere does it seem to be more seductive and persistent in its temptations than here, out on the decks - a combined effect of the rich, oxygenated air perhaps, along with the inevitable sense of anticipation and adventure that journeying to the island-home of the Queen has upon anyone who dares risk coming under its spell.

'Are you of the photographic persuasion yourself?' the gentleman inquires rather awkwardly, choosing to forego the stimulation of his newspaper for a moment. He has a ruddy, weathered complexion and, bare-headed, seems to be not in the least bit disturbed by the wind, which ruffles his whiskers and hair from time to time. Perhaps, Amos surmises he would be connected to the navy or merchant shipping; inured to the rigours of the crossing.

'Yes. Though first and foremost a painter by profession, I have been an admirer of Mrs Cameron's photographs for many years,' Amos replies, aware that his own voice sounds unusually loud, as if shouting against the din of the engines and the wind combined. 'And, of course, the photographic image can aid the artist in his endeavours. My mission here for these next few weeks, however, is to complete a portrait in oils - a distinguished client, you understand'

'They say just about anybody who's anybody went to her to have their likeness captured,' the woman remarks, nestling into the flank of her companion as if for warmth. 'All the artists and poets ...'

'And Darwin,' the gentleman chimes in. 'And Hershel – scientific men, those.'

Amos nods with suitable deference at this injection of masculine name-dropping – though hardly much impressed by it as he returns to his sketch, quickly rendering the head and shoulders of the women in a matter of minutes.

'Lots of interesting news lately, would you not agree?' the gentleman adds proffering his folded newspaper to Amos for his edification, but perhaps realising the futility of such an exercise confines himself to further observations of the artist's drawing technique instead, regarding Amos's increasingly rapid and unconstrained movements with some alarm as his hand flits across the little sketchpad in quick, ever-more spontaneous strokes of the heavy, dark pencil until, with a final frantic flourish, he tears off the page and presents his sketch as a souvenir to the lady herself. Taking his leave, he wanders along and up some steps to the much narrower top deck, behind the bridge and a place reserved for first class passengers – in truth, glad to get away. Whatever the news in the papers (and it would surely be something miserable) he did not wish to know. He was not a political animal. And really, he thinks, what would anyone want to be doing with their nose stuck inside a paper when you have all this around you? This glorious vista! So many ships to wonder at, so many different vessels sharing the narrow stretch of water – fishing boats with their hoards of crying gulls following in their wake; navel vessels or big clippers and seafaring ships out of Portsmouth, their white sails filled and from which, sometimes, carried on the wind, the distant sounds of shanties being sung from the men working on the decks can be heard. And then, of course, there are all the spectacular yachts, the sleek, elegant toys of the rich and famous – all their colours and pennants flying, their masts leaning and dipping at precarious angles to the foaming brine. Everywhere such open space, such vitality and freshness in the air!

On board meanwhile, and in terms of opulence and high fashion, the scene must be the equal of any street in London or Bath, Edinburgh or Brighton: the ladies in their sumptuous, colourful seaside fashions and beautiful touring hats of chiffon trimmed with bright flowers; the gentlemen, some in formal attire but others already in the mood for the seaside - their flamboyant straw boaters upon their heads, the newly fashionable stripped jackets upon their shoulders – blazers, as they are coming to be called, with their shiny buttons - and all attended upon by grooms, footmen and servants who appear to be equally as excited and relieved to be so far away from all the stifling customs of the family estates and the towns. He feels happy for them, and even finds himself smiling at strangers who smile back. Remarkable – the liberating prospect of the seaside. He had even noticed this subtle transformation earlier, at all the various stations and halts along the way as the train headed south through the countryside of Hampshire – of how invigorated it made him feel as each passing mile of the journey took him further and further away from all the filth and grime of London, further away from the bleak industrialised world of business and commerce that he and so many of his contemporaries have come to think of as being in some sense 'normal.' This is different; so very different - and he wonders why he has never taken the trouble to venture upon such a fabulous and stimulating journey before.

From his present vantage point, his back to the towering, black-painted funnel where the steam and smoke of the engines pour high into the sky, he is able to survey the approaching coastline of the island with the tall spire of Ryde church upon the horizon and, to the west, the distinctive Italianate skyline of what must surely be Osborne House with its broad terraced gardens just visible between the trees of Scots pine and cedar: home to Queen Victoria herself for these past thirty odd years and from which, it is said, since the death of her beloved husband Albert, she now rarely if ever ventures forth. Instead, the entire world must now beat a path to her door, the mighty British Empire that has thrown its embrace around the entire globe and upon which the sun therefore never sets, all directed towards and centred upon this one tiny spot in the English Channel; visited by celebrated statesmen and princes, alike; by obsequious courtiers and ambassadors by the carriage-load; all followed by a never-ending procession of cultural luminaries, artists and poets. The like has never existed before and perhaps never will again, he concludes, as he glances around once more at his fellow passengers, most of them on their feet now and, like him, gazing out with keen anticipation as they approach the pier onto which, once the steamer has drawn alongside, they will soon all be put ashore.

But abruptly his attention is diverted elsewhere, because out of the corner of his eye he spots none other than Daphne. He can scarcely believe it – but yes - just along towards the stairway, her lovely slender waist arched as she clasps the deck rail and leans back, one hand shielding her eyes against the sun! Sporting a flat cap with plumes of ostrich feathers set on her head at a jaunty angle, her lush dark hair pinned up beneath, it can only be her - a fashion statement as unconventional and yet as practical as ever out here on the windy deck. *But what is she doing here?* Surely she is already over on the Island, with her husband, and has been for over a week! Extraordinary. He hurries to meet her - but she, not having seen him, has already made her way down to the main deck and is walking away from him, back towards the stern of the boat, moving with amazing speed even on her elegant heels and out of sight among the crowd already gathered and waiting to disembark. He pursues her, knowing she cannot be far away. And a moment later he catches sight of her once more – this time at the top of a further set of steps, those leading out of bounds to passengers, oddly enough. For a moment all he can discern is the top of her cap as she pauses to negotiate the steep descent before she finally vanishes from view.

Within seconds he has thrust his way thought the mêlée and has descended the steps also, very steep and almost ladder-like as he discovers almost to his cost. But here he encounters merely the noisy business-end of the boat, the ropes, capstans and pulleys and all the other working paraphernalia of the ship and its crew. No sign of her, no sign of Daphne at all - and no way up from this section either, everything being closed off by the large enclosed paddle wheels. How bizarre! The only souls present are a couple of seamen, their backs bent to the task, busy preparing for the docking of the boat.

'The young lady, where did she go?' Amos questions them, calling loudly above the din of the paddle wheels, aware also that he is slightly breathless from the chase and, unhatted, his long hair blowing across his face and eyes.

'Young lady?' one of the men roars back with a certain incredulity and annoyance. 'No young lady here, Sir. We'd have noticed one of those, wouldn't we Jack!' he jests with his companion.

'I'd say so!' the other replies, not even bothering much to look up from his labours.

'Then she must have gone overboard. Quick, we must look, over the side!' Amos cries, genuinely disturbed now by what he has seen, and worse by what he *cannot* see any longer.

'Overboard!' the men cry in unison, straightening their spines and now suddenly very alert and interested indeed, for it is an important word when used at sea – as all three, including Amos himself, race to the stern and stare down into the turbulent waters and the foaming wake created by the paddles – the whole vessel just about to commence the process of reversing in order to manoeuvre closer to the pier.

But there is no sign of anyone or anything in the water, nothing at all. And the men become firstly mystified, but then stare in irritation, more than a little morose at the ravings of the young exotically dressed intruder in his reefer jacket and bright red cravat. 'Is he drunk – or worse?' their questioning eyes seem to demand as they glance at each other, and then quickly ignore him – with far more pressing things to busy themselves with now than some phantom of a young dandy's imagination.

Dazed and stunned, tottering on unsteady feet and realising that he has probably just made himself look a complete idiot, Amos makes his way back to the centre of the vessel which has now drawn alongside, adjacent to the blackened timber and ironwork of the pier and to where everyone, amid a buzz of laughter and anticipation, is preparing to brave the rickety gangways and to disembark. Even the elderly couple he had been sitting with earlier have gone by now.

Indifferent to all the excitement, and noticing the newspaper that the gentleman had been reading, Amos sits down here again and, waiting for the crowds to disperse, picks it up for a moment to peruse its headlines. Neatly folded in the expert manner of one used to manipulating the vast expanse of the typical broadsheet into something more manageable, the text displayed here on one of the inner pages causes him to shudder with surprise. It is a piece about the skeletal remains found at The Tower, the very ones he had been called in to sketch only a few months ago – an update, it seems, on the story of the finds. Hoping he might discover here some acknowledgement of his own labours he reads through quickly. But there is no description of anybody making any drawings. No credit for his work: nothing. Just some non-committal quotes from the administration, explaining that the restoration will take some months yet before completion. They are pleased, however, to announce further bequests from one or two wealthy benefactors, including, he is surprised to learn, Lord Oliver Ramsey – whose regiment has always been proudly represented among the Warders of The Tower. The bones of the Tudor queens discovered there, meanwhile, are now gathered safely and placed in caskets that will, at a later date, be interred beneath the flagstones once more, close to the altar.

He is so engrossed in the news, that he does not notice that someone is talking, speaking softly to him from behind his shoulder; he is simply too deep in thought to register the voice at first - until he receives a hand upon the shoulder by way of emphasis. He notices the braided cuffs and shiny buttons; and it is this little sparkle of reflected light that finally snaps him out of his reverie, making him flinch.

'Is everything in order, Sir?' comes the voice. Amos turns and looks up. It is an elderly seaman in uniform and by his gesture of an outstretched arm indicating the vista of the empty deck around him, it becomes clear to Amos that he is the last one remaining on board – and upon which he is ushered gently off the boat by the kindly ministrations of the other man, whose face seems strangely and unaccountably familiar for a moment, and who guides him along with a look of genuine concern still upon his old gnarled face as he enquires once more of his health before finally allowing him to depart.

And so it is for Amos that his first steps upon the magical island that he has heard so much about, and which he has been looking forward to seeing with such enthusiasm, can now only be taken with a sense of trepidation. Not the most propitious of starts, he thinks to himself as, still confused and visibly shaken by the experience of a moment ago, he can only speculate with a profound unease now upon what else might be awaiting him here during the coming days and weeks.

Once re-united with his painting equipment and other items of luggage, and following an excellent lunch of local lobster ashore in Ryde, a further journey by chaise-cart is required to take him to his destination and the small villa in the south-west corner of the island that he has rented for the coming weeks. It is a peculiar feeling for Amos, arriving in an unfamiliar place and to a house that will, of course, be empty. No servants will be there to welcome him, he realises; no friendly neighbours will call with messages or with items of mislaid mail; no familiar animals will bark or purr at his coming - and he wonders just how he will feel about it all as his carriage driver negotiates the approach along a leafy lane up to the gate. As a matter of fact, first impressions of the exterior of the building are not at all disagreeable: tall, stone-framed windows stand either side of a fine elegant doorway with stained glass lights above - all reached by a winding path from the lane itself and surrounded by a pleasant wooded garden with drifts of wild garlic and bluebells, all in flower. It is also, by the sounds of it, a place not too distant from the sea and, perhaps more importantly, not too distant from the far-larger neighbouring building called 'Parnassus' - the imposing residence and summer retreat of none other than Lord and Lady Bowlend. He had passed it just a moment ago, noticed the nameplate on the pillar of the gateway: a magnificent villa built in the revivalist style with tall gables and mullion windows, surrounded by extensive gardens and terraces. The whole area in fact, he realises, is a well-ordered and affluent part of the world, and all set in breathtakingly beautiful surroundings - wooded, leafy and verdant - and slightly exotic, too, with cordylines and phormium plants proclaiming the warm, almost semitropical climate that prevails here, their tufts of spiky leaves thrust towards the sky - all of which pleases him enormously.

After paying the driver and enlisting his help with unloading and bringing in his luggage, Amos is able to inspect the interior of what is to become his home until at least the end of May. Here, unfortunately, all is not quite as inviting as the exterior. It has a bleak, empty feeling - with the typical worn and dilapidated furniture, grubby kitchen and suspect plumbing of a property that changes hands as often as every few weeks and is therefore cared for by nobody in particular.

Ascending the stairs, he walks through the echoing bedrooms on the first floor. There is a smell of mothballs here, the curtains are hanging in shreds and there are no carpets at all upon the bare boards. Beth will no doubt be able to put this to rights in her usual capable way when she arrives in a few days, he thinks, as will the ministrations of his occasional valet, James, also due. He takes some solace from that prospect - and also from the fact that, for all its pitiful neglect, there is still a certain dignity and aesthetic appeal about the place, which has clearly been constructed by craftsmen, with elegant, dark-panelled wood everywhere, some of it beautifully carved with spiral and acanthus motifs, and small roundels of stained glass, too, amid the tracery of the windows and doorways, all lending a certain aesthetic appeal and dignity. By fortunate design, moreover, the house does have a substantial conservatory, embracing the whole of the southern aspect of the building. On an overcast day, therefore, Amos surmises, he might be able to wheel his easel out beneath the long glass roof overlooking the garden. If, on the other hand, the weather were sunny, there would always be the large empty rooms at the front of the house, north-facing with their substantial windows and which could also serve as studios. One way or another the cottage will be suitable enough for the occupation of painting.

Moreover, there is something here that does succeed in lifting his spirits quite substantially – for downstairs, upon a table in the kitchen an envelope awaits him, sealed with a daub of shiny red wax, and with the impression of a signet ring upon it that he identifies straight away as Daphne's. Eagerly he opens the envelope with his penknife. It is an invitation. His company, it states, is requested for high tea tomorrow at Parnassus. And there is a postscript, too, written in Daphne's own distinctive copperplate hand: 'Amos, do come! I have been here for a week already; have hardly left the house, and am absolutely dying of boredom. You should stay here under our roof if it is too dreadful for you there. Yours, Daphne.'

How lovely to have her greeting and her familiar handwriting that he recognises instantly to welcome him. But it is also a message whose words confirm the awful truth: that it could certainly not have been her on the steamer earlier today. Not at all. And this, of course, only begged the question: who or what had it been, then - that strange and beautiful apparition in the plumed cap that had appeared and then vanished, seemingly into thin air? Was it just an extraordinary case of mistaken identity? Or was it rather a mirage of his own making, a product of his own fevered and troubled imagination? He simply did not know.

That evening, following a brief exploratory walk around the nearby bay with its turbulent seas and crashing waves, its broad crescent of sand and shingle beach and its fine hotel in the lee of the cliffs where the lamps already lit in the windows had beckoned him in for an evening meal, he returns to the cottage and retires to his bed, untypically early for him as with more than a little reluctance he faces the prospect of a night alone in the unfamiliar, creaky and draughty building. It becomes cold, and very obvious to his chilly bones that spring has not quite arrived, not yet even to these southernmost shores of England which are normally renowned for their balmy and temperate climes. It could be the depth of winter out there, he thinks, listening to the whistling of the wind and the various unfamiliar voices of the seashore: the ever-present rhythmic noise of the waves, a deep pulsating sound, but also with the added descant of what he supposes must be large pebbles or flints of some kind being dragged in and out at the foot of the cliffs by the powerful forces of the tide. It is almost a screaming sound, a sound of voices in distress, reminding Amos with his ever-present vivid imagination of the sounds of a shipwreck. Yes, it could be just that kind of a night, a night on which ships could go down; or upon which the watery graves of generations of mariners might open and eject their contents and their scattered, rattling bones upon the shore. And if it had been a singular experience for him, arriving earlier to an empty building with no one to acknowledge his coming, then it occurs to him now that this must also be the first night that he has really ever slept alone, totally alone in any place for many a year. Always he would have had someone close by - a companion, a lover, even one or two household staff in other rooms: always at least one other living soul somewhere under the same roof. But here in his loneliness he is very much forsaken. Nature rules in a place such as this, so distant from the familiar urban world. It is the primitive, unforgiving mistress and governess now who is at large out there, eerie, commanding in all her mystery and unfathomable reaches – *there*, just beyond his door, rattling the shutters of his windows, begging to enter. And then with a chilling clarity he happens to recall the image in his mind's eye of the old seaman who had guided him off the boat earlier, the one who had found him dazed and staring at the folded newspaper on deck after everyone else had gone ashore and whose face had also seemed so very familiar at the time. Because now at last Amos is able to place it. He realises that it resembled none other than that of the old Yeoman Warder at The Tower – the very same who had sat with him that evening while he sketched the bones: he who even then was supposed to be no more than some wretched figment of his imagination – or so they had assured him, the fools!

And as he reads again for solace the brief message left by Daphne today and which, he is delighted to discover, still bears some traces of her perfume. And as he smoothes the folded paper between finger and thumb to help release the comforting fragrance, imagining that perhaps she would have had traces of it on her hands as she wrote, or that the paper itself might have rested on her dressing table where her scent bottles would have left their subtle imprint, he is compelled to face the terrible, chilling truth. For he knows now, beyond all shadow of a doubt, that he is a haunted person, driven and pursued by some terrible spectre – be it within or without – something almost demon and savage and over which he has no powers or means of control.

'You may be dying of boredom, Lady Daphne,' he mutters to himself with a grim smile, recalling her words. 'But you should perhaps spare a thought for me this night – for I may well die of fear.'

Chapter Eight

Portrait and a Conversation

'Huh! Made me a bit on the corpulent side, haven't you?' are Oliver Ramsey's first observations upon being shown through into the conservatory where the almost-finished portrait stands in readiness between the tall twin uprights of its easel. 'Make me a little slimmer, eh? Or can't you do that now?'

Ramsey is here today for what, Amos hopes will be a lengthy uninterrupted sitting in which he will be able to observe and study how the man's face and complexion behave in daylight and consequently to render the finishing touches to the head and shoulders. A coat of varnish could then be applied in a few weeks time, and then the job will be done – and it can't come soon enough for Amos, because the whole enterprise continues to fill him not only with repugnance, but with anxiety, too. For just as the powerful Lord Bowlend is someone who could further his career as a painter, with introductions to any number of prominent individuals and their families, he is also someone who could just as easily wreck it if crossed or displeased.

'You would not wish me to flatter your Lordship unduly,' Amos replies with a note of banter. He would only ever address him as *his Lordship* when being slightly ironic. The rest of the time he was permitted to call him Oliver, of course. 'The art world would not forgive me, nor your friends forgive *you* if we were to manipulate the truth for the sake of vanity.'

'Yes, yes, you're right enough, I suppose,' the big man replies while continuing to sidle up to the work, producing his monocle from his waistcoat pocket, attaching it to his eye socket with a rough screwing motion and, with the inevitable squint and lopsided facial expression that the instrument invariably produces in those who insist on using it, continues to give the painting his critical eye.

The canvas itself is over six foot in height so that the subject can be shown full-figure, legs astride, quite imposing and almost regal in appearance with an ivory topped cane brandished in one hand like a royal sceptre, the other hand holding a top hat and leather gloves. The figure itself is clothed in a formal black morning suit, double-breasted and with a crisp white collar, the chest and stomach in its white waistcoat forming a rather bulbous shape in front. The eyes, meanwhile, are depicted looking straight ahead, towards the viewer, who is caught in their gaze - the large, square-shaped face commanding in appearance, grave and serious, challenging all comers. Serving as background to this modern-day emperor of industry, meanwhile, is the magnificent country seat of Bowlend Court, with its distinctive gothic-style portico and tall pointed windows, standing foursquare in all its glory - that most conspicuous and most tangible outcome of all his labours.

'I must get more exercise, do more riding,' Ramsey concludes, his fingers stroking his chin in contemplation of the rotund image staring back out at him as if looking into a mirror. 'There's a local Hunt, and they're doing point-to-point racing this weekend. I'll see if I can ride with them.'

Although the wearing of the monocle does make him look at lot older than his forty years, Ramsey does appear in good health, and also particularly well-dressed and scrubbed this morning: his face, apart from his long sideburns, clean-shaven and his skin as shiny as an apple (and almost of a like colour in places.) The worst of it, however, is that he does appear to have put on even more weight than before - so much so that Amos, in comparing him to the painting, is almost of a mind to increase the girth of the subject even further just in order to keep pace with developments. He is becoming a very big man, the rate of growth accelerating all the while, exponentially so.

'Settling in all right are you?' Ramsey inquires once he has had his fill of the work - though with a distracted look now that betrays a lack of genuine interest in any answer that might be forthcoming as he allows his attention to wander instead to a perusal of his surroundings, the elegant though modestly appointed conservatory, untidy with its profusion of overgrown pot-plants and assorted items of oddly matched furniture - mahogany, rosewood and wicker – and then, through the tall windows and French doors, to the sprawling garden outside, appearing no doubt every bit as disorderly, wild and unkempt to his discerning eye.

'Yes thank you,' Amos continues by way of reply, feeling confident and at ease in his smart suit and ascot tie; determined not to make any concessions to the nature of the work he is engaged in by dressing down, therefore, and already making ready with some suitable paints squeezed from tubes onto the surface of his palette. 'Local knowledge has been invaluable, I must say, and everyone so helpful - the best places to shop, the best places to have lunch, the best way to order up wood for the fire or wine for table. In the absence of my staff to minister to my needs, I simply would not have been able to get along without it. It was good of you to offer to put me up at Parnassus, of course. But as you can see, I shall be able to manage quite well, thank you.'

Ramsey, however, appears not altogether pleased at having his offer of hospitality rebuffed – since he likes everyone to be beholden to him, of course: under his control. 'What a pity! Lady Bowlend will be so disappointed,' he declares, making it clear that it would have been Daphne's idea, after all, not his. 'Anyway, where do you want me?'

Ramsey does not need to stand, Amos tells him. A stool is provided, and it is upon this creaking and woefully insubstantial structure that the big man lowers his immense bulk - reminding Amos for one bizarre moment of an elephant at the circus, reluctantly sitting back onto his haunches at the ringmaster's command. Accepting a glass of claret, he eventually manages to stop fidgeting, however, to strike up a neutral pose and to relax. Outside, the skies are already turning overcast and drizzly, occasionally peppering the windows and glass roof with tiny hailstones. But at least the light remains adequate, Amos thinks as he takes up his brushes and palette in earnest now. As always when he works, he encourages his sitter to converse with him, and to this end, after a few moments, he embarks upon some pleasantries:

'And may I enquire after Lady Bowlend,' he begins. 'Is your good wife well?'

'Not bad, not bad at all. Considering we're no longer exactly a couple of newly-weds, I'd say we're doing quite well.'

'And the pitter-patter of tiny feet? Are we to expect something of that nature shortly, perhaps?' Amos continues – it would appear by the expression on the noble lord's face rather impertinently.

'Naturally, I would expect to leave my estate to a son and heir in good time,' he responds. 'My first wife was unable to oblige in that department, so we are hoping for a blessing shortly - that Daphne might prove more compatible. We are deploying all of our resources, I can assure you - in the matrimonial department, you understand - to make it happen.'

As ever, Amos tries to conceal his distaste at any allusion to what Ramsey and Daphne might be engaged in between the sheets. Try as he might, he simply cannot get used to the idea, and the thought of Daphne crushed beneath the bulk of this enormous beast of a man continues to appal him.

'There is no one else who can inherit, anyway,' Ramsey continues, accompanied by a little sniffle, designed perhaps to convey a certain impression of sorrow. 'We lost my elder brother, sadly when still quite young. Everything fell to me - all the wealth amassed by my father over the years during which time he built up the company from nothing to what it is today.'

'Ah, so that's where you get your business acumen from, your father?'

'Taught me everything I know.'

'Did you get on all right with him?' Amos inquires, his fine sable brush hovering above the surface of the canvas as he peruses the man's face with expert eye time and time again, only just occasionally adding tiny dabs of thin glaze to the work itself.

'Oh yes ... as well as any son ever gets on with his father, I suppose. Strict disciplinarian. Made damn sure I made the grade for the guards.'

'Strict, you say?'

'Oh, I say so! Children were to be seen but not heard, otherwise we'd cop it, I can tell you! Ruled with not exactly a rod of iron, then at least a formidable switch of birch, if you know what I mean. Never did me any harm, though. Our home was a well-ordered place as a consequence – and a quiet one. He always used to insist on silence at meal times, the old man – in fact, as I seem to recollect, he always insisted on silence at just about *any time*. Funny, I suppose, when I look back on it. Even our toys - you know, when children have toys that make all kinds of sounds and squeaks and things. We had those, of course, only he used to take the toys apart and remove all the squeaks. Yes, odd in a way. But as I say, never did me any harm.'

'No, clearly not,' Amos concurs and quickly hides his face behind the canvas for a moment in order to control himself.

'The Crimea was what made his millions,' Ramsey continues. 'He saw the war coming, miles ahead of the competition. He knew that modern inventions were making warfare an ever-more lucrative enterprise, too. He anticipated that the railways would allow troops to be moved around in greater numbers and far more rapidly than ever before, and he realised that the invention of the telegraph would mean that messages and dispositions could be communicated much faster than ever before. War was becoming more manageable, in other words – he knew that, and invested heavily in what was making it manageable. Yes, the Crimea was excellent for us. We are hoping for another similar opportunity again in the not-too-distant future - perhaps some kind of action in the Transvaal with the Boers or the Zulus – or even both! Not quite sure yet. Time will come, though, when we won't have to suffer any more of these wretched lulls, these inconvenient pauses in-between wars. I mean how can a firm develop and sustain a viable business strategy when its source of revenue is forever fluctuating? No, time will come, mark my words, when we'll convince the politicians and the public to exist in a perpetual state of warfare, always riled up with one foe or another. Then we can plan more efficiently for the future in terms of raw materials, labour and projected costs and so on, with a steady revenue stream instead of always stop-start as it is at the moment.'

'Perpetual warfare? Won't you run out of people though sooner or later if you do that?' Amos inquires through gritted teeth, wondering just how he is going to get through the next hour or two without telling his distinguished sitter what a first rate bastard he is.

'People? What do you mean, people?' he says, looking more than a little puzzled by Amos's latest observation.

'Yes, you know - cannon fodder – soldiers.'

'Oh there'll always be plenty of those!' Ramsey cries with a dismissive wave of the hand. 'Too many damned unemployed out there, as it is. Warfare – it's an economic strategy, Amos. We manage the population just as we manage the herd – through culling the surplus men whenever necessary - otherwise the strain on our economy from all the poor would be unsustainable. Besides, I wouldn't object to a world in which the girls outnumbered the boys, would you, ha, ha!'

'As a matter of fact I think I might,' Amos replies coldly while continuing to work with increasingly petulant and rapid little movements of his brush – and realising with dismay that his brush-hand is trembling and that the work he has intended to do today, refining and finishing the head and shoulders was actually now looking worse than when he had started.

'I say, you're – er – not *one of those* are you, Roselli? One of those homos?' Ramsey inquires, beginning to regard him with a look of suspicion - so not for the first time, therefore, must Amos remind him that he should relax his face and try to look reasonably calm, as he would wish to appear in his portrait.

'Don't worry. I'm not *one of those,*' Amos assures him. 'Though would it matter if I was?'

'Criminal offence, young man. I would have to disassociate myself from you and your work if that were the case.'

'Just try to relax the furrows in your forehead,' Amos

urges him again.

'Sorry. Anyway, don't you opium-eaters lose all interest in fornication anyway after a while? Isn't that so?' he observes, becoming ever more importunate and downright rude, in fact, by now - using the derogatory term, opium eaters, for those who take laudanum in excess.

'You could be right - though I can't say I've noticed anything untoward just yet,' Amos replies urbanely. 'Absinthe tends to compensate for that, anyway.'

To which Bowlend laughs and says, 'Emm! So I still need to keep an eye on you, eh - if we are to execute my lady wife, next.'

'*Execute?* What an odd word to use!' Amos says, and laughs.

'Why that's the term for it, isn't it? You are to do her, execute her portrait next, as we have agreed,' Ramsey continues with obvious irritation that he might be showing himself up by employing the wrong terminology. 'You will be alone with her for extended periods.'

'You could always send a chaperone - as one would for a young girl.'

'Don't be ridiculous!'

'I am not the one who is being ridiculous.'

But Ramsey's patience is at an end. He breaks from his enforced pose, gets to his feet and marches towards Amos.

'You will learn quickly enough how ridiculous I can be if you start stripping her - *au naturel* - for one of your filthy allegorical nudes again!' he roars coming up close and pointing an intimidating finger towards Amos's face. 'Those days are over, Roselli.'

'Oliver, calm down, please!' Amos declares, one hand imploring the other man to return to his place. 'Daphne and I have known one another since childhood. She is like a sister to me - you must realise that, surely?'

Ramsey, with grudging acquiescence, returns to his stool where, to Amos's surprise, he quickly lifts his chin and assumes the studied pose of calm and tranquillity once again. 'You will do the work over at Parnassus,' he states, trying to speak without moving his lips, but managing to lay down the rules already, nonetheless. 'You can bring your brushes and bits over, can't you - that big wooden box of yours?'

'My elm chest? Yes, if you can provide a north-facing room with large windows and space enough for my easel, yes, I suppose that will be in order,' Amos agrees though with obvious reluctance.

But just before they can finalise the arrangements, there is the distinctive sound of a carriage drawing up on the cobbles of the lane at the front of the house. Wonderful! Because this is surely his trusty staff arriving from London - at last! Feeling excited all of a sudden, and with brushes and palette still in hand, he hurries through to answer the door even before they can ring at the bell. It is, indeed, his valet and maid arriving, and he ushers them in with a heartfelt warmth. Beth is as bright-eyed and inquisitive as ever as she steps over the threshold in her little blue bonnet and Sunday-best cambric dress, looking as if she is taking part in the adventure of a lifetime - while James in contrast gives the impression of being utterly exhausted from the journey, his heavy-lidded basset eyes as droopy and as disdainful as ever as he trudges into the hallway in his old-fashioned black frock coat and glances around at the sorry state of the interior with already a look of some despair.

'Here is the kitchen, Beth,' Amos announces straight away, showing her through without too many cumbersome formalities and realising as he does so that he is feeling unaccountably happy at her arrival, and hungry too. 'It's a bit dilapidated, I know, but there are provisions aplenty in the larder, and the range is in working order - I've seen to that already - though a bit grubby. Feel free to make yourself a pot of tea after your trip. And you may bring in another for my sitter and myself, as well, when you are fully refreshed - shall we say in ten minutes'

'*Ten minutes!*' Beth exclaims and wipes a little bead of perspiration from her dusty forehead, at which he is compelled to see things from her perspective for a moment. Coming thus into an unfamiliar house straight after having spent a whole day travelling by rail, steamer and carriage from London to the Island, they would probably both be hungry, as well as tired, he thinks. 'Well then, fifteen minutes will do fine, Beth,' he concedes, with a smile of compassion that, oddly, still seems not particularly appreciated and merely causes James to raise an ironic eyebrow as if in despair as he continues to haul in the luggage from the chaise-cart and to negotiate with the driver his fare.

Upon his return to the conservatory, Amos finds Ramsey up on his feet and, monocle re-attached, bent forward and studying the painting at close quarters once again, his nose only inches away from it as if totting up some kind of valuation by examining the number of brush strokes upon its surface.

'Emm, fine work!' he admits, grudgingly. 'Anyway, you will, I take it, at least be honouring us with your presence at dinner this evening?' he inquires, resuming his place on the stool once more and striking up the required pose with the by-now practised movements of a seasoned model.

Amos, however, does not answer right away. Taking high tea for one brief hour over at Parnassus yesterday afternoon had been strained and awkward enough, he recalls. The prospect of a whole evening in Ramsey's company was positively daunting.

'Well?' the big man demands. '*Respondez s'il vous plait.* I shan't ever hear the end of it if I return home without your agreement.'

Thinking of Daphne and of how good it will be to see and speak with her again, he accepts, though at the same time he is also pleased to announce that he fully expects to be able to dine at home from tomorrow onwards, since his people will have got it up nicely for him by then. He feels a sense of relief, therefore, that he will not be incumbent on his illustrious paymaster any more than is necessary, and Oliver seems to sense this, too, and to acknowledge it with his usual air of irritation and disapproval. In this huff of a mood, therefore, a period of sustained quiet ensues in which Amos is able to concentrate and to accomplish some useful work, his brush hand resting on the long mahl stick for steadiness as once again he attempts to apply the necessary finishing glazes to the face of his subject. Delicate work and for a while all seems well – but it is not to last, of course. The artist becomes acutely aware that the other man is examining him all the while as he works, watching him closely out of the corner of his eye, as though sizing him up, trying to fathom his mysteries. It is an uncomfortable sensation.

'Y'know, you're a rum sort of fellow, Amos,' Ramsey begins again, reverting to first-name terms once more and clearly wanting to alleviate the discomfort of what, to him, would be an unnatural silence. 'You don't like shooting; you don't like riding; you're not excessively promiscuous, or so you assure me. In fact you seem to be the perfect saint. Bit too good to be true, eh! I'm still in the dark about you, Amos, and I don't like that. Enlighten me, won't you? You must have some kind of passion in life? What is it?'

But Amos, again, is not to be intimidated. He works on in silence, continuing to treat Ramsey's curiosity with suitable indifference for quite some time before finally responding.

'My passion? Well, precisely what I am doing now, if you must know,' he replies at last, though still without glancing up to acknowledge the other man's attempted interrogation. Instead, with palette and brushes in abeyance, he transfers his attention to the contents of his wine glass which he swirls and brings to his nose for a moment before imbibing. 'I love my work,' he continues. 'It has taken many years of study and endless practice to have developed my skills and a style that I can call my own. That doesn't come without sacrifices. And it doesn't leave an inordinate amount of time left over for frivolous things like hunting, fishing and shooting, if that's what you mean.'

'What you describe as *frivolous*, Amos, are the time-honoured occupations of the countryside, and of the gentry,' Ramsey counters straight away taking up the challenge. 'They are in fact the pursuits that go to make up the complete gentleman, the right stuff for defending Queen and country.'

'*The right stuff?*' Amos inquires, putting down his glass and allowing a look of some perplexity to settle upon his brow.

'Yes. We have to continue to breed men with the necessary backbone, the capacity for competition and leadership in order to preserve the hierarchy of command that governs society. We need to maintain a resource of strong individuals who can draw blood, Amos, if we are to survive and not just become a nation of shop assistants or, if you'll forgive me, aesthetes.'

'And blasting dozens of helpless creatures from the sky with a shotgun – that's how to go about it, eh?' Amos inquires as he draws forth one of his brushes again ready to continue.

'No, not entirely. No one thinks that. But the business that goes with it – the business of riding, competing, chasing – the business of quick unselfconscious slaughter – that *is* the way. Without the ability to do that in peace time, we're done for when we need to take to the field or rouse ourselves to fight.'

Amos feels a chill descend down his spine. *Quick, unselfconscious slaughter.* Is Ramsey trying to tell him something? Is that how he would like to deal with his enemies, with anyone who opposes him or threatens the equilibrium of his smug little world – his home and country, his marriage? Amos gives a further shrug of the shoulders before responding.

'Each to his own,' he states as he breaks again to pour a little more wine for his guest. 'For my part, I believe the arts are more important than any of that, supremely important. The arts inspire, civilise and moderate our baser instincts and are a source of happiness. Without them we merely exist as a kind of rabble – perhaps with all kinds of noble appendages, like heraldry, chivalry and all that, but a rabble all the same. It is beauty and the quest for beauty that inspires me. I don't expect you to understand anymore than I can understand you because it all begins at an early age, doesn't it – if we are lucky enough to be exposed to something more inspirational, something decent at the start.'

'What do you mean? Are you talking about childhood?'

Amos has to think deeply. How can he make an oaf like this understand?

'Well, yes, that's right,' he says. 'My earliest recollections, for example, are of imaginative and creative experiences – like being at home, at Christmas – things like that – with me seated at a big table, my feet hardly touching the floor and surrounded by lots of paper and paints and coloured crayons and things. That's what I mean. Looking back now, it seems quite idyllic, really. I can remember doing Christmas cards, little scenes of cottages in the snow, icicles hanging from the gabled roofs, and pine trees and holly bushes in the gardens. I would fold the cards and present them to my mother who would comment on them and we would talk about who we would send them to, and of how I might improve upon the pictures next time. Remarkable - how certain memories like that stay with you. Father was away working in the city I suppose, and my sister already at school, so it was just the two of us alone with the staff in that great big old building. It was probably perfect bliss - I realise that now - me messing about with brushes and little trays of watercolour, and my mother busy about the place, conjuring up all the Christmas treats, the mince pies and puddings and all that. And then we would sit together and talk about painting. I would be shown how to draw perspective, and how to make a window and a door into my cottage, and how to paint a light in the windows, too, when the skies were grey and full of snow outside. I realise now that must have been true contentment. In fact I sometimes fancy that even if I should live to be as old as Methuselah, even if I should become the most successful and wealthiest painter in the world, I doubt that I will ever be able to recapture such a state of perfect contentment ever again. But of course that doesn't stop me trying. Every portrait every sketch I do is probably done in the hope of capturing again, even if only for one moment, that state of perfect serenity and happiness.'

Oliver Ramsey continues to regard him with a look of distaste, however - and Amos feels suddenly a little sick in his stomach, that he has laid bare so much of his inner self to such a reprobate.

'All sounds a touch unhealthy, Amos, if you ask me - such an unnatural longing for ones mother.'

'Ah, but surely even you had a mother once, Oliver,' Amos responds, 'in addition, that is, to a father who dismantled your toys,' he adds, maintaining his voice of nonchalance still, but knowing instinctively that he was hitting a raw nerve. Without looking at his guest he can sense the stiffening of his limbs, the straightening of his spine.

'Correct! But that, as I said, is the stuff of childhood. I'm a grown man, now, Amos, and I have a thriving business constructing and deploying my very own special toys - ones that squeak and go bang very loudly, as a matter of fact. I am also in possession of a wife, and a particularly attractive one to provide for my needs and diversions. I have Daphne, and I mean to hold on to her. I hope I am making myself perfectly clear, Amos?'

'You have made your point eloquently enough on more than one occasion already, thank you,' Amos replies, lifting his face from his work at last to look the other man squarely in the eyes. And so an understanding is reached. Both are satisfied it seems and gradually a workable atmosphere envelopes the room once more during which Amos is again able to put some meaningful additions to the canvas – until, that is, the silence is broken by Beth who, with a little rap of the knuckles upon the French doors into the conservatory finally brings in some tea, all neatly presented on an enamel tray that she must have discovered in the pantry, plus milk and sugar and even a little lemon juice should it be required (heaven only knows where she found that!) – and at which the noble lord's face transforms itself dramatically. Examining the young woman, still in her travelling dress with its fashionable figure-hugging lines, he has the unselfconscious stare of a farmer at a cattle market, Amos thinks, his thick, wine-stained lips smacking with salacious interest as he watches her set down the tray with a little curtsy and then continuing to regard her thus unabashed until she leaves the room.

'*Ingénue!*' he remarks, somewhat cryptically as usual for anyone who might not have a French dictionary immediately to hand – while glancing in Amos's direction and beginning to regard him with an altogether new and disturbingly higher level of esteem. Unnoticed by the departing Beth, Amos glares across at him with cold disapproval and shakes his head in despair by way of response – a gesture of censure which snaps the big man out of his reverie. 'Emm. Neat little bunny, what!' the sitter concludes. 'Wouldn't win any beauty contest, but a nice little bottom all the same! She could come over to Parnassus and *sponge my aspidistra* anytime! If you can spare her, that is.'

'Ah, you are an aficionado of bottoms, then, Sir?' Amos observes, as if thinking aloud as he brandishes his brush with a little flourish in the air above the surface of the canvas. 'Female ones, I presume. You're not *one of those,* after all, are you?'

But Ramsey merely points a menacing index finger at him once again.

'Careful, Roselli! I'll have your guts for garters if I have anymore of your cheek.'

'Cheek!' Amos fires back, with brazen audacity still – and to which both men laugh at themselves and laugh heartily as Amos breaks off to pour the tea. Then, to the accompaniment of a deliberately loud and provocative tinkling sound as he cleans his brush in a little jar of turpentine on the window ledge, he returns patiently to his work.

Chapter Nine

A Secret Caress

The strength of the wind is almost overpowering up here, vicious in its intensity as he walks against it, struggling at moments to stay on his feet as he fastens the lapels of his trench coat with its high collar that he endeavours to keep up around his ears for protection. It is not a cold day but the wind here on the downs can penetrate to the very bones. He has been warned of this, and of just how swiftly the weather can change – with his having already experienced at least a dozen permutations so far this morning, from pleasant sunshine, to drenching rain; from sea mist, rainbows and hailstones to something not dissimilar to a tornado, and then back again to sunshine. It is, he reflects, nothing if not *lively*, the weather here.

Upwards and onwards he walks, climbing steadily above the bay up to the highest part of the downs, almost five hundred feet above the sea, they say – the high-lined horizon and waters of the English Channel all capped with turbulent waves and 'white horses' rolling in from the south-west. What a sight! What's more, it matches his mood just perfectly today, the contending of the elements against all manner of romantic notions within, stirring and inspiring him to rejoice in his own youth and vitality amid the vastness of nature. Marvellous.

It soon becomes apparent, however, that his sense of romantic isolation is about to be challenged as, advancing towards him from a lane leading up through a fir copse in the lee of the hills, there comes a most peculiar-looking elderly gentleman. Dressed in a long cloak and with an improbably large broad-rimmed hat, like something one might behold on the London stage, he walks erratically with big, bold steps, his head bowed forward as if muttering to himself. So quickly does he advance, that it is impossible for Amos to avoid him, and within seconds the old fellow has spotted him and drawn alongside,

'What are you doing here?' the fellow demands, thrusting his long walking stick into the ground with an emphatic gesture, like brandishing a staff of office - and as if the whole of the downs belonged to him alone.

'I beg your pardon!' Amos responds, astonished by the man's rudeness and ignorance. 'I don't believe we have met before, Sir. I would certainly remember one as discourteous as you!'

'This is no weather for touring the island,' the old fellow continues, ignoring Amos's protestations, 'not up here on the wind-swept, high backed down! You'd be better off below there in the Albion, the hotel of yonder bay. That's the place for tourists today.'

'I am not a tourist,' Amos states angrily. 'My name is Amos Roselli. I am a painter ...'

'Oh a painter, eh!' he exclaims, his eyes squinting somewhat as if struggling to see what exactly such a creature might look like. 'Well, we've got far too many of those as it is, young man. Tourists, and painters and poets. Two-a-penny here. You'd do much better in Bath or Brighton or somewhere like that, and so Good Day to you, Sir!'

'And Good Day to you!' Amos replies indignantly, as the old fellow bounds away, climbing and striding out along the crest of the downs with the accomplished dexterity of a mountain goat, his dark-cloaked figure receding into the distance at amazing speed.

How very peculiar! Amos thinks, and it takes him quite a while to regain his composure after such an onslaught – almost as tempestuous as the weather itself! But he refuses to allow anything to trouble him or spoil his mood this morning – this very special morning, in fact, because now it is time to retrace his steps back down to the village and to a very special assignation at the Villa Parnassus – there to embark on the very first stages of a new portrait of none other than his beloved Daphne, Lady Bowlend. This is going to be the first time since his arrival on the island that he will be alone with her – without the presence of Lord Bowlend. No tortuous high teas or stuffy dinners staring at each other across a table listening to Ramsey's pompous conversation this time. This morning is to be theirs, and theirs alone - and so it is with a sense of growing anticipation that he quickens his steps, pursued as he goes by another squally shower that has sprung up from nowhere it seems in a matter of seconds until he finds himself beneath the canopy of cedars upon the sheltered drive leading to Parnassus, flanked on either side, he notices once again, by a decidedly overblown profusion of cement statues and urns. These tend to be lined up in almost regimental fashion, in the manner of troops on a battle field and would, most likely be the result of the noble lord's penchant for order and formality – qualities which, when combined with poor taste, as here, make for an rather unfortunate combination.

By Ramsey's insistence, stating that it would be inappropriate for Daphne to be alone with the artist in his 'grubby little cottage' as he had put it, Amos has had to move all of his equipment, his easel and his paints over here to the villa. For here at Parnassus, there would always be other people, staff and visiting tradesmen, plenty of keen eyes and ears, all of which fulfils Ramsey's purpose of having his wife kept under surveillance while she and Amos work together on her portrait. All very bizarre – though in fairness Ramsey had sent men yesterday to assist with the moving of the heavy easel and other equipment, so really Amos could not complain.

The butler answers the door, and then Lady Bowlend's chamber maid leads him upstairs to the library, also serving as morning room, and to a waiting Daphne who has it seems been examining the tarot cards, having laid them out in some arcane, time-honoured pattern upon the top of her Davenport in the corner - but which, upon his entrance, she swiftly clears away, presenting him with a mischievous smile as she does so and an almost imperceptible yet typically *Daphnesque* pout of the lips - as if thereby acknowledging a guilty secret but not really caring much who notices. A large vase of suitably mirthful hyacinths is placed upon the mantelpiece proclaiming her mood.

'Hello, dear one,' she says, coming over and taking his hands in hers for a moment. 'I have been so looking forward to this! Polly is downstairs still, but he will be leaving us shortly, don't worry.'

She is looking especially lovely this morning, he thinks, having put on a simple kimono-style gown for the purpose of modelling, silken and loosely draped and therefore something that can easily be undone or removed if need be. Her rich chestnut-brown hair is brushed and loose about her shoulders, ready for whatever styling is required; a substantial jewel box, spilling out with hair clips, brooches, necklaces and strings of pearls, is also available, placed upon a little dressing table replete with mirrors, brushes, combs and powder that she has had moved into the room - everything prepared and ready for the kind of work which, after all these years, she is so familiar with and so capable of performing for him. It is an arrangement, however, clearly not much to the liking of her husband, who - territorial in the way of some rutting beast sensing an intruder on the scene - charges in for a moment to make his presence felt. In appearance he is just the antithesis of his wife: all buttoned-up, polished and gleaming in red coat and riding boots, and is about to 'leave them to it,' as he states rather gruffly with a threatening glance thrown specifically in Amos's direction before stomping down stairs and out of the building altogether. And a moment later when Amos glances down from the windows he can see him mounting and then riding off on horseback - in the company, it seems, of a friend from the local hunt. It would be the point-to-point race he mentioned the other day, no doubt. With a feeling of immense satisfaction, Amos watches him go - the man's unfortunate mount already seeming to be buckling under the strain - exercise of a kind for the big man, yes, though the poor animal beneath him would be the unwilling recipient of most of it, Amos concludes.

'Very impressive!' he observes, not referring to Ramsey

but returning his attentions to Daphne once again and gazing with admiration around the beautiful room with its towering bookshelves of oak wood, fashioned from timbers once salvaged from a local shipwreck, she tells him, and all bristling with expensive leather-bound volumes of the classics together with works by contemporary writers, including plenty of Tennyson and Thackeray, Dickens and Swinburne – writers and poets that, he realises with amazement, have all either lived or worked upon the Island at some stage in their careers. There is a sense of being at the very hub of things in this extraordinary part of the world, he thinks as he attends to his easel which has already been put up for him by Ramsey's staff. Quite inspirational.

'One of my rooms in the cottage also contains books – though nothing quite like this,' he remarks as Daphne takes her seat before him. 'I was reading last night, as a matter of fact - quite late. And then I had the most peculiar dream.'

'Oh, poor thing! That's what always happens to me if I read too late at night,' she says with a somewhat disinterested attempt at paying heed – and evidently far more excited by the prospect of modelling than anything he might have to complain about. 'How shall you paint me? Half-profile perhaps? This is certainly my better side, would you agree?'

It is all deliberate, of course, her time-honoured way of teasing him and getting his hackles up. The hyacinths – symbolic of playfulness - on the mantelpiece should have been sufficient warning to him of the mood she was in. If her husband could have a day of sport, so could she.

'You don't have a better side,' he says. 'Both are perfectly lovely.' Anyway, as I was saying – *pay attention!* - in the dream I seemed to have been drifting through all kinds of corridors and rooms, like in a great building, and I was dressed quite outlandishly, as well, in clothes like they had in the olden days, you know.'

As he speaks he secures a large canvas to the easel and prepares a blend of linseed oil and turpentine, just the right consistency for the paint - quite fluid in texture in this instance for the purpose of quickly blocking in some background and getting the whole of the canvas covered, something he always likes to do at the start of any new work. Although this is to be another substantial piece, four foot in height, he has decided to paint Daphne's portrait straight off, without preliminary sketches of any kind. After all, hers is a likeness he could, if need be, paint from memory - almost with his eyes closed. The only decision needed today is how best to render her – though in this respect he is somewhat restricted since they have agreed with her husband who is, after all, paying the bills, that things should be kept simple. Lady Bowlend is to be seated, and dressed formally in a fashionable ball gown almost bare-shouldered with a low décolletage and cuirass bodice – though much of the clothing can be added later, of course, using a mannequin. Above all, it is to be a conventional rendering, something acceptable to hang on the walls at Bowlend Court. No fancy allegory or symbolism, he has been warned. And though not entirely to Amos's liking, these instructions barked out to him by Oliver Ramsey at dinner yesterday evening, still the prospect of being able to paint Daphne once again was such an enticement that he had agreed to the terms unconditionally.

'I suppose we all have funny dreams like that from time to time,' she concedes, responding to him at last in a quite serious way now, as if there is something she also wishes to tell him. And yet she does not. Preoccupied still, availing herself of her little hand mirror, she takes a pair of tweezers to an unruly eyebrow instead, and then settles down to observe his preparations.

'Yes,' he agrees, 'and the funny thing was, you were in the dream, too, I'm certain. Only it didn't look like you exactly. I can't explain. I've forgotten the half of it now. Anyway, I think I'm still reeling form my encounter up on the downs this morning - some mad old chap!'

'What? We don't really have too many mad old chaps here,' she replies.

'Well, I must have been unlucky, that's all I can say. He was walking around in a big cloak, and he was most rude. Thought I was a tourist. He didn't quite tell me to pack my bags and go home, but almost.'

Daphne looks at him with a combination of disapproval and alarm and then lets forth a great sigh.

'What is it?' he asks.

'Amos, you do realise who that was, don't you? That was Tennyson – Lord Alfred Tennyson – you know: *Poet Laureate.*'

At which Amos responds with an appropriately penitent groan and rubs his palms over his face. 'Oh dear,' he says, 'It doesn't look as though I've gotten off to the best of starts with our esteemed neighbour, does it.'

'No, not exactly,' Daphne agrees in a waspish kind of way. 'And I was relying on you to secure an introduction to Farringford and all the local set.'

'Sorry,' he says, feeling bad, but quickly endeavours to dismiss the incident. 'Watts will introduce us later – don't worry,' he adds, and then comes over to the dressing table and embarks on the preparation of her hair, something he is well used to, arranging it in just the way he wants by firstly brushing it straight, tying it off from the crown and then compiling a triple braid which he carefully and skilfully twists and pins into place, secured with a beautiful comb featuring a butterfly motif of enamel and various semi-precious stones. The result is an elegant, woven wedge of hair at the back, a chignon that extends, garland-like, out and a little downward almost without touching the base of her neck at all. Excellent! He then deliberately loosens a few strands from the area around her temples, and these he moistens and curls adroitly around his fingers to create a stray curl or two that falls seductively around her cheek and throat. For him this is one of the most delightful elements of the work, the process of arranging her hair, her clothing and jewellery before painting her, to play with her gorgeous long dark tresses like this. She enjoys it too. It is something they have always done together, since as far back as they can remember.

'One of the earliest memories I have is of you doing my hair,' she suddenly whispers as if reading his thoughts – and so close to him that she need not project her voice at all.

'Funny, I was just thinking the same,' he echoes in an equally soft and tender voice. It's been a long time since we've had the pleasure of anything quite like this, hasn't it!'

'Yes, far too long. A lot has happened since then. I mean, thinking about it now, I realise I never really knew what I wanted from my life – not until quite recently. That sounds absurd, doesn't it, for a grown woman. But, you see, having been married to Polly for over a year now has at least enabled me to identify what it is that I *don't* want. And that, in a funny sort of way, has also taught me to recognise what it is I really need.'

How should he interpret this, he wonders, as he continues his preparations. What is she asking him to say?

'No one ever touches me in quite the way you do, Amos,' she whispers softly as he completes the arrangement of her hair. 'No one is ever allowed such liberties, nor ever shall.'

Her voice is changed, he notices: and though still quiet and gentle it is also edged with excitement. There is something new here between us, he realises – something different and irresistible. And although he did not set out today with such a mission in mind, it was happening nevertheless, happening in the way of some powerful, inexorable event of nature over which neither of them seem to have much control. They are becoming lovers, or could become so if they were to continue thus – and he realises, therefore, that Oliver Ramsey had been correct, perfectly correct to insist that the painting of her portrait be done here in his home, here at Parnassus with so many other people around – for had they been totally alone and at liberty, he and his beautiful Daphne, they would surely have fallen into each other's arms already.

With an abrupt and decisive movement that surprises him for a moment she raises her hands and unfastens the pins and the comb from her hair, whips away the braiding, pulls off the ties and allows everything to fall again, her lovely hair again all long and lush about her shoulders. Then she hands him the brush once more and with eyes as large and bold as he has ever seen them says: 'Now do it again, dear one. I want you to start all over again. Would you?'

And gladly he obeys – beginning with the brushing, then the weaving, and then the arranging of locks of stray hair. Her breathing deepens; she is alive to her own pleasure and he is more than willing to oblige.

He loves the fragrance, the special scent that is always associated with her, some rare and very special perfume no doubt brought over from Paris. But there is more today ... there is, in fact, the thrilling and unmistakable allure - a sigh, a breath upon the air and hardly perceptible to any of the five senses, of a woman being pleasured, and one, if truth be told, that he recognises all too well of late since the departure of his fiancée from his life some months ago, a rift that has been filled with many a fleeting and promiscuous liaison with other women - and those, moreover, that he should probably have known better than to associate with at all. Since then, in fact, he has become what is politely described as a 'man of the world,' and well on the way to what others in a less tolerant frame of mind might venture to term a rake and a scoundrel. Consequently, the tiny, almost imperceptible thrill and shudder he senses in her limbs as his fingers touch her face and her shoulders and her hair, is an all-too-familiar one - though never until now has he noted anything of the kind in Daphne, not until this morning for the very first time. How much of this might be due to her experiences since marriage, he cannot tell - nor does he wish to speculate or dwell on the idea too much. He knows only that it is here, now, fully present between them, that certain frissance, and he is intrigued by it.

Well, we shall never get any painting done at this rate, he thinks to himself, with a little rueful smile - but keeps his peace - surrendering instead to the delight of the moment - such a banal, ordinary occupation, this, arranging her hair, and yet he finds himself wishing it would last forever.

Eventually, however, his preparations are complete and they are both faced with the decision of what might come next. Painting a portrait seems the least that is on either of their minds, he realises - but then suddenly he is aware, and she is too, that there are voices in the corridor outside, perhaps others out there curious over the prolonged silence here within - and who knows whether anyone might be watching them even now! - peeping through doors ajar or even through keyholes from adjoining rooms. And so he removes his jacket, takes up his brushes and palette and begins to paint - to embark at last upon the delightful task that has brought him here, and which, he concludes, is probably not such a bad substitute to making love, after all.

Time passes. The minutes combine to make an hour as, with admiration she watches him from her own position of stillness, following his movements out of the corner of her eye, as so often she has followed him in the past and in places as varied and as different as could be: as a child in her parent's morning room; in the stately drawing room of his own family home; or outside in gardens or upon the prow of a tiny boat on the river that ran between their homes – and yet always displaying the same confidence and refinement, always the same accomplished manner and special *panache* that was all his – and his alone. At work he would act without awareness, with perfect spontaneity which was a joy and fascination to behold for any of his sitters – stepping back from time to time for the wider view, or else bounding forward for closer examination, his palette of colours renewed constantly by the squeezing of lead tubes or moistened with dabs of oil and turpentine, blending themselves almost without his conscious effort, exactly the right consistency and tone – the brushes bunched in his hand and bristling out from the space between palm and palette like arrows from a quiver, and from which he would withdraw deftly one or another from time to time, applying his colours according to its size and texture of each one before restoring it to the same place and with the same smooth, accomplished movements born of years of constant usage. She has known him as a child, and as a young man, but now she sees him as a mature and finished gentleman there before her. He has altered so; he has grown to become the most handsome of creatures. And as she continues to observe him with such fascination the lines from one of her favourite poems dance in the air about him as she watches:

> From underneath his helmet flow'd
> His coal-black curls as on he rode,
> As he rode down to Camelot.

She remains silent as he works, maintaining her composure perfectly, but eventually she does begin to speak, for speak she must – and in a voice of such intimacy it is almost palpable.

'Amos, I also had a dream last night. I wasn't going to tell you about it, not after what you said, because it all seemed like too much of a coincidence, and it wasn't altogether pleasant, either, I have to say. I was in some queer, dark building – not alone. There were other people with me, other women, and I thought I was going to die, and I couldn't understand why. I mean, why would anybody want to hurt me, I thought? And then you appeared. You were not supposed to be there, somebody said. But there was an old gentleman in the dream. I'm not sure whether he was in uniform or something like that, but he seemed to be in charge and he had contrived that you should visit me, and I told you I was so afraid, and you said I should not be, that I should not worry because there would be a reprieve. A reprieve, you said – what did you mean?'

'Well, don't ask me - how should I know! It was a dream after all,' he replies, his brush suspended above the canvas for a moment and pretending that he was not disturbed by what she was saying. 'Why were you going to die, anyway?'

'Oh, I don't know. I suppose I must have done something beastly and had been condemned. I felt so relieved and happy you had come to speak with me, and you took my hand and smiled and it felt lovely. And then the old gentlemen in the uniform returned and took you away. There were lots of heavy doors closing with the sounds of big iron keys turning in locks, and then I was alone and it was dark again.'

She slides her hand across her forehead for a moment and seems a little dazed, and when she next speaks it is in a voice that is unusually faint and weak: 'Amos, have you got any loddy on you?'

Leaning over, he reaches inside one of the voluminous pockets of his coat, draped over a chair nearby, and hands her the little brown bottle, the laudanum from the village chemists, complete with its rather melodramatic skull and crossbones symbol denoting 'poison' and the neat little measuring cap on top.

'Monthly pains again?' he inquires.

'No, no ... I just want some, that's all. I don't feel right.'

'Come on! It was only a dream,' he says smiling reassurance. But he too continues to feel uneasy. He has rarely if ever seen her behaving with such strangeness - her moods so changeable, like the very weather he had been walking through this morning, one moment radiant and playful, the other dark and tormented.

He watches her as she adds the capful of laudanum tincture to a glass of water, her hand trembling just a little as she does so - watches her with fascination, beguiled by her lovely profile as she sips the gentle opiates, the nectar of tranquillity that he knows will wash over her in just a few moments. But there is no time for this to happen. Because suddenly everything changes. Abruptly she turns and stares at him, stares wide-eyed, her nostrils a little flared with excitement and alarm.

'Amos, something dreadful is going to happen ...'

'Don't be silly. Of course it won't.'

'No - I mean now, this very minute - something is about to happen *now*.'

Abruptly, with these words and the expression of terror on her face, he feels the muscles of his scalp creep upon his head - to be followed just a second later by the distinctive sounds of horses and a wagon moving at some speed along the lane outside and then turning and sliding quickly and with untypical violence and commotion into the gravel drive leading up to the portico below. By the sounds of it there are a good number of people on horseback in attendance, and some of their voices are raised and agitated. Amos and Daphne both rush to the nearest window and look down - she clasping him by the arm immediately because the sight they behold is indeed dreadful. Below, stretched out on an open farm wagon, wrapped in blankets is none other than her husband, Oliver Ramsey - unmoving, his face as pallid and inexpressive as wax. Another man, smartly dressed, is in the wagon alongside him, seated upright, one hand holding his wrist as if taking a pulse, while others on horseback have joined them and have drawn up alongside, too. The expression on all of their faces, to a man, is one of the utmost gravity and concern.

'Oh my God, is he dead?' Daphne cries, the words almost stuck in her throat.

It appears that Ramsey's body has been laid out and

secured to an old door which serves as a field stretcher, and this is drawn off from the back of the wagon by several men and then, with considerable hardship, eventually dragged rather than carried in any dignified fashion up the steps and into the hallway. Amos and Daphne run down the stairs and within a moment are there amid the commotion and confusion, with many of the servants and house staff already gathered around the stricken master, still attired in his ostentatious riding coat of scarlet, and the doctor still trying to minister to him. Daphne eventually pushes her way through the crowd and is quickly given the information she needs:

'It was a bad fall – a ditch,' says the local huntsman with whom Ramsey had ridden off earlier, looking anxiously up from a kneeling position there at his side. 'The horse pulled up suddenly, stumbled beneath him and off he went. Landed on the front of his head. He is alive, but completely out of it, and we don't yet know the full extent of the damage. We had to shoot the poor animal.'

'How long has he been unconscious?' Daphne demands.

'Almost an hour so far. We have tried everything – smelling salts, cold water. We just can't get him to come round.'

The bruising to his forehead is clear now and seems if anything to be darkening even as they watch. Amos voices concern that there could be internal bleeding but the doctor, convinced to the contrary, merely shakes his head at such conjecture. Instead, he orders that Ramsey is carried into the drawing room, where already a makeshift sickbed has been set up on the settee. But this is quickly determined to be too small to accommodate the huge girth of the man, and so the silk-covered duvet and pillows are laid out on the floor instead, and it is onto this improvised nest that Ramsey is eventually manoeuvred in as dignified a fashion as possible by the collective efforts of no less than six able-bodied men, including Amos who a moment later also applies himself to the task of removing the man's large black riding boots. The weight and bulk of the fellow is astounding, rendered somehow even heavier by his state of unconsciousness – though no one has yet ventured to use the term 'dead weight' to describe their plight.

Not yet, anyway.

Daphne, meanwhile, endeavours to take charge of the situation, doing her best to send everyone away and to urge the servants back to their duties – though this with only limited success - while Amos, and with no thought of returning to his work, of course, can now only continue to pace up and down aimlessly the length of the drawing room where various members of the household staff continue to congregate, all flustered and in a hubbub of disputation and ominous conjecture as if some terrible judgement from on high has suddenly been inflicted upon them. Everyone's life could be about to change now - irrevocably, they all seem to realise; everything could be so very different if the worst were to come to pass.

Meanwhile, Amos can only gaze in silence beyond the tall mullioned windows, out towards a garden that is opening and blossoming to spring – so that for a moment he becomes lost in its cruel, uncaring beauty. The fresh, silky greens and bronzes of all the young budding leaves, the lilac and apple blossom – everything so vigorous, bursting forth in a gentle riot of colour and scent, totally oblivious and disregarding of the little human tragedy here within, a drama which remains so very important, so insistent to everyone involved. Again he turns to look into all their faces, tries to become engaged in some sense with what is taking place. It doesn't look good. With every passing minute they become increasingly anxious and pessimistic, and there is already talk among the senior staff, he notices, that it might be appropriate to send a telegram to the family solicitor in London. If their master were to die they would need expert advice, and quickly; and the firm's own team of lawyers, too, would need to be notified. At one stage he overhears Daphne speaking with David, their steward. And her words are portentous indeed.

'Yes, David, do telegraph Mr. Jenkins and tell him to prepare all necessary papers and to be ready to take the overnight train if need be. God pray his journey will not be necessary. He should do nothing further, therefore, unless we confirm the worst. Is that clear?'

The steward nods his understanding and within moments

has run from the house towards the village post office to send the telegram.

Chapter Ten

Dreams and an Invitation

Recollections of the events of the day weigh heavy on Amos as he takes a turn around the bay, walking this evening upon the broad arc of sand and pebbled beach where, in the lee of the rising downs to the west, the twilight always seems to arrive so much earlier than anticipated - the final cheerful rays of the sun glinting only far out to sea now, or else across the white sparkling hulls of boats and ships towards the distant horizon. An ominous feeling haunts him, knowing that something terrible has occurred today, and that perhaps even worse might yet transpire – almost as if it were a kind of condemnation that had been laid upon him, a punishment from the heavens for his flirtations with a married woman. Yet here as always, outdoors, in proximity to the vastness of the sea he finds some measure of equilibrium. The shady atmosphere of the bay is ideal for cooling his fervid brain, and it is with this renewed sense of tranquillity at last that he is able to settle down, even to enjoy a glass of wine in the hotel before returning home along the leafy lane to his cottage and where, after a little routine book-keeping and letter-writing, he retires early to bed. The whole building, he feels, has definitely become more agreeable and welcoming now that his servants are present. He likes the occasional sounds they make about the place as they go about their business. Everything has been cleaned, scrubbed and polished to perfection by Beth, who even takes the trouble to place little vases of flowers here and there - he has seen her gather them from the garden in her spare time. The curtains have been repaired, and rugs have been brought in to cover any naked floorboards. There is hot water on hand every morning when he rises, and the sheets are clean and pressed and the pillows fluffed up nicely for him each evening when he retires. Tonight, his bedroom is perfectly silent, as well, the weather outside clement and calm - and he should, he knows, be able to sleep. Yet he cannot – he simply cannot rest: his heart continually springing into some kind of impulsive, erratic rhythm the moment he closes his eyes.

It is a little disappointing that the celebrated photographer Mrs Cameron has left the island, he thinks. And no matter how many times he passes her former home or wanders as he did this evening into the little roadway in which it stands, there is nothing left for him there to see or marvel at, nothing for him to learn or take inspiration from. The lovely tragic heroines in their elegant, flowing gowns that she once photographed have all gone; the children with wings made of goose feathers attached to their shoulders are no longer enlisted to pose as angels; and any tall, reasonably distinguished gentleman possessing a beard and who might be passing along the road outside is no longer hauled in and compelled to sit before the lens for hours clad in the paraphernalia of some Arthurian knight or ancient god. All is deserted now and silent as the grave, while nearby, down the road, the home of her friend Lord Tennyson stands in its own way equally uninviting - out of bounds for visitors and tourists alike and as indomitable as a fortress. Amos's own senior colleague from the London art scene, the celebrated painter George Frederic Watts has also yet to put in an appearance for the season – and will, they say, be absent from his island residence for at least several more weeks. And as for the forthcoming evening of entertainment with the famous Russian medium Madam Alenushka that Daphne has scheduled for tomorrow – well, that would surely have to be abandoned now, he realises. How very disappointing!

Yet in the place of these several frustrations and setbacks

there have been for Amos, a number of unanticipated and quite spectacular victories, and regardless of what might happen for the remainder of his stay, he knows it will have been well worth the effort – for already there are several fresh commissions for portraits that have come to him since his arrival, and it seems possible that a return visit later in the season could be particularly lucrative if he should so choose – though it does occur to him, also, that if the worse should come to pass just down the road at Parnassus where he had just a few short hours ago left his patron Lord Bowlend possibly at death's door, that his major source of introduction to all these local, well-to-do families might well be about to evaporate and vanish into thin air. Even by late this evening there has been no fresh news as to his fate. For all Amos knows, the portrait he has been working on might no longer have a living recipient to take delivery of it: only a widow remaining to accept it on his behalf. And for one bizarre moment he sees in his mind's eye the large canvas framed and hanging on a wall somewhere surrounded by a bevy of admiring onlookers – and with a little gold R.I.P. plaque attached beneath, and the lovely Daphne in black widow's crêpe standing nearby, a handkerchief to her cheek, dabbing a wayward tear. 'Yes, he was a good man,' she sobs, rather unconvincingly before lowering her heavy black veil once more across her face. It is all nonsense, of course, and Amos endeavours to dismiss these visions from his over-active imagination – in case, by some form of innate sympathetic magic he should influence events and cause the poor man to die. Surely not! Surely a man as robust and pig-headed as Oliver Ramsey could pull through a mere riding accident!

And so the thoughts continue to come and go; a grotesque assortment of illogical, morbidly dark thoughts. And when he does finally drop off, far into the early hours, his slumber is fitful and full of equally disturbing dreams. At one stage he sees the face yet again of none other than the Yeoman Warder from the chapel on Tower Green. The old fellow is opening a door for him this time which, accompanied by the sounds of heavy bolts and creaking hinges, swings wide, allowing Amos to step out from what seems to be a dark tower within which he has been kept and onto a long narrow walkway outside –

flanked by a low wall, its base covered in lead as if at a juncture of a rooftop - and which itself appears to be set between his tower and another very similar one with a large oak door straight ahead. The abrupt change of light as he steps outside between the towers is too much for his eyes and for a moment he is dazzled and rubs them with his palms, and when he opens his eyes again he realises that he is, in fact, very high up, that the walkway and the tower behind him are bathed in glorious sunshine and that the birds are singing. It is early morning, in springtime and there is a fragrance of elder flowers and wild garlic in the air. How lovely! But then as he glances down over the crenellated stonework and rooftops that border the walkway he notices in the shady area down below a crowd of people who have gathered, all dressed strangely in long robes and jostling together in a green space bordered by the walls of stone and who in deepest silence are all looking at Daphne who is in the centre of them, bare-shouldered and kneeling. She looks up and meets his eyes for one moment before there is a terrible flash of steel and her head is cut clean off with a single stroke of a great broadsword from a man who has been standing behind her. A terrible fountain-jet of scarlet blood shoots into the air and he screams and sits up in bed, the sweat pouring from him in the cold darkness, his nightshirt clinging to his damp flesh. Footsteps, running towards him, are heard and in rushes James his valet, as if emerging from a great distance, with a lamp held aloft, quickly followed by Beth who takes him by the hands.

'Sir! What is it?' she entreats him, her face anxious, peering into his eyes at very close quarters.

'You were having a nightmare, Sir! All is well,' James adds from behind her shoulder.

But already Amos is up on his feet – horrified by their faces staring at him, their disembodied heads illuminated, floating in the darkness.

'Where is the door?' he demands, loud of voice - frantic. 'I must get out there. Quick! Where is the door? Where is the Warder?'

'Sir, there is no door. Beth cries, endeavouring to hold on to his arms as he searches the blank wall of his bedroom with desperate palms for some way out. Gradually, he realises where he is, that his servants are around him and that it has, after all, been some terrible nightmare from which he is only now just beginning to emerge. James, meanwhile, has lit some candles, and with the advent of the additional light their bodies, not merely their heads are revealed to him - and gradually some sense of calm and decorum is restored. Amos sits down on the edge of the bed for a moment and rubs his eyes. He endeavours to smile and to laugh it off, but the others continue to look at him with the gravest concern.

It is really too late to go back to sleep now, he realises, and when he goes to the window and pulls back the curtains the first light of dawn is already just visible and the melodious sounds of a blackbird comes up to meet him from the garden, reminding him again of the dream, oddly enough, and of the birds that were singing then as well. This horrible experience, he knows, has all been to do with the disturbing events of yesterday afternoon, of seeing Ramsey stretched out there on the floor like that. It is guilt - ridiculous, futile emotionalism that has been fuelling his nightmares. He can hold back no longer, therefore. He simply must know what has happened to his illustrious neighbour. And so - early or not - James is enlisted to go over to Parnassus straight away to make inquiries.

Downstairs, Beth, meanwhile, has brewed a pot of tea and sits with him in the parlour while he gratefully imbibes the hot, refreshing beverage, both still in their dressing gowns and Amos with a blanket about his knees. She does not feel she should leave him just yet, she says. She will stay, if he does not mind, as she has one or two bits of darning and mending to do anyway, which she can manage quite comfortably here on her lap - and this she does, taking needle and thread to a torn pillow case, working with amazing dexterity in the poor light and merely getting to her feet from time to time to attend to a little fire she has quickly set in the hearth or else to take a sip of her tea. And as they wait for the valet's return, he looks across at the diminutive figure of the young girl in her seat opposite him, her head bowed forward close to the sewing, her normally tidy and neatly pinned red hair a mass of sleepy, tangled tresses, and he wonders at her kindness. The business of staying up like this, tending to a mad fool who has bad dreams in the early hours is not part of her contract of service. She needn't bother. Yet she has.

Of course, none of this would ever have happened under normal circumstances. Had they been in London, for instance, he would have been left to get on with it; the ranting and raving of the master of the house would have gone unheeded, tactfully ignored. But here on this unique little island it was all so different, as if the normal rules of accepted behaviour and tradition could always be stretched a little or even totally abandoned.

'It was in colour, the dream - or nightmare, I should call it,' he mutters, as if talking to himself, but he glances her way, knowing she would be listening. She cuts the surplus thread she has been using with her teeth before turning her face in his direction, her eyes fixed upon him for a moment, and still with the utmost care and concern, he thinks. He wonders if she can perceive how terribly shaken and upset he still feels. 'And there was a sense of smell, too,' he adds. 'All kinds of fragrances, and all so real! In a funny sort of way, the colours and smells were more real than normal perception - what they call preternatural, I suppose.'

'People say it does sometimes happen, Sir - that we dream in colour,' she ventures to reply at last in a more practical turn of phrase, which makes him smile.

'I was at the Tower of London, Beth,' he continues. 'It was so real!'

'Oh, that's a horrid place, Sir!' she exclaims with a little shudder of the shoulders, though softly still. 'I went there once as a young girl.'

He does not respond, feeling stunned for a moment that she should regard herself as anything other than a *young girl*, which is how he has always thought of her, of course. But then, after all, she is growing, he thinks. She must have been in his service for a year and a half already. And in that time she has changed, of course. She has become taller, stronger and altogether more confident than when he had first taken her on - and she knows her own mind, too, it seems. He does not wish to agree or disagree with her verdict on The Tower, since it has always been a part of the City that he has been drawn to, a place where he has spent many a pleasant hour with his sketchpad, studying the extraordinary diversity of different styles of building and masonry – studies that have aided him in many of his paintings. But she is entitled to her opinion, he thinks – one which, he knows, many would certainly share.

'Beth,' he says, 'tell me – do you believe in ghosts?'

'In ghosts, Sir?' she echoes, and thoughtful for a moment as she folds the mended pillow case neatly in her lap and smoothes it with her hand. 'Well, Sir, I cannot recall having any dealings with them directly. Only I think if there are any spirits up there they would not be troubling themselves too much with our affairs. They would surely have more important things to be doing than to be running about frightening us.'

'But what about if they had a message – if, for example, they needed to tell us something - something important? Then don't you reckon they might come to us, reveal themselves or give us a sign?'

'Perhaps they might, Sir. But that is different. It's no use in our asking for them to come, as people do. That is what I mean. They will not come just because our vanity calls for them to appear – unless, that is, they are of the mischievous sort and playing games with us anyway.'

'Emm. So all these mediums and psychics that are everywhere and so much in demand these days, they are all a waste of time?'

Again, Beth appears to ponder carefully before replying.

'I am not altogether certain about that either, Sir,' she says. 'I did go to an evening once at the spiritualist church in New Eltham where I used to live before I came into your service. People say that they invent things, and are very clever at deceiving – while others say that some of them, the best of the bunch, are honest and would never lie or pretend to people. They say that there are spirits, genuine and loving spirits who watch over us, too – which I like to believe in sometimes. But I think if we cannot know for sure whether they are truthful or not, any of these things, we should be cautious, lest we be deceived also.'

'You are very diplomatic, Beth, and far more clever than you let on,' he laughs.

Through the parlour door, he notices that the early sun is beginning to shine through the stained glass of the front porch, casting bright ripples of dancing colour across the walls of the hall. It is going to be a lovely morning. And now, having spoken with her like this, having conversed calmly to someone so down-to-earth as Beth after his night of horrid dreams, he feels for the first time strong enough to face the day, to go on with some measure of equanimity. And then, through the same windows, the tall, black-clad figure of James can be seen returning to them, hurrying up the pathway. Without ceremony, he comes straight in and through to the parlour – at which Beth gets to her feet and so does Amos – both searching into the valet's big, drooping eyes for any signs of good news. For a moment James is as impassive and inscrutable as ever. But they need not fear. There is something most encouraging to report, he finally announces – namely the welcome news that Lord Bowlend has woken from his coma several hours ago and is already speaking to the doctor, albeit non-too coherently as yet – but at least he is already starting to complain and to grumble about lots of things, they say – which is 'probably a good sign.'

'Thank heaven!' Amos declares by way of a suitable demonstration of concern for the welfare of the unfortunate man, while at the same time feeling just the tiniest twinge of guilt that the greater part of his joy is in knowing that the portrait he has laboured so hard over these past weeks would still have a living recipient to pay for it.

'Oh, yes and a message, Sir, from Lady Bowlend also,' James adds – though at the same time throwing a hesitant sideways glance to Beth who is still present, perhaps questioning whether it is altogether appropriate that she be privy to something of so personal a nature.

'Well, come on – out with it, man!' Amos demands, feeling irritated by any allusion, even an unspoken one, to Beth's lowly status. What a pompous ass this man is!

'That the séance with the Russian medium, Madam Alenushka, is to proceed as planned this evening. That is the message, Sir. Oh, and that you should feel free to bring a guest or any other person with you of like interest.'

'Really!' Amos responds with surprise, turning to Beth. 'Well – it seems you shall have occasion, Beth, to make up your mind more fully on the very issue we have just been discussing, that is if you would care to accompany me this evening?'

At which Beth nods vigorously by way of reply, and with her folded pillow case still under her arm, runs from the room accompanied by an incredulous stare from James who turns to examine Amos's face a moment later with a look of utter astonishment. That he should so honour the young serving maid! That he should even have the slightest interest in her opinion on such matters!

'Thank you. That will be all, James!' Amos declares and dismisses him with an imperious wave of the hand, privately wondering at his own peculiar behaviour - but glad of it, nonetheless: that he was able to be so bold, to snub his nose at James and to defy his snobbery. The island air continues to work its unconventional magic, it seems. And he cares not one bit for the consequences. Excellent!

Chapter Eleven

Motif of Roses

The drawing room and its inhabitants have been cast into almost complete darkness as the exotically dressed Madam Alenushka in a floor length gown of purple satin with an extravagant shawl of damask draped around her shoulders, wanders as a restless spirit back and forth before a small, select audience of awe-struck humanity – friends, neighbours and some local dignitaries all ranged in a broad semi-circle in the drawing room of Parnassus and availing themselves of an assortment of cushions, sofas, ottomans and armchairs upon which to place themselves for the purpose of observing the celebrated medium at close quarters. The silence that punctuates the Russian woman's strange and otherworldly pronouncements is almost palpable as everyone waits with baited breath for whatever words of ghostly wisdom might yet proceed from her prophetic soul. Amos, however, is not entirely captivated by her rather extravagant, theatrical style. With her face heavily powdered, a dark pencilled liner around her exotically made-up eyes, she seems to have as much of the circus about her as anything else, added to which he feels uneasy and tense inside anyway because he knows just how much emotional capital Daphne has staked on this very unusual event and how diligently she has been working towards its success; everything from hand-picking the guests to hiring the famous psychic herself at considerable expense.

'I feel there is somebody coming through by the name of William or Wilhelmina ... and this person is having difficulty breathing,' announces this modern-day priestess of the mysteries, looking towards nobody in particular but clearly wanting a response from among those gathered before her. 'There is something I am feeling here, in the chest or – er – abdominal regions. Does that make sense?'

'That could be my father,' a woman in the audience states a little tentatively, one hand raised and looking round at the others with a face that betrays a certain embarrassment and diffidence – as if attempting a dare of some kind and wanting to be egged on by the others.

'And his name was William, yes?' asks the celebrated psychic.

'Well, he went by the name of Bill most of the time, but William would have been his full name, yes.'

'And the pains here, in the chest – I am being told of a heart condition or breathing?'

'Yes, he died of pneumonia, I think - or had trouble breathing, anyway, just before he went,' the woman responds, continuing to appear transfixed by the towering visage of Madam Anelushka and still, curiously, with one hand raised above her head.

'Bill says to tell you he is happy,' Madam Alenushka continues with growing confidence, her eyes lifted as if in receipt of some benefaction from on high. 'Also I have a female here, an important female at his side, his dear mother and ...'

'Oh his mother is still alive,' the woman states rather uncooperatively. 'I was speaking to her only yesterday and ...'

'Sorry, *his grandmother* I was meaning to say – he is with his grandmother, and they are happy, and they are both telling me that all will be well for you, also, so that you are not to worry.'

'Really. That's so right. I do worry sometimes,'

'Of course you do. You are thinking about changes that have to be made in your life, is that not so, my dear?'

'Why yes... yes, that's true.'

'But he says not to worry, my dear. He wants to tell you it will all be – how do you say – all for the best.'

'Oh good! Can you just ask him something, though?'

'*Ask?*' Madam Alenushka echoes with a suspicious look on her face, as much of it as can be discerned in the gloom at any rate before adding in a voice and an accent, which at this stage Amos realises is beginning to sound a little northern English, 'Well ... I can try, luv.'

'Does he remember where he left the gold fob watch that the regiment gave him on his retirement when he moved to Brighton last September and that might have ...'

'He is very faint now ... I am losing him,' Madam Alenushka interrupts, a hand pressed to her forehead as if in some distress. 'No, sorry, he's gone. I cannot answer that question. Anyway, I have here another person from the world of spirit here with me now, very insistent, oh my goodness, yes: a gentleman – or it might be a lady – directing me towards someone here in the centre. Or perhaps a little further over ... yes is it the lady here in the black veil? Yes, it is somebody who has recently passed over that was close to you. Is it your husband, my dear?'

At which the elderly lady in mourning gown and white widow's cap promptly bursts into tears. 'Yes, yes,' she sobs, 'we buried him only last week.'

'He wants you to know that the flowers were lovely!' Madam Alenushka cries in a note of exaltation. 'He did so appreciate them.'

'Flowers? Oh no, you must be mistaken. He left directions in his will, quite adamant, that there should be no flowers at his funeral.'

'The flowers *in the garden*, my dear,' ... responds Madam Anelushka straight away with a beatific smile. 'He means those of your garden. They have been such a delight this year, he says.'

To which the woman nods her understanding and, thus reassured of the authenticity of the Madam Alenushka 'second sight' after a moment's foolish doubt and indiscretion lifts her veil momentarily and dabs at her eyes with an elaborate lace handkerchief.

'You know what - this is all a load of bloody codswallop,' Ramsey whispers into Amos's ear, a whisper which is quite loud, for all that, and to which Amos merely nods uncomfortably realising that others in the room have heard.

After regaining consciousness yesterday from what was described as a deep coma, the Baron has been restored to something approaching his old morose and ill-tempered self with amazing rapidity thanks to the ministrations of a small army of doctors and pharmacists – so that he sits here now in all his pomp at Amos's side, ensconced in a vast armchair, his forehead heavily bandaged and appearing a little groggy and distracted at moments but in every other respect in reasonable command of all his faculties once again. 'And I've paid good money for this old tart to come here this evening,' he adds.

'Sssh!' somebody behind hisses in his direction, confident in the gloom that she will not be identified or have to deal with any later repercussions – and which causes Ramsey to become even more irritable, as Amos can discern by his constant fidgeting in his seat, adjusting the tails of his coat with irritable little flicking movements as he looks around endeavouring to locate the source of his censure.

The performance, however, continues to gain momentum and to persist for a further thirty minutes with several more fleeting spirit visitations recounted in vivid and cogent detail by Madam Alenushka, until eventually it is time for the interval. The lamps are turned up once more, rising from their tiny blue embers to broad yellow orbs of light and everyone breathes a sigh of relief to be back in the land of the living and where, amid the welcome and amiable clatter of teacups and spoons, everybody is able to converse with one another in something other than hushed whispers.

'Not impressed?' Amos enquires of the big man as they get to their feet.

'Huh – Russian medium!' he exclaims, and not altogether discretely again, either. 'If you ask me, I'd say her base of operations would be located more likely at the end of Morecambe pier, rather than anywhere near St Petersburg. Ha! All I can say is that everything has been going wrong in my life since we've had all this nonsense coming here under our roof!'

But at this he catches a look of reproach upon Amos's face, mingled with a certain amusement, moreover, and this is sufficient to pacify him, at least for the present. He is being foolish, and he knows it. 'Anyway - it's unwholesome, that's all I have to say,' are his final comments as he heads off towards the drinks table. Here, Daphne, looking fabulous in a black velvet gown bound with mauve and lilac, the ties of her velvet neckband trailing behind where it merges with little braided strands of black hair, tries to intercept him and by the look on her face is trying to caution him over consuming alcohol in combination with whatever medication he has been prescribed. But self-denial has never been Oliver Ramsey's strong point, of course, and he will have none of it, and even shoulders his wife out of the way none too gently as he pours himself a whisky. That's odd, Amos thinks. He may be a gruff and uncouth oaf by nature, but rarely has he ever demonstrated it in such a graphic and forceful manner. Luckily no one else seems to have noticed the physicality of it, or observed Daphne's cleverly concealed embarrassment and distress as she turns from him and, with hardly time to hoist her skirts, hurries from the room - the flounces and hems of her beautiful crafted and embroidered dress trailing the carpet awkwardly as she goes.

For a moment, Amos considers hurrying after her - but noticing Beth standing at the back of the room, and looking more than a little awkward and self-conscious amid the dozens of well-dressed and cultivated people who all seem to be assiduously ignoring her, he strolls over in her direction instead and inquires whether she has found the proceedings of interest so far.

'Oh yes, Sir, thank you,' she replies. 'It is most educational also to observe the reactions of the other people.'

She is wearing her best cambric dress and a little tunic on top, fastened with silver buttons, the same as she travelled in the other day, and has pinned her hair up and added a wooden comb, which looks quite presentable, though he notices that the lenses of her spectacles are badly scratched - and that her attempts at applying a little powder and rouge to her face this evening in order to look more sophisticated perhaps - something which would be a rare enough exercise for her at any time - has not succeeded particularly well. Her normally delicate and flawless young skin now appears blotchy and dry looking. What a shame! Appearing to sense his observant artist's eye upon her, and seeming to perceive that something is amiss, she removes her battered spectacles with a rapid, anxious little movement and sequesters them into her canvas handbag. The little bag has a motif of roses embroidered upon it, he notices, crudely executed, and the clasp is also rather tarnished – and this she clutches nervously with both hands in front of her, almost as if protecting herself. Poor girl.

One of Ramsey's servants in a black frock coat, probably the butler, passes by at just that moment and throws a cold, disapproving glance in her direction. Oh dear! Was this quite the right thing to have done, Amos asks himself, inviting her to come along this evening? For, if the truth be told, his little maid here is all rather betwixt and between at present. By her attire she is neither humble enough to be a servant nor affluent enough to be a guest, and therefore becomes a puzzlement to most people present - who simple resolve therefore to have nothing to do with her at all. Feeling responsible for having thrown her into such a social maelstrom, he remains with her a little longer, therefore, exchanging pleasantries; and then, a little later, at the conclusion of the second half of Madam Alenushka's reading, he makes certain that she is at ease and comfortable enough to return the short distance back to the cottage alone, which she assures him she is quite happy to do, and subsequently draws herself up to her full height and strides out with dignity past all the other servants as she goes.

Eventually, with all the invited guests having left, and following a supper of smoked salmon and champagne, Amos, Daphne and her husband find themselves alone with their enigmatic visitor from Russia and also her companion, a tall woman by the name of Frances who always travels with her apparently and acts as her assistant. All the servants have been dismissed, each to their own quarters, and thus the house itself is more peaceful and settled than it has been all day, and also pleasantly void of the smells of singed hair, an unmistakable redolence which many of the ladies have about them these days from the over-use of hot crimping irons. But this, mercifully, with the aid of an open window or two through which the warm, rose-scented air of the summer's evening might enter, has now become almost completely vanquished. Seizing the moment, and following a delightful and entertaining recital of music upon her piano, Daphne rises and asks Madam Alenushka if she would agree to hold a special private session to contact 'the other side' – a request, Amos surmises, the visitor would probably have anticipated already, in any case. Graciously, Madam Alenushka agrees to this request. A final glass of wine is taken and then the small, circular table that Daphne herself is wont to use for séances and which, Amos is astonished to discover, has been brought with her all the way from the mainland, is moved into the centre of the room and everyone, upon directions from Madam Alenushka herself, places their finger-tips down upon its polished surface in readiness – for what, exactly, nobody quite seems to know as yet, except perhaps for the celebrated medium herself who still has a most commanding way about her – so that those present obey her instructions to the letter, not least of which is to stay silent and calm as she utters some prayers in a strange and unfamiliar language. Oliver Ramsey, meanwhile, takes the opportunity to attach his monocle to one eye, the better to examine his guest and her shenanigans at close quarters. Nothing much happens for quite some time, and it is becoming obvious by the deep vertical creases in the skin above the bridge of his nose that the noble lord is still as sceptical and as hostile towards his guest as ever – until, that is, the table starts to vibrate beneath his finger tips, and to do so, moreover, in such a curious fashion that, everyone instantly realises, it could not possibly be the result of any human intervention – everyone, that is, aside from Ramsey himself who still obstinately tries to maintain a stance of scepticism and so has to call across to wife: 'Is that you, doing that, my dear. Your knees?'

Daphne shakes her head in vigorous denial, as does Amos in anticipation of the same question being directed at him – while Madam Alenushka and her companion merely regard his interruption with a look of utter contempt, before turning their faces away and ignoring him entirely as the lady herself stares ahead, her eyes wide but unfocused, as if awaiting inspiration, her finger-tips still firmly in position.

To everyone's surprise, the table then makes a sudden jolt to the side and, a moment later, to the accompaniment of a collective and audible intake of breath from all present, rises a good several inches from the floor. Amos feels his shoulders lifting themselves up around his ears in order to accommodate its movement as, simultaneously, Ramsey's monocle pops from its socket and dangles on its cord.

'Who are you?' Madam Alenushka demands in a loud sonorous voice to no one in particular.

A peculiar sound like a muffled scream, very faint but chilling, seems to fill the space between them which compels even Ramsey to shudder in astonishment for once – and then a second later the table rises again, even higher, and begins moving off to the side, rotating horizontally in mid-air as it goes – a spiralling motion compelling everyone in contact with it to abandon their chairs, therefore, and to follow - their feet shuffling in rapid little movements as each one tries to anticipate the trajectory that the table itself might choose to take. Daphne looses touch for a brief moment before chasing after it and restoring her hands to its surface. It simply has a life all of its own, strongly animated – so that within moments they find themselves at the other end of the room, having been hauled along a good twenty feet from where they started. For a moment, all seems settled again. But any lull in proceedings is destined to be short-lived and a moment later the table suddenly twists and rotates so violently that this time it is Ramsey who is thrown off and he stumbles quite awkwardly. Amos is about to go to his aid but is halted by an angry frown and the exhortation from Mrs Alenushka herself to: 'Stay! Keep your hands on the table, young man!' Amos obeys, trying to hang on - but it is too late, the table comes crashing to the floor again with an enormous thump, at which Madam Alenushka almost charges across the room to the unfortunate Oliver Ramsey, still slumped on the ground and having difficulty getting himself to his feet, and cries: 'Baron, baron!' and points an accusing finger so alarmingly close to his nose that his eyes appear to cross as he looks up towards its menacing tip.

'Yes, that's me. I am Baron Ramsey, Lord Bowlend,' he responds irritably, managing to sit upright by this time and to reattach his monocle. 'You must know that much, woman! The name is on the cheque, after all!'

Amos and Daphne, meanwhile, have hurried across to his aid and are helping him to his feet by taking one arm each - while also urging him by frantic whispers to hold his wrath.

'No! Barren - barren of child!' Madam Alenushka cries, correcting his misconception. 'You shall remain barren of issue. No child, no heir! Barren, barren!'

Ramsey is furious, Daphne most distraught. But the amazing seer is not done yet. She next turns on Amos, thrusting an accusing finger this time in his direction, her voice deep and resonant and speaking as if she were not in control of herself at all, but instead channelling the words of some other disembodied entity - one sentient only to her.

'And you, Sir! You failed her! You lied! You knew there would be no remedy. Oh, how will you ever be forgiven!'

'What do you mean?' Amos demands, frozen in terror at the woman's mad, staring eyes - but at which Madam Alenushka suddenly wobbles alarmingly on her feet and then collapses as if hit by a train - falling flat onto her back with a loud thud that, by all appearances, has rendered her completely unconscious.

Everyone rushes to her aid; smelling salts are applied and little by little she is brought back to consciousness - as the second person to be rendered horizontal on the drawing room floor of the villa Parnassus in as many days opens her eyes and looks around with at first a look of stupefaction but then suddenly one of frantic disbelief as if not quite knowing where she is. At length she is pacified by Daphne, persuaded of her continued safety by her companion Frances, and finally bought to her feet by the efforts of the two men until she can eventually be deposited safely on the settee. Her companion, Frances, joins her and, once reunited with her glass of wine, appears, like Madam Alenushka herself to be entirely unmoved by anything that has taken place - as though it were all perfectly normal.

Amos takes the opportunity to ensure that everyone else is comfortably seated and that their glasses are also filled until eventually there is an opportunity amid the restored atmosphere of calm and conviviality to discuss what has just taken place. And as Madam Alenushka begins to regain her composure, some quite astonishing facts concerning the medium's life are gradually disclosed. Allowing everyone into her confidence, and in a voice which becomes less and less of the exotic and foreign and more and more of the familiar warmth of colloquial English, she admits that she has, as Amos suspected, been born in England – 'up north' in Blackpool, she says, but then happened to marry a fabulously wealthy Russian and consequently spent much of her formative years in St Petersburg at the court of the Tsar. There she learnt much of what she knows from the powerful and celebrated mystics of that country. And no, she insists, it is not entertainment that she is engaged in, as some might believe. She knows what he – Oliver Ramsey – is thinking of her, she says, fixing him with a penetrating eye for a moment, and it is not true. Many of the voices that she hears are genuine spirits longing to communicate with their loved ones. She is not a charlatan. He is mistaken if he supposes that.

Ramsey, for his part, shakes his head vigorously by way of protest – that he should ever entertain such a notion. Why the very idea!

'You see, luv,' she continues, addressing Daphne mostly now, 'the work of a medium or psychic – it's not an exact science. Sometimes we do see things and hear the voices, and at other times not. But when there are none, when you draw a blank and yet people are watching, when an audience of dozens or even hundreds have paid good money to attend, well what can you do! The show must go on. And so we avail ourselves of ... well, certain techniques. We invent things a little. It doesn't harm anyone. I am not fraudulent, my luvs. The spirits speak through me ... sometimes. And that's what's happened this evening. I know that's true because I cannot remember anything of what happened.'

'Don't you think that's somewhat of a contradiction?' Oliver Ramsey suggests, lighting up a cigar and reclining now more into his seat on the sofa. 'How can you know if you can't remember?'

'I know, that's all,' is the sum total of the exotic Madam

Alenushka's response, and to which Ramsey merely lets forth a guffaw of renewed scepticism before sitting back once more and returning to the ecstasy of his smoke.

'So there really is something ... something after death?' Daphne asks, ignoring her husband's boorishness, her lovely brows furrowed in concentration. 'Should we really allow ourselves to believe in that?'

'Of course, my dear. Of course. Belief is important. All this scepticism that we hear so much about these days - it is misguided. Oh, it is of no consequence that we dispensed with God - or stopped believing in him through all our learned works of science. God will survive that! What is far more dangerous for us is that we stop believing in the Devil, to dismiss evil as simply human nature, something we can put to rights with a little reason and sweet talk. For he hasn't gone away, *Old Nick*, but still works his evil through people just like he always has, and all in the most clever and devious ways, still, working to unravel all the goodness and grace of the world.'

Daphne nods her comprehension and smiles, grateful for the other woman's candour, while Ramsey for his part continues to look unsettled, his habitual sullen expression returning to his face whenever Madam Alenushka ceases to observe him, his mouth puckered in a most unbecoming fashion. This weird, uneducated and simple-minded woman clearly has Daphne under her spell; and he is none too happy about it.

'Madam Alenushka, what did you mean about Mister Roselli having lied?' she inquires in a soft and gentle voice, which the older woman and her companion both seem to appreciate.

'I don't recall. Is that what I said?' Madam Alenushka replies, glancing at Frances for confirmation and then apologetically with a little hint of a smile towards Amos himself. 'Well, there you are - it must mean something, my luvs! But what it is, I cannot tell you. Like I say: when the voices come like that, I'm not aware. I am only the channel for them.'

'Do you think you might be able to do it again ... now?'

Daphne asks, clearly also disturbed by her pronouncement about her husband being barren.

'I can try,' Madam Alenushka replies – though with little conviction it seems. And, indeed, after twenty further minutes of fruitless endeavour, with all seated unproductively around the circumference of the little table, they are forced to abandon their efforts for the evening and Madam Alenushka and Frances rise and prepare to go to their room. They will depart in the morning after breakfast, they announce - the destination of her very next venue, everyone is astonished to learn, none other than the residence of Her Majesty the Queen: Osborne House. Quickly Amos jumps at the chance and asks if he might accompany them. He will arrange the carriage himself, he says, and call for them in good time in the morning. This really is a heaven sent opportunity, he knows – for if only he could get a foot in the door at Osborne, to secure an introduction no matter how tenuously with those who would be close to the Queen, who knows what distinguished people he might meet or what commissions might come his way! To his delight, the esteemed and clearly *very* well-connected Madam Alenushka agrees, and they resolve to meet early the very next day.

At the cottage, and after instructing his valet James, and Beth also, of his intentions to rise early the next morning, Amos retires to his bedroom and endeavours, as best he can, to quieten his thoughts and settle down to sleep. But he knows it is not going to be easy. What a curious and disturbing experience this evening has been! And now, outside, the wind is beginning to stir quite loudly through the branches of the trees, as if some rain or even a storm might be on the way - the pale curtains of his partly open casement casting gusty moon-shadows across the floor of his room. It is, however, far too warm to draw shut the window, so it is something he must simply endure.

Tomorrow will be different, though, he tells himself, trying not to heed the tiny whispering voices of ivy and rose leaves as they scrape their fingers across the walls of the building outside. Tomorrow will surely be a triumph! Osborne, the glorious palace of his dreams where he will ride up the drive in a smart carriage with the ladies at his side: the opportunity of a lifetime. Even if he gets no further than the Gate House it would be an achievement. At the very least perhaps he could persuade Madam Alenushka herself to mention his name in the presence of the Queen! Well worth a try! And if it really is true, as he has always believed, that there is a special place destined for him in the upper echelons of cultured society – a place where he, as a talented young painter already knocking on the doors of fame and fortune, rightfully belongs – then this would surely hasten the process and become his entrance ticket and calling card combined to that exalted world. He might even become a regular fixture at Osborne in time, celebrated and feted just like the painter Lanseer had once been; welcomed and sought after in aristocratic circles everywhere.

'Her Majesty will receive you now, Mr Roselli,' the footman would say and show him through into the morning room overlooking the broad terrace and gardens at Osborne and where the diminutive little woman dressed in black would offer her hand to him. He can see it now, hear her voice. 'Mr Roselli, how good of you to come. If you could run up to Sandringham this year and produce portraits for some of the lovely young princesses We would be so grateful!'

'Thank you Ma'am,' he would reply with not too deep a bow of the head, appropriate to his elevated status. How fabulous! But then gradually the lovely dream dissolves and transforms itself into a vision of home – not his humble rented accommodation at Mornington Terrace in London, but the family estate in Kent. Rarely would he ever think of it these days, or even visit much at all since the death of his mother so many years ago. It is now in the sole possession of his father, a man who has always disapproved of Amos's career as a painter and who has even cut him off from any allowance or financial support in recent years – his childhood home once so beloved by people, so full of music and light, now merely somewhere to be avoided: dour and uninviting, only to be visited with reluctance when duty demands. He sees it all now in perfect clarity, the landscaped grounds and Palladian walls and terraces of what, many of his friends would be surprised to learn, is still a substantial and affluent country seat, a prestigious estate whose foundations were built on monastic lands, whose inhabitants once hunted in the parks of the royal estates and who had once even entertained kings at their table. But in his dream it looks unfamiliar, dilapidated, like a romantic ruin - the paved court at the rear of the building where he once played as a child amid the wisteria and climbing roses now desolate, eerie and bleached of colour, composed of half-ruined arches like some deserted cloister in the moonlight. How very strange!

He hurries around and up to the portico - and here at the familiar double oak doors with their beautiful carved motif of roses that he remembers so well, he fumbles in his waistcoat pocket for his key. Inside all is deserted, dark, musty in fragrance and everywhere the sinuous shrouds of spiders' webs covered in dust hang from banisters and picture frames and from all the once-beautiful carved tracery of doorways and widows. The floor, no longer graced by lavish carpets or tiles, is now covered in dried leaves; while each lamp, each chandelier, each nook and recess of each elaborately carved bookshelf or gilded cabinet is likewise tarnished and flecked with disuse and humbled by exposure to the elements. Bewildered, he sits down at the bottom of the grand staircase in the entrance hall, and wonders, feeling guilty that he journeys here so rarely. What on earth could have occurred in his absence? Where on earth has everyone gone!

Then he sees coming towards him a beautiful woman, graceful and elegant, clothed in a long cuirass gown of cloth of silver with skirts of sepia and grey taffeta silk, her shoulders bare. Tiny but spectacular glimmers of opulence shine from her person, from her earrings, and neckband, a lovely corsage of flowers, pale lilies and carnations upon her chest. It is Daphne, dressed as if going to a ball, her hair piled high in an elaborate chignon entwined with a string of pearls and a black velvet neck band from which a great diamond set in silver hangs like a gigantic sparkling tear-drop upon her breast. She would be no stranger to this place, of course; she would have visited it a hundred times as a child and as a young woman, and so he should really not feel at all surprised to discover her here. She approaches closer, almost gliding towards him, apparitional and stunningly beautiful, and stares at him in a puzzled way, her lips smiling very slightly, as if amused to find him seated alone at the foot of the stairs.

In silence, he climbs slowly to his feet and takes her gloved hand with its delicate lace cuff and silver buttons and she brings her face so very close to his.

'What they say may well be true,' she whispers, 'that I have only ever kept his love through practising spells and enchantments.'

'Yes, you are a sorceress – I always knew it!' he says, and nods his understanding, for it all seems reasonable enough to say such things in a dream as, arm in arm, they wander through the spaces of the deserted building, through the morning room, the library, the dining room, once such busy parts of the building but now merely populated with white dust sheets shrouding and protecting the furniture, the curtains flapping as the wind cuts through the tall, half-opened casements - stirring the leaves in little whispering eddies upon the floor. Even some wayward tendrils of ivy and the white flowers of columbine, he notices, have wound their way inside and around the tracery of the windows and pilasters. And then he turns to her and looks into her lovely face, as he has done a thousand times before and waits for her to speak.

'Oh, if you will only kiss me!' she whispers, again so close.

'Why? What is my kiss to you?' he asks.

'Then I shall be able to forgive you,' she replies. 'Then I will have restored to me my soul and will be able to rest in peace.'

Their lips meet for a tiny, fleeting moment, and then she hurries from him. He gives chase, seeming to fly through the rooms rather than run until, just as he is about to catch her in his arms, filled with such desire and passion, she is gone. He is merely left clutching at the dusty folds of the curtains - the open window through which she has flown revealing only the garden beyond - its tall, nocturnal hedges of yew and laurel bathed in moonlight. She is gone. And as he opens his eyes he realises he is in his own bed, safe enough but alone – so very alone – the curtains in his room flapping from time to time across the small window recess nearby, the rose leaves still whispering as they gently chaff the walls outside. And then, softly at first, the rhythmic sound of falling rain begins to make itself known. Beautiful, cool, gentle rain. The air becomes fresh – so fresh, until here in the darkness, a feeling of utter peace descends upon him, just seconds before he turns over and falls into a deep and grateful slumber from which he does not wake until dawn.

Softly, the morning comes; slowly his sleep and sweet dreams subside and give way to consciousness. He is aware of the sounds of Beth bringing up the water and towels and, with a deliberate rousing noise, setting down the two polished brass cans outside on the landing and pouring their contents into the hot-water jugs ready for him. His wake up call! All melancholia and gloom of the night is vanquished by the sound of her busy feet about the house and by the bright sunshine and exultant bird song outside – and a sense of optimism and excitement takes a hold as he rises. He sharpens his razor on the strop, shaves the stubble from his throat and cheeks and with a tiny pair of scissors carefully trims his remaining half-beard into shape – sprucing himself up for the important day ahead, for he must, he knows, look his very best for Her Majesty.

Still full of anticipation and excitement, he takes an early breakfast, as arranged, then returns to his room where James has already laid out his very best morning suit and cravat, his ash wood cane, best kid gloves and plush top hat, all in readiness for his journey by carriage to Osborne with Madam Anelushka and her companion. All seems set fair; the carriage already having been sent for by James, and he is just about to wander over to Parnassus to meet it when his progress is halted by the arrival of a telegram, an event that most people of his station in life invariably interpret as only ever signifying bad news. And it *is* bad news. His father has died suddenly overnight. Amos must take the earliest ferry back to the mainland, and thence to the family estate in Kent - while Madam Alenushka and her companion must journey alone to Osborne, taking his cherished though slightly unrealistic hopes of ever meeting Her Majesty the Queen along with them.

Chapter Twelve

The Gable Hood

Proudly, with a little polish of her new spectacles and a swift glance at herself in the hall mirror, an exercise which for once does not put her in a bad mood, Beth fastens the ribbons on her new bonnet, all trimmed with fresh cornflowers and violets, and sets off – feeling so excited – because today is going to be all hers, the first time in weeks, completely free for one whole day. What with Mr. Roselli being out and about in the City and the sun shining on a perfect summer's afternoon, it is just a delight to savour - and to be outdoors, even better. She has also been invited by none other than Mrs Edwards for tea and scones in the bakery just down from the market – though what exactly might be the purpose behind this unusual request, if in fact it is anything special at all, she cannot imagine. But it is a rare treat to be asked out - and one which, despite the fact that during their last encounter the woman had been tetchy and a little unkind to her, Beth herself is not about to forego.

For Beth, the high street is a place that never fails to excite and intrigue. Even when she must go to it for supplies and trudge its length with great baskets and bags of goods under each arm, for her it is still a joy – a place where half the world gathers and puts its wares on display. She loves the haberdashery, the green grocers, the fishmongers – she even loves the tobacconist! She adores the sounds and smells, the brightly coloured striped awnings hung above the shop windows, the calls of the hawkers from the stalls that line the curbs. Here, the window of the jewellers becomes a royal treasure house, a kingdom of rubies, sapphires and jet; and the pharmacy a place of almost mystical fascination with its medicine bottles, its capsules and pills, the alchemy of its great glass carboys with their brightly-coloured liquids to represent the four humours. Even if she were compelled to come here every day until she were a hundred years old she would never be able to comprehend the half of it. She feels so very happy.

'I must say you do look well, Beth,' Mrs Edwards declares as they meet and then hurry along the busy street to the bakery – there to take their seats at a table set in the window, covered by a beautiful lace tablecloth and where they can enjoy their tea together, watch the world of London society go by and gossip to their hearts content. 'Such a fine little bonnet, and lovely ribbons! Why they are beautiful, quite beautiful,' Mrs Edwards adds, continuing to heap praise on the somewhat transformed visage of the young girl there before her who has grown somewhat in height since their last encounter and whose face displays a firmer jaw-line and more elegant brows, so that she seems to have taken on a far more open and alert appearance. Quite pretty, in fact.

Beth can well-perceive the curiosity in the older woman's eyes as she dishes out the compliments every bit as liberally as the cream she spoons upon the range of cakes and patisseries set before her and which she is clearly about to devour with an eagerness which is almost frightening. 'I can see your circumstances have improved somewhat from the last time we spoke, young lady,' she adds glancing up with a look of inquiry that seems to demand that at least some degree of explanation be provided.

'Well, yes, things have altered, Mrs Edwards, you are right,' Beth admits and then goes on to explain exactly why – though the story does begin with a little piece of sad news.

'Mr Roselli's father passed away only a few weeks ago,' she begins, 'and everything by way of inheritance has gone to Mister Roselli and his sister Margaret. Mister Roselli himself has come into possession of a manor house and lands in Kent, and quite a fortune as well. My wages have increased as a consequence - and so I have not done badly either - and we have more staff now at Mornington Terrace. The country estate, though, is really spectacular! I have been there already. It's so historic and very grand - I never realised just how grand. The foundations of the building, they say, go right back to Tudor times. It has even a courtyard with fountains, and there is a glasshouse full of the most beautiful flowers and exotic palms. There is ever-such a long drive with big iron gates, that leads through the front gardens, and a coach house and stables for horses, too - and there are acres of apple and cherry orchards and pasture for sheep, and the lawns at the back of the property slope down to a beautiful river - with swans - which Mister Roselli likes because he says they are the creatures closest to the Muses - which, I think has something to do with the arts and all that kind of thing. Oh, I am getting quite breathless thinking about it! Mister Roselli intends still to keep the town house at Mornington Terrace, though, because of his work. But finding money to pay the bills is no longer a struggle. The allowances for everything, food, coal, wood for the fires and oil for the lamps have all increased and I have a full purse these days when the tradesmen come to call. It's all so much easier now, and I may ask for anything I want ... within reason.'

'Emm!' Mrs Edwards remarks, trying to sound appreciative, but evidently also a little put out that her former predictions of Mr Roselli's inevitable spiral into decline and penury appear to have been postponed - at least for the time being. 'So there's not much point in my trying to tempt you away again. What does he pay you now?'

'If it please you Ma'am, twelve pounds per annum.'

'But you have education, don't you, you can read and write? - I remember you told me so. You should be earning far more money than that, working in a far better position.'

'Perhaps I should,' Beth concedes, 'but remember, when I first came to Mister Roselli I needed to find work quickly. I was quite desperate at the time. And, as I say, I have received a generous increase in recent weeks. So really I am content with that.'

'Ah, but are you content with your prospects, Beth?' Mrs

Edwards counters, her shrewd little eyes narrowing with thought. 'Consider this ... that you are still a young woman, how old now?'

'I am eighteen Ma'am,' Beth answers, almost certain this is the case – though the sad fact is she does not know the exact year of her birth – an embarrassing gap in her personal knowledge she has always endeavoured to keep to herself.

'A young woman of eighteen years living with a bachelor pushing thirty, and one moreover of dubious reputation and with money to burn – what do you think people might say? What do you imagine this will do to your own prospects of ever finding a respectable and loving husband as I have done? Think carefully.'

Beth does indeed think carefully – in fact she rarely passes a single day without doing just that, though perhaps not quite in the same way as Mrs Edwards might be expecting. Even as she sits at the table this afternoon trying to field all the probing questions Mrs Edwards sends her way, a certain persistent anxiety plays on her mind. In particular she is concerned over the welfare of Mister Roselli himself, who seems most perturbed of late, wandering aimlessly about the city, sketching old buildings and river wharfs and altogether too many places of dereliction and decay than, she would imagine, would be at all good for anyone, let alone one suffering the pangs of bereavement. She has seen the sketches he brings back and they are very morbid – despairing, almost – though she does not convey these details to Mrs Edwards, of course – since the older woman is already convinced quite sufficiently of Mr Roselli's unworthiness. So she continues to keep her peace; she sips at her tea in its delicate little blue china cup; she cuts another scone, butters it, applies some strawberry jam with a finely engraved silver spoon and resolves not to say a further word on the subject. Mrs Edwards, however, is still not about to abandon her bid to capture her and save her from the clutches of her dissolute master.

'Beth ... you are a bright little thing, very bright, and you could rise to a position of responsibility if you stay in this line of work – a mistress of a worthy household. But, remember, the best situations generally come with husband attached, as a working pair. Nobody is much interested these days in employing a spinster or an old maid. And to escape that fate you must withdraw yourself from the present situation. Don't ruin your future for this ungrateful man. As for his new-found wealth – well, how long do you imagine that will last? The hardest thing about having money, young lady, is in keeping it. A fool and his money are easily parted, as they say. And where will you be then?'

'I think ... I think I should be just as content as I was a few weeks ago, before things altered,' Beth answers with decision. 'As long as I can be of use, that is. Because even if it does all go wrong for him, the way you say, how much worse would it be without ... well, without somebody to look after him?'

'Oh, you are such a naïve little fool, Beth!' Mrs Edwards exclaims and crashes her cup down so forcefully into its saucer that the sound turns heads in the shop. 'Women must do their duty,' she whispers aware and slightly ashamed of her own untypical outburst of passion. 'And the men we choose to associate with must do theirs. All Mr Roselli will ever do, I fear, is dream. What use can that ever be to you? More to the point what can you ever be to him?'

'Please Mrs Edwards, do not become angry with me. He is a fine man and very clever. It is not just my opinion. I have many times heard people say so.'

'What people? His rowdy friends with all their champagne, their loose morals and fornication? Oh it all seems such fun now, that sort of society – but you wait, young lady, wait until you're older.'

'Many of his friends are famous and successful artists ...'

'Ha, famous for what! For painting harlots with pouting lips and bare legs? Disgusting.'

'No, that is not what they paint,' Beth argues with a confidence that appears to amaze the other woman who stares for a moment open-mouthed in astonishment at being contradicted so firmly. 'They paint feelings and ...'

'Feelings! Don't be ridiculous. How can anyone paint feelings!' Mrs Edwards continues, her heavy, bovine features appearing suddenly to be very swollen and hot-looking – and in response to which she opens her fan and waves it rapidly under her chin.

'If it please you, Ma'am, they do say that a true painting cannot be of anything other than feelings. A painting, they say is not just a likeness of something that we put in a frame and hang on our walls. They say it is something that has a depth and a meaning far greater than what is visible. It is about things that we dream of, things that we live our lives for and things that we may even die for - and that I have heard them say when they talk together. I know I cannot always make it clear what I mean when I speak like this, but I believe that they are people who are devoted to what they do and that they are sincere - as, too, are many of the fine young women they have as models. *They* are the ones who are sacrificing their lives. They are servants of beauty and truth. Against that my sacrifice is hardly anything at all. What little I can do, therefore, I shall do - and bear it gladly even if I am not given credit.'

'So you will remain with him. Stick with the wastrel to the last?' the older woman demands with an air of dismay and a voice of feigned exhaustion - and to which a demur and determined nod from Beth confirms the worst, at least from the other woman's perspective, and following which she does not seem to want to look into Beth's eyes any longer at all. Instead, she searches in her purse in order to settle the bill, and by her movements about the table - tidying this or that bit of china or cutlery in the habitual way of one who is used to doing such things and yet who cannot quite give up, even when paying for the privilege - it is clear she is preparing to leave. How ungracious! And Beth knows now - whatever the future holds, whatever the consequences of the radical choices she has made and announced today, it will not be one shared with Mrs Edwards or anyone of her kind; and when they part a few moments later outside in the hot, dusty street it really is, this time she knows, a final farewell.

Sandstone and flint ramparts, herringbone brickwork, and ancient foot-worn pavements edged in moss and lichen, the Tower of London is a place he never tires of visiting - a place of endless fascination, and today once again Amos has surrendered to the desire to come here to the Inner Ward with its lawns and open spaces in order to sketch and also to read one very important letter. Being forced to remain in the capital in order to deal with legal formalities following the division of the family estate, he has used his visits here to find a certain solace, a certain forgetfulness regarding his plight – not the plight of having inherited a small fortune in land and capital, of course, but that of being estranged and so far away from Daphne – who must remain on her distant island, along with her unfinished portrait, both waiting for his return. His visits here have become a sedative, therefore, something to settle his turbulent mind – so that already he has become a familiar face among those who work here, among the many warders, gardeners, masons, carpenters and cleaners who reside within the precinct itself or who else come and go on a daily basis from their homes nearby. They are used to his presence – clothed in his smart fashionable jackets or, on the sunnier days like today, in his flannel shirts and wide-brimmed straw hat; they are used to his little folding camp chair upon which he sits for hours on end with a large sketch pad perched on his knee; and they are used to his questions, his jibes and passing observations. He feels reassured by their acceptance of him, even perhaps by their sympathy towards his eccentricities. In a peculiar kind of way, also, he is able to find some resonance to Daphne in places such as this, places that inspire him to draw or to paint. It is most likely the reason, too, why he spends so many hours wandering the streets of the capital, browsing around the various curiosity shops in Fleet Street or Leicester Square, or even further afield to Kensington or Hammersmith, collecting items of jewellery or other exotic and unusual accessories that could prove of use in his paintings – anything that might be suitable for Daphne: a decorative brooch set with pastes that she might wear on her gown or in her hair, a necklace of tiny enamel squares or opals, a filigree headband or barrette of copper that could be employed to denote a certain style or allegory. He loves shopping for such things and imagining how she might look when wearing them. It provides some measure of compensation, the next best thing to being in her company. And thus the lonely hours have turned to days, the days to weeks. It has been over a month now - and still always the demands of the solicitors detain him, keep him captive in the hot, stifling atmosphere of the capital at the height of summer and, most of all, keep him away from the one place in the world now to which he longs to return. And although he has become more proficient of late at controlling the sense of anguish and impatience, he suspects he will have to address the issue head-on shortly because this morning he received a letter from her, a long-awaited letter by private courier from the Island, registered and sealed and which he had realised straight away, therefore, must be of importance. He has made a pledge with himself to read it here a little later, as soon as he feels more composed - something which, he knows from experience, an hour or two of sketching is sure to achieve.

Unfolding his chair and placing it down in a quiet leafy area north of the White Tower, he sets to work this afternoon drawing the scene before him using a combination of charcoal and coloured chalks. Such an assortment of fascinating buildings and architectural styles from so many periods of history - it never fails to excite him. There is Medieval and Gothic in abundance, of course - and a more perfect example of Tudor building you could not expect to find in all the world than here in the cottages to the West of the precinct: the old picturesque cottages ranged along the inner wall and flanked by the Bell Tower and Beauchamp Tower. And so it is that he realises that he is also looking across to the execution site, the very spot where in the past so many enemies of the crown had met their bloody end, a place recently transformed for the benefit of tourists into a prominent attraction with decorative posts and chains around it. And then beyond that, behind the rooftops of the cottages, there would be that walkway - the leads - between the towers and from which a man might look down upon the site of the block itself. Yes, he was looking towards the very place where he had stood at that horrid moment in the nightmare – the vantage point from which the gruesome spectacle he had witnessed so vividly a few weeks ago had taken place. The recollection causes his heart to race for a moment, his mind churning in a sudden frenzy of profound comprehension because the truth is obvious to him now - that everywhere, at all times, everything he sees reminds him of the extraordinary and peculiar destiny in which he and Daphne have become entangled - feeling almost powerless to step outside of it, this dark, supernatural power that has such sway over him. And now, of course, there is the letter. What could it contain? Realising that he is ready now, and that he will probably not be able to apply himself to any further work until he has discovered the answer to this question, he stows his sketch pad away into his folio case and locates a quiet, shady bench in a peaceful corner where he sets about reading, imbibing every word and wishing she were here to speak it herself.

She is still on the island, she tells him, missing her horses – for, apart from the coveted animals owned by the local huntsmen, there are only 'stable nags' here for the hauling of coaches, she says. She is still enjoying her life of leisure or, as she describes it, the round of endless dinner parties, soirees and high teas that polite society demands in such a place.

'Yes, it is an enviable life, I dare say,' she writes as the second page begins. 'There is hardly an evening when we do not have some engagement. Consequently, we do not rise all that early as a rule. During the mornings I devote much of my time to the spaniels, walking down with them to the bay, then letting them off and throwing sticks for them into the waves, an occupation which I enjoy well enough and which they adore, of course, their little tales wagging - and their barking, so happy that it is infectious and it makes me smile and forget my cares for a while. The bay is a busy little place, as you recall, with those garish-painted bathing machines that they push down into the sea for the ladies. It is hot here now, and everyone is flocking to them in order to swim without being seen – though the men do not seem to bother with these constraints, and continue to swim wherever they will. There are boat tours now, as well, since you left us. They set off from the little jetty by the hotel - with hawkers coming along with their tickets picking up anyone who is brave enough to hop into their little row boats and take to the seas and where, I am reliably informed, they explore the caves beneath the cliffs and even have the occasional picnic therein among the company of the gulls and bats.

There is a Punch and Judy stall that has sprung up on the beach, as well - very tall with a red and white apron, always surrounded by children and consequently very noisy. And there are men and women further along, away from the crowds, clambering all over the rocks and cliff faces with little hammers, searching for fossils - that is, impressions in the rocks of creatures and plants that, they insist, lived millions of years ago. They say that here is one of the best places in the whole world for such diversions. But there is a sinister side to it - because I hear them mumbling among themselves that, because the rocks in which the fossils are embedded are all so old, that the Bible must be wrong when it tells us the age of the creation as being only a few thousand years. And if it is wrong on that score, then what else might it be wrong about, they ask, looking at one another in a dark sort of way? The Ten Commandments perhaps? I must say I find it all more than a little unsavoury and in fact quite disturbing. Do I really wish to be told that the earth might be millions of years older than what the bible teaches, or that the same kind of logic should urge us to disobey the commandments and therefore to steal or kill or commit adultery with impunity? Really, what possible use is that to anyone!

'So I give the fossil hunters a wide birth and prefer instead to remain in the here-and-now. We find a quiet spot further along the coast, my canine friends and I, and sit and look out at the water, instead. I inhale the aroma of the brine and the seaweed and watch the waves in all their changing moods and tides - and then I walk again onto the downs, perhaps. And thus the morning passes until it is time for lunch. I have encountered your funny old gentleman in the big hat and cloak, by the way, and we have become the best of friends. He is perfectly charming.

As a rule, the afternoons are spent in the garden where I am trying with varying degrees of success to extend the herbaceous borders to the north and east, never the sunniest corners of course. But I have hopes for next year when many of the plants will have matured and be bedded-in nicely. Sometimes I read a little in the summerhouse or, if the weather is bad, upstairs in the library, the room where you painted me – remember? I press flowers there - or I do a quick reading of the cards for myself and wonder at my destiny, as if for just that one moment my whole life might be encapsulated in those twenty two peculiar little vignettes of the major arcana – their message weaving in and out before me like so many chapters in a story. In the fashion of the fossil collectors, I pretend I can read the story, and that it has some kind of meaning. If only! The piano is also a great comfort. And then it is time for dinner and the prospect of whatever engagement awaits us thereafter. So you see, dear one, I am as gainfully occupied and productive as ever. Polly sometimes comes to examine the garden, when he is in residence that, is, and not away on some business trip or the other. He approves and tells me I am very clever - though that is about the extent of his kindness these days.

'Dear one, I was so saddened to learn of your loss, and of your dear father who has passed away. It was terrible that you had to rush away and I could not take your hands in mine and comfort you. I have written also to your sister Margaret, my dearest friend in all the world, as you know, to convey my sympathies and to tell her she must come and holiday with us just as soon as circumstances may permit, and that wherever in the world I am there will always be a welcome and a warm heart waiting. I have known her and regarded her as the most agreeable of companions almost as long as I have known you, dear one, and I hope always that she will think well of me.

'Your sorrows must be grave indeed, and against that I feel that any grumbles or gripes that I might have must pale into insignificance, but I must tell you that I am not the happiest of creatures at this juncture, and that things have not gone altogether smoothly for your faithful muse during your absence. There has been a crisis. I think you can probably divine the nature of it. I did not tell him, I could not tell him at first, and I am positive it was right not to because even though I suspected I was with child it came to nothing, and I lost the tiny embryo after just a few weeks. It was quite painful, quite bloody and an altogether rather sordid experience. I meant to have kept it private, but the good doctor, who I had thought was my confidante, must have let the news escape, because now Polly does know, and it is as if the whole world has fallen apart. Disaster! Catastrophe! It has if anything made him treat me with even greater unkindness than ever before – even, I dare to say, extending to a certain animosity, as though I have in some sense failed him.

'Even the staff here seem to be against me of late – and of course the entire household are cognisant of what has taken place. They regard me with suspicion and irritation when I speak to them, as if it were somehow a crime I had committed. David, the steward, even had the cheek to suggest the other day that I was too thin, and that to be thus ill-disposed in any female creature is never a good state for the bearing of offspring. Do they expect me to eat myself silly and become fat with hanging udders? Really, I feel I am viewed now as some kind of prize Friesian cow that is expected to become inseminated at the earliest possible opportunity and bring forth the pedigree stock for the benefit of all concerned – though never is there much of a care for my welfare or whether I should ever live through my travails.

'To be perfectly frank, the prospect of another pregnancy fills me with horror, and the very act by which it might be attained now repulses me more than ever as a consequence. It quite literally makes me nauseous. Because of this, Polly has become very unkind and morose of late; he loses his temper at the slightest provocation, and it can be quite intimidating when he gets cross like that. Ever since his accident, it seems, there has been a gradual descent into a terrible state of insensitivity and even a kind of brutality that effects everybody around him and which I feel powerless to forestall.

'The other evening, he even threw in my face the encounter with Madam Anelushka that time - remember? - and her dire pronouncements. He went all shouty-crackers and said that I had made a fool of him and that it must be true, after all, what she told us – that we shall remain barren, and that this is what comes of dabbling in the occult. He even told me I had been a fool to have brought all this "mumbo jumbo," as he refers to it, into the house, and that we are cursed for being so dishonourable and perverse. For a grown man - and one, moreover, that purports to be rational and scientific, I must say he has proved very much the contrary of late, behaving quite hysterically, grumbling about evil influences being brought in, and that I have encouraged him to black magic and table tipping. He can be very cruel when the mood takes him, even calling me a witch.

'What have I done to deserve this? I cannot tell you how very peculiar it all seems, how very strange after a lifetime of being valued and looked upon with such fondness by you, dear one, you who have been a friend to me without ever once demanding anything in return.

'Do I sound a hopeless case? Am I being too precious? I know you would be teasing me something rotten if you were here with me now. But do not be too harsh, my dear Amos - for it is you, after all, who have put me up to it - you with your dedication and love – you who have always listened to me and understood every flight of fancy, every idea and avenue of exploration I have ever allowed my thoughts to wander along – always, and without ever once complaining or judging me. For if you could be here, if you could see us here at Parnassus when he walks past me each morning at breakfast without even once meeting my eyes, or when he roars at me and tells me off because the servants have been culpable of this or that minor misdemeanour and I am somehow meant to be responsible for it; if you could comprehend the unkindness of our nights together when there should instead be the sweetest pleasure in its place, then you might be more lenient on your muse and grant her some token of your sympathy.

'Tell me you can come soon! I know you have been so very taken up with your affairs in London, but please do not forget your friend who looks each day for a letter or telegram to announce your intention of returning. The portrait waits still for your finishing touch. The very same cottage you took before has, I hear, become free for the remainder of the season: an opportunity for you to return to our island, therefore, for an extended stay as you promised and to become our neighbour once again. Your friend and colleague Watts has arrived at last,

I am told. Why not follow him? Exchange the soot and smog of London for the air and freshness of the seaside! Replace the noise and commotion of the city for the call of the gulls and the whisper of the wind through the cedars and the bracken. Everything calls you back, dear Amos, not least your restless muse who pines so sadly. Come soon.'

Daphne

Slowly, he reads through the whole letter again before folding it and replacing it in its envelope. Inevitably, he pictures the scene at the villa where she resides, the ivy, the wisteria and roses on the walls outside, and the little Davenport desk and writing table in the library where in private moments she lays out her tarot cards and where she would have sat perhaps only yesterday to seal her letter and then perhaps have taken it personally herself, for reasons of discretion, down the lane to the corner store and post-office in the village; he imagines how she must be feeling, tries to interpret her words, to read between the lines, and the more he does so the more troubled he becomes. Should he really desert London now at this stage, cast aside all the legal commitments and obligations he has set for himself and return to the Island? There is so much here still to be done. Yet how can he possibly refuse her? How can he fail to respond to her need?

He strolls back to the spot to the north of the White Tower where he had been sitting earlier and begins to sketch again, brandishing with swift and expert eye his charcoal stick or pastel crayons upon the surface of the paper, concentrating, channelling his thoughts. It is the only way he knows to steady his mind, to find some measure of equanimity in the face of what he has just read and the restlessness it engenders in his own heart. Gradually, however, he becomes more settled, more engrossed in his work and lost in the timeless, living theatre of history set there before him.

As always there are a number of tourists milling around, ladies from the country in their out-of-fashion bustle skirts, their parasols over their shoulders, and with the darker, taller figures of gentlemen in fine cravats and top hats walking at their sides. He incorporates a few of these into his drawing –

they are part of the scenery. Nourished by an endless diet of penny novelettes or popular stage-plays, they have come here to look upon the many places where the stories and chronicles of The Tower have been enacted over the centuries in so many bloody episodes of royal intrigue. With a macabre curiosity, a longing for the barbaric eccentricities of the past, they peer around every corner, behind every doorway to seek out the legends - places where a witch might have been racked or a Duke imprisoned; places where one might climb the stairway of a tower that once housed a princess or to behold in awe the sumptuous jewels, the crown, the orb and the sceptre once carried by the Queen at her coronation. Here one can stand upon the very spot where a traitor was once executed, or pay ones respects at the gravesides of all the famous black ravens that have dwelled here over the centuries, those poor creatures with their wings clipped ever since the prophesy so many centuries ago that the nation would fall into ruination and calamity if they were to ever leave the Tower.

And then, as so often happens as he sits here, one or more of those very same tourists would creep up behind him, hover just over his shoulder to examine his efforts - sometimes speaking to him and leaving compliments, at other times several of them conversing amongst themselves, talking about him as if he did not quite exist in the living flesh but was instead some bizarre automaton or animated wax-works set out there on the Green for the edification of all concerned. He doesn't mind, of course. It is a small ordeal to bear in exchange for the privilege of being allowed to work here, and he usually manages to tolerate any interference of this kind with a dignified and stoical silence.

'Those are the Queen's Lodgings, aren't they - them buildings yonder?' a gentleman asks, pointing with his cane and placing himself alongside for once instead of discourteously leering over his shoulder as most spectators do.

'That's right,' Amos answers, tilting his head so that he might look up from beneath the brim of his straw hat. The intruder in this instance is on his own, quite young and with an intelligent face; kindly enough - so that Amos feels reluctant in this instance to see him off as he might normally have done with a well-rehearsed, icy stare. 'It is the residence of the Lieutenant of the Tower, in fact' Amos continues with an authoritative air, happy enough to respond to someone else who clearly also knows his way around reasonably well.

'Ah! So that was where they kept poor little Jane Grey - just before her execution?' the man continues with a rueful shake of the head, shielding his eyes from the sun for a moment as he looks across towards the buildings - for such was the widespread knowledge, the common currency of the Tower's history that people will regard the characters associated with it almost as personal acquaintances - as if Jane Grey herself who lived and died over three hundred years ago would be privy to his concerns and would be just about to pop over to the window herself and give him a wave.

'Yes, executed at the age of sixteen, I understand,' Amos observes.

'That's that Bloody Mary, then, we've got to thank for that, I suppose!' the man declares, referring to the Tudor Queen of the time and continuing to speak of her as one with whom he would have had at least a passing acquaintance.

This really is too amusing! Amos thinks, as he laughs and turns to look at the man once again - but as he does so, he notices he has been joined by a young woman, the dappled sunshine dancing across her face, her eyes regarding him with intense curiosity for a moment - and yet kindly, too,

He does not acknowledge her interest, however, but merely turns his attention back to his sketch - before suddenly realising that the woman herself is wearing a most strange bonnet, like a gabled hood that you find in old paintings, trimmed with tiny pearls. How odd! But when an instant later he turns to look again, the young woman is gone. Only the young man is standing there, looking down at him still - though this time with a slightly perplexed look on his face.

'Where has the lady gone?' Amos inquires.

But the man merely stares back at him and shrugs his shoulders. 'Eh?' he says.

To which Amos gets to his feet and looks all about him. There is no sign of anyone else within a hundred yards. There is no woman in a gable hood, or any woman for that matter -

yet he had seen her, just five seconds ago!

'Where is she? Where has she gone?' Amos demands, feeling that the words escaping his lips are already sounding faintly hysterical and absurd.

The poor man, meanwhile, is beginning to look alarmed by now, as if regretting having ventured to speak to such an odd and eccentric person. He should have known better, his trembling lips and startled eyes seem to suggest.

'S.s.orry ... sorry to have disturbed you,' he finally stammers, already making his retreat and moving away from him.

'Where is she?' Amos demands again, though speaking to no one in particular, since the spectator of a moment ago has by this time fled back to the safety of a small crowd of onlookers near to the Waterloo Barracks and who are already shaking their heads and muttering among themselves at the ravings of the mad artist. *The mad artist* ... that was him.

Oh dear! This won't do, Amos, tells himself, as he slowly packs up his belongings, his charcoal sticks and coloured chalks, his sketchpad and folding chair. This won't do at all. You are a wealthy young man now, completely free and at liberty. You could travel anywhere in the world – get away from all this bedevilment, escape forever from all these morbid fantasies.

And suddenly he arrives at a very important decision.

Upon his return from The Tower to his home in Mornington Terrace that evening, Amos informs Beth and his valet-cum-butler James – now a permanent member of the household along with his wife - that they should prepare themselves for a lengthy journey, perhaps as early as next week. The business with the family estate will simply have to look after itself, he announces, confident that his solicitor will be able to take the strain. James's wife, however, should stay behind in London to look after the property – a suggestion to which, oddly enough, James seems perfectly agreeable. Beth meanwhile is barely able to contain her excitement and spends the rest of the evening and much of the next day in busy preparation, not least of which appears to be the cutting of material, with the aid of a pattern taken from a magazine, and the sewing and making up of a new cambric dress that she might wear for the forthcoming adventure.

'May I ask where we might be going, and for how long shall we be gone this time, Sir?' She inquires, quite reasonably enough, he thinks, as she serves breakfast one morning shortly after his announcement - since he has kept them in the dark about it so far, not really certain himself of where and for how long – not certain at all, that is, until this very moment: because now he knows exactly.

'Well, Beth, I think you should prepare for a lengthy absence,' he answers, setting down his cup and saucer for a moment so as to attend to her question with due diligence. 'I believe it might be possible to negotiate a lease on the cottage right through until the end of the summer.'

'*The cottage?* What, you mean on the Island, Sir?' she asks with a look of surprise and bewilderment. 'Where we have just been?'

He smiles at her surprise. He can't help it. Would she have been expecting some exotic foreign journey, he wonders? Italy or Greece? Paris or Istanbul?

'Yes, that's right. We might even remain into the autumn months if necessary,' he hears himself saying, his voice full of enthusiasm now. 'There is, after all, Lady Daphne's portrait to complete. That will take a while. And who knows what further commissions I might pick up along the way. There are lots of well-connected people there. Though, to be frank, there are other things afoot, Beth – important things over which I will not trouble you at present, for I am not all that certain myself what they are. Suffice to say that I believe there is something that has to be settled there, one way or another, something involving our distinguished friends at the Villa Parnassus, and that I must be a part of it. So, in answer to your question, yes - we shall stay there for as long as it takes, until it's finished.'

'The portrait you mean, Sir?'

But to this question he does not volunteer an answer.

Chapter Thirteen

A Thing of Beauty

With amazing rapidity the sun has vanished beneath a towering confluence of rain-bearing clouds bubbling up from the south, appearing out of nowhere it seems in what has hitherto been a clear blue sky. Looking at it all with some apprehension, they know that a storm will almost certainly be upon them – and within minutes.

'We must take shelter, ladies, and fast!' Amos announces. He is here with Daphne, in the company of Beth, all three together this afternoon within the old deserted keep of Carisbrooke Castle located in the centre of the Island and where just a few short moments ago they had strolled through the twin-towered gate house and into the large, sunlit open expanse of the castle bailey. Here they stand, dressed in their light summer clothes and straw hats, dwarfed amid the tall ivy-clad ramparts of a bygone age, the buildings mostly left derelict now, the walls already presenting the appearance of so many ancient cliff faces - all covered in vegetation, with slender harts-tongue ferns joining the occasional primrose or pink campion that has made its home amid the crumbling masonry.

With Oliver Ramsey away on business in Manchester, it was an opportunity far too good to miss, or at least that is how Amos perceived it – a chance to do something exciting, almost forbidden, in the company of Daphne. Deciding to take Beth along with them has given the whole venture a gloss of propriety – at least he hopes it will suffice should anyone familiar see them here. But so far, having managed their journey together, firstly by carriage and then by foot, without encountering a single acquaintance, Amos has hopes that they can remain undetected and that at the end of the day no one will be any the wiser – that he had taken a married woman off on a sightseeing tour without the knowledge or sanction of her husband: not really the *done thing*, even among the eccentric and bohemian circles of the Island. But he simply had to do it, had to do something to lift her out of her depression – for that, he suspects, is what Daphne has descended into of late. He had noticed the deterioration in her straight away, upon arriving back on the Island just a few days ago. It was immediately apparent to him that she had lost even more weight, if such were possible, wraith-like almost, and that her complexion had if anything grown even more pale than was usual - this despite the sunny days and the ministrations of the sea air that normally encourages even the most spectral of faces to blossom into a rosy glow of health and vitality.

But suddenly there are more pressing concerns for him to consider - because the rain has begun in earnest now and it is obvious that they are in for a drenching. Taking flight together and giggling with excitement, like children, they run to one of the derelict buildings that cluster round the ramparts, locating a place inside where they can sit comfortably, the ladies upon their shawls, Amos upon his rucksack, and watch the rain through the many broken spaces in the walls – apertures and cavities where once fine crafted windows of diamond-shaped glass or study doorways of English oak would have rested, but which have by now become merely gaping, empty spaces open to the sky. Thunder and the occasional flash of lightening follow on now, as if a host of cannon were demonstrating the martial spirit of the place - rain turning to fierce hailstones at moments which bounce off the ground like grapeshot fired from some celestial garrison above until, after some minutes, they realise that their plan to walk to a nearby railway station later on must now be abandoned. The ground would be completely sodden, Amos concludes – and so, at a suitable lull in the intensity of the rain, he volunteers to run down to the village and hire a carriage instead, leaving the ladies to fend for themselves for what he assures them should be an absence of not longer than one hour.

'We could wait until it passes – and then all go together,' Daphne suggests, clearly not keen on being without male protection in such a strange and eerie location – for they appear to have it all to themselves today, and the deserted atmosphere is slightly forbidding. The one serviceable building, the house occupied occasionally by the Governor of the Island, stands empty and silent, its shutters closed, and even the workmen usually engaged on the modest restoration work of the Castle Keep seem to have deserted the place for the summer.

'Ah, but it might *not* pass,' Amos argues. 'And even if it does, the ground will be treacherous – and it will be very late before we reach home. No, there's nothing else for it, ladies. I'll have to go fetch a carriage. Sit tight.'

And with that resolution, his jacket removed from his shoulders and held aloft to ward off at least some of the rain, he sets forth, through the gateway and out into the remnants of the storm.

In fact, the rain does abate, and the worst of the thunder does roll away quite rapidly – something which makes both Daphne and Beth feel a little more at ease; and in order to while away the time Daphne takes Amos's sketch pad from the rucksack he has left behind, and with the little block of paper perched on her knee sets about, a little bashfully at first drawing what she sees with a combination of pencil and charcoal. To begin with, she turns her attention to the remnants of a fallen tower outside that, rather ominously, presents the appearance of having been struck by lightening at some time in its recent history but which has now become the home to colonies of noisy jackdaws. Eventually, however, and realising that Beth would be far more interesting material, she transfers her attentions to the younger woman instead – much to her surprise - and with a note of encouragement to her voice says: 'Come on, little Beth! Strike up an heroic pose and I shall portray your likeness in my own hand. I cannot promise it will be to the same standard as our eminent and gifted friend, but I haven't spend all those years in Mister Roselli's studio without picking up a thing or two about drawing, you know. And I promise to give it my best.'

'I hope he won't mind Ma'am, will he?' Beth inquires a little hesitantly, not quite knowing what to do by way of striking *an heroic pose,* but removing her straw hat and spectacles and sitting very upright anyway.

'Just relax and be yourself,' Daphne laughs. 'You have an interesting face, Beth. I have seen you alter even in the short time I have known you. You're still growing, aren't you! And no, he won't mind.'

But Beth cannot relax, cannot let go. It is a most unusual situation, being the focus of somebody's attention like this, and she continues to sit with her spine perfectly erect, bolt upright, a look of some petrifaction on her young face. Daphne laughs, which causes her, if anything, to become even more self-conscious.

'Sorry, Beth, dear,' Daphne apologises. 'It's just that you looked for a moment just like your James the valet: all stiff and pompous.'

'If it please you Ma'am, he is not *my* James,' Beth states with bold determination to put the matter to rights.

'No – no, of course not. Sorry,' Daphne replies with kindness, for she cannot help noticing that at the mention of the valet's name Beth has become disturbed and almost tearful. 'I'm being silly, Beth, aren't I. What's wrong?'

The young girl does not reply at first, so Daphne asks again, 'What's wrong, Beth? You can tell me, don't worry.'

'Well, he – James – is part of the household now, as you know, Ma'am. And everything has been fine until he joined us here on the Island. That meant he was away from his wife. And, well, you know what men are like when they don't have the steadying influence of their wives to hand.'

'Emm ... so tell me more, little one,' Daphne says, continuing to work with the charcoal sketch but also having to resort quite often to the eraser and suspecting, too, that she will have to start again on another page once Beth has relaxed a little more and got whatever it is off her chest.

'Oh, there is really nothing much to tell, Ma'am,' Beth replies, looking down at her interlaced fingers and trying to drop her shoulders – though still with little success in that regard. 'I have nothing to complain about, not at all. And when I think of those poor souls, those girls of my age or younger who are working in factories and mills even as I speak, I know I am the most fortunate of people. It's just that the other day, while I was ironing Mr Roselli's shirts, James reprimanded me and said I was doing it wrong. Well, I have ironed more shirts that he has had hot dinners, and I knew well enough I was doing nothing wrong. But then he came up behind me and put his arms around me - to take the iron and guide my hand, so to speak. And his face was very close to mine, and he smelt of onions.'

'Emm ... that's not so pleasant, is it!' Daphne remarks. 'Beth, you must tell Mr. Roselli of this. Don't feel awkward. He would want to know. And, for your part, you must not give James the slightest encouragement. You are perfectly within your rights to protest if he becomes too intimate.'

'I have known girls in my position to get into trouble from that kind of thing, Ma'am. It is difficult – because I think it's only natural to respond to kindness.'

Yes, but there is appropriate behaviour. Kindness is not the same as impropriety. And, as I say, you should do well to report what you have just told me to Mister Roselli. We can speak to him together on the return journey, if you like. I shall help you. And now, Beth, I wonder if you could relax those shoulders of yours and think upon nicer things than men who smell of onions - for I am about to begin a fresh page.'

Feeling relieved and suddenly very happy, Beth smiles and slumps back against the warm stones of the wall as a long sigh of contentment escape her lips.

'Are you enjoying being here by the sea, Beth?' Daphne inquires.

'Oh yes, Ma'am. It is like a paradise compared to London with all its horrid smells and dusty air. I think I am really a country girl at heart.'

'Were you born in the country? Is that where you come from?'

Beth is silent for a moment before answering, and then speaking with care, 'I do not know exactly where I was born, Ma'am.'

'Oh, I'm sorry, Beth ... I didn't mean to be ...'

'Oh that's all right, my Lady. I don't know because I grew up in an orphanage. They say my mother left me there when I was very small. She left no token, no information of any kind. So I suppose I will never know who she was or her whereabouts.'

'That's a rotten start in life - for anyone,' Daphne observes, still working diligently on her sketch, but in fact every bit as intrigued by the young girl's story. 'What was it like? Did you receive any schooling?'

'Oh yes. I was allowed to attend a ragged school right up to the age of ... emm, I think it must have been about eleven, because I remember asking if I could stay on longer to help out. I did an extra year, helping all the other children with reading. I used to look forward to that, even though it was quite a long walk from the orphanage to the schoolhouse each day. But I didn't mind because there were always so many nice front gardens on the way. I loved those, all the grand houses with all the beautiful plants and shrubs that people grew - and also all the wild flowers. I should say I came to know every flower there is and all their names, and through all the seasons, too, upon that walk – or at least those that were upon the journey I took each day. I loved the primroses and the violets the best, I think, because they were always so brave after the winter and stuck their tiny heads up even through the frost. You would think they were nipped and dead, but then the next day you would pass and there they were again, all chipper and with the first bees visiting them. My most favourite of all, though, were always the roses. Such lovely scented flowers. I would sometimes crush some rose petals between my fingers or rub them onto my sleeve or hem and take that wonderful memory back to the children's home with me, so even when I was shut up inside for being naughty I could still somehow catch the fragrance on my clothing and it would take me back to my favourite walk and to being at liberty, outside. I much preferred being at school to the orphanage, of course. And the lessons I enjoyed the most were the history ones. All the kings and queens - I learned them all, and all the dates when they lived and died; all the battles they fought, and the great fire of

London, too. I could tell you the dates of anything you care to mention: the noble King Richard, and the wicked King Henry who murdered his wives, and the poor King Charles who lost his head after the civil war.'

'Well ... here we are, Beth. This was where he was imprisoned.'

'Really?'

'Yes, exactly. They kept King Charles here at Carisbrooke until they took him to London where he was executed.'

'That was in the year sixteen-forty-seven,' Beth states, demonstrating that her earlier assertion of knowing all the dates was a genuine one, but also reporting the matter in a voice of such sober reflection, like some old school Ma'am, that it makes Daphne smile – a reaction which she conceals this time by lowering her face over the sketch pad for a moment. 'What a thing to come to pass!' Beth continues, now more than happy to talk, it seems. 'To cut off the head of a king? I should say the people of those times should be right ashamed of themselves to have done such a wicked thing.'

'It feels suitably sad and tragic, here, though, don't you think?' Daphne observes, casting her gaze around the walls with all their broken stones and the stray mosses and ferns of neglect growing out from between them. 'I do love it, I really do.'

At which there comes a sudden loud din and the insistent calling of young crows and jackdaws, probably just out of the nest - very noisy, and clearly not to Beth's liking.

'Oh Ma'am!' she laughs. 'What a harsh sound they make! I don't like those.'

'Don't you? Oh, I do,' Daphne confesses. 'They remind me of the rooks and ravens we have at Bowlend Court. I adore them and all their black plumage; and when I am in a dark mood I like to go for a walk alone through the rookeries and listen to their cries. It makes me feel better for some reason. Funny. I wonder if any of these old jackdaws here are descended from those who would have peeped in the windows at King Charles when he was having his supper. What do you think? Do you have any relations, Beth, brothers or sisters or anything?'

'Yes, Ma'am I do have an older half-sister. She was also put in the orphanage but she left early on, because she got married. I never saw her again – not all the time I grew up there, anyway. And then I had to leave school and go into service. It was at New Eltham, in London where there are lots of wealthy families. I was twelve years old or thereabouts. It was very hard work and quite a jolt coming from a poor children's home into a well-to-do household like that with all its new furniture - and so clean! I liked being clean and tidy, and having my own uniform - and living so close to London, too, and in such an historic location! I used to love going to the palace grounds nearby on my day off – something they let me do one Sunday every month as soon as I had finished my chores for the morning - though that usually meant only just the afternoon that I had for myself - but I preferred the palace to going to church, even though I could not afford to go inside. It was good to be outdoors, wandering around the park and the moat - and even in the winter I didn't mind being out there. Only, the rest of the time, during the week, life wasn't quite so nice. It was very hard work. I was expected to make the beds, clean all the fire places and lay and light the fires for the homecoming – as well as bringing in the water and scrubbing and cleaning the big building from top to bottom. And so much dust – I swear there was never a place like it for collecting dust so close upon the main highway! And then of course there was always the silver to polish and the cutlery to shine up. One evening I was so tired I fell asleep on the stairs going up to my room. Honestly! I don't know how it could have happened. I suppose I must have sat down for a moment, and then I didn't remember anything else. I woke up in the same spot when the morning came and just got on with my work again.

'But that was not the worst of it. I used to be left on my own in the house, you see, locked inside from around eight in the morning to four in the afternoon because the family were all out at work. So even though I was busy, I was still lonely and often quite frightened because there was no one else about - and I wasn't even allowed to answer the door unless we were expecting a delivery from the shops. One day I came downstairs and saw a big shadow of a man outside on the glass of the front door in a stovepipe hat. I swear he was a giant. I sat there on the stairs sobbing until he went, and when the mistress of the house came home at four she found me still sitting there and she beat me for being idle. She had a big strap like a belt, and she would hit me on the legs with it. I do not suppose, looking back on it now, that she was all that nice, do you? And I do not think either that they were really quite so well to do as they made out – because it was a cheap option for families like that to get a girl from the orphanage. I was there for almost five years.

'Really!' Daphne responds, stopping for a moment to hold the sketch out at arm's length and looking reasonably content with the outcome so far. 'Five years – that's a long time, isn't it.'

'Yes, only I suppose at least I had a room of my own, there. And after having to sleep in a crowded dormitory at the orphanage that was just marvellous. Of course, when you are in service in those kinds of houses, your room has to be kept simple and uncluttered. You are not permitted to have anything of your own in it - no paintings or books. That was not at all to my liking, so I sometimes kept a little library book tucked away in a box. Then it was like coming upstairs at the end of each day with my candle into a little part of heaven - to a special place that belonged all to me. The worst of it, though, I suppose, was being so hungry, which I seem to have been quite often. And there were always so many temptations - so many lovely things to eat in the house that I had never seen before and which were all forbidden to me – like biscuits. I had never seen the likes of a biscuit in all my life when I first went there, and I remember one morning I lifted the lid of the biscuit barrel they kept on the sideboard and there were custard creams inside. They do smell delicious, don't they! I had never smelt anything quite so tempting. So I took one and had a bite. Well, you can imagine what happened next. During the course of the day I kept coming back and managed to eat almost every one. I couldn't resist. When the mistress found out she not only beat me but I had to pay for them out of my wages for the next six weeks. They resented me having anything nice like they did. I remember one day after serving the table at tea time, there was the new season's jam, and at the end of the meal when I could always have whatever bread was left over for myself when I cleared up, I helped myself to some of the jam as well before putting it away in the pantry, and the misses saw me and smacked my hand and said: no, the jam was not for the likes of me! There was a young man staying at the time, their son I think, and he said to his mother that she should let me have some – which she did, but only that once!

'It wasn't always bad, though. When they were out, and whenever I could find a moment to spare I would sneak into the front room where they had a big bookcase and I would take a book from it and sit for a while to read. It was like being back at school, only even better – because I was at liberty there to pick up whichever book I liked and read the words that so many clever men and women had written – people that were no longer alive, and yet their thoughts were there, in my hands, to marvel at. But of course I was not supposed to be doing things like that, and when they found out I was looking at their books – because I sometimes left a marker or a little slip of paper or something in them to find my place the next day – they locked up the front room and would not let me in even to dust - accept on weekends when there was always someone there to watch me.

'I used to think to myself that I had been wicked, and that I must have done something terribly wrong at some time or other to be treated this way. Only I couldn't ever remember having done anything wrong. And then it was Christmas coming, and I knew that people would give presents to one another. What could I give anybody! I had hardly any wages at all, you see. But then I got an idea, because once every week the misses used to send me to the main market for special groceries and to the butchers, and because it was quite a distance from where we lived, she would give me the omnibus fare for the return journey. Well, I never spent that money on the omnibus – unless the bags were really, *really* heavy, that is. Instead I would walk home with the bags, and keep the money, which I then saved in a little purse behind the wardrobe in my room. And then one day just before Christmas I had enough to buy something really fine for the misses, and I went into a haberdashery with my purse and told them I wanted the lovely parasol in the window that I had been looking at for the past few weeks. Well, the woman there wouldn't believe me – she looked at my clothes, which were quite humble I suppose, and more or less implied that I must have stolen the purse from somewhere. No, I said – this is my money. *This is mine!* So I did get the parasol ... eventually after speaking with the manager. It was made of paper and had paintings of people from China on it and mountains and lakes, all dark and with silver threads running through - and the handle was so pretty, too, all lacquered and shinny. It was very smart, I thought. I even had enough money left over for some special wrapping paper, too, and so when Christmas Day came I was able to give my present to the lady of the house all tied up with a ribbon. I don't know if she ever used it. I heard her say to somebody that it was old fashioned. I didn't know what that meant, because it seemed beautiful to me and something like that is forever lovely. Anyway, I suppose that must have been the final straw, like they say. After a while I thought to myself – "I can't take any more of this." I saw other families when they visited, or saw people walking together in the streets arm in arm and speaking nicely to one another. Even in nature, even the wild animals have other creatures among them, I thought, who show them love and kindness in their own way. Why should I be any different? And so one day when the weather seemed set fair for a spell I ran away. I walked all the way back along the London Road out into the Kent countryside, sleeping out at nights under bushes or anywhere that seemed safe, and then to Chatham and then along to a little village outside where I had an idea my sister was living – because I did get a letter from her when I was at the orphanage, and there I asked for her among strangers until I found the place where she lived. It was a lovely little cottage near a churchyard with roses around the porch. And when I rang the door bell she came to the door in her apron and saw me – it must have been the first time since we were children – and all she said was: "what do you want?" She was angry I had found her, I suppose. And she only took me in for a couple of nights and said that I would have to go and enter a position in service again somewhere. It was then that I found a newspaper on a bench at the railway station and saw that Mr Roselli was advertising for someone to do for him in the West of London, and so off I went the very next morning. What a lucky day that was. I have been so very happy working for him. It is so different. I can have whatever I want in my room, and all the books I could ever wish to read. He doesn't mind. And to be here today in this wonderful place with you Ma'am – it is like I am in a lovely dream. I can't tell you how happy I am.'

Still at her drawing, Daphne does not respond right away to Beth's story, but keeps her peace, hoping that when she does speak it might be something relatively unemotional and simple. She locates a coloured chalk among Amos's sketching items – a reddish, ochre one – and with this she puts in a little colour to her subjects hair, which has a remarkable vibrant lustre to it, she notices, especially when caught in the sunlight. The reddish chalk goes quite well with the grey of the charcoal, she thinks to herself with a look of approval. And now she is ready to speak.

'You know, you just said something, Beth – what was it, about the parasol; that it was beautiful and that something like that is forever lovely. Did you know that our great poet, John Keats, once wrote "a thing of beauty is a joy forever" – did you know that?'

'I don't think so, Ma'am, no,' she replies, wondering at the other woman's intensity.

'Well he wrote that here, perhaps on this very spot or very close by, many years ago. He knew this castle in his time when he too visited the Island.'

'Perhaps I would have had it in school, or read it somewhere,' Beth suggests, not wishing her ideas and ramblings to be compared to those of a famous poet.

'Yes, perhaps – but you put it in your own words. I sometimes think we are living in times of such wickedness, Beth. Everywhere there is so much poverty and squalor taking hold. There are more and more factories, so much more smoke and grime and ugliness every day and so many awful cities growing up everywhere in which people live out their lives as little more than slaves. I think those of us who understand there is an alternative – well, we must resist and fight against that decline, and never forsake beauty. Anyway, on that note of rather unrealistic optimism, I shall now reveal to you my finished sketch – which I am not altogether convinced will be a joy forever. Look – what do you think?'

At which, she turns the paper towards the young girl and shows her. Beth takes a peep, frowns at it and then puts on her spectacles to look more closely. The hair plaited and wound round her head has been beautifully rendered, and her profile looks quite strong, she is surprised to see, and with a noble nose and jaw. 'Oh Ma'am, I fear you have made me look like a princess. That will never do,' she says, making light of it.

But Daphne is not sharing in her levity and in fact looks displeased. Before Beth can apologise, however, for any note of ungraciousness, the other woman has leaned over and placed a hand upon her shoulder. And Beth is astonished to see there is a tear in her eye.

'Beth, you must never sell yourself cheap. You are a very rare and special young woman.'

'Oh, Ma'am!' she protests, but just then they hear the approach of a carriage coming up the cobble lane towards the castle. Amos is returning, and now they must prepare for their journey home.

'No, listen to me, dearest Beth,' Daphne begins again, with a note of haste to her voice now. 'You must understand that what I say to you is true. I am so glad you came with us today – and not just because of being chaperone, which is not necessary for us, in any case. Mister Roselli and I are quite adept at meeting in secret and being together against other peoples' wishes. We have been doing it most of our lives. You are here because we each wanted you to be. You have all your life ahead of you, Beth, and it will be a fine life, I am sure, and with perhaps children of your own one day that you will love with all your heart, for certain. As for me – well, I do rather suspect that I might remain without those blessings. But if ever I were to have a daughter, and should such an unlikely event ever occur in what short time remains to me, I should feel proud and honoured if she were to turn out to become someone just like you.'

There is no time for Beth to respond as she looks into the other woman's extraordinarily beautiful eyes and which for that moment seem to regard her again with such intensity – because suddenly they both notice that Amos is there, nearby standing beneath the towering arches of the Gate House waving his cap in the air. 'Noble ladies, your carriage awaits!' he cries out to them and laughs – and they, laughing too, gather up their belongings and run to greet him.

Chapter Fourteen

A Crescent of Green Lawn

'James – you should fetch your wife over to stay with us,' Amos suggests, intercepting his valet as the man descends from the bedroom one morning where he has been laying out the clothes that Amos has chosen to wear later on - including, since the day is to be very warm, a fashionable flannelette shirt and light beige trousers.

'My wife Sir?' the valet echoes, looking a little baffled.

'Yes. After all, we are to be here some weeks, if not months. That would be a comfort for you, would it not?'

'Oh really, Sir, I don't think that will be at all necessary …' James responds, his heavy-lidded basset eyes downcast in his typically annoying and censorious manner – and evidently not at all inspired by the prospect.

Amos, however, who has conversed with Daphne and knows exactly the reasons for his reluctance, is not to be deterred. 'Oh, but I insist, James!' he says. 'The sea air will surely be to her liking, and she can be gainfully employed here, taking on some of Beth's duties. There is space enough, and we can bring in a double bed for you both as you had in London.'

'I am not at all convinced, Sir, that she would relish the journey by sea,' he persists - though rather forlornly by now.

'Come now, it's hardly an ocean crossing, the short distance across the Solent!' Amos argues, still with a smile on his face. 'And as I say, *I really must insist*. It will be company for you.'

Beth, meanwhile, in her working clothes, her white apron and mop cap, hovers nearby, busying herself dusting the umbrella stand in the hallway, clearly following every word while also trying not to appear too interested. For a moment, James catches the look in her eye and seems to realise what has happened. Conceding defeat with a brisk, curtly delivered nod, for clearly the game is up for him now, he turns and marches off, none too pleased it would seem judging by the heaviness of his gait – upon which Amos exchanges a look of some complicity with Beth, but they say nothing more on it. He does notice, however, that she appears not quite so relieved as he had anticipated upon having the matter resolved so promptly. Instead, she continues to look pensive, almost tearful he suspects at one stage as, a little later, he encounters her in the conservatory. She is busy applying some much-needed wax to the table and chairs; the sun is pouring in and it feels gloriously warm – so that the smell of beeswax polish in the hot air is quite intoxicating: a very homely and domestic kind of fragrance.

'Are you well today, Beth?' he inquires, pretending to be busy himself, taking up his brushes and inspecting them.

The young girl bites her lip, and it seems to Amos that she is struggling between trying to find some suitable reply or else refraining from speaking at all. Instead she diverts her energies into ever greater and more robust movements of her arm as she puts an amazing shine upon the wood. Realising he is still observing her and waiting for a response, however, she does eventually speak. She throws down her cloth and turns to him, her fingers interlaced tightly.

'Oh Sir, I was just wondering – I hope it is not impertinent of me to ask – but is Lady Bowlend unwell?'

'Unwell – why no, not that I am aware of, Beth. Why do you ask?'

'My apologies, Sir. It's not for me to question in this way. Only from what she says sometimes, it is just as though she feels she has not long to live.'

Amos stares at her for a moment without speaking. If he already feels unsettled by Daphne's erratic behaviour, then this latest remark from his maid certainly only adds to his sense of agitation. That Beth should make such an observation is disturbing enough, but that he, upon hearing it, should not feel at all surprised is perhaps even worse! So it's not just him, he realises. Others have noticed, too.

'Has she said that to you?' he asks.

'Perhaps not in so many words, Sir. But I felt it was implied rather by the way she spoke the other day.'

Amos falls silent for a moment. He wants so much to let her into his confidence. He longs to share his own anguish with somebody, but is Beth the right person? A young serving maid? And then he realises that he is being an oaf, an absolute snob. Here is a delightful, caring young woman. She has put a question to him in all humility and out of a genuine regard for another's welfare. If he were to fail to provide her with at least some semblance of an answer now it would be little short of a disgrace.

With a gentle wave of the hand he suggests that Beth take a seat, while he pulls up another close by.

'Beth,' he begins in hushed tones, 'what I am about to say must go no further than these walls. I appreciate your concern, and, yes, you are correct. The lady of whom you speak is distressed over a number of things - and a little frightened, too, no doubt. Firstly, she is frightened of another miscarriage and of what it might do to her already delicate constitution. She is frightened of her husband, Lord Bowlend, who - to put a not too fine a point upon it - is rather a bully. I suspect she is worried, above all, that she might not be rising to the challenge and expectations heaped upon her of bringing forth the requisite male heir, or *any* heir, in fact. All of this is taking its toll upon her well-being. To be honest, Lady Bowlend is not quite the woman I knew even a year ago. She has changed rather for the worse, I fear - you would have noticed also, because you are well-familiar with her likeness in all the paintings I have back in London. So there you have it, Beth! What do you think? Am I being foolish telling you all this? I know, of course, that I can trust you - is that not so?'

'You can indeed trust me Sir,' she replies with amazing seriousness.

'Perhaps Beth, you could endeavour to glean a little gossip

or information yourself sometime – I mean, from the staff over at Parnassus? I know it's your afternoon off today but perhaps I could write a message for you to take over on some context and then ...'

'Oh Sir, I am to go over later today anyway. Lady Bowlend has kindly offered to teach me about the language of flowers, the meanings that people convey to one another with their bouquets and décolletage.'

'Really! The mysteries of the *Tussie-Mussies,* you mean. How kind of her!' Amos responds, though realising that such singular treatment would probably render his maid an object of suspicion below stairs at Parnassus almost instantly, and that there would be little she could glean now from any of the servants there. 'Be discrete, though, Beth, won't you,' he suggests. 'Most of the staff there are naturally loyal to their paymaster, and will always take Lord Bowlend's side on any issue of controversy.'

She seems to understand and, shortly after, makes ready for her appointment. She puts on her wide-rimmed Sunday-best bonnet against the already-strong sun and hurries off with an obvious excitement in her step – and upon which Amos settles down to write one or two letters and then to clean and to tidy up his paints and equipment as planned. This accomplished, and ensuring that his brushes are set out carefully on the inside window ledge of the conservatory to dry, he elects to take a turn around the garden for a while, admiring with pleasure the glorious roses as they climb the southern walls and interweave with the honeysuckle and ivy there. What fragrance! And he takes a little yellow bloom from them for the buttonhole of his shirt – and also, on the path where the stones are already warm in the sunshine, picks a young primrose, too. Looking down in this way and attending to the flowers he does not notice the entrance of somebody into the garden via the wicket gate to the side, nor the man's stealthy approach until suddenly there he is, Oliver Ramsey himself, standing almost right in front of him, dressed casually in a white waistcoat and flannels, as if having just come from a game of croquet and looking rather hot and bothered.

'I believe you own me an explanation, Sir!' he states, his

deep, booming voice very loud, so that Amos almost jumps into the air with the force of it.

'An explanation – what for?' Amos demands, a little irritated over the absence of any formal greeting and also over being shocked and made to look foolish by the intruder's sudden appearance. 'Why didn't you ring the door bell and have yourself announced properly if you wish to speak to me?'

'The purpose behind your little excursion the other day, Roselli, if you wouldn't mind,' Oliver Ramsey goes on, not in the least bit impressed with the other man's attempt to lay down the rules. 'You were seen in Carisbrooke with my wife. What is the meaning of it?'

Amos attempts a smile, making light of it. '*Oh that*! Well, we had a day out, that's all - with other people.'

'Other people? What *other people* are you referring to? Your girl - is that who you mean?'

'Beth was in our party, yes.'

'You play the fool with me at your peril Roselli! I know from your valet how many were in your confounded party – your cosy little *ménage a trois!*'

Ah, of course! Amos thinks. Now it was all falling into place. James has obviously been spying and telling tales, perhaps even as a result of being reprimanded earlier. Had he gone over to Ramsey afterwards? It seems more than a coincidence that just as James had been forewarned of impropriety, so Amos himself should now become the recipient of the same accusation from the noble lord. The tables have been turned. Not pleasant – to have a servant betraying him like this. But at least it has made his decision for him all the easier. His valet will have to be dismissed.

Ramsey, meanwhile, and much to Amos's surprise, appears no longer quite so explosive or even at all disgruntled any longer. Having changed his entire mood and demeanour within a matter of a few seconds, he allows a thin kind of smile to spread across his face. He then takes out a cigar from his waistcoat pocket and even offers one to Amos – who, determined not to play Ramsey's game of being chums all of a sudden, firmly declines to take it. However, with both men realising that there might be matters to discuss, they agree to go inside together, to the conservatory at Amos's invitation where they seat themselves in deck chairs by the doors and where, after a moment of looking unproductively at one another, each keeping his own counsel, the noble lord, speaking from amid an acrid cloud of cigar smoke, calmly inquires: 'Tell me, Amos, how often has she had other men?'

'I beg your pardon?'

'How often – how many men has she had before me, and since? Come on, you must have some idea.'

'I can't imagine what you're referring to,' Amos responds as if slightly puzzled, while also noticing with consternation that the big man's backside is almost touching the ground as the canvas of the deckchair strains to contain his mighty loins.

'You told me she was a loose woman once, don't you recall?'

Amos has to think long and hard about this one. 'Oh did I!' he exclaims and chuckles. 'Well, perhaps not quite in so many words. And anyway, that was probably at the start, wasn't it – when you had just met her and invited her out. I wasn't being serious. I was probably just trying to put you off the scent.'

'You wanted her for yourself then?'

'As my model and my companion – yes, of course. And to be frank, I didn't believe you were the right man for her. The truth is that Daphne has never been anything remotely approaching a loose woman. As far as I am aware she was a maid when she married you.'

'What at thirty years – still a maid! Come on Roselli, I'm not that naïve.'

'I think we should always caution ourselves against judging others by our own standards, don't you?' Amos replies with an acerbic smile. 'That is what I believe to be the case. And anyway - even if I knew anything to the contrary, why should I discuss it with you?'

'Because she's my wife. She belongs to me, and I have every right to such knowledge!' Ramsey suddenly bellows - and very loudly, too, once again - leaning forward in his chair, like a bull about to charge. So sudden these dramatic changes in demeanour! 'I have powerful friends, Amos – in the art world as much as anywhere else. Unless you fall into line I'll make sure you never work again among the elite as a portrait artist. You'll finish up painting dogs' arses for a living if you're lucky. And you can kiss goodbye to ever becoming an Academician.'

Amos remains silent for a moment, cautions before replying - still the two of them seated in their deck chairs, facing each other, feigning nonchalance - Ramsey almost chewing his cigar instead of smoking it, and Amos occasionally examining the fragrance of the little yellow flowers of his buttonhole. 'Don't you think you might be rather overstating your influence?' the artist finally suggests.

'You believe that, do you?' Ramsey chuckles, though still with palpable menace. 'Well, we shall see about that in due course – only by then it'll be too late for you, my friend, far too late, make no mistake! *How many men*, I say? I've seen how she twists everyone around her little finger – the power that she has. She's a whore, isn't she? She's a witch, and a whore!'

But at this Amos sees red. The limit of his patience has now been reached and in fact overstepped by a mile with these latest profanities. What an vile creature Ramsey was becoming!

'I'll punch you on the nose Ramsey if you would do me the honour of getting up off your fat backside for a moment and joining me outside.'

At which, to his horror, Ramsey agrees - stubbing out his cigar in one of Amos's porcelain paint dishes and then, accompanied by several ripping noises as he extricates his enormous bulk from the canvas chair, getting to his feet and marching out of the conservatory ahead of him. Consequently, the two men find themselves out in the garden, squaring up to each other on the lawn, their sleeves rolled up in readiness. It looks like it's a proper boxing match he is after, Amos concludes, judging from the way the other man is shaping up - fists raised and attempting to prance about, looking ridiculous on his relatively tiny feet – Queensbury rules and all that – so he, too, raises his fists. But suddenly he feels a blinding pain in his shin, and he realises that Ramsey has kicked him. This is rapidly followed by a malicious right hook to his jaw that almost knocks his head off, and the next thing he knows he is flat on his back, looking up at the sky and the puffy white clouds sailing round in little circles above him – while somewhere, as if in the distance he can hear Ramsey's thundering voice bawling out at him: 'I am furious with you, Roselli, do you understand. I am bloody, furious!'

Worse, when he looks to where the voice is coming from he discovers Ramsey towering above, about to hurl his entire bulk down on top and to crush him - a catastrophe that Amos averts only at the last split-second by rolling over sideways and away. His assailant, instead, falls flat on his belly, which seems to wind him and brings forth a long and resonant fart. By the time he is up Amos is fully recovered, therefore, ready and prepared now for anything, kicking included.

'I'll kill you, Roselli!' the Baron roars pointing a threatening finger as he staggers to his feet - but then abruptly he stops. His eyes are staring instead straight ahead at something behind Amos's shoulder.

Alert to any possible diversionary trick, it is only very gradually that Amos turns to seek out whatever his opponent might be staring at, and there standing stiff and uncomprehending behind him is the astonished visage and basset eyes of none other than his valet, James himself.

'Ah, my good faithful James!' Amos cries as, advancing on the man and grabbing him by the arm none too gently, he propels him forward towards Ramsey. 'Now, you over-starched, stiff upper-lipped bastard. Tell the noble lord here exactly what you know about my relationship with Lady Bowlend.'

'Nothing, Sir, I know nothing.'

'Precisely. You know nothing, my friend, because there is nothing to know. Only tittle-tattle, of which you seem to be an altogether accomplished and seasoned veteran. Well now, I want you to tell this gentleman the truth. Tell him there is nothing between myself and his wife - nor ever was. Tell him it is a perfectly innocent and decent friendship!'

'It's true, Sir! Yes, it's true!' James blurts out in a strangely high-pitched voice. 'Mr Roselli is an honourable man. And I doubt not that Lady Bowlend is also a most honourable lady. Whatever impression I might have given you, Sir, it was false –

out of - out of my own displeasure at being reprimanded by Mr Roselli earlier. That is the truth, Sir.'

With one final yank of the arm, Amos pushes the valet away, so strongly that he almost collides with Ramsey who, with a withering scowl in Amos's direction, pushes the poor wretch back again - returning him to his owner like so much baggage being hurled to and fro before stomping away angrily back around the perimeter of the house to negotiate his exit via the wicket gate, clearly the means of his entrance earlier and now the route back to his own home.

'Your services will no longer be required, James, and you have the rest of the afternoon to pack your bags,' Amos states calmly and with a final dismissive wave of the hand, not bothering much to look at the man. 'Don't even try to protest - unless, that is, you would like a written reference with the word *treachery* emblazoned upon it. Go on now - off with you!'

And James, with the greatest alacrity, obeys.

'Cornflowers invariably signify the concept of refinement, of *delicacy*,' Daphne remarks to Beth who, with a fine pencil, makes another little entry upon her note pad before nodding to the older woman to indicate her understanding of this latest valuable snippet of information. The two are seated here side by side in the library of Parnassus busy sorting and arranging a prodigious quantity of fresh colourful blooms, including a variety of wild flowers, leaves and grasses, upon the surface of a large, polished mahogany table - items all gathered fresh from the garden and nearby meadows this afternoon where, in the glorious warm sunshine, dressed in their light linen clothes and straw hats, they had filled their trugs of willow to the brim and carried their specimens underarm, back upstairs here to the welcome cool of the oak-panelled room - a room clearly very much in regular use and enjoyed by its owner, Beth concludes, pleasantly untidy with books left out all over the place, opened on tables or armchairs, and with what would probably be pressed flowers, too, she imagines, slipped beneath stacks of heavyweight volumes on various shelves or cupboards. It feels exciting just to be here - the heady combined fragrances of so many flowers filling the air - and all so refined and peaceful as well, the only sounds being the distant pendulum of the great clock in the hallway downstairs, and the trickle of song from the occasional blackbird or thrush perched in the honeysuckle beyond the windows – these being left ajar at present expressly to let in the lovely warm scented air from outside.

'How do you feel about it all so far, little Beth?' Daphne inquires.

'Oh thank you, yes, Ma'am, I do understand,' Beth replies, commenting on what she has already learnt. 'So, let me see, a person might give cornflowers such as these to another as a token of friendship? A young lady to another lady, perhaps?'

'Yes, that's right,' Daphne replies, smiling and clearly pleased with her pupil's progress as she takes one of the little blue flowers and presses it gently between her fingers to explore its shape and texture before handing it along to Beth. The slightly bristly stem can be felt between the fingers, as she takes it, and the paler blue of the outer florets she notices are complemented by those of a more purple colour inwards towards the centre: so very lovely, even though it has no fragrance.

'Of course,' Daphne continues, 'it would normally be more acceptable for the cornflower, which is quite a humble little flower, after all, to be included in a more sophisticated arrangement - a bouquet conveying not just one sentiment, but perhaps several all at the same time.'

'I see.'

'For example, if I were to place the cornflowers like this, together with a sprig of lavender and tie them with a ribbon thus it would suggest that I was not only expecting delicacy from someone but also that I might be slightly mistrustful and anxious over whether their discretion could be relied upon. You see, lavender, and for all its gorgeous aroma, signifies the emotion of mistrust. So the person in question would jolly well have to prove their worthiness.' Upon which she pauses for a moment and twirls some fresh lavender flowers between her finger and thumb to provoke their scent. 'It is a way of informing someone of ones expectations, of how one would wish them to behave. You don't have to go through any embarrassing speeches to express your feelings, in other words. Nor is it always necessary to present the flowers directly in order to convey your message. Even if I were to wear these as a décolletage upon my wrist, for example, it would still signify my misgivings, albeit in a more general sense. But that is not all. If you do give them to another, you should also always bear in mind just how you actually present them. For example, if I take this bouquet and hand it to you thus, inclined to the left, towards my heart, it means I am making a comment on my own state. Fair and good. But if I do it the other way around, inclining to the right, towards *your* heart, it shows that I am communicating my feelings about you. An important distinction.'

'Indeed, yes, Ma'am,' Beth replies, sounding quite breathless with all these revelations. 'And may I ask, would it be important which hand I use to give my flowers?'

'Oh yes, that too - absolutely!' Daphne remarks with pleasure, delighted at how engaged the younger woman seems to be with the entire topic and all its subtleties. 'As a rule, you should present them with your right hand. To do so with the left would have a negative connotation, suggesting that you were displeased with someone. You are learning fast, little one, don't you think!'

'It really is so interesting, Ma'am. I always knew there was something going on that I did not quite understand, the way well-bred people use flowers, when they stare for so long at each other's pretty hats and whisper to each other when the florist comes. But this is the first time anyone has ever explained it to me. I am so thrilled!'

'Oh, but you must be careful, at the same time,' Daphne cautions her, seeming to be enjoying the process of teaching every bit as Beth is relishing her own role as a student. 'You must understand that if you mount them in the wrong way it can prove very embarrassing. Supposing you wore your cornflower in a prominent position, but allowed it to point downwards. I'm afraid that would reverse the whole sentiment of delicacy, and would in fact be telling the world that you do not consider yourself to be delicate at all!'

At which she breaks off to register Beth's sudden intake of breath. 'That would not do, Ma'am,' the young girl declares. 'I'd be a strumpet!'

'Worse – supposing you presented it to a gentleman, placing it in his lapel upside down. What would that say about how you were disposed towards *him*?'

At which Beth and Daphne together laugh quite heartily as Daphne gathers up a further combination of flowers in her hands and imbibes their collective scents with obvious enjoyment. Perceiving that Beth is so completely at ease with the process of study, she suggests that they should next each construct a modest posy for the other – a Tussie-Mussie as it is was once called way back in Tudor times - in order to convey a relatively complex message or sentiment. Beth agrees, and several further minutes pass in almost complete silence, therefore, as the two women work away, sorting flowers, trimming them with scissors and arranging them in the time-honoured fashion – that is, into small, tightly-gathered circular groups, each bound with decorative paper or a ribbon.

At one stage, Daphne's serving maid enters with some hot chocolate - as ordered up earlier - and places the tray with its fine bone china cups and silver spoons onto a nearby coffee table, casting a decidedly suspicious glance in Beth's direction, however, as she does so, as if astounded by all the attention and fuss her mistress was lavishing on an inferior – someone of the rank of servant like herself. Extraordinary! Beth notices this, senses it almost without looking up from her endeavours, and realises too that Mister Roselli has been correct in assuming that there would be no allies here. They would already be regarding her with jealousy and even a little hostility perhaps. But none of this is of any concern to her now, so engrossed is she in her task of compiling her bouquets. Even more extraordinary, before she can stop and attend to the task, Lady Daphne herself has begun to arrange the china and to pour the chocolate. A generous spoonful of cream is dropped on top of the chocolate for her guest, and a tiny bowl of golden Demerara sugar is on hand should she wish to partake of a little extra sweetness. The fragrance of the chocolate as it is poured is so rich and inviting, Beth feels! She can hardly believe what is happening. It is so utterly blissful. Even better, she is beginning to notice a certain new vigour and happiness in the other woman's face. It is almost as if she were enjoying the afternoon as much as Beth herself!

'You know what, Beth,' Daphne begins with the first appreciative sip of chocolate, 'this sort of thing is really too good for men, isn't it!'

Beth laughs, wondering though whether it is quite appropriate to do so. 'I think so, yes, Ma'am,' she finally replies with a little giggle of delight.

'Speaking of which I wonder where Lord Bowlend is this afternoon? The last I saw of him I think he was going over to visit Mister Roselli. I expect they are having a nice little tête-à-tête, don't you?'

Oh … yes, Ma'am. In their own fashion, I'm sure. Though probably without the hot chocolate.'

Further laughter is followed by a little more application to the matter of the flowers, until each has finished her bouquet - and these, therefore, can be duly exchanged and examined so that the interpretation can begin.

'Well let me see …' Daphne begins, holding Beth's decorative little posy up to the light and twirling it between her fingers to take in the sight of each flower and stem before placing it to her nose to also imbibe the fragrance, which again she seems to relish with the applied skill and perceptions of a seasoned connoisseur. Beth has created a combination of Magnolia, White Bell Flowers and sprigs of Parsley. These are also supported by some leaves of cherry - all tied neatly with a little silver satin ribbon. The expression here is *a love of nature and study* augmented with the more personal intimation of *I am grateful and willing to learn*' - all of which appears to please Daphne greatly. 'Oh, thank you, Beth!' she says. 'What a kind and sweet message to send!'

But then she falls silent for a moment, thoughtful, as she continues to ponder the flowers.

'Could I have done better, Ma'am?' Beth inquires, filling the silence.

'Well, the only thing I would say is that it is all just a little pale and anaemic-looking, don't you think. Rather like me. Perhaps you could embellish it with some lemon zest to provide colour and a certain piquancy to the scent.'

'Lemon?' Beth says, surprised that fruit might be included.

'Oh yes. Zest signifies ... well, *zest*. Precisely that! Look, here ...'

Upon which Daphne reaches over to a fruit bowl and quickly locates a plump little lemon. With a sharp knife she then very artfully pares away a thin yellow strip of rind, and this she entwines through Beth's bouquet – and to very good effect. It really does look so much more colourful and inviting, Beth realises, while Daphne herself smiles with pride at her little addition before placing it down upon a napkin on the coffee table.

'That is what you have brought to me this afternoon, Beth: a little zest,' she says smiling with genuine tenderness. 'And actually, I am very grateful for it.'

Beth, meanwhile, and almost overwhelmed with such kindness, has adopted one of her wonted, bolt-upright postures, more than a little tense now, because it is her turn to interpret the bouquet that she has been given. The flowers themselves she is able to identify well enough. Naming them is not the hard part. The challenge for her is in remembering what they all mean according to the lore she has been schooled in today. Lady Daphne's posy is much larger and bolder than her own, moreover. It contains several stems of yellow coronella complemented with the dark green of spearmint leaves – unmistakable, that fragrance! These express sentiments of warmth but also of something more subtle such as *may success crown your wishes.*' There are, moreover, also sprigs of Rosemary included, with their tiny and distinctive pale blue florets and which – she discovers as she checks her notes – can only mean something like *your presence revives me*. How kind! So, now Beth is able to give voice and to present her interpretation in full - which is met with a most genial smile and a nod of appreciation from the older woman.

'Spot on, little one!' she states with merriment. 'You are a brilliant pupil!'

'Thank you, Ma'am,' says Beth, but then abruptly and

much to Daphne's surprise, a look of sorrow seems to darken the younger woman's face - as if a cloud has gone over the sun - and which she manages to dispel almost instantly with a thin smile, as if hoping it would not be observed.

'What is it, little one?' Daphne inquires.

'Oh, if only there was somewhere where I could put all of this into practice!' Beth answers. 'All these fair and dainty little things - I doubt that for me there will ever be much chance of doing anything with it at all, not really.'

'Don't you be so sure!' Daphne interrupts, wagging her finger - and there is laughter in her voice. 'Actually, I foresee that one day you will be a lady, Beth. Yes - my legendary psychic powers are at work here, you know. You will be a lady, and then you will need all these cultivated skills in abundance, principally to amuse yourself with all your admirers - there will certainly be dozens of those - while keeping all the others, the ones you don't want, at bay. You will wear glorious roses for the former; vulgar marigolds for the latter - and a thousand other combinations in-between.'

'Oh, Ma'am, how funny you are!' Beth declares, quite tickled by it all, and she giggles deliciously for quite some time.

'You don't believe me, eh!' Daphne exclaims. 'Well then, let's see what the cards have to say on the matter. Let's clear all these flowers and bits away - you do that - and I'll fetch the tarot cards.'

To which Daphne, with great enthusiasm, goes to one of the more secretive draws of her Davenport and returns with her deck of cards, which are wrapped in a square of finest black silk, Beth notices, and which she next hands to Beth in order to shuffle, with the instructions that she should think very hard and contemplate her prospects and wishes as she does so. These being returned to Daphne, now seated on the opposite side of the table, a number of cards are withdrawn from the pack and placed, one by one, into a special and precise arrangement. One card is placed overlapping another, for example, while others are laid out in a column, all with their faces down while Daphne herself takes a moment to meditate quietly before the reading itself can start.

'Well now ... let us see if I can weave my customary

magic!' Daphne begins, her long, tapering fingers with their rings of emeralds and diamonds poised above the cards. And then, accompanied by little snatches of interpretation each time she gives her verdict, the cards are gradually turned over, one by one, face up, to reveal their own unique pictures and symbols – strange, arcane images of medieval figures in rather coarse colours of red yellow and blue; kings and emperors, magicians and lovers, along with one or two more sinister images of fallen towers and even one of a hanged man. Beth should not feel disturbed by any of these, however, Daphne assures her, as they only indicate difficulties and hardships from past rather than what might lie in the future. Instead, the cards she seems most interested in are what she names for Beth as 'The Wheel of Fortune' and another called 'Justice.'

Beth's eyes fill with attention as she surveys the depiction of the wheel itself with its human figures perched upon it, some rising to greatness, others falling from it as it turns, and also to the other card – with a noble lady holding a sword in one hand, the scales of justice in another. What could it all mean?

'These both indicate positive change,' Daphne declares with confidence, her voice soft and steady in tone, almost without emotion of any kind. 'Ultimately, though, we are being led to this one,' she adds as she carefully turns the final card over –'Ah, ha! Look, Beth. It is Le Monde – The World.'

Staring intently at the image on the card, Beth waits for the verdict. This one depicts the figure of a woman, unclothed, encircled with a wreath of some kind and also the heads of a lion and a bull. Perched higher up, meanwhile, can be seen three eagles, one with its wings spread. Quite a formidable combination, surely?

'Attainment, completion, success,' Daphne intones solemnly by way of interpretation. 'So you see, little Beth, I was right. There are great changes afoot - somewhere or other! What do you think of that? Or is it all a lot of nonsense?'

'Oh no, not at all. I hope it is true, Ma'am!' Beth responds. 'How thrilling that would be. Whatever it is!'

'Emm! Sorry I cannot be a little more specific.' Daphne says, aware of her own shortcomings as a seer and noticing also a renewed pensiveness in the young girl who is looking all about her now in a most strange way again, as if examining the contents of the room, the sideboards and dressers with their profusion of china and plate, the curtains and valances with all their flounces, swags and extravagant folds – almost as if she were mesmerised. 'What is it Beth? Have I upset you?'

'Oh no Ma'am, Beth replies swiftly, anxious not to convey the wrong impression. 'It is just that ... well, I do not think I have ever been in a more lovely room. How beautiful it is here! I felt that when I first came in. The little pieces of stained glass in the windows, the beautiful curtains, the lovely paintings and mirrors. How peaceful, how clean and comfortable and how very interesting it all seems.'

Daphne smiles, particularly pleased, because the library is rather her own personal domain. To have Beth say such things, moreover, almost thinking aloud in her own simple, direct way is much to her liking because it has been such a joy having the young woman as a guest this afternoon. It has lifted her spirits far more than she could have ever anticipated. But sadly, she knows, it is already becoming quite late, and she rather suspects that Beth will soon have to leave – a decision somehow hastened all the more by the sounds of a door slamming downstairs and of loud voices raised in the hallway, signifying the return of Lord Bowlend for sure. Both women sense a change in the atmosphere of the building straight away – not altogether easy to explain, but they both feel it, and there is no need to put their shared understanding into words. For words to them after such a delightful few hours together seem quite superfluous and obsolete all of a sudden. Instead, Daphne picks up a marigold flower and a sprig of forget-me-not and with a petulant movement of her arm throws them together into Beth's lap - and everything about this gesture she understands.

'I have had the most lovely afternoon, Ma'am,' Beth states in a very simple and unaffected way getting to her feet. 'Thank you so much.'

'The pleasure is mine, little one!' Daphne replies. If you have time next Sunday, do come again.'

To which, disposing of the marigold in a nearby waste-paper basket, but clutching the precious forget-me-knot to her breast, Beth cordially accepts the other woman's invitation with the briefest of curtsies, before leaving the room.

The long summer's day draws to a close, and the lingering twilight illuminates stretches of warm garden and strangely luminous lawn - as if the heat of the day were stored up in the soil and being surrendered only very gradually back to the sky above - as Amos wanders out to enjoy the fragrant air and the occasional glimpse of sea-view visible through the trees of ash and Scots pine. A chance to think! For he must try to find some measure of renewed tranquillity and peace, he simply must!

To be here at such a time is a rare enough event, anyway, he reflects - because for once there are no social engagements; no parties or recitals or murky séances to attend to. He is alone, therefore, without demands upon his time, strolling peacefully, albeit not entirely without pain in his injured shin, contemplating the turbulent and frantic train of events that have occurred since returning here just a little over a week ago. How extraordinary it all seems. If anyone would have told him he would be spending his summer months in a place such as this, so remote from the hubbub and excitement of London and the social scene, so very far removed from all his friends and fellow artists and poets, he would have regarded their pronouncements with utter disbelief. But it has happened.

As he walks, it becomes a little darker, and swift-winged bats begin to populate the sky - a sky which, at this time of the year, he knows will never become totally dark, never quite surrender its memory of the daylight hours. Here, where the ground rises a little from the house there is one very special crescent-shaped stretch of lawn, bordered by natural balustrades of green hedging. He loves this spot because it affords an excellent view of the sea with its amazing variety of vessels ranged upon it. Here, sometimes, the local fishing boats are joined by other much-larger, ocean-going vessels, steamships crossing the English Channel to France, others sailing along and out into the Atlantic - among them, too, the elegant, tall-masted schooners and clippers, built for speed and all puffed up with sail. And then there are the occasional yachts, of course, those fabulous boats of leisure and conspicuous wealth with their distinctive club ensigns out from Cowes or Yarmouth - so many busy comings and goings of which he plays not the slightest part and which breeds in him this evening a most unfamiliar sense of tranquillity - so that suddenly he realises in a bizarre kind of way that he has found contentment, after all, and that there is actually nowhere else in the whole wide world where he would rather be than just here at this very moment, standing upon his little crescent of lawn and looking out to sea.

In no hurry to return inside, and with slow and unhurried steps, he continues to wander through the garden, imbibing its mysterious and silent atmosphere that seems for him this evening so steeped in magic, so fertile with inspiration that for a moment he half-expects some winged angel or ethereal woodland spirit from a watercolour by Blake to come dancing through the undergrowth of furze and bracken towards him. Again and again he stops to listen, alert to every possibility, wanting to be at one with his feelings, to lock them into his memory for all time - for even the sounds of this place are special, he thinks. Even at a distance the sea gives forth a subtle, mesmerising noise like no other. Wherever you go on the island you are inevitably surrounded by it, supported by its endless rhythmic presence. The voice of the sea is carried on a breath, on a sigh that reminds him of poetry perfectly intoned; of whispers and secrets uttered - almost a kind of symphonic sound. Yet even when unheard, even when overpowered by the noises of the land, by wind or by rustling trees, it could still be perceived in other ways - by the freshness of the air, that briny, seaweed fragrance. Or else there would be that deep, deepest resonance - a kind of thud, a heartbeat engendered by the waves that could be felt rather than heard. The ever-present sea. Living in a place like this you become sea-struck, a glorious sickness like being in love - which brings his thoughts back to Daphne, of course. And he knows now more than ever that he needs to be close to her - not just for a few more precious weeks like this until he finishes her portrait, but for always. What the solution to that longing might be, he cannot say nor does he dare contemplate it too much as yet, but it is a fact of life now, something which he recognises and can comprehend with the utmost clarity. And he knows now, too, that he will have to respond to it somehow - and act upon it sooner rather than later.

Continuing on his way, he discovers a little outcrop of laurel and lingers here, examining with fascination its structure, its leaves, shaped like arrowheads, its stems and branches supple and very slightly tinged with red. How marvellous, he thinks, that we have kept the laurel to crown our heroes and our poets, just as the ancient Greeks did - that we have come to honour these aberrations of history even in our own times: the mythology, the stories of the Gods whose improbable and extravagant antics are retold anew by each generation, not least his own in the paintings and poetry that he and others like him are constantly creating. They say it would have had narcotic properties – laurel – and that the half-crazed priestesses of Apollo's shrine at Delphi would have burned it upon their altars, a combination of barley and laurel leafs to help induce a trance that would allow them to speak the oracle to anyone who came to them on the seventh day of the new moon.

And then, suddenly, above him, so straight and silent, like the flight of arrows themselves, a dozen or so ravens cross the sky in single file, returning late to their roost – they whose plumage the God Apollo once turned to black. Apollo, that beauteous god of poetry and prophesy, of archery and the games - the overseer of every creative spirit that has ever lived. How encouraging, to have his own meditations this evening confirmed by so many outward signs! And so it is that with these strange and varied reflections he continues his journey through the twilight of the garden, retracing his steps along the little stone pathway where he had picked his primrose earlier this afternoon - until eventually his attention is drawn back to the house. Here, suddenly, a glow of light from a window has pierced the darkness and then, a moment later, the sound of a horse and carriage can be heard approaching and drawing to a halt outside the front gate, its wheels rumbling on the cobbles and sounding all the louder in the hush of the evening. This is surely the carriage come to collect the departing James, he assumes - and so he wanders around, through the wicket gate to the front garden to watch him go.

He is correct. The carriage that will take James to the harbour at Yarmouth has arrived. He sees Beth there as well, outside, still in her working clothes, an apron and a shawl about her shoulders, too - tiny patches of whiteness in the fading light. She has assisted the valet out to the highway with some of the lighter pieces of his luggage and is even magnanimous enough to exchange some parting words with him it seems and to wave him goodbye as the horse and carriage with its little glow of a spirit lamp aloft turns and clatters off down the lane once more. She is a good soul, Amos thinks. She will have to take on some of the departing man's duties now, as will he himself, of course.

'Would you like someone local to come in, Beth, to assist during the daytime?' he inquires meeting her as she returns along the path to the front door. Her face is illuminated by the light from the house, and there are garlands of celandine in her hair.

'Oh no, Sir,' she answers cheerfully. 'We can manage all right. It is not a large house to keep.'

And for some strange, unaccountable reason he feels immensely happy with her reply.

Chapter Fifteen

Laurel and a Cuirass

He can only hope and pray that Ramsey will not disgrace himself – though so far his behaviour does not bode at all well in that respect. He seems especially full of himself this evening, bumbling and galloping his prodigious frame around the whole of the building, knocking over jardinières and pots of aspidistras as he goes and not paying much attention to anything at all other than the sound of his own voice which, as always, is loud and strident - and so overflowing with irritating and pretentious phrases in French once again that there is a very real risk of him becoming entirely incomprehensible. Amos is worried. Having courted the friendship of their host this evening, the celebrated painter George Frederic Watts, assiduously over the years, this is the first time he has ever visited him at his home here on the Island. An intimate gathering, hand-picked from the literati and many of the good and the great of the local art world, to be invited here was certainly an honour. Unfortunately, from the moment Amos received the invitation a few days ago a certain problem had also presented itself. Knowing Daphne's inevitable interest, Amos was compelled to take the enormous risk of inquiring whether Watts might also like to extend his hospitality and to make the acquaintance of the Lord and Lady Bowlend. At first the great man seemed reluctant; having declined the offer of a baronetcy himself only quite recently, he was not overly impressed by those with fancy titles to their names. His lukewarm response was brought to a more respectable heat, however, when Amos informed him that the said Lady Bowlend was none other than the lovely young woman who had modelled for so many of the paintings that he had shown him over the years. Having not too long ago entered into a very brief marriage with the young actress Ellen Terry, thirty years his junior, Watts was a man who was well-known for his appreciation of beautiful and captivating young women. The promise of meeting Daphne in the flesh, therefore, proved more than sufficient to persuade him to countenance the proposal.

And so it came to pass that Amos, in the company of Lord and Lady Bowlend, and guided by the evening star peeping ahead between the trees, walked together the short distance from their homes to the substantial thatched cottage owned by Watts nearby and where, amid a noisy gathering of various eccentric and colourful individuals, Daphne - in her stunning black sheath dress of lilac and brown taffeta silk - has already become the very centre of attention and can be seen mingling with the likes of Anne Thackeray or chatting avidly with Lady Tennyson. Amos, meanwhile, feeling at ease in the company of so many artists, their wives and mistresses, is able to engage Watts in conversation and even Tennyson himself who, mercifully, fails to recognise him at all from their encounter on the downs one windswept morning earlier in the year and who, this evening, has become the very exemplar of charm and courtesy - very much in contrast to Oliver Ramsey, who still appears to be champing at the bit to be introduced to everybody of any importance or notoriety as quickly as possible - including the famous and celebrated Watts, of course.

'Ah, *Enchante!*' Ramsey declares,' as Amos does the introductions - and upon which the noble lord takes the painter's hand so firmly in his own and shakes it with such extraordinary vigour that is causes a sharp intake of breath from everyone in the vicinity - an act of crass stupidity upon an artist renowned for his sensitivity of touch and delicate brush work, so that the sixty year old Watts looks understandably distressed as he withdraws his by-now somewhat crumpled hand and examines his fingers one by one with some consternation – a gesture of disapproval completely lost on Ramsey who instead clasps an arm around Amos's shoulders and roars with laughter.

'Amos here is one of my favourite up-and-coming young painters,' he continues effusively and much to Amos's astonishment. 'Oh yes – *formidable!* I'll have you know he is engaged at this very juncture in painting my dear wife, Lady Daphne, and he insists, the rascal, on an allegorical theme, portraying her as her namesake, the beautiful nymph from Greek mythology, no less. I tried to persuade him against such a challenge and to stick with a more simple, formal portrait, but he *must attempt to scale the heights,* he tells me – so who am I to argue!'

Amos, perplexed, his brows furrowed, is scarcely able to contain himself. That Oliver Ramsey should praise and commend him so highly was peculiar enough, but that he should wax lyrical about some sort of allegorical painting he has never commissioned and about which Amos himself knows nothing whatsoever is little short of preposterous.

'The nymph Daphne? Oh my! Yes, that really would constitute a challenge,' Watts declares by way of response, stroking his long silver-grey beard and eyeing his young colleague with a look of some suspicion, as if examining the credentials and vaulting ambition of one who aspires to become his equal and doubting, too, that he would ever really be up to it. 'As with Bernini's masterpiece, which of course is in marble, it would normally show the subject at the point of her transformation, which requires not only enormous subtlety but also considerable boldness and technical strength. I have never attempted to emulate anything of the kind myself – not even on canvas. I wish you luck, Amos my young friend and shall look forward to perusing the finished article.'

'Oh *certainement!*' Ramsey chimes in on Amos's behalf, 'I understand it's already well under way, and to be completed quite soon – *n'est-ce pas*, Amos?'

'If you say so, my Lord,' Amos replies with more than a little irony and a shrug of the shoulders – at which Watts, still appearing to be more than a little mystified himself, wanders away to more pleasant and fruitful ground, namely three lovely young women gathered in a group nearby admiring one of his paintings, providing Amos, therefore, with an opportunity to corner Ramsey at last and to illicit some kind of explanation.

'What the devil is all this about?' he demands above the sudden din of a nearby piano striking up - and lots of raucous sing-along noises from the other guests. 'The portrait we agreed on was to be a simple likeness - nothing remotely allegorical. Don't you realise the whole thing will have to be virtually repainted to accommodate such a ridiculous shift in motif.'

'Yes ... sorry about that Amos. Forgot to tell you about my little change of mind. Silly of me. But the myths and the classics really do appeal to me of late. It is the kind of mandate you are more comfortable with, anyway, isn't it - your usual obsessive, turgid style? I haven't seen one of your damn paintings yet that doesn't take an hour to decipher, or else isn't like some bloody poem, half in Latin, half in Greek. It would prove embarrassing for you, moreover, if you failed to comply - especially now after the great Watts has learned of your endeavours. He will expect to see it. And I would of course have to remind him should you disappoint me or ever fail to complete it.'

'If you imagine that such a work is somehow beyond my powers, I have to tell you, my distinguished friend, that you are mistaken. And if this is your pathetic way of wreaking revenge ...'

'Revenge!' Ramsey exclaims. 'Why should I be seeking revenge, Amos? *Au contraire!* It was I, after all, who cuffed you the other day and knocked you over - not the other way around. Myself, I doubt you'll manage it, especially with a model you are so emotionally attached to - *so besotted with.*'

'Wrong, your Lordship - as so often.'

'Really. Well, prove it, Amos! Prove me wrong! Tell you what, I'll even permit Daphne to come over to you for the sitting. You can start tomorrow. No more dragging yourself across to our place with all your paints and brushes. What do you say?'

It would be churlish to turn away such an attractive

proposition, Amos realises – and so he nods a grudging acquiescence before walking away - though he does realise as he goes that he might well have fallen into a trap here, the entire implications of which he does not particularly wish to contemplate as yet, preferring to postpone any attempt at doing so until at least the morning when perhaps he will feel a little more sober. It is, in any case, such a delightful, exhilarating experience being here this evening, and he remains determined to enjoy it. Daphne, too, he notices, seems quite intoxicated with it all, as if drawing vitality from the pleasure and stimulation of being in the midst of so many interesting and amusing people for once – a kind of conversational feeding frenzy, that results in a quickening, dazzling gleam in her eye whenever he catches her attention. She has never looked more lovely, he thinks, or more animated. The champagne is flowing and what's more several partygoers have suddenly taken it upon themselves to make a human chain and to go dancing together out through the doors and into the garden, and he is being enlisted into this enterprise without any possibility of escape. Oliver Ramsey, too, is to be seen in the midst of it all, his fat hands groping around the waist of a attractive young lady he has managed to get behind, everyone singing as they go and with Daphne in good voice too, desperately trying to lift her skirts and to follow along in the line not too far behind. But then just as he begins to negotiate the opening into the garden, Ramsey stumbles and falls onto his backside, almost dragging everyone else down with him in the process.

'Oh bugger!' the great buffoon declares, smiling stupidly as he staggers to his feet. 'Apologies for the bad language!' he adds – at which Daphne is upon him in a flash, darting towards him.

'Oops, don't you mean *pardon my French!*' she squeals all of a sudden – to which the entire room explodes with raucous laughter, with many, including Daphne herself, unable to cease giggling for several more moments – because it really was very funny - wickedly so, exposing her husband's habitual affectation. But Ramsey is not laughing. His face, in fact, does not display any humour whatsoever. He is clearly incandescent with rage.

'Oh, pardon – pardon Monsieur!' Daphne declares, trying to pull a straight face and wave the matter aside but only succeeding in plunging herself into a coughing fit, and at which Ramsey merely turns and stomps away, inconsolable at this final outrage - or so he has clearly perceived it - and he becomes a chastened figure for the remainder of the evening: silent, brooding in a corner, like some monstrous wounded animal.

When morning comes, the late, late morning directly after the party, Amos's first perception upon waking is that he is lying on top of his bed rather than in it – and with a raging headache, too, testifying, no doubt, to all the various excesses of the previous night. Finding himself to his consternation still dressed in his shirt and trousers, moreover, gradually a far more realistic understanding of the consequences of Oliver Ramsey's new instructions for his wife's portrait begins to dawn on him – and he can only stare up in horror to the ceiling and contemplate the terrible error he has made in accepting his challenge to paint her as her mythological namesake: Daphne, the beautiful nymph pursued by the God Apollo and from whose lecherous intentions she can only save herself by calling forth her own metamorphosis and self-destruction. As Watts had stated himself with chilling accuracy, it would be the kind of thing that even the most accomplished master would baulk at, and it was little short of a provocation on Ramsey's part to have committed him to such an ambitious enterprise.

Rising, and with the ministrations of water upon his face and strong tea in his stomach, Amos finds himself still contemplating the whole appalling episode; he cannot dismiss it from his mind, until finally, over breakfast, it becomes clear to him what his response must be: he will simply refuse to do it. He will just say no - and let the devil take the hindmost! If Watts comes to think any the less of him as a result, it would just be too bad. And in any case there are other, far more exciting things to occupy his thoughts this morning, because one thing that was very positive about last night was Ramsey's change of mind, permitting Daphne to sit for her portrait here at the cottage. Marvellous! And a little later, therefore, he wanders through to where the canvas is already set up in its easel in the bay of the front room, a place which has, he realises with satisfaction, already come to look very much like a typical artist's studio – that is, untidy and pleasingly fragrant with the odour of linseed oil and turpentine - and where he stands now amid the glorious chaos, hands on hips, examining his work with a critical but also, for once, approving eye. Yes, he reflects, not bad - not bad at all! It shows the almost completed image of Daphne, clothed in a modern ball gown, seated in repose, her hair woven and pinned into a sophisticated chignon, her face with its slightly mischievous, slightly tragic dark eyes in half-profile, dreamy and meditative as if gazing through a window, the source of the light in this instance, out towards some distant horizon - an excellent contemporary likeness which would grace the walls of any home. Perfectly adequate, in fact.

'Yes, he mutters to himself, 'that will just have to do, Oliver, my friend. That will just have to do.'

And yet as he looks more closely, and as he contemplates picking up a brush for a moment to undertake some work on the hair, an area which remains still a little coarse and incomplete, his imaginative inner eye cannot help considering how one might actually go about depicting the mythological Daphne in a work such as this. He considers the challenge it would entail. Inevitably, too, he thinks of the achievement it would represent in the eyes of the world, the prestige, the adulation it would bring.

'Difficult, yes – and yet if only I could pull it off!' he mutters to himself as he returns to the breakfast room and sips a little cold tea. 'What a triumph that would be!' And so, seated thus once again, his hands up behind his head, daydreaming, he allows himself to contemplate the consequences of his success, including a scenario in which he becomes the recipient of Watt's admiration, publicly acknowledged: 'I say, well done! Well done my boy!' the old fellow would say in an almost fatherly way and with a slap of approval on the back as together they struggle to get a glimpse of the masterpiece itself beyond the multitude of bonnets and top hats at the summer exhibition of the Royal Academy - all of his adoring public crowded there, jostling to find a space from which to dote upon the object of their homage. He can almost hear the adulation - even see that longed-for invitation to Osborne, sealed and stamped with the royal coat of arms, landing on his doormat at last!

And so he continues to dream, almost unaware of his surroundings at moments, unaware of the puzzled and slightly disapproving expression on Beth's face as she enters - seemingly baffled over his untypical silence as she clears away the breakfast plates – and upon which he even takes up a little sketch pad and plays with the idea there and then, drawing with a dark pencil the figure of a woman, someone of just above medium height like Daphne, running, pursued, hunted, as if in flight - until eventually he convinces himself that he does, in fact, want to do it. He even grabs his watercolour box and applies a little wash of colour in places to bring the image more to life.

Time passes rapidly, so rapidly that he is surprised when Beth appears again – prompting him to take a glance at the clock on the mantelpiece and by which it is confirmed that that over two hours have since elapsed, and that she is, in fact, already bringing in his late-morning tea which she sets down upon the dining table, though not before having to make a space, rather demonstrably he thinks, for the incoming tray and tea pot amid the dozens of sketches, paints and brushes that have become scattered thereabouts since breakfast - almost as if by unseen hands.

'Ah, thank you, Beth!' he says. 'Heavens, is it really eleven o'clock already! I think I ought to stretch my legs, don't you. I wonder, would you come through with me to the front room for just a moment and tell me what you reckon on our Lady Bowlend this morning?'

Beth, with a look of infinite patience and all due solemnity as she often feels is necessary on such occasions, removes her apron and goes with him to where the current portrait is waiting in its easel. She comes close and examines it, as she has done surreptitiously, in fact, already several times over the past few days as it has progressed from a rough blocked-in surface without much form to the now almost finished product. She remains silent for a moment, as if bestowing upon it a suitable period of concentration before delivering her considered verdict in her usual forthright manner. 'I should say it is a perfect likeness, Sir. It is Lady Daphne as we would all wish to think of her – at her happiest and most serene.'

'You mean it's all rather superficial?' he suggests, not pleased - because she is right, damn it! As always, she is absolutely right.

'Oh no, Sir … I didn't mean to suggest it was superficial or anything like that,' Beth responds with urgency, wanting to put the record straight.

'Don't worry, I understand,' he assures her, displaying a grim kind of smile while at the same time, and to her horror, taking up a sponge and wiping some of the still-soft paintwork from the surface in broad sweeps of the arm – until he realises there is no way it can be rescued or redeemed, not at this late stage. If a perfect likeness were the only requirement for a great portrait, then this would be fine. It would, in fact, be excellent. But that is not sufficient, and never can be - not for the lofty heights to which he aspires. No. This, as Beth rightly states, is merely the public face of Daphne, the one the world would be expecting to see, calm, confident, dignified – but there is nothing of the real woman underneath. There is none of her vulnerability, none of her intelligence, her fragile longing and passion for life. And if he is to transform her likeness into the troubled and tragic Daphne of the myth and legend, expressing all those inward qualities, he knows he must begin afresh, with an entirely new composition. So he unlocks the painting from the easel and places it in the corner. Daphne's face is still intact, looking as lovely as ever, and it might serve for a later endeavour, but for now it has become history. It is obsolete. Instead, he resolves to set to work on a brand new canvas, the frame for which he begins to assemble there and then on the dining room table, enlisting Beth's help to stretch the coarse, unbleached calico fabric taunt while he hammers the tacks into the stretchers to secure it. He then slots the little wooden wedges into the corners of the frame, tapping them into place until, with the aid of a gigantic set-square to check the right-angles, the whole structure gradually becomes firm and symmetrical. Priming the surface comes next, without a moment's delay - applying a ground layer of white gesso with a large decorator's brush, hoping this will have dried sufficiently by the afternoon - in readiness for Daphne's arrival. And as Beth retreats silently away into the kitchen with a look of some bewilderment and exhaustion on her face, he carries the whole thing through into the conservatory where the warmer air should, he hopes, speed up the drying process. This accomplished he wanders out in his shirtsleeves to find a shady nook in the garden where, still with his mind buzzing with ideas, he settles down with his sketch book on his knee, attempting to summon up again all the various images and representations of the subject he has seen and admired over the years.

Firstly, of course, there is the famous marble by Bernini which he had once seen in Rome as a student. Watts had mentioned it yesterday. It has become the standard, the template almost, upon which so many inferior works, usually paintings in oils, have been attempted over the years by various French or Italian painters. As in all of these, the nymph would usually be depicted in some form of flight, or with arms raised above her head: a good start for any composition. As in the Bernini, her face would be turned slightly towards he who was pursuing her, the robust figure of the god Apollo. For the present work, however, Amos realises he does not really need to include Apollo at all – and in fact it would be far more satisfactory, more subtle and clever if he did not do so - while perhaps only her eyes of Daphne need to be averted, not the entire face. Above all, he wants it to be tasteful, not to become at all obvious to the casual observer what the subject might be at first glance. He even suspects, as he sketches away with rapid, excited movements, that it might be feasible to portray the nymph herself in contemporary clothing, featuring a cuirass bodice, almost armour-like, and in which Daphne herself always looks so stunningly beautiful, of course. Emm ... so much to ponder, therefore – such a fascinating idea to contemplate! And as so often when a fresh composition is germinating in his mind, he becomes thoroughly absorbed in its all its subtleties and permutations – so much so, in fact, that as he works away, he is unaware of the arrival of the mortal Daphne herself, standing there in the garden nearby, her figure bathed in dappled sunshine and watching him at work with a smile upon her face.

'Amos,' she calls softly. 'Amos?'

'Ah, sorry! What time is it?' he asks, his face lifted towards her, almost as if puzzled by her sudden appearance – as if arriving in a dream. She is dressed in a long white-linen dress with short, off-the shoulder sleeves, loose-fitting apart from a silk scarf tied about the waist, and with a plain, wide-brimmed straw hat trimmed with yellow flowers. Oh yes, she is indeed very lovely, he thinks, while still half-lost in his imagination.

'It is well past noon, my dear,' she replies with a note of admonition to her voice, closing her parasol with a vigorous little snap, 'and I am here for my sitting. I glanced into the bay window as I passed - and you have put me in the corner. Why am I so abused? My husband tells me you are going all allegorical on us. Can it be true?'

'Oh, yes, that's right,' he replies, getting to his feet and taking a purple iris flower for her and smiling with confidence as he threads it into place into her hat-band to join the little 'hopeful' sprigs of yellow gorse that she has already woven into it. The hat itself has a perforated brim, which casts little webbings of sunlight across her face.

'An Iris!' she murmurs with comprehension. 'Oh, you have a message for me, then.'

'Well, I'm hoping that you might be a little intrigued, at least, by what I have planned,' he says, allowing her to take his arm as they saunter back towards the house – having by this stage completely dismissed from his mind any suggestion that he might have been coerced or tricked into this new initiative. It is *his* idea now – of course it is! It has been all along - though by the look of amused suspicion on his visitor's face, bestowing upon him a typical *Daphnesque* pout of the lips, it would seem that she remains yet to be entirely convinced.

Back inside the conservatory, the blank canvas he has left out to dry is ready for use - and with the sun too bright today to consider working anywhere other than the studio with its north-facing windows, they continue through to the front of the house. Here, Amos locks the new canvas into his easel and soon they are both at work, she posing in her usual adept way, running through a few variations until she can provide him with what he wants, and he busy meanwhile with the blocking-in of background colour, employing for the purpose bold strokes with a large brush and thinly mixed paint. The position she must adopt this time is a little different from the norm, he tells her. For one thing he wants her arms raised, and for her to be glancing back, perhaps turning to look over her shoulder, as if being pursued. To this end she must extricate herself from her sleeves, and he must fasten her wrists so her arms will not tire, securing them with a thin strip of gauze attached to convenient nearby picture rail and into which he drives a strategically placed nail for the purpose. Eventually, settling her into a position that satisfies him, and making sure she is comfortable with the ties, he even goes to the lengths of hauling in a mattress from the spare bedroom, which he places between her body and the wall for her to lean against, so she does not have to strain in order to maintain her balance. Though elaborate procedures of this kind are all perfectly normal for an artist and his model during any lengthy session such as this, it would of course all seem somewhat bizarre to the layman – or at least that is the impression Beth conveys a little later by the astonished look on her face as she ventures in to deliver a message. It is from the steward at Parnassus, to the effect that Lady Bowlend's brother Gerald and his wife have just arrived a few minutes ago from the mainland.

'Oh, good!' Daphne declares, taking care not to move her arms. 'They are due to spend a few days with us,' she adds, turning her face towards Amos for a moment as Beth takes her leave.

'Will you have to go over?' he asks, feeling disappointed.

But Daphne smiles and merely shakes her head. It seems that their arrival is not unexpected. She will remain, as scheduled, therefore, perhaps even until dinner, she says – whereupon he decides it might be time to indulge in a little absinthe. Putting down his palette and brushes he goes to a table, set well out of sight from the window and where a number of special bottles and glasses are kept, his latest discovery from Paris, in fact - the increasingly fashionable drink of absinthe, or the *Green Fairy* as it is fondly called in bohemian circles. Daphne, glad of the break in proceedings, releases herself from her bonds and watches with some amusement as he progresses through the elaborate ritual of preparing the drink – firstly placing the special perforated spoon over the wide-rimmed glass; then pouring chilled water over a sugar cube he has placed upon it, allowing the water to percolate down into the absinthe itself - which subsequently undergoes all manner of delightful variations of colour and texture as the alcohol and the herbal ingredients are diluted.

'It should be proper iced water, I suppose,' Amos grumbles, his face intent with concentration and pleasure as he observes the swirling green mixture undergoing its transformation, 'but there's none available in these parts, of course - not at this time of the year, anyway.'

Pulling her sleeves up over her shoulders once again, she comes over to take her glass – an expression of mock-astonishment across her face, making big eyes and feigning as if she would not have seen it all before. She is in excellent humour this afternoon, he thinks.

'Is Gerald still embroiled with the firm?' Amos inquires as he takes his first appreciative sips of the drink and then returns to the easel, mixing up more colours with his palette knife, soft ochres for the background and some purple for the shadowy areas beneath the figure, making ready to begin again.

'Oh yes – on the board of executives now,' Daphne replies, sipping appreciatively at the contents of the long, slender hand-crafted glass - which has exquisite scrolls of silver upon it, particularly around the stem, and which she raises to the light and examines occasionally in-between sips. 'I don't profess to understand it all that well, but he agrees with me that the firm should be scaling down on armaments and turning more towards civil engineering. Gerald is convinced that's where the future lies – in transport, he says. I do hope Polly is willing to listen, and I'm doing my bit to nudge him in that direction – only I'm afraid it's not at all easy.'

'No, I'm sure it wouldn't be,' Amos observes, though in a voice which, she knows, signifies that he has already become absorbed again in his task and is perhaps only adhering to the conversation with some difficulty as he continues to brandish his brush again in wide, spontaneous sweeps and flourishes upon the canvas. The coarse hogs-hair bristles make a busy, scratching sound as he works – shaping up the background once more while his model is otherwise engaged – producing some sky and an horizon behind the figure itself, quickly blending the colours in a rough, superficial frenzy of skill and dexterity upon its surface.

'Polly is becoming frightfully stubborn of late, and rather volatile too,' Daphne complains as she returns to her position in case he needs her again. 'He loses his temper now at the slightest provocation – especially if he suspects anyone is trying to boss him around. As if anybody dare do *that*! Oh, if only I didn't feel so ashamed – I mean about the source of our wealth. I felt it yesterday evening, the contempt everyone had for Polly, knowing he makes his millions through slaughter.'

'Tennyson snubbed him,' Amos observes. 'He hardly spoke a word to him all evening.'

'Yes. I only hope we didn't embarrass you too much, dear one.'

Amos gives a little shake of the head by way of polite denial, but he knows well enough, as he takes up his glass again and sips meditatively at the green nectar, that it had been a mistake, a terrible error on his part to have brought him to meet Watts. For her part, Daphne had been a great success, of course, almost an object of veneration with her gorgeous extravagant evening clothes and fabulously exotic jewels, her natural refinement and clever conversation, but most of the other guests had regarded her portly, bumbling husband with a mixture of alarm and embarrassment, while Daphne's demolition of his character with her quip about his French had certainly done little to help matters.

'Polly is no fool, of course. He would have sensed their hostility from the outset,' Daphne, observes, as Amos breaks off for a moment once again, this time to manoeuvre the easel a little closer to the light of the window. 'So now he's putting on a party himself by way of response.'

'A party! Really?'

'Oh yes. We don't just have Gerald and Mopsy this weekend. I'm afraid there will be heaps of others: including a lot of his old cronies from the mainland, politicians, bankers - all frightfully impressive, or so he seems to think. He's even invited that awful Tommy Newman – you remember that knave I sent away from Bowlend Court for firing from the window? This is all done to upset me, of course - to spite me. I told Polly in no uncertain terms that I wanted him *disinvited* at the earliest opportunity, but he refused. This is his answer to the Tennysons and the Watts of this world - the arty-tarty set, as he calls them - and to the lovely evening we had there yesterday. As a matter of fact, he's calling it the Anti-arty-tarty Party, the one he's arranging.'

'How ridiculous!' Amos mutters, realising that he will certainly not be on the guest list himself, therefore.

'Yes,' Daphne agrees, 'it is ridiculous. Anyway, dear one, I don't want to talk about it anymore. It's so distressing. In fact, the time is long overdue for you to tell me your customary story. I want to hear all about my namesake from the universe of ancient mythology. If I am to depict such a celebrated creature I must know who she is and what she stands for, don't you think?'

He is more than happy to comply with this request, of course. The composition is taking shape before him already; his earlier idea of a cuirass line to the figure has proved a good choice, that fabulous pointed sheath-like bodice - so dramatic, so armour-like: shaped like a gothic arch inverted upon the female form. What could be better! And he is thrilled by the whole idea now in all its shades and nuances.

'The story of Daphne!' he begins as if announcing an act from a play as he works, she seated a little behind, still with her absinthe, watching him over his shoulder and listening with pleasure. 'Well, we have to go back to ancient Greece for this one. Your Daphne was a nymph, a beautiful spirit of the river who attracted the amorous attentions of the God Apollo. But it wasn't just a typical bit of pagan hanky-panky, this. Also interwoven in the story was the God Cupid. Now, Cupid – you might also know him by the name Eros – was the little chap you find in all the baroque frescoes and sculptures – you know: cute, chubby and very cheeky – so cheeky in fact that he boasted to Apollo one day that he was the better archer of the two - to which Apollo began to chide him, remarking that such a puny little fellow couldn't possible match someone like himself, the tall, handsome God of beauty. So Cupid, his pride more than a little deflated, decided to play a trick on Apollo. He made some special magic arrows. The best were tipped with gold, and whoever they pierced would fall passionately in love with the first person they set eyes on. The other arrows were blunted and tipped with lead, quite dull, so that whosoever they pierced would lose all desire - would become cold and void of passion for any unfortunate soul they happened to encounter. Anyway, Cupid let fly one day and he pierced Apollo with one of the golden arrows just as his eyes were about to alight on Daphne – who just happened to be passing by at the time one presumes. But at about the same moment he also let fly at Daphne herself with one of the lead-tipped arrows, so that she could only regard Apollo's advances with horror and revulsion. Frustrated beyond measure, Apollo decided to take her for himself anyway, to violate her if need be, and a chase ensued. The lovely nymph, in fear and horror, called upon the Gods to end her life and to transform her into something that Apollo could not violate or have his wicked way with, namely a laurel tree. This wish was duly granted, and quickly too – so that just as Apollo was about to catch her up in his arms, she was transfigured there and then. The laurel stems twisted about her waist; her limbs turned to bark; her hair to foliage – so that instead of the lovely nymph, all Apollo had to grasp at were branches and leaves. All he had remaining to lavish his caresses on was rough bark and sharp twigs. Now that sounds like a sad ending, but Apollo was magnanimous in defeat and chose thereafter to honour Daphne and the laurel and have its leaves woven into a wreath and awarded to all those he favoured. That's why we still crown our heroes with laurel, of course. It's why Tennyson and his predecessors have had the title of Laureate bestowed upon them. The golden and leaden arrows, meanwhile – well, it's almost like a kind of alchemical formulae enshrined in the legend itself, don't you think? Amazing! The only question I'm pondering at the moment is just how much of the composition here should be taken up with the human figure, those lovely slender limbs of yours, and how much the foliage and bark of the laurel'

And thus Amos reaches the end of his story - all the while working at the canvas, blocking in the background and the shape of the cuirass – something that does not demand too much observation. So it is only now at the conclusion of his tale that he turns to seek out Daphne's reaction, if any, to his story. But to his surprise she is no longer there. She has left the room. Putting his brushes and palette down, he searches and eventually locates her out in the conservatory, seated on the window ledge, her empty absinthe glass still in hand and staring out to the garden where some drops of rain are just beginning to fall.

'Are you all right?' he inquires, coming up slowly behind her. But as he attempts to place a hand upon her still-bare shoulders, she gives forth a little cry, hardly audible. And then she shudders, and turns her frightened, tearful face towards him.

'You fool, Amos. You bloody fool! He wishes me dead – and this wretched picture of yours will be my memorial.'

Chapter Sixteen

Cigars and Brandy

'What time does our friend Gerald get back?' Tommy Newman asks, his voice edged with more than a little irony at the use of the word 'friend' and imbibing his claret in long unruly gulps. Newman, is someone who does not savour wine as would any normal civilised being but instead consumes it like a man dying of thirst seizes upon water, his moist, swollen lips sometimes hardly able to mould themselves around the rim of the glass without dribbling half its contents down his lapels.

'In about an hour, I understand,' Ramsey replies from the other side of the dark-panelled and dimly lit study, dressed already for dinner, pouring brandy and availing himself of a large Havana cigar which he twirls artfully and ritualistically between finger and thumb before cutting and lighting up. 'I thought it would give us an opportunity to talk first,' he adds, explaining the inversion in routine of taking the customary masculine pleasures before the meal rather than after (though it is a common enough oversight, anyway, in the Ramsey household), and upon which he tosses another cigar across into Newman's lap before ensconcing himself between the arms of a settee, an item of furniture that barely encompasses the huge size and bulk of his body.

'What's he been up to, anyway?' Newman asks.

'My dear brother-in-law? Oh he's been up at Cowes, apparently, trying to worm his way into the Royal Yacht Club, or Royal Squadron or whatever it is they call it. He hasn't got a hope in hell of getting in, of course. Bloody snobs. Anyway, they'll only have to take a look at that tart of a wife of his to make up their mind!'

'What Mopsy?'

'Yes – you've seen her, haven't you. Oh, she's all right, really, I suppose. But as for him ...'

'Bit of a pain in the arse, what?' Tommy ventures to suggest without fear of reprisal, knowing how very much his friend detests him.

'All he talks about these days is bloody transport - *the future* he assures us,' Ramsey continues. 'If he had his way we would never manufacture another bullet, let alone cannon. Doesn't he realise that we are on the verge of a golden age in artillery! Myself, I reckon we'll have an automatic gun soon. It can only be a few years away, a real machine gun - industrialisation of warfare on a scale inconceivable only a decade ago, especially in Europe - and he, the bloody fool, wants to develop horseless carriages so people can drive to church on Sundays without getting their shoes dirty!'

'We've already got the railways for all that, anyway, haven't we?' Newman protests, making a mess of lighting his cigar and succeeding only with difficulty in extinguishing the taper used for the purpose before burning his fingers.

'Exactly. But what can I do! My wife insisted I give him a seat on the board before we got married. Now I'm stuck with the imbecile – and his friends.'

'Major shareholder?'

'Not too significant. He's always selling stock – his main source of extra revenue from what I can make out, and that won't last forever – not on his life-style. We could boot him off easy enough. But it's Daphne, you see - I know she wouldn't stand for it. So we have to tolerate him ... for now at least.'

'Em, that's not very helpful for you, is it, Oliver old boy!' Tommy observes in his usual jaunty way, though thoughtful, too, as if scheming - his heavily oiled, silver-grey hair all shiny in the candlelight and which, in combination with his thin pointed chin, all conspires to emphasise his rather unfortunate rodent-like appearance. 'I mean, in business, if you don't grow and expand, if you don't grab the opportunities when they arise, your competitors jolly well will – you can rely on that, what!'

'Exactly!' Ramsey agrees. 'Anyone with half a brain knows that. Why the hell can't *he* see it?'

Newman climbs out of his armchair and, wine glass still in hand, wanders around the room, admiring as best he can in the dim light all the various trophies on the wall and the paintings and little pieces of sculpture in marble or bronze that Ramsey has either acquired locally or else brought over from his residence on the mainland - all typically depicting warfare or various scenes of rape and plunder, and each employing a respectable gloss of historical subject-matter to make it acceptable. Ramsey likes that kind of art.

'Ha, warfare! It was all so simple – so dashed intimate back in the old days,' Newman observes with a sigh, casting his eye over a painting of Waterloo and the swath of wounded and mutilated bodies spread out on the battlefield. Some gallant cavalry are to be seen riding among them, brandishing sabres and regimental flags, their coloured uniforms of scarlet or blue so decorative amid the typically grim patina of smoke and mud that warfare always brings to the landscape. 'Pity, in a way, that it all has to change,' he adds returning to his seat again and tending to fall down into it instead of negotiating a civilised descent, so that his wine is spilt once again. 'You're right. Soon it will all be done at a safe remove – so far away from the action that the chaps who give the orders will never need to see the outcome of it at all - clinical, scientific warfare, conducted at a distance by the generals and politicians. Should make it a lot damn easier on their consciences, what!'

'And with any luck the public will become less squeamish about it, too,' Ramsey agrees in a tone of genuine deference, rare in him.

He is fond of Newman – Newman, this peculiar, clumsy and unattractive little man who resembles nothing so much as a well-groomed rat and yet who has such a sharp and penetrating intelligence that he can somehow always anticipate what it is that Ramsey himself desires – *always*, and with that uncanny, clever knack of putting into words precisely what he might be thinking or planning, as well – even before he does so himself at times. And if there is any special effort called for, be it at work or at play, any coercion or any significant degree of bribery or corruption required in high places, it is always Tommy Newman with his quick, cunning brain who manages to fix it for him. Invaluable.

Newman himself, meanwhile, is peering back at his friend with a strange, calculating kind of look, stroking his narrow little chin between finger and thumb as if demonstrating a renewed measure of admiration; and then a moment later he chuckles and says, 'Well, Oliver, my friend, I have to hand it to you, this is a nice little domestic arrangement you've got up for yourself here - keeping the wife stuck away on an island all summer while you hop off on your business assignments every few days. Rather convenient, what?'

Getting to his feet in silence, and not responding straight away to his friend's audacity, Ramsey waddles across to the door of the study and takes a peep outside along the corridor, making sure there is nobody around within earshot, before slowly returning to the settee where he leans back once more, draws on his cigar and, after puffing a vast cloud of smoke into the air, allows a salacious grin to spread across his broad, fleshy face. 'They've got some new girls at Purdy's, they tell me.'

'Madam Purdy's establishment. Oh, really? I should think another trip to Manchester might be on the cards for you, then, eh?' Newman suggests.

'You should come this time. I've been reliably informed there are special offers.'

'What, two for one again? Ha, the bloody stupid tarts - they have no idea, do they! As if the likes of us would be bothered about *special offers*. We could have ten girls a night if we wanted to and still have change left over from our travelling expenses. Ha! Speaking of which, old boy, that's why it was a bit of shock to us all, you know: you getting hitched like that last year? Getting married, like that. Still can't quite get over it.'

'Had to. Duty calls. Had to start on the campaign of making heirs ... sometime.'

'Still enjoying the experience?'

'Oh yes. Lady Daphne's obvious displeasure at having me on top, crushing her, excites me still. I enjoy corrupting her cultured mind every once in a while. Though I must say that lately it's becoming more and more expedient for her to demonstrate her skills as a horsewoman, if you understand my drift? I really should exercise more; lose some weight.'

Newman grins and nods his understanding, accompanied by a moment of dark introspection that seems to jog a memory somewhere. 'Talking of cultured minds, what happened to that painter-chap, Roselli, wasn't it – the one I met at Bowlend Court? I hear he's become one of your neighbours here. Wasn't he supposed to be doing a portrait of you or something?'

'Oh, that's all finished. Coat of varnish drying on it at the moment, apparently, and to be delivered in a few days. As a matter of fact it's not bad. I shall probably hang it in the boardroom. Oh yes, our friend Mr Roselli has proved quite handy - more handy, in fact, than I could ever have anticipated. Most important of all he's kept Lady Daphne amused over the summer, and given me the liberty to pursue my other amours. You see, Newman - and in confidence now – you are not to tell a living soul – there is someone else. I want to marry again.'

'Really – so soon?'

'I must. Daphne will never do. There was that miscarriage business, of course. Yes, I know what you're going to say – you'd suppose we could try again – but damn it, she doesn't even have her monthlies now, not from what I can make out, just ruddy headaches. And she's taken to mocking me these days, humiliating me in public. No, I can't go on like this, Tommy. People talk, they whisper – you know, innuendo: that I'm not man enough to produce the goods. It's embarrassing. In an odd sort of way it's probably even bad for business - the image of the firm and all that. No, I have to marry again, Tommy – and I've just the girl, or should I perhaps say *Fraulein* already lined up.'

'You don't mean ... not the one I'm thinking of?'

'Yes, that's right. The very one. Seriously well-connected young lady, eh!'

'Rather! Worth a few bob, what!'

'Exactly. And all-woman! Not some precious touch-me-not aesthete like Daphne. Granted, she is German, doesn't speak much English and isn't particularly blessed in the brains department, either; but for all those minor inconveniences she does compensate by being extremely wealthy - and with the most gorgeous bottom you could wish for. I simply have to remove a certain obstacle from my life, firstly, of course.'

'Ah, so that's where your artist friend comes in! Divorce from your good lady wife on the grounds of adultery, am I correct?'

'Precisely. You see, at the start, when he commenced on her latest portrait, I insisted that he come over here to do the work. But then I realised I was missing a trick - so I've become more amenable lately and been allowing him to receive Daphne down the road in his studio. His latest masterpiece is to be a particularly saucy portrait of her, I understand. They've been alone enough now and fumbling about in each other's underclothes often enough, too, no doubt, to provide all the evidence my solicitor needs. Even if not, we'll come up with something.'

'Emm ...' Newman sighs, puffing at his cigar, his eyes unfocussed and directed upwards, as if weighing up the feasibility or otherwise of his friend's ambitious game plan. 'I have to hand it to you, Oliver, old boy. That's clever. But a divorce - even if you have a watertight case - well, you do realise, don't you, it might still take a while? Just as with the first Mrs Bowlend, you're probably looking at years rather than months. And you're not getting any younger, my friend. Is your nubile Fraulein prepared to wait that long?'

Oliver Ramsey stares back long and hard at the face of his colleague. It seems he is being serious for once, and it does, after all, makes sense, what he says. There would be plenty of other huntsmen sniffing about that particular quarry - many a suitor far younger and more handsome than himself lining up to put a ring on the finger of that particular lady, whose family even enjoys royal connections.

'You're right,' he admits. 'It would take an age, wouldn't it, especially if Daphne objects and contests the whole thing, as she probably would. Damn it! I hate you, Tommy - you're always right, you bastard. We need to come up with something else.'

Footsteps are heard approaching along the landing outside. There is a knock at the door, decorous and soft - the butler announcing that, 'Lady Bowlend's brother and his wife have returned from Cowes, and Mrs. Rivers is enquiring whether she might come up.'

'Ah Mopsy! Come in, sweetheart!' Bowlend declares loudly, glancing over the butler's shoulder towards the voluptuous, blond-haired young woman advancing up the stairs and along the corridor toward him. 'Back safe and sound, I trust!'

'Hello Polly, darling,' she says and, as soon as the butler has closed the door, sweeping across the room and placing herself down onto Ramsey's knee. 'Yes, safe and sound. Gerald is hobnobbing with his sister, so I thought I would come up and see what her gorgeous husband is up to.'

Having already it appears dressed for dinner after her trip to the north of the Island, Mopsy is clothed magnificently as always in the very latest fashion, her tight-bodiced dress hugging her waist and thighs and only flaring out in a riot of flounces, pleats and ruffles at the level of the knee – an appearance, therefore, that could be described, were one to be unkind, as resembling a somewhat over-plump mermaid. A triple string of pears hangs about her throat, which also sports an attractive velvet ribbon.

'Charmed I'm sure!' Ramsey purrs like some monstrous, satisfied tomcat as the young woman wriggles into a more comfortable position, one arm around his neck as she kicks of her shoes, the other resting a little immodestly across her abdomen. 'Some champagne for the young lady, if you please Newman!' he calls to his friend. 'As you can see, I am rather pinned down at the moment!'

'I say old boy, wouldn't want me to make myself scarce, would you - tactical retreat, and all that?' Tommy himself inquires feigning embarrassment as he eventually manages to pop the cork and pours some bubbly for the new arrival.

'Don't you dare Newman! I wouldn't want to be held responsible for what might happen if you were to leave me

alone with this goddess for too long.'
All three laugh together.

'Not with Gerry downstairs, anyway,' Mopsy interjects with even more outrageous intimacy, taking the glass of bubbly and draining it almost straight away. 'Anyway, Mopsy's been thinking of having some of her ribs removed,' she states, changing the subject with bewildering rapidity and referring to herself in the *third person* in a childish sort of way as she often does. 'You know, the bottom ones – just here, so Mopsy can have an itsy-bitsy tiny waist again. Gerry won't let her, though – he says it's frivolous – that there are people starving in the streets and that it is immoral for Mopsy to spend money on operations to make her waist pretty and tiny again.'

'Well, all I can say,' Ramsey begins with a grin, 'is that if Adam once spared a rib so you could come into being, then the least you can do now it whip out a couple for the pleasure of Adam's descendants.'

'Oh, I like that. That's good. I'll say that to Gerald,' she says with a serious air, very deliberately as if making a note of the precise arrangement of the words so that they might be recalled at some later date from the distant recesses of her brain.

'Anyway, the poor are only starving because they're bloody idle,' Newman chimes in. 'Don't start feeling guilty about the bloody poor!'

'Oh, I say – I quite like your friend!' Mopsy exclaims upon hearing this. 'He talks sense!' she adds, turning her face towards Newman himself for the first time to deliver the compliment – though also with one outstretched arm proffering the empty glass to him to be filled again, which it duly is. She then brings her attentions back to Ramsey, a far more important individual, and gives him a little tickle under the chin. 'And Polly is so good to us, too, isn't he!' she coos. He's such a pretty Polly, and helps us earn lots of lovely money for me to spend, doesn't he!'

'She knows what side her bread's buttered,' Newman observes, addressing still only the back of Mopsy's head – and to which she herself, without turning this time, summons up an expression of disapproval. That is going a bit too far, her scowling face seems to suggest.

'Don't you start, you two old reprobates!' she declares wagging a heavily bejewelled finger at any suggestion of bawdiness on their part. 'A girl has got to have respect, you know.'

'That's right, Ramsey responds, chuckling loudly. 'You just ask my ruddy wife about that!'

'Oh don't talk to me about your wife!' Mopsy declares rather drunkenly already. 'If you want my opinion, I would say your wife is an absolute mess. If she's not completely loopy, I don't know who is!'

'*Loopy!*' Ramsey echoes. 'Are you suggesting Lady Daphne is mentally unstable?'

'Why yes,' Mopsy replies, 'as a matter of fact I am. The way she goes on sometimes with her wretched tarot cards and astrology and all that tripe. Ha! And all those dreary artist friends of hers – they're even worse! That pretty Roselli boy you're always inviting round has completely turned her head, I swear, and sent her into a permanent state of melancholy.'

Ramsey, catching Newman's eye, discerns that his friend is equally alive to the implications of this highly pertinent remark and he becomes unusually pensive thereafter, lost in thought – so much so that his attentions tend to stray from Mopsy's blandishments for a moment, much to her disapproval because in response she gives out a little squeal of protest into the silence that ensues and, with amazing audacity, even gives a little tug at Ramsey's earlobe to regain his attentions.

'Polly!' she squeals, 'he's ignoring Mopsy! Mopsy's very upset,' she adds, hooking the fingers of her other hand over the fabric of her dress and giving her décolletage a little shake by way of emphasis – which to her surprise merely draws forth a stern expression and a clearing of the throat from the noble lord, followed by the instructions, softly spoken but firm, that she should perhaps pop downstairs again and join the others, as he has something further he would like to discuss with his friend Newman.

Reluctant, a little wounded and obviously mystified she

does obey, however. She climbs down from the gigantic thigh, slips on her shoes with the unsteady movement of one who has perhaps already had too much to drink, and with a studied tremble of mortification upon her scarlet lips and, finally, a frown directed specifically in Newman's direction, turns and leaves the room, closing the door a little too loudly behind her as she goes.

Newman examines the face of his friend with a blend of admiration and suspicion. 'You rascal!' he says. 'I suppose you've already bagged that one, eh?'

'Never you mind Newman. Never you mind!' Ramsey replies. 'She wants her pathetic husband to do well. What am I to do if she enjoys my company?'

'Looks like it's a bit more than company she's enjoying,' Newman observes.

'Shut up Tommy, and listen! Didn't you catch that? The silly bitch had something important to say for once just then – and I don't just mean having her ruddy ribs removed - as if anyone in the real world could ever be found to do a thing like that! No, listen ... Lady Bowlend is going loopy, she said. Insane. Well, there's the answer! Don't you think I could obtain a much quicker divorce if my poor wife were to be declared insane? I could, couldn't I? You remember our old friend, Smithy? He got his wife diagnosed with hysteria and had her locked away, didn't he? The divorce followed soon after as I recall. And didn't he say something about them throwing away the key and all that if you get it right with them – you know: a few discrete charitable donations through the right channels? Yes. Then at a stroke we can remove any obstacle to my marrying my German heiress. Even better, without Daphne around to shield him we can kick that arse of a brother of hers off the board at the same time.'

'I say, Ramsey, that's not bad, is it, what!'

'No ... and it's not that there isn't ample evidence, after all. She virtually lives off laudanum these days. Like Mopsy says: she's a mess. Morally weak, too, of course - carrying on with her artist friend. Heaven knows what perverse, activities could be envisaged going on over there in his sordid little cottage. I shall be deeply shocked, a broken man. With the most profound reluctance I shall have to send her to an institution for the terminally insane, or whatever fancy term they give to the loony bin, these days. And after a short pause, I shall marry my little bit of totty.'

'The totty with the botty, what!'

'Precisely, Newman, precisely – the totty with the botty. And with an uncle who owns a munitions factory, as well! Onwards and upwards, eh!'

But Newman doesn't respond. With another protracted sigh, he gazes upwards into space once more in his habitual way, still thinking, contemplating this latest strategy with all the cunning and penetrating logic of a general in the field. Much to Ramsey's disappointment, he still seems unable to countenance the proposal. 'It's still going to take time, though' he says, fixing Ramsey with a steady eye - all the banter and clumsiness having dissolved now, revealing a rarely seen dimension of latent intelligence and foresight beneath. 'You can have her locked away quick enough, but the legal formalities that follow ... well, that's a different business altogether. You mentioned our friend Smithy – but his affairs took over a year before everything was settled.'

Newman is right again, of course. And Ramsey's fleshy jowls sink so far downwards in despondency that his face becomes almost entirely square for a moment, the flab of his various chins spilling out from the white-starched wings of his shirt collar in a most unbecoming way.

'Do you hate her. Do you loathe and despise her?' Newman asks at length, his words plunging into the silence that seems to have engulfed the room with this new and sinister mood of concentration and purpose.

'Why ask?'

'Just speculating, old boy! Just speculating. I mean, would you miss her – Lady Daphne – if, for instance, she were suddenly, *very suddenly*, no longer around?'

Ramsey thinks long and hard. And his lack of a reply speaks volumes. What has he really ever got from this marriage. What will he ever likely get from it in the future, he asks himself, other than perpetual irritation and embarrassment, endless delays and frustration? All his bravado, masquerading as someone who regularly enjoys his wife's favours is false, of course. She does not mount him like a horsewoman, as he implied in such a jaunty fashion earlier to his friend. The truth of the matter is that his marriage is a failed and dismal ordeal; binding him to a frigid and unresponsive woman who literally vomits in the bedroom every time he puts a hand on her; a woman who has confessed to him that she will only ever love one man for the rest of her life? And that man was, of course, not him. His colleague seated opposite, moreover, seems to comprehend all of this, to be able to read his mind with some extraordinary sixth sense, some filthy animal instinct that only he possesses.

'Tell you what, old boy,' Newman begins again, taking up a brandy glass this time and pouring some for himself from the crystal decanter. 'You carry on with your little scheme - insanity or adultery or whatever combination of the two you'd like to try. It might come up trumps. But in the meantime I'll see what I can do, something that might prove a little more immediate and - er - shall we say decisive. Leave it with me, Oliver, old boy! Leave it with me. I reckon I can fix it for you - if you really want it, that is.'

'What do you mean?'

But Newman merely places a finger of silence to his moist lips and says no more - and a moment later, they hear the sound of the dinner gong in the hall, anyway - a noise that almost immediately begins the process of salivation and upon which they both get to their feet and shuffle their way downstairs to join the happy party already gathered in the dinning room below.

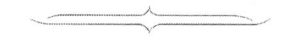

Transcript of a Letter from Beth, serving maid to Amos Roselli, to her sister Jane, August 1877

Dear Sister,

I trust you will forgive me if I write to you, but I wish that we do not lose each other through neglect or indifference. Blood is thicker than water, they say, and you are all I have by way of family.

I have not been able to sleep this evening and have been up reading. It gives me time to put pen to paper and tell you my news of the past year or so. A letter once in a while is no strain for either of us, so let me begin. If you cannot read this, you may show it to someone who can, and they will read it for you.

Since we last saw each other I have come into service with a Mister Roselli who has property in London and in Kent. At present I am writing to you from the Isle of Wight. We are staying here in a cottage for the summer. The weather is lovely – though very hot just now. Mister Roselli is an artist. He is a bachelor. He is tall and has long black curly hair. He is a very kind gentleman and never raises his voice to me even when I do things wrong. His valet has had to leave him, and I have taken on some of his duties, which I enjoy. I have a good wage, and the work is not hard. So I am happy. Also, on top of this, I receive an allowance – I call it my 'mystery allowance,' for I know not from whom it comes. It is not much – only a few shillings - but it means that I can afford small luxuries like a magazine or flowers from time to time. It arrives by registered post every Tuesday from a solicitor in New Eltham. So I can only think it is to do with the family where I once worked. Perhaps they have passed away and remembered me in their will. Their son was always good to me (I remember he let me have the bread and jam that time when the Missus slapped my wrists). Perhaps it is to do with him. Anyway, the solicitor says he is not at liberty to divulge (I think that is the word he used) the name of whoever is responsible. And he cannot tell me how long it will last.

I often think how nice it is that you have found a husband. I am so happy for you. And wherever our mother might be, if she is looking down from heaven, I am sure she would be proud. I hope you are well now and that you might be blessed with children soon. Perhaps you are already! How thrilling it would be to be told I am an aunt – that I had a little niece, for example. I would be so glad to share my good fortune with you and help in the child's education.

I feel that us women should be educated as much as men.

We should not have to sacrifice ourselves to drudgery or a loveless marriage just to survive. To be able to read and to have a voice that is informed by wisdom must be the most precious of things in all the world. Every person should have such a chance in life. If I was very wealthy and had lots of time I think I should devote my life to it.

Do not feel bad about sending me away like you did. I know how hard it must have been for you - another hungry mouth to feed, and all the extra worry when I turned up on your doorstep that time. I hope we can be friends still. What with my change of fortune I really would not be a burden to anyone now. So please write to me at the above address when you have time.

Your loving sister,
Elizabeth

Chapter Seventeen

A Mysterious Book of Verse

He realises it is the best chance he is ever likely to have of asking. He simply must persuade her to return to sitting for him, to convince her that she need not fear, that her husband does not have any baleful or sinister intentions. But as he examines the face of the lovely Daphne walking at his side, her lips tightly compressed in thought, he knows it is not going to be easy. Dressed incognito today in a simple grey linen dress, buttoned at the front, and with a decorative straw hat with veil, she might easily be mistaken for a tourist, a young woman from the clerical or commercial classes with her thin summer shawl tied around her waist, visiting the island for a few days from London or the Midlands. Amos, for his part, wears a full beard for the occasion, borrowed from the many props and accessories kept among his studio equipment – an addition to his normally sparse, wispy half-beard and which, with the addition of a flat cap pulled down over his dark locks, succeeds in disguising him tolerably well from any prying eyes – for today, with Oliver off the Island once more on business, they have had little need of encouragement to arrange another tryst, though this time in complete secrecy, alone. Excuses were easy to come by. She was to go shopping on her own, he was simply to go walking along the coast - and so, with the aid of the local railways and a swift 'fly' or two that have hastened them along the island's leafy lanes and roadways towards each other, they are met here today beneath the famous Undercliffe of the south coast, strolling arm in arm along one of the many shaded pathways threaded with babbling streams and where the trees and lush wooded glades, rich with honeysuckle and purple foxgloves, cluster down to the very margin of the sea itself. To their left hand side as they walk, meanwhile, row upon row of steep and spectacular escarpments of sandstone, covered in Sycamore and Holm Oak, rise up towards the tiny glimpses of blue sky above. It is, Amos concludes, quite simply sublime. And for a painter or poet of any kind it is a very heaven on earth.

'Ah, isn't this just glorious!' he exclaims as they catch sight of a ribbon of blue sea between the trees, wanting so much to draw her out of what appears to be an untypical heaviness of spirit – but to which she merely smiles a kind of vapid agreement in lieu of voicing any kind of opinion. This is not like her, he thinks. Something is troubling her, for sure. So to entertain her further he peels off his disguise - accompanied by a little theatrical squeal of pain on his part and rubbing of the chin before stowing the furry object away into his pocket. But even this extravagant act fails to rouse her from her dark mood. Again, he looks into her face – a face that, he notices with approval, is beginning to develop a little unfashionable colour in the cheeks, the sea air working its magic at last, even on Daphne. In time, she will disclose her thoughts, he knows. So he waits in silence, waits patiently as they stop and admire together the faded petal sculpture of a local well dressing, its once-vibrant colours and textures now almost disintegrated in the August heat. It is a place of such vitality, the bird-song so fulsome in proximity to the running water, that gradually he senses a change in her mood. It is as if the sight of the well with its crude and simple piece of local art - a triumph of patience and dedication to produce a picture solely from the petals of flowers - has settled and focused her thoughts, for it really is quite humbling.

And so it is that when she does finally speak, it is like a torrent of words issuing forth. What she has discovered just these past days, she tells him, as they set off once again, arm in arm, is simply awful and has done little to dispel that persuasion so deeply seated in her mind that her husband wants her out of the way. Oh yes, she insists, shaking her head with dismay at Amos's protestations, it is true. He will stop at nothing now. She is not mistaken and the reasons for it are fully known to her: because her husband is having an affair.

'An affair!' Amos echoes, trying to sound surprised - though from what he knows of the man and his character, not really all that shocked by the revelation.

'Oh yes - or perhaps even worse than that!' Daphne continues. 'I heard it from Gerald. He accompanies him on business trips sometimes - during which Polly is forever chasing women, apparently - and, worse, perhaps even visiting prostitutes. I am appalled. I cannot bear him to even talk to me now, let alone touch me, and I have insisted that we sleep in separate rooms. His response is ...' She breaks off for a moment and brushes a loose strand of hair away from her face, and he can see there is a tear in her eye as well, which she discretely wipes away at the same time. 'His response is that I must discuss my plight with a doctor. Yes - that I am perhaps suffering from frigidity or hysteria and loosing my mind. Can you believe it! It would be laughable if it were not so appallingly dreadful. And what am I to do? How can I protect myself? I am only a wife, Amos - when all is said and done, merely a chattel. And if my good husband thinks I might be going insane ... well then, something must be done. The doctor must be called. And when the doctor calls, as he did yesterday, he must ply me with all kinds of stupid questions. Do I know of anyone in my family who has suffered from insanity, he asks. No, I reply in rather a droll fashion, that as a matter of fact we have usually all quite enjoyed it! He does not find this amusing, however. Instead, he chooses to interrogate me about all my vices and nasty habits, about drinking alcohol and taking loddy. He wants to know all about my excessive interest in occultism; he asks me if I hear voices; asks me if I indulge excessively in onanism. Can you believe it! The audacity! Anyway, the upshot of it all is that he is going to refer me to a specialist in London, so I can be properly assessed. We might be going as early as next week, and it's all for my own good, Polly says. In truth, of course, it's all about clearing the way for his new conquest.'

'I just can't believe it!' says Amos, endeavouring again to sound dismissive, though at the same time knowing full well how easy it remains, even now, to have an inconvenient wife locked away in an institution, often for the remainder of the her life on grounds of so-called insanity - a kind of living death in a way for the poor woman merely so that the husband might be free. 'Don't you think you might be mistaken?' he suggests, still trying to make the best of it. 'I mean about this other woman?'

'Oh no - I'm afraid not,' says Daphne. 'I've even seen her now, the object of his latest ambitions. That was my joyous weekend taken account of. It's just as well you were not there, after all, dear one - the Anti-arty-tarty Party and its aftermath. There we were, Gerald and I, trying to make an impression and hold our own - with Gerry, as ever, trying to put his case for developing the business and all that kind of thing - all to no avail - when I noticed this woman among the guests - the Prussian, I shall call her for purposes of discretion and ease of reference - who is the one who has clearly caught the eye of my husband. She is an heiress, a friend of Mopsy's it seems and, perhaps a trifle more importantly, the niece of a prominent German who owns a munitions factory - all of which can only assist in raising her profile in Polly's estimation. Oh I suppose she is also quite presentable - in a buxom, Germanic kind of way, if you like that sort of thing. The men seem to adore her, at any rate. She is distantly related to royalty, I understand.'

'Really!'

'Oh yes - I told you the other day it was an impressive guest list. Anyway she is young, rich and on the loose. If anything untoward were to happen to me, I'm certain Polly would be making a beeline in that direction, if he hasn't done so already, that is.'

'For heaven's sake!' Amos protests again in his own gentle way. 'Nothing whatsoever is going to happen. No doctor in the world will ever find anything wrong with you mentally - and nor is there any reason, by the way, why we shouldn't continue with your portrait. You know that, don't you. If you do not confront these anxieties, Oliver will have succeeded in what he has set out to do - that is, to frighten you, to dominate and oppress you and therefore bring you under his control like everyone else in his universe. Don't be deceived!'

She takes his hand and gives it a grateful little squeeze by way of agreement, and eventually she even allows herself a smile. 'You know, I remember as a child I once had hopes that your sister and my Gerald would fall in love one day and get married. Margaret and Gerald. Funny how one has those kinds of fantasies when young. But that was not to be, was it! Instead my brother finished up wedded to somebody with a name like Mopsy! Strange girl. And now she's procuring lovers for my husband. I'm certain she hates me.'

'It's of no consequence even if she does,' he observes, trying to sound rational.

But Daphne can only smile rather grimly, pensive again. 'I wonder,' she says. 'Sometimes I'm not so sure about that.'

A few steps further, and the whole landscape changes. They emerge from the dark and brooding trees into a bright open lane flanked by fields of barley sheaves – all the men and women busy with the work of the harvest, great horse-drawn wagons flanked by labourers with pitch fork and scythe. It is in a far more cheerful mood, therefore, that they continue on their way - further down a long hillside, still always in the sunshine – and Daphne, therefore, with her parasol raised - until eventually they come upon the outskirts of a little town by the sea.

Having been little more than a collection of tiny fishing villages just a few decades ago, the whole south-east corner of the island has already evolved into a network of fashionable communities and seaside resorts, their popularity being driven by the especially warm and balmy climate here. Many of the towns like this one have long piers of wrought iron and timber, magnificent feats of engineering which extend hundreds of feet out into the sea. Here the buildings, too, can be very grand, with hotels and restaurants, bookshops and picture galleries clustered alongside the many newly built villas of stone and flint that have so quickly sprung up all across this glorious part of the island - and some hugging the cliffs so tightly, so high above the sea in places that the boats out at sea appear to sail between the very rooftops themselves, amid all the weathervanes and chimney pots.

After a lunch of delicious local crab at one of the seafront hotels, they take a turn around the busy town itself – a bustling place, full of summer visitors at the very height of the tourist season now, the streets noisy with the rumbling of horse drawn carriages, cabs and vintners wagons, the pavements and seafront promenades teaming with ladies in elegant crinolines, their parasols upon their shoulders, and garrulous gentlemen in bright-coloured jackets with canes and straw boaters walking at their sides - and everywhere the strains of brass bands marching in some unseen hinterland of pavilions and parks.

'Amos, I want to go into this bookshop,' she says taking his arm and giving it a little squeeze. 'Would you mind? I just need to check on something.'

He agrees, but to his surprise once inside, embraced by the cool welcoming silence of the shop, Daphne does not appear to want to linger. Instead, she simply examines a few titles amid all the dusty leather spines and towering shelves that would normally tempt them to stay for hours, and then, with a discrete and rather disagreeable glance of curiosity towards the staff behind the counter – two elderly gentlemen – she takes his arm and urges him to walk straight out again.

'No ... it was not this one,' she whispers once outside. 'Or if it was, then the woman who was in charge that day is not present this afternoon. I will explain everything in a moment, don't worry.'

Following the sun, they wander along a lane of fishermen's cottages until, turning a corner, they find themselves suddenly almost on top of the sea, the waves thundering and roaring in towards them and where upon a wide paved walkway a number of welcoming benches have been set. It is here, away from most of the crowds that they agree to take their ease, an opportunity at last to sit and to admire the foam-topped turbulent waves, the soaring gulls and black cormorants passing by – an opportunity, too, for her to tell him the reason for wanting to bring him here to this particular place today - and this she does.

'It was some weeks ago, while you were away in London, dear one, when I surrendered to a desire to explore this magical part of the island on my own. I came here and went into that shop – I am almost certain it was that one back there. There were lots of second-hand books; and you know what a fool I am for those! Simply cannot resist. Anyway, I had not been in there more than a few moments, on my own and feeling not unlike a child in a sweet shop, when a woman, the proprietor I presume, called out from the back of the shop my name: "Daphne! Daphne!" She called twice, "just look around and I'll be with you in a moment. The poetry section is just to your right, down the isle!" Well, that was odd, I thought because before I could manage to examine the woman's face she was gone – away into what I assume was the storeroom or her office. But I did go to the poetry section, as she suggested, and I did find some unusual and utterly irresistible books, one of which I have with me today. I will show it to you in a moment. Anyway, when I was ready to pay, I rang the little bell on the counter to summon the woman and asked her if she was acquainted with me. I certainly couldn't recognise *her*. "Oh, no Madam," she answered. Well, you would think I would have persisted and inquired of her there and then how it was that she had known my name but somehow I neglected to do so. I suppose I was so excited about the books and things that it just didn't occur to me, or else I probably wasn't certain whether she had really called my name or whether I might have simply imagined it, or even if it was the same woman whose voice I had heard. It was only much later, that evening back at Parnassus when I recalled the event that it struck me as most singular. Anyway, here it is Amos. Only a tiny thing, but packed full of gorgeous poetry: *A Treasury of English Verse*. Look.'

He takes the little volume that she has had buried away in her handbag all this time and gently turns the pages. It is a broad selection of poems, finely printed, spanning the centuries from Chaucer to Tennyson, and sometimes with an annotation or an introduction placed alongside. Amid the modern works of Swinburne and Keats, therefore, the language and style of bygone times also comes up to meet him – the wonderful sonnets of the Tudor and Elizabethan age - some of the earliest in the English language, and with Shakespeare featured again and again, of course. But he knows there would be others of importance, and it is not long before he encounters some by Wyatt. She has discovered them already, in fact, and a bookmark guides him to the one she has been reading last and which he therefore examines now, knowing by her untypical silence that she is waiting for him to do precisely that.

Request to Cupid for Revenge of His Unkind Love
By Thomas Wyatt

Behold, Love, thy power how she dispiseth;
My grievous pain how little she regardeth:
The solemn oath, whereof she takes no cure,
Broken she hath, and yet, she bideth sure,
Right at her ease, and little thee she dreadeth:

Weaponed thou art, and she unarmed sitteth:
To thee disdainful, all her life she leadeth;
To me spiteful, without just cause or measure:
Behold, Love, how proudly she triumpheth.

I am in hold, but if thee pity moveth,
Go, bend thy bow, that stony hearts breaketh,
And with some stroke revenge the displeasure
Of thee, and him that sorrow doth endure,
And, as his lord, thee lowly here entreateth.
Behold, Love!

'Yes, it's interesting, isn't it' he begins by way of response, his arm resting again across the top of the bench so that it encloses her shoulders gently. 'It could even have been a lyric for a song. Cupid was a popular theme among writers of those times. But usually, for them, he was a pleasant God. Here he seems to be the instrument of vengeance and spite.'

'Exactly,' she agrees a little ruefully. 'I thought it would be right up your street, Amos my dear - very apt, considering that you insist on painting me as the victim of Cupids arrows. The strangest part of it all is that I obtained this book weeks ago, long before you had your brainstorm!'

'Could I borrow it?' he asks,

Willingly she agrees – almost relieved to be rid of it, he suspects - this strange object that has come into her life under equally strange and bizarre circumstances. It is just another source of anxiety for her, she who of late is already so apprehensive and highly strung, he feels. It is as if a scream is bottled up inside of her at moments.

Nearby they notice a gentleman standing, looking out to sea, very dapper in his colourful blazer and straw boater, typical seaside attire. Always mindful of their delicate situation, they regard him with suspicion for a moment until they are satisfied that he is no one they recognise. He is, however, a spy of sorts, Amos thinks to himself with amusement, because he has in his hands a small telescope - and this he extends and trains on something further along the beach - evidently an assortment of colourful bathing machines, garishly painted wooden boxes on wheels that are hauled by horses at regular intervals down into the sea and back again for the benefit of swimmers. The object of interest in this case, therefore, Amos realises, would most likely be the scantily clad ladies stepping down from them into the water – though there are men among them, too, today, as Daphne is quick to point out.

'Look there's no segregation of bathers here at all!' she exclaims with surprise, shielding her eyes from the sun. 'It is astonishing, isn't it - that people should behave with such liberty here when back home they would never dare even contemplate such a thing. I'm afraid, the seaside, it is becoming a place of utter sauciness, don't you think!'

Smiling, he agrees. And if it is true, as many social commentators are beginning to note with typical British distaste for the pleasures of the flesh, that the seaside is gradually becoming a culture apart, almost, a fresh principality of sand and sea that has been appropriated by the youth of the nation and where consequently many of the conventions and boundaries of class and good taste appear to be breaking down, then nowhere is that transformation more apparent than here today, in this very special place so far from the gloom and priggishness of the town and city. Emboldened by it all, and by the unusual sight of so many men and women in the water together, Amos suggests that they stroll along and see if they can hire one of the bathing machines themselves for an hour.

'What!' she exclaims, drawing herself back from him in astonishment.

'Don't worry. We won't be swimming,' he assures her. 'I can't anyway. But we could get really close to the sea, couldn't we - and maybe even dip our feet in the water. Come on, what do you say!'

To his surprise and delight, she agrees. 'It is an absolutely brilliant idea,' she says, giggling, getting to her feet and taking his arm. And thus within moments they have run along to the beach, past the crowds of people reclining in deck chairs, past the ever-popular donkey rides and busy Punch and Judy stalls surrounded by children, out along towards the water line and the waiting bathing machines. Here, with Daphne having already relinquished her shoes so that she might feel the hot sand upon her feet, they pay their fee and are ushered down among the huts by one of the attendants.

Theirs, it seems, is to be a rather ostentatious yellow-and-red stripped one, parked in readiness just above the water line - with a prominent and equally vulgar advertisement for mustard emblazoned on its flank, and into which they enter via a small set of steps at the rear. Once alone inside they need only endure a few moments bumpy ride within the darkened interior as the wagon is hauled down into the sea before, breathless with excitement, for it really is a totally new experience for them both, they are able to fling open the seaward-facing doors. A burst of bright fresh air assails them - and there it is: the sea in all its loud, foaming magnificent glory, roaring away there right under their very noses.

'Oh my God this is so beautiful!' Daphne exclaims, shielding her eyes from the sun and stepping out onto the topmost rung of the little set of wooden steps that extend down into the water itself. Holding onto the handle of the door, she then leans out and takes a peep around the edge of the hut itself. 'I say, I hope that chap with the telescope isn't still around!' she declares in a brilliant imitation of some disapproving schoolmarm. And then, with a little squeal of mischief, she turns back to him, wide-eyed, a guilty hand to her mouth to conceal her laughter, her shoulders up around her ears. It is the young girl he remembers from childhood all of a sudden, an aspect of Daphne he has not seen for a long while and which he finds an absolute delight.

'Don't be daft!' he says, admonishing her. 'That's the whole point of these things. People can slip into their bathing costumes and climb down into the water without anyone on the beach being able to watch them. It's only if you venture right out that you can be spotted - and that, I can assure, is not something I will be contemplating. Though I must say I do rather fancy a bit of a paddle. How about you?'

Upon which, removing his shoes and socks, he rolls up his trousers, steps down and dips a foot into the water to test the temperature. It feels surprisingly warm here in the shallows and so he sits himself down on the lowest dry rung of the steps and allows his feet to become immersed, catching little pieces of seaweed between his toes as each pulse of the incoming tide washes over them. And then, to his delight and amusement, she joins him, bare-legged and daring - still full of laughter as she snuggles up alongside him and there also dips her feet in the sea. A new experience for her. After a while, she removes her hat, too, with its thin white veil, and allows the sea air to penetrate her lovely hair, letting it untangle from its combs and pins so that strands of it become lose and chaotic, falling in several little serpent coils about her cheeks.

'I'm so glad you agreed to this little piece of madness,' he says, his eyes fixed on the gulls as they wheel and circle in the sky ahead but really full of care only for her.

And then as they continue to sit closely side by side and watch the waves rolling and pounding in towards them, she rests her head upon his shoulder – in perfect innocence, as she once did when they were children but which she has not felt free to do for many a year. The only difference now is that her fragrance is something sophisticated and musky from Paris or Cologne, whereas once upon a time it would have been simple crushed lavender or thyme from the meadows around her home.

'Oh, Amos,' she says, 'I am so happy. So perfectly happy. Nobody knows we are here, do they? Nobody knows who we are. We can become whoever we like in this magical little box. Why can't we just stay here forever?'

Although separated by a respectable distance, the other bathing machines adjacent to theirs are all occupied it seems as he begins to glance along the water line and take account of his surroundings. The structures themselves are not so far apart as to preclude anyone being able to hear what is going on next door, therefore, and so he is glad that she is speaking still in whispers. Not that anyone here seems to be in the least bit concerned or curious about anyone else, because there is laughter and screeching everywhere. A portly gentleman with a vast moustache and beard, all wet and bedraggled around his cheeks comes floating by on his back, his feet paddling - and not much more than a few yards from where they are seated. They watch him with amusement as he passes, looking not unlike a stranded whale as he draws to a halt further along and then, as he emerges from the water, searching for one of the huts, his own presumably. There he stands in his skin-tight bathing costume, the hoop design of the fabric doing little to flatter his decidedly corpulent figure. He is, for all that, an athletic-looking gentleman – in a way similar to how Daphne's husband would probably look without his clothes, Amos reflects. Some ladies are giggling and beckoning the gentleman towards them from the interior of the hut, cooing and waving to him from the steps. Amos can just glimpse the provocative bare legs and bloomers of the Sirens themselves, as the gentleman, who goes by the name of Henry apparently, wades towards them - all bristling with desire and pumped up by the vigorous sea-air.

Not at all English, this kind of behaviour, Amos thinks, though also recollecting that it was only a few decades ago when it was perfectly respectable for men to swim in the nude in places like this, and restrictions on mixed bathing have always been flouted, of course. Local bylaws struggle to impose propriety, and here today they seem to be totally non-effectual. It is really quite amusing.

Daphne, meanwhile, and having decorously replaced her hat and veil, does not seem so entertained by the spectacle. She is frowning and observing the man with a certain distaste as he climbs the steps into the other hut and from where, moments later, the sounds of some kind of masculine grunting and female giggling are to be detected – the hollow wooden structure tending to act as a sound box, amplifying every sigh and whisper of delight. What on earth could they up to in there! Amos wonders. Lucky chap!

'Amos, tell me, Daphne begins again, fixing her hat pin into place with a vigorous little movement, 'what is it like being a man?'

He turns to look at her – examining her lovely eyes, her troubled brows where two very untypical little furrows have formed above the bridge of her nose. 'What a curious question!' he says. 'What do you mean - in what sense?'

'I mean, I cannot understand why people are all so physical about one another. Why is Polly always chasing other women, craving always to possess them? What is the drive you have, the animal lust you all seem to be ruled and governed by at almost every moment? I don't understand. How is it – what does it feel like?'

He has to consider this with some care, since he has never really had occasion to analyse such a natural and basic instinct before. He listens to the slow rhythmic thud of the seawater beneath the floor, watches the great foam-topped waves rolling in towards them still and is lost for a moment in the power, the relentless energy of it all.

'Well, I suppose it's quite agreeable most of the time,' he responds kicking back at the waves as they advance and making little puddles on the steps now. 'It's a feeling of strength and of lust mixed with the thrill of the chase and all that. Think of all those rutting stags and things and that deep, throaty roar they all make when they're excited and you won't be far off the mark.'

'Why do you say that?'

'What'

'About *stags* and *being off the mark* – it's the language of the hunter.'

He agrees - though he hadn't thought of it quite like that because, he complains, it then all begins to sound so brutal and he has never thought of his manhood in that way. It was that wretched book of verse he'd glanced at early answering for him.

'Yes, but I am afraid it is brutal,' she murmurs, still with her cheek upon his shoulder, speaking now only very slowly and with a steadying hand upon his knee as if she would cease his kicking of the waves. 'It is brutal. It is quite humiliating as well at times, and I have already had quite enough of it, I think, because it does not suit me at all.'

Aware that she might actually be crying, he keeps still now. With tender care, he keeps her close at his side until they both become calm again. 'Well, it doesn't matter,' he murmurs, returning to the conversation. 'If it doesn't suit you then you should certainly not feel guilty about it.'

'Oh, I don't feel guilty,' she insists as she lifts her face from his shoulder. 'It's just that ... well, to be indifferent, like I am – it's not really what is expected of one, is it?' At which she takes her handkerchief to her eyes to deal with the teardrops, pretending it is the wind that has caused them. But then she laughs. 'You know, I remember once, one evening, going with Polly to a music hall – somewhere desperately sordid in the East End, I suppose. There was an act in which a man, quite an elderly man I believe, appeared as a female impersonator upon the stage. Dressed in a gown, with a gigantic bustle, a false décolletage all padded out and a glorious curly wig piled almost to the ceiling, he was more female than any female one could ever meet, if that makes sense, and with an affectation of youth - singing all the while in some dreadful falsetto voice. I wonder if that is what so many of women finish up doing in our own way. We aren't ready for marriage; we aren't really in the least bit interested in any of it, some of us – the rules we must obey, the men we are supposed to serve with such admiration, the physical torment they inflict upon us in the bedroom which we are expected to enjoy, the babies we are expected to bear. We don't really want these experiences, or else we do not understand how to enjoy them - but we are expected to embrace them all with enthusiasm nonetheless –

and to play the part demanded of us. We become female impersonators - every bit as bizarre as that poor fool in the music hall that evening, demeaning himself on the stage, selling all of his dignity for a few shillings a time.'

Attentive as ever, he continues to look into her face, fascinated, registering with the ever-observant eye of the painter all the subtle changes that the immediate locality and the play of light generates upon it - the rippled, glancing water dancing their reflections up onto her white skin, the net-shadows from her veil casting their webs across her face, moving as she moves or as the occasional breeze lifts the fabric, the light forever changing, moulding itself to the contours of cheek and forehead as it goes - only her eyes remaining untouched, constant in their dark intensity and youthful vigour. So very lovely. 'Well, it's an intriguing thought,' he admits, trying to reassure her with some measure of empathy.

She gives forth a long, protracted sigh. 'Oh, Amos, I think I should like it all a lot better if only it made me feel the way I do now, here with you. I am never frightened when I am with you. It's like that marvellous comforting feeling – you know, when you're just on the edge of slumber, or just waking from a glorious sleep. So calm and peaceful - like being carried away on a little boat, floating down a river, safe and yet all the time full of all sorts of exciting possibilities. That is what I feel anyway. Does that make any kind of sense at all, dear one?'

'Yes, of course.'

'But with Polly it has never been like that. It is like being violated, hunted down - until now he no longer even has the grace or decency to distinguish me from any other quarry. And all the while there is your wretched little god with his arrows - who has enchanted me all my life and yet who has only turned my heart cold it seems, so that every man I now meet seems dull and crude by comparison to you. Only what about me ... me inside? Who am I? I do not know any longer, Amos. I am caught in the middle, expected to be your model on the one hand and a trophy for my husband on the other - really just something to be hung on walls along with all the other treasures and acquisitions. I belong only to others. That is what I feel, and that is why I am so afraid – that I should care so little for my future because of it, that I no longer own my own future.'

In silence, he considers what she has told him and tries again to find a rational response that might comfort her. But it is not easy. It troubles him, too, because it seems her husband is succeeding in what he has clearly set out to do, that is to break her, to extinguish her spirit - especially during these past few weeks. Perhaps she is right. Perhaps it really is all part of some devious and unwholesome plan. She is made to feel anxious now – inadequate for not becoming a mother, for not becoming what everyone expects of her - while he, Amos, can only look on, powerless, unable to offer any remedy and instead only seeking to satisfy his own selfish craving to paint her and capture her beauty, an exercise which would seem to her in her present state to be every bit as disturbing as the designs of her husband.

'I won't ever let anything terrible happen to you - you know that, don't you,' he says, taking her hand again. 'Listen, let's finish this damn painting. Let's get it out of the way, and then, well ...'

'I know - then we can run away together!' she laughs, though it is an odd, haunted kind of laughter. 'What an odd couple we shall make. We shall grow old together in some strange far-away country, and have grey hair, and people will wonder over our secrecy or that we are alone with just each other and without children or anybody to claim our time for theirs.'

'So you *will* allow me to finish it, won't you?' he interrupts, gathering up her hair as the wind takes it and keeping it from her face - and resolving not to respond to her strange fantasy except with a smile. 'Neither of us needs to run away from anything. So enough of all this nonsense!'

'Yes, all right,' she says with untypical obedience, summoning up a smile of her own again from somewhere remote. 'And I will let you finish your masterpiece. Promise. Only I shall never give up on nonsense. Not all the time I have you to listen to me.'

'Well, that's a relief – on both counts.'

Reaching into his waistcoat pocket and glancing at his

watch, he realises their allotted time in the bathing machine is almost up – and so, in accordance with the rules, he must now take the flag given to him earlier and slot it into the little receptacle outside, so as to signal their readiness to be hauled back up onto the beach. This being accomplished, Amos closes the seaward doors and then, taking their seats inside on the broad ledge that runs around the interior, they dry their feet on the towels provided as the little journey begins. There is a sudden jolt as the wagon is hitched onto the horse and within moments they are up on the beach again and ready to leave.

Outside, where the attendant responds to Amos's generous tip with an extravagant wink of complicity - fortunately not noticed by Daphne - they discover that the beach has become altogether less crowded now, and that long shadows are beginning to engulf the bay and render it all quite dull in comparison to the warmth that shone upon the sands earlier. There is a chill in the air, and in response to which Daphne wraps herself in her shawl – a thin, plain cotton taken from around her waist as together they climb up to the promenade and walk back along the lane to the railway station, a place where they must begin their homeward journeys – which must be undertaken separately, of course. Parting is not easy, but at least it is all agreed now: Yes, she will come, she tells him. She will come to him tomorrow at noon to sit for him and his wretched painting.

'So there you are, Amos, you have what you want from me after all,' she concludes with a wistful though also somewhat rueful smile. 'You needn't have feared. It has been such a perfect day, hasn't it! I wonder, though, if we will ever have occasion to be alone again quite so often once this glorious summer is through?'

'I'm sure we will,' he insists.

'Yes,' she says. 'Only it's just that life seems so intense at the moment, like watching the sand trickling through an hour glass – you know, when it moves so quickly at the end. It all feels like that to me lately. I am so thrilled at moments, and yet so frightened all at the same time.'

At which she learns across, one hand on his shoulder and kisses him on the cheek by way of parting. 'I love you, dear one,' she whispers and, for once, it seems there is a special and altogether new level of intensity behind these familiar endearments.

Chapter Eighteen

Now Cease, my Lute

That he would think of her this night as he lay in bed is no surprise to him – for how could he do otherwise after such happiness in each other's company today! But he also wonders just how she might be feeling at this moment, alone at Parnassus in her own separate bed chamber, with her husband due back any day now and finding himself yet again denied his conjugal rights. How long would the brute put up with that! Again and again he is able to envisage her, imagine and recall her lovely face through the ever-observant faculty and memory of the artist's eye, that special inner vision that he, in the way of some ancient conjurer, is so accomplished at summoning to his command - and relishing thereby more than ever the prospect of her returning to the portrait tomorrow. Will she really come? Dear Daphne! The prospect and sweet expectation of her presence in just a few short hours the other side of the night links him to her in thought - and so it is really only a natural transition into his dreams that she continues to be here, her image playing upon his inner eye, a place where they have somehow found themselves together and alone once more in the little rowboat that they used to take up and down the river between their homes when they were young, so that behind her now there is the background of water and above this a number of white, fair-weather clouds scurrying by in the blue summer sky. He is busy at the prow of the boat, rowing but also looking towards her all the while, speaking, laughing, responding to all her smiles and fleeting glances: Daphne in all her states of metamorphosis, as all his women, in every picture he has ever done of her – as Circe and as Elaine, as Guinevere and as Ophelia, yet all blended into one eternal image.

Where are they going? he wonders. It could be any one of the many places they have loved and visited over the years, any one of the little streams and tributaries and special bays of green reeds where willows trail their branches over the sparkling water; where carp and pike hide themselves in watery hollows. It is all so familiar, yet here they are not dressed as normal but in clothes that he does not entirely remember as having ever worn. He has his cap still, but it is somehow different, very flat, he senses, and perched on his head at a jaunty angle. And then he is aware out of the corner of his eye of the tip of a plume of some kind attached to it - and yet it all feels perfectly ordinary to him, perfectly natural to be wearing such things. She, meanwhile, has no hat or bonnet at all but instead a delicate jewelled head-piece that, unlike today at the beach, succeeds this time in securing her hair against the breeze and keeps it drawn back, away from her face. The dress she wears is of a beautiful golden colour, trimmed with purple and crimson brocade and has a tight bodice and a curious straight neckline, almost from shoulder to shoulder – something he has never seen her wearing before. Upon her fingers, she has many precious stones and rings, far more than usual. She is very carefree and happy, and he feels so very happy, too. The sunshine on his back is warm, and the languid pulse and plash of his oars through the water so very rhythmical and reassuring, carrying him deeper and deeper into his delightful dream, so gorgeously sensual and warming of heart that he never wants it to end.

He continues to row, and as he becomes more aware of his surroundings, the broad expanse of the river and its scenery, he notices that the banks of the river are becoming quite wild, exceptionally lush and verdant. The buildings and homes that he feels should be there, moreover, the familiar houses with their manicured lawns that normally run down to the water's edge, are absent; the various safe moorings and river steps and all the other familiar landmarks of his childhood, are nowhere to be seen. Instead the only buildings visible are formal, stone-built ones: castles, churches or abbeys, while beyond these, everywhere, the wide open countryside runs unencumbered across what should be familiar roadways, bridges and railways. Why is this? What has changed? And then suddenly all the doubts vanish, and he feels perfectly at one with his surroundings, no longer needing to doubt or to question, as if he and she have never known anything else. He is no longer dreaming, he is simply there. It is like being in heaven, he thinks for one final moment before all self-consciousness vanishes.

Daphne smiles at him. They have come to rest, and he is no longer rowing because they have moored up somewhere secluded. Here it is shady and pleasantly cool - the trees with their long weeping bows and finery of leaves overhanging them. He is holding a stringed instrument, which he knows is called a lute, and this he begins to play upon. It is the most marvellous feeling to be able to do this, to have such finesse, such dexterity and natural ability at his command, so that his accomplished fingers work instinctively, without his conscious effort, powerful, creating the most beautiful sonorous chords and melodies without the slightest effort - the most enchanting music he has ever heard. And when, with gentle and lilting voice she sings to his accompaniment it is like a choir of angels - the words belonging to songs or poems intoned in a language that, though sometimes familiar, is yet strangely unlike what he understands as English. He also has the sensation that the words she sings are *his* words, and that he has made them for her. He is a poet, and a singer and a musician. He has arms strong enough to row a boat, and yet fingers delicate and skilled enough to accompany her in song. He is a proud, swaggering young man, tall and sturdy, overflowing with strength and desire.

In a moment his song is completed. Something has altered. It feels suddenly less sunny, less warm. The afternoon has turned towards evening and a more urgent breeze ruffles the canopy of leaves about them. 'Will you take me home?' she asks him, still seated in the stern of the little rowboat, but with a wide-brimmed bonnet and a cloak now about her shoulders wrapped against the chill of the evening. And he agrees, without urgency, however, for there is all the time in the world. But then suddenly it becomes very dark indeed, and when he hears her voice again it is more insistent and just a little tinged with urgency. 'Will you take me home now, dear one?' she asks him again. And when he looks around he finds himself back in the Chapel at The Tower of London, back in Saint Peter ad Vincula – he recognises it instantly and can even smell the dank odours and incense of the interior there. By the meagre glow of a solitary lamp, he sees that he is with his sister Margaret and two other men, bearded, with caps like his own, jewelled and opulent and whose faces seem kindly and yet are strangers to him. Together he and the men lift the long wooden box, an arrow chest of elm wood, from the ground and carry it upon their shoulders from the Chapel. It is very dark outside, without a moon, and they are guided towards the river stairs by a soldier whose face reminds him of the ghostly Yeoman Warder with whom he had sat that evening when he was called in to sketch the bones that were discovered here. And as they reach the steps, all dank and awash with the black tide of the river, and as they load the box onto a nearby barge that is waiting already on the water, he hands the gentleman a small purse of coins before jumping on board the vessel itself. And then he is rowing once again, but this time together with the other men. They stay close to the riverside, the dark inky channel of the Thames, down beside the creaking hulls of great vessels and ships whose companies are all asleep and waiting sail, along to a place he knows is called Deptford, where they moor at the foot of yet more stairs. The arrow chest is again lifted and carried upon their shoulders to a wagon which takes them through silent midnight streets and lanes until he finds himself inside another building, feeling safe and secure within a house that he knows belongs to his sister and her husband.

Time passes and then it is daylight and he is riding on horseback alongside the wagon with the arrow chest again, this time covered by some kind of tarpaulin to disguise its presence. It is a long and solemn journey, shrouded in secrecy that seems to endure forever, through days and nights, along further rivers and yet more roadways, all merging, one into the other. Nobody speaks, or if they do it is but rarely. All are stony-faced, silent and dedicated to the enterprise of taking the arrow chest to its rightful destination. Already they are far away from London, and again night has fallen. Ahead, he can just detect the outline of a church at the end of a lane, upon a slight mound of a hill set amid flat fens and wide horizons, a place surrounded by yew trees - themselves much darker than the starry sky - and a graveyard adjacent all bristling with stones, crosses and monuments, all ancient with time, some fallen, others leaning. Inside the building, meanwhile, a hasty service is being performed, discretely with only a few candles and no choir. There is no playing of music or chanting of hymns - but merely the pale moonlight through tiny arched windows of stone mullions whose colours are all turned grey with the darkness outside, and with the priest muttering his prayers and conducting the mass so quietly, almost in silence. It is unfamiliar and disturbing, not as he expected at all - everything so forbidden, everything furtive, secretive and edged with danger.

The arrow chest is then taken away to a place where it will be safe for all time - a place ordered by a noble family struck by misfortune and tragedy - but still a better place, for all that, than where they had laid her before. He has taken her home, exactly as she had requested of him, and all is well. All is well. And he wakes from his dream for a moment in tears before falling once again into a deep and blissful slumber where he hears the half-familiar words whispered gently as if through leaves of rustling trees:

Now cease, my lute! This is the last
Labour, that thou and I shall waste,
And end that I have now begun:
Now is this song both sung and past,
My lute! Be still, for I have done.

The morning comes; a blackbird is singing outside his half-open casement of his bedroom window – piping up so loudly that it almost splits his ears! Already, the dream is fading and half-lost now amid the glorious sunshine. Yet he does not want to lose touch with it. Not yet. Ignoring for now the rituals of the morning routine, the jug of warm water and towels already set out for him by Beth in the hallway, he wanders down and into the garden instead, clad only in his dressing gown. The sun is still low but gaining in strength and vigour, already pleasantly warm. It feels like he has not been to bed at all, but has returned instead from a special tryst, a night with a very special friend or lover, and there is a sense of excitement and intrigue that still thrills in his heart and allows him to feel strangely intoxicated, like the sensation of being in love mingled with the sweet torment of being parted from the object of ones affection. How wonderful. And yet it had been only a dream. Only a dream.

Gradually, a sense of anticipation takes over. It is going to be another glorious summer's day, and – even better – there is Daphne's portrait waiting - so much to look forward to! And with these expectations driving him forward, he returns to the cottage and his bedroom, washes and dresses, wanders back down into the dining room and takes his seat for breakfast. Beth has prepared a feast this morning - and at his invitation joins him for a pot of tea afterwards.

Noticing Daphne's book of verse on the table, and knowing full well he had placed it elsewhere yesterday before retiring he realises with a sense of growing curiosity that Beth must have been looking at it herself. Upon checking with her, she replies, 'Oh yes Sir, I hope you don't mind. I love this little book. It is one that I would read when I was in service in New Eltham – that's where I used to work before I came to you, as you recall. They had it in the library. I could not sleep last night, and so I lit a candle and came out here to read.'

'I didn't realise you could read – I mean poetry,' he says, and immediately realises he is sounding pompous. Why should she not read poetry!

'Oh, I love this one, Sir!' she remarks with a little giggle of excitement, leafing rapidly through the pages with the confidence of one who knows its contents intimately and can always locate the place in question. But on looking up to meet his eyes, she seems suddenly anxious, that she should be troubling him with such trivial matters instead of getting on with some proper household business or chore instead. But he is not cross; he smiles, pours a little more tea for himself and – to her astonishment – some for her as well, and then with a nod by way of encouragement in her direction indicates that she should read. And this she does, in a completely natural, accomplished and fluent manner.

'It is called 'Isabello; or, The Pot of Basil, by John Keats,' she announces:

> 'And she forgot the stars, the moon, and the sun,
> And she forgot the blue above the trees,
> And she forgot the dells where waters run,
> And she forgot the chilly autumn breeze;
> She had no knowledge when the day was done,
> And the new morn she saw not: but in peace
> Hung over her sweet Basil evermore,
> And moistened it with tears unto the core.'

Noticing that he does not respond right away, she fills the silence hastily with: 'I think it is lovely, the lady's devotion to one who has passed away. And I like the basil because it reminds me of cooking. And Mr Keats visited the Island, too, so I think it is one of my favourites in the whole book.'

'Very fine, very fine,' he declares at length and, although he could hardly say it was one of his personal favourites, still he remains impressed and he can only marvel at how well she has read it. And then, noticing a bookmark protruding from the pages he takes the little volume from her and opens it there – only to discover, to his astonishment, the very same lines he had heard in his dream. *My lute! Be still, for I have done.* He had not inserted the bookmark in this place himself, so it must have been Beth who had done so.

'Were you reading this last night?' he questions her.

'Yes Sir,' she answers, leaning across to check or to remind herself. 'Yes, that's a lovely one, too, isn't it!' she continues with a renewed flurry of vivacity and pleasure. 'There is quite a few from Tudor times. They're wonderful.'

He does not remark on her observations straight away. He wants to evade the subject now because it is bringing him back more and more to the night, and abruptly he feels he has had quiet enough of it. Yet even here in the harsh light of day, even now he cannot quite let go. Dreams and the waking world are all beginning to merge as one to him. Most disconcerting.

Glancing out the window and suddenly anxious to change the subject, he rubs his hands and declares, 'Look, what a lovely morning it is going to be, Beth. I am going to be at work on the painting with Lady Daphne, who is to arrive at noon. So if you wish you can take the day off and do some sightseeing. How would you like that? You can take the book of verse with you if you like.'

Beth needs little persuading to such a venture, but does not wish to take the book - because, as she says, Lady Bowlend might wish to have it back. It is hers, after all; and he is compelled to agree, amazed at how often he seems to be in agreement with his maid, who has more common sense at moments than it seems he could ever aspire to. He watches her clear away the dishes, watches her as she returns with a little vase of freshly cut lilies with green fronds of maidenhair which she places on the table - and within minutes she is dressed in her best clothes and off on her day's adventure - with a smile on her face and with just the faintest hint, he fancies, of complicity in her eyes as she goes, as one who, knowingly and with tact, must withdraw from the scene – allowing lovers to be alone.

The appointed hour comes at midday but it is still some time before Daphne puts in an appearance, ringing the door bell and waiting in the shelter of the porch in the light rain that has just begun to fall until he comes to open it himself and to show her in.

'No maid to answer the door to you today,' he announces by way of explanation as he takes Daphne's cloak and umbrella himself and ushers her through to where he has already set everything in readiness for the work he intends to do this afternoon - in the conservatory this time, as the light is quite dull elsewhere. 'Though I reckon poor Beth is going to get a drenching if she's out for any length of time in this,' he adds. 'That'll be my fault because I did suggest she take the afternoon off.'

'Oh, don't worry,' Daphne says with a grin. 'I saw her down at the bay sitting in the tea rooms - in the company of a rather handsome young man, as a matter of fact.'

'Young man? Handsome! What do you mean?' he demands with some consternation, a reaction which encourages Daphne's smile to become even broader.

'Why Mister Roselli! I do believe you might be just the tiniest bit jealous,' she declares with mock astonishment, raising her eyebrows and imitating his own troubled voice with uncanny accuracy. Clearly in high spirits, she is wearing one of her lovely arts-inspired gowns, loose, silky and unwaisted and with a simple straight line descending from the shoulders, suitably liberal and free-flowing - as if the dress itself is able to express all of her feelings - and all of her laughter let loose as well. 'I'm afraid you cannot expect Beth to be here alone all these weeks and not attract some attention from the local lads,' she adds, admonishing him still further. 'How very unreasonable of you! She is a fine young girl, and someone will be snapping her up soon enough, don't you worry.'

He is angry with himself now, embarrassed that he has let his feelings show.

'I'm not worried,' he insists. 'I'm not in the least bit worried. It's just that ... well, I need her.'

'Oh yes, you need her; we all know that! You need her to make your breakfast, to sweep out the ashes from that big black stove in the corner there, and to wash and change your linen. But that is not the most attractive of prospects for a bright young person like Beth. I'm afraid, you can't keep all your women forever, Amos, like some permanent harem around you: all your female admirers that you never satisfy!'

He feels his back stiffen with indignation. This is getting

worse and worse. What on earth could she mean by that last remark? She also seems slightly incoherent, he thinks, and he wonders, too, whether she has been drinking or taking laudanum already, so early in the day. Meanwhile, she has wandered over to take a look at the painting fixed already in the twin uprights of its easel, awaiting what he hopes will be the final touches this afternoon. Hands on hips, she stares at it for a while, also comparing it with a number of sketches of herself scattered around, some already propped up into position for reference. And then suddenly her face drops and all her banter and good cheer vanishes. It is as if a terrible dark cloud has descended, as gloomy as those in the leaden sky outside, casting its shadow across her lovely brow.

'I seem to have already become more laurel-tree than nymph,' she says, gazing at the canvas again – and still with a look of disapproval. 'I have a face, yes, and it is as good a likeness as any - but the rest of me is almost vanished, look!'

'Emm, you may be right,' he admits. 'I reckon it probably needs more of your lovely bare shoulders restored to it, don't you?'

Responding to this suggestion almost instantly, she slips off her dress and throws it over a chair, not in the least bit self-conscious, clad now only in her petticoat - her corset and chemise clearly visible beneath - a particularly appealing combination of pale-blue satin with fine white lace, tight-waisted and exceptionally supportive of her cleavage. He cannot recollect her ever wearing such extravagant and seductive clothing before when modelling for him. Nor is it altogether logical, he thinks, for her to be tightly corseted when she was a moment ago wearing such a loose-fitting dress. He offers her a towel to wrap around herself for comfort and modesty, but this she declines – dashing it away with her hand and instead setting herself straight-away down onto the somewhat threadbare chaise lounge and into the familiar position she knows he wants of her, with arms above her head. She does it all so naturally, without needing to be prompted: the perfect artist's model still. But she seems particularly feisty today, he thinks. How odd!

For a while he works in silence, mixing, testing his colours, observing with satisfaction the exact level of pathos he is looking for in her face and which seems so natural to her. Excellent. And to be alone with her like this is simply a delight.

'Aren't you going to tie me up again today,' she asks, her voice rather languid he senses, referring he realises to the last occasion when she needed the assistance of a strip of gauze to keep her arms suspended and stretched on high for such a lengthy period.

'No, not today, he replies, more preoccupied with her face in the painting and indicating, therefore, with a gesture of his working hand that she can lower her arms, anyway. 'Not unless you really want me to, that is.'

'Don't worry, I'm not that kind of girl,' she counters straight away and, dropping her shoulders quickly she emits a strange little sigh of despair. 'Though I sometimes rather suspect that my husband would like me to be!'

'Really! Another one of his quirky ways?'

'I believe so.'

'Hence the mistresses. Emm, do you really think it's all true – these rumours?'

'Oh yes, they're true. But, as I said the other day, they are not just mistresses, Amos. That is far too grand a term for them. Heaven only knows what terrible diseases he is exposing himself to, and me of course when he returns home from his antics. Oh God! You know, if I felt I was going to be syphilitic, if I felt that was going to happen, I would rather not go on. I would top myself. I would want to die rather than go through something so frightful as that. You've been to those museums, haven't you? – the anatomy museums where they have all those unspeakable things in jars of formaldehyde and those horrid wax models to demonstrate the effects of venereal disease – the sores, the pus, the ugly bloated faces. And then what about the loss of hearing and sight! They say you go mad, don't they, before your joints seize up and your skin begins to rot? I sometimes wonder about Polly – his sanity – because he is so radically changed of late – so aggressive, so unreasonable! I had thought it was all down to that fall from the horse, the blow that he took earlier in the year – remember? But perhaps there is more to it than that. I'm afraid I just don't know how long he has been carrying on like this, you see. Maybe he is ill, seriously ill already: the wages of sin and all that. And it will be my turn next!'

'Now, now, don't you go getting yourself all upset again,' he admonishes her. 'You are wonderfully well, perfectly healthy and very lovely.'

Downing tools for a moment, he urges her once again to relax and sit back while he goes off to fetch some champagne.

'What are we celebrating?' she asks as he returns, the bottle proudly resting in its ice bucket, though in this instance containing only moderately chilled water from the cellar.

'The completion of your portrait, of course!' he declares as he pops the cork 'We really are almost at the finishing post!'

She sips gratefully at the cool, sparkling drink, while he persists in his work just a little longer with a very fine sable brush, working with considerable finesse by this stage, applying the thinnest of glazes on the flesh-tones and referring also just for a moment to one of the sketches nearby – done some years ago, in fact, but useful now for the current work. It is just a matter of final adjustments now, he tells her as he works on in silence, revealing more of her shoulders in the composition, as suggested. Just a little more.

'Polly will be returning this evening,' she announces a little later, her voice deep and suitably foreboding, observing him closely over the brim of her glass as he works. 'I shall have to go back to the house in an hour or two, to prepare.'

'Pity ... but look, we're more or less done now. Come on - tell me what you think of it.'

Rising from her seat, a little unsteady on her feet, she steps up alongside to examine the painting, leaning a hand upon his shoulder and giving an approving nod.

'All done - and you have survived it, after all,' he reminds her a little ruefully as he breaks away to take a sip of his own champagne at last.

'So far – but you have yet to hand it over to he who commissioned it,' she adds, serious now as she turns away from him to look out of the windows. 'Then he will own me entirely, body and soul.'

There is nothing he can say to this. She is clearly aware

that it has been her husband's idea, all these additional elements added to the new portrait – sinister ones, as she would perceive them – and so she is allowing herself to be scared by it all over again. But then all at once she seems to alter. She kicks off her shoes and wanders further along the length of the conservatory, champagne glass still in hand and relishing the sensation of the warm flagstones upon her feet it seems while examining with a critical eye still more of the sketches laid thereabouts of her own face and also one of her torso, naked which she takes up and looks at as she walks back towards him along the length of the room.

'Do you have any idea, Amos, what it is like to be naked and to model for an artist? I can tell you it has been the most liberating of all experiences. To have a man look without judgement upon all those parts that I as a woman must hide from the world. How lovely it has been over the years! To have had moments of being almost divine in somebody's eyes. Such a contrast to the present business of marriage. I imagined it would all be quite thrilling, you see, married life. I thought of my body as some kind of musical instrument that was wanting only for a skilled musician to come and play upon. But then I married Polly. I married an ape who can only pound on the keys and make a din. The body that I once was so proud to own because of you is now something I loath because it is taken and lusted after by him, to be mauled and drooled over with wet, disgusting kisses and foul breath. I cannot reconcile the two experiences, you see, and I don't suppose I ever shall. I am afraid it has been such a shock that it is quite enough to turn one mad. And now you have given him my soul as well in this painting. I am lost now ... completely lost, don't you see?'

And then suddenly he realises she is crying, quickly turning her back on him completely in a bid to hide the fact, her little shoulders shuddering with the misery of it all as she throws the sketch down on the window ledge.

'I'm so very sorry,' he says, coming up behind her and taking her hand, urging her to turn to face him – and upon which she becomes unusually bold and insistent in her movements, turning and holding on to his sleeves, clutching the fabric tightly in her hands.

'Oh Amos, it is hardly your fault! Come on ... come here!' she urges him in a strangely whining voice, tugging at his sleeves as she brings him to the long, chintz-covered seat, where she almost hauls him down alongside her, a place from which she rests her head upon his shoulder and sobs away, so desperately that he feels powerless to stem the tide - and with a need for the comfort of his touch which is amazing to him. Rarely has he ever felt that intimacy of hers, so desiring of his physical presence. He places an arm completely around her therefore, and here they remain for some time, silent except for her fitful sobbing and full of care for each other.

'Oh dear, look!' She exclaims softly under her breath once the tears have abated a little. She has spilt some drink on her petticoat and so she gets to her feet and simply peels off the garment in one carefree sweep of the arm, leaving herself in her corset and chemise beneath, bare-legged, her body animated by an involuntary shudder of pleasure that seems to ripple through her entire frame before taking up her glass again and draining it.

Amos watches her lovely throat and mouth as she imbibes, one hand on her hip, her long neck arching back so she might strain ever last drop of intoxication from the vessel. Yes, he has seen her without clothes before, naked before – in fact more times than he or she would probably care to admit to any stranger - only the way she looks now, half-undressed, seems to him more risqué somehow than mere nakedness. More naked than naked.

Curious, and recalling some words she spoke earlier he asks her: 'Daphne, what did you mean ... just now, about never satisfying any of my women. That was what you said, wasn't it? I'll have you know I have had a number of very encouraging reports over the years ...'

'Did I say that? Oh Silly!' she croons, returning to the seat and sliding back into his arms. 'Only you do rather fancy yourself, don't you, dear one - so aloof!' she adds bringing her face and her lovely dark eyes so close to his. 'That's why I am trying to be your tart today. I am teasing you. Only you cannot see that even now. I am telling you that there is no requirement for you to live like a monk here on the island just because you are parted from all your loose women in London. Foolish boy! You could have your wicked way here, I'm certain - with Beth, for example. She's utterly devoted to you. You could have your wicked way with me, too. It doesn't matter now, because I am no longer your sacred muse, Amos. I am just a woman of the world, and I am already quite corrupted. The worst of it is I don't think I entirely object to the idea of being corrupted sometimes - by the right person I'm still convinced it could be quite thrilling.'

She glances up at him just then and again he returns her gaze, looking deeply into her eyes. He has never heard her speak in quite that kind of dissolute way, this new creature of physicality there before him. He becomes intrigued and suddenly immensely curious about the new Daphne, while all the time feeling an inevitable sadness and tug of regret for the one who has somehow vanished, the one who might never return.

'Do you remember what we used to do together when we were young?' she whispers, seeming to be looking inward for a moment, as though the recollection had just occurred to her. 'I mean with each other - our little games?'

He knows what she means, and it is a bit shocking that she should bring it up. 'Yes,' he replies, 'but that was a long time ago. Anyway, young people always do that kind of thing ...'

'Yes, but we could do it again, couldn't we - now!' she continues to urge him, not much interested in his protestations - and glancing up at him once more with those incredible dark eyes, larger and more inviting than ever, framed by those glorious long black lashes of hers. 'Why don't you just kiss me?' she whispers.

There is no answer to this - because he wants to kiss her, and so without another word he does, lingering for some time, and it is sweet. He has never kissed her in this way before, full on the mouth, at least not for many a year, and the shape and sensation, the moisture and revealed secrets of her lips is thrilling to him. Moreover, it brings him back to a recollection of that dream he had not too long ago, the dream in which his kiss was to restore her soul to her - so that for a moment he is there again in the deserted home of his youth, amid all the dried leaves on the floor, the shredded curtains flying in the half-opened windows and the moonlight in the garden beyond. How delightful!

'Do something nice to me, dear one,' she murmurs. 'Give my body something lovely to hold in my memory. He's back this evening, and you know what that means; what I might have to endure in just a few hours from now. It's so awful. I need to have a memory from today while I'm lying there – something lovely to dwell upon. Do you understand?'

He does. He is suddenly aware of just how much his own body is tempted to oblige. And yet even now he knows there is something not entirely right about what is happening. If it were any other woman he would not have minded - not one bit. He would have read the signals, known she was ripe for the taking and would have installed her naked in his bed by now. But here with Daphne something is wrong; some primal instinct of self-preservation is urging him against it, and she seems to sense this, too.

'You don't have to take me to bed,' she whispers more insistent now, as if reading his thoughts like a sorceress, unbuttoning his shirt so that he can feel her trembling, uncertain palm upon his chest, and already one leg hooked over his as, instinctively, they twist their bodies further towards each other. 'Oh, come on! No one will know,' she whispers. 'We can just do it here now, here in this lovely warm room under the sky. Look at us! We're done for now, anyway. What would anyone think if they were to come in now and see us like this - me half undressed; an empty champagne bottle and ...'

But just at that moment she falls silent. Abruptly, she sits up straight, staring ahead as she points vaguely with one unsteady finger towards the windows and the wet, misty garden beyond and says, 'Amos is there somebody out there? In the garden, *look!*'

He does look, even getting to his feet in some alarm – knowing, indeed, that it would look pretty incriminating, should anybody discover them thus.

'Can't see anybody,' he replies, approaching the French doors, which are steamed up somewhat. 'I don't have the key on me, damn it. I can't get out there.'

'Oh God! This is what I feared,' she cries, getting to her feet also and crossing her arms across her chest - a futile exercise in modesty, since she is already running around barefoot in one of the most exquisite and seductive corsets ever fashioned by human design. 'Polly might be away but he will have one of the servants spy on me. They are all against me - all of them. I will have to go, Amos. You will take me home, won't you.'

'What? Why did you say that?' he demands, suddenly, his heart pounding, disconcerted by her turn of phrase which has brought his extraordinary dream of last night back to him with a vengeance - so many diverse dreams now, all crowding in on him at once.

'Why, what's wrong with asking you to do that?' she snaps, genuinely upset now. 'Oh never mind, I can find my own way back!' she adds, grabbing her petticoat and dress and clambering into them with haste - dreadfully unbalanced, and clearly the worse for drink, and snatching up her book of verse as well to take home with her, while Amos continues to rub the mist from the windows and to peer out, still seeing nothing much at all, however, other than the swirling sheets of drizzle and the scarlet drifts of flowers, begonia and dahlias all drooping in the wet garden.

And within moments, before he can even finish his inspection of the outside, or locate a key to unlock the doors, she is gone. He hears the sound of her heels clattering along the hallway; the front door slams and suddenly the house is silent - a silence, however, that is soon filled because just a few moments later, as ill luck would have it, the rain comes on apace and beats down - so loudly upon the glass roof above him that he knows she will be drenched in no time. There is a flash of lightening next, moreover, followed very closely by a clap of thunder, indicating that a full-blown storm is soon to be upon them. For a moment he considers rushing out after her - but there is nothing to be gained by that, of course. It would only create a scene and consequently land her even deeper in trouble should anyone notice. Instead, amid the noise of the downpour, he resigns himself to the task of tidying up, removing the excess paint from his palette, cleaning his brushes - all the while trying to make sense of what had just happened, or *nearly happened*. Something inside had told him it was wrong - and then suddenly he understands what it would have been. Could this, in fact, have been little more than a brazen, desperate attempt on her part to become pregnant, to produce a child for Oliver Ramsey – and with him, Amos, to provide the seed? Yes, of course! It comes as a chilling and sobering revelation to him now. And as he sits himself down once more on the chaise lounge to contemplate its implications, he is not entirely sure it is to his liking. It is almost as if the woman who had been with him in this room a moment ago had not been the Daphne he knows and loves at all, but some dreadful impersonator, devious and cunning. What could possibly have possessed her to attempt such a thing?

But just then the hairs on the back of his neck begin to creep and he becomes acutely aware that he is being watched, stared at. He turns quickly and Daphne herself is there, standing outside in the rain, staring at him through the glass. Without the key still he cannot let her in but only stares back at her, waving to her instead, imploring her to come back around to the front again. But she does not move, not one bit, but simply continues to stare. She is as pale as he has ever seen her. And her eyes are bloodshot - so red. And then he realises, as best he can through the misty window with the raindrops pouring down its surface, that her eyes are not just simply bloodshot. The sockets of her eyes are turning to blood.

'Daphne!' he cries and shrinks back from the awful spectre - and then he runs. He runs from the windowed room, runs through the house to the front door, runs out into the driving rain, around the house to the rear and the conservatory, his heart pounding in his chest like it would burst - runs upon the slippery paving stones to where the dreadful apparition was standing just a few moments ago in the soaking garden, terrified of what he will find but unable to hold himself back from looking. But no one is there. No one!

'Daphne!' he cries, wanting the sound to be louder than it is but discovering that it cannot escape his throat which has become so tight now he can scarcely draw breath anyway.

'Sir! Sir!' a young voice calls from a distance. And suddenly Beth it there, rushing around the corner of the building and into the garden, her presence lit by a sudden flash of lightening in the gloom, her umbrella held aloft - though this she quickly hurls away as she reaches him - thrusting out both her arms instead to hold him tightly by his wrists. 'Sir, what is wrong?' she asks, her face agitated, full of concern.

'Lady Daphne? Where is she?' he cries.

'She got back safely, Sir, don't worry. I just saw her home myself. We met down the lane.'

Utterly distraught, soaked to the skin, almost paralysed with terror and hardly able to stand any longer, let alone walk, he leans on the young woman as she guides him back round to the porch and the open front door, which is loose and swinging in the wind, her umbrella once more in her hand and held above him all the while as if to offer protection - something which even then strikes him as faintly ludicrous, that she should protect him! Inside, she continues to fuss, however; she guides him - shivering uncontrollably now - to the settee in the parlour, fetches some dry towels, puts some tinder and a log on the fire and in time is able to prepare some hot tea - as, bit by bit, he begins to gather himself and to explain what has happened. She listens patiently, remaining with him while he sips at his tea until, through her presence and occasional conversation, some degree of welcome normality is gradually restored.

'Do not be anxious, Sir, All is well,' she says in a voice of remarkable maturity, he thinks - and which is somehow immensely reassuring.

He notices a little drop of rainwater that falls from her hair as she is standing there, and realises for the first time that she must have received quite a drenching as well. 'Your hair ... it's all wet,' he murmurs, getting to his feet as if surprised, reaching out to her and holding a wayward strand of red hair between his fingers. Embarrassed, she tries to ignore him. But he takes a towel and bids her to be seated, pulling up a free chair for her into the centre of the room and where he gently dries her hair, so bedraggled, caressing away the nest of tiny red tangles that the rain has made of it.

'Sir, I do not think it right that I should receive this attention,' she whispers sitting bolt upright. 'It is I who should be helping you.'

'Daphne's hair was not wet at all, Beth,' he murmurs, realising that he is still in a state of shock and that his own voice is probably sounding distracted and rather weird. 'How is that possible? She was out there in that downpour, but her hair was dry. And her eyes ... ' at which he breaks off and lets forth a cry of anguish, so that straight-away Beth is up on her feet again looking at him with such pity, he notices, so that he feels embarrassed.

'I am fine, Beth,' he says, holding forth a reassuring palm, the towel draped around his neck so that he looks not unlike a boxer, stunned, coming from the ring. 'Do not be alarmed, please. And I would be grateful if you would not repeat what you have seen or heard here today, not to anybody.'

She agrees of course. And a little later, once she is satisfied that he is fully recovered from whatever has so disturbed him, once he is settled in his armchair and appears at last to be gently falling into a merciful sleep, she finally tip-toes upstairs and puts on some dry clothes herself. She then returns down to the conservatory where, amid the sounds of raindrops still falling loudly on the roof and the occasional distant rumble of thunder she gathers up the champagne bottle and empty glasses from the floor, and slowly steers her mind back to more mundane things – namely considering what she should do next by way of preparations for an evening meal. But then for a moment she is unpleasantly reminded of the whole terribly upsetting episode again when she discovers a reflection of one of his sketches, a portrait, head and shoulders, which has been propped up near to the easel. A remarkable likeness in coloured chalk, there it is: the face of Lady Bowlend looking out at her, reflected upon the glass of the window - while at the same time, outside in the garden itself, some bright scarlet begonias have conspired to merge with the image of the face. And it is clear to Beth now that this must have been the source of his hallucination. Prudently, she lays the sketch down, so that its spectral presence will no longer appear in the glass should he return, and then she gets on with her duties in the kitchen, working in silence as best she can so as not to wake him, looking in every once in a while to make sure he is safe, her face full of concern, watching over him like some hovering angel, fearing for him now more than ever.

Chapter Nineteen

The Magician

Everyone is excited. Tennyson is to do a reading in the library of his home nearby, followed by a walk up to the beacon on High Down, the most elevated point of the cliffs above Freshwater. It is to be staged just for friends and acquaintances, he has announced - though he will also be holding a collection later to be set aside for a certain charitable cause in the village involving a needy widow. Guests are expected to contribute whatever they deem appropriate, according to their means. It is as simple as that and quite spontaneous. Mindful of the fine weather and that there is to be a degree of outdoor activity involved, Amos chooses a light flannel suit with jacket instead of a regular coat. Beth lays it out for him, ready and waiting in his room after breakfast along with a freshly laundered shirt.

'You will make a fine valet yet!' Amos says, a little quip in response to her busying herself to make certain he has everything he needs for the big occasion.

She often takes it upon herself to help him these days, making herself useful where once his valet would have fulfilled the duty – a daily routine that she would undertake to ensure that all was well with his attire and during which, once the shirt and collar were ironed and laid out, she would return to him and attend to minor details, to assist perhaps with the securing of a cufflink, or the pin in the cravat or tie that he might have fixed imperfectly in his haste to be up and away. It amuses him, that she should bother. She is becoming quite a capable and clever girl, he decides; and Daphne was right enough in what she said the other day, that it will not be easy to keep her. After all, she is no ordinary maid. She can read exceptionally well, for one thing, and write - and is far better at the arithmetic of the household than he will ever be! She is over-qualified for all the menial tasks she must do, he thinks, and she probably deserves better - thoughts that provoke an untypical feeling of anxiety in him for just a moment: that one day she will no longer be here.

'I hope I am not fussing, Sir,' she says in her usual cheerful and simple way. 'It's just that it reminds me of one of your paintings - one that you have back at Mornington Terrace.'

'Oh really, which one is that?' he inquires, gaining interest.

'One of those that you never sold …'

'Well, there are quite a few of those, Beth, he reminds her with a dismal smile.

'No, the one about olden-days, in the castle, with the knight about to set forth to look for a dragon or to go into battle - I'm not sure exactly, Sir, where he is off to in the picture - but anyway, there he is in all his mail and armour and there is a young lady who is leaning over a stairway and fixing her token to his arm as he goes. Well, I think that is what I do when I make everything ready for you, knowing I have played a part in whatever you are going out to do. Does that sound silly?'

He smiles and regards her closely for a moment, aware of her proximity, the gentle sounds of her breathing, her clothing, rustling as she moves about the silent room, the subtle fragrance of lily of the valley that surrounds her at times. She is, to be sure, a fine replacement for the dour attentions of his former valet James. And he is forced to ask himself, therefore: might this all just be a shade inappropriate, a serving maid performing such intimate duties? Yes, perhaps it is. Do I mind, he asks himself - do I care much for the consequences or what other people might think should they for a moment be able to see through these walls and observe what is going on? No, not at all. It is all perfectly delightful, he concludes as, once again this morning he stands in front of the long, full-length mirror in its oak frame and thrusts out his chin proudly to receive her blandishments, which today includes a small purple heliotrope for his lapel, presented with a little giggle of merriment as she reaches up on her toes to secure it quickly into place. Would she have known the significance of the flower that turns its face always to the sun – the heliotrope, for devotion and faithfulness? After Daphne's schooling, probably yes.

'You are going along, too, I hope, Beth?' he asks. 'To Tennyson's reading, I mean.'

'Me Sir! Oh, may I?'

'Yes, of course. I would like you to, and I am certain that Lady Bowlend, also, would wish you to accompany us on such a special occasion.'

'Oh, but what shall I wear, Sir?' she asks, suddenly less sure of herself and wringing her hands a little. He always finds it amusing, the way her emotions can swerve and vary so swiftly from one moment to the next.

'Why, you have a lovely cambric dress, don't you, the one you wore the other evening? That is also quite suitable for a summer's day – and Lady Bowlend will lend you a smart new parasol, I'm sure, for it is likely to be a hot walk up to the downs.'

'Yes, it surely will be, Sir.' she agrees. 'And I have modified my dress and sewn some flounces and ribbons into the skirt lately.'

'That's right, for I have noticed you at work on it with the sewing machine,' he affirms with suitable enthusiasm for the poor rag she is forever altering with every little scrap of lace or ribbon she can find in the haberdashery or second-hand clothes shops. She looks so pleased at his approval, and it is with a flurry of genuine and irrepressible excitement that she hurries to her own room to make herself ready.

And thus the preparations for the great event continue until by around midday they are able to go along to Parnassus to meet Daphne – who, for her part, greets them in one of her arts-inspired, loose-fitting garments, rustic of hue with panels of beige and lilac satin and tied at the waist with a wide belt of brocade. Here, Beth chooses a smart parasol to her liking from among Daphne's collection, and then all three together stroll the short distance along to Farringford, up the graceful curving drive of cedar and willow to the home of the Poet Laureate and where, inside, sherry and wine are already being served - or tea for those of a milder persuasion, for it is hardly afternoon yet – and where everyone eventually gathers in the darkened library and settles down into various chairs, settees or nests of cushions in good time for the reading. Watts and his new wife are here, he notices - both loyal admirers - and the parish vicar too, along with many other dignitaries from local society.

Written over forty years previously, the poem that Tennyson is to recite today is his famous *Lady of Shalott*. Beloved and celebrated pictorially by so many of Amos's most successful contemporaries from the artistic world such as Morris, Holman Hunt and Rossetti, it is one of the works to have made the poet a household name. An entire generation has marvelled at it, spoken of it and speculated over its meaning. Amos is also well aware that the Lady of Shalott is a poem that has fascinated and captivated the attention of Daphne throughout much of her life. And he loves it too.

Tennyson is advanced in years now, with a full long beard and still a figure of considerable dignity and charm to all who encounter him, so that as he makes his entrance from the hallway this afternoon in a formal black suit and with a theatrical bow to the audience everyone falls immediately silent and watches as he takes his seat upon a tall, finely carved, straight-backed chair, sitting upright, his hands placed upon his knees. He does not need to bother with a script, of course. He has read his famous poem aloud in public on countless occasions, and its familiar lines roll forth as naturally from his lips as if he were talking to a gathering of friends – only with an astonishing, robust and drum-like rhythm to his voice as he intones his words with such gravitas that all who are gathered in this room today are immediately under his spell.

Unnoticed and almost invisible in the semi-darkened room, Daphne, seated on a cushion at floor level beside Amos's chair, leans across and takes his hand, and by the intensity or otherwise of her touch he immediately senses those passages that conjure up the most meaning for her as, together, already entranced by the great magician, they continue to listen with rapt attention to the story of the lady on her island in the river, condemned to observe the world not through a window, but instead by reflected images in a mirror:

> *And moving through a mirror clear*
> *That hangs before her all the year,*
> *Shadows of the world appear.*
> *Then she sees the highway near*
> *Winding down to Camelot,*

... until soon it is as if they are there, transported into the presence of the Lady as she sits weaving at her loom and subsequently discovers the beauteous knight outside her window, passing down towards the fabled castle of Camelot. They share with her the very moment when her destiny changes. The mirror through which she has hitherto viewed the world suddenly breaks, the rules that have governed her for so long are forgotten, overwhelmed by the all-consuming reality which she now turns to behold with her own eyes - and nothing, for her, will ever be quite the same again:

> *She left the web, she left the loom,*
> *She made three paces through the room,*
> *She saw the water-lily bloom,*
> *She saw the helmet and the plume,*
> *She look'd down to Camelot.*
> *Out flew the web and floated wide;*
> *The mirror crack'd from side to side;*
> *"The curse is come upon me," cried*
> *The Lady of Shalott.*
>
> *In the stormy east-wind straining,*
> *The pale yellow woods were waning,*
> *The broad stream in his banks complaining.*
> *Heavily the low sky raining*
> *Over tower'd Camelot;*
> *Down she came and found a boat*
> *Beneath a willow left afloat,*

And around about the prow she wrote
The Lady of Shalott.

The minutes pass, and as the final stanzas take the tragic lady along the river in her boat of death, down to the fortress of the Arthurian knights and where her lifeless body is discovered to such consternation by all who dwell there, the tale reaches its strange and poignant conclusion as Lancelot, unaware of her love and devotion for him, enters the scene:

But Lancelot mused a little space
He said, "She has a lovely face;
God in his mercy lend her grace,
The Lady of Shallot.'

In the dark library at Farringford, there is only silence now, as Amos looks around at all those present. People are reclining, some their heads cast down, others looking up into space, stunned, contemplating the lines they have heard, so familiar to many, and yet so powerful still to all. It is as if he is observing the conclusion of some extraordinary living drama, almost like the aftermath of a scene of battle. Eventually, however, the old sorcerer rises and, without applause of any kind – as per instructions - leaves the room. And so, by slow degrees, everyone gets to their feet and gradually tiny threads of conversation return, becoming gradually more and more vociferous and animated until laughter joins the sighs and a certain normality is restored. What an enchanting, unique experience! What an honour it has been they all say, the popular cry. And for once he is inclined to agree.

After luncheon, they all assemble outside on the drive in readiness for the walk, some guests exchanging their fine clothes for outdoor cloaks and jackets, their fine leather shoes for stout walking boots, others defying the demands of the great outdoors completely and willing to embark upon the three-quarter-mile trek uphill dressed just as they are, in morning suits and fine silk dresses. Daphne's only concession to the elements is to don a large, floppy straw bonnet with a white veil to protect her face, and Beth does likewise, though in a somewhat more modest way in her little flat bonnet bordered with wild flowers. And here they wait, until Tennyson eventually emerges in his legendary and altogether highly unseasonable cloak and black hat; and with his elegant wife Emily wheeled in her chair out to his side to bid him God speed – for she is clearly unable to accompany him today – off they all go following in his wake - firstly along a pleasant lane to the rear of the house, named *The Primrose Path of Dalliance,* apparently, and which in spring, they say, really is lined with deep clusters of yellow primrose all the way but which now is lush merely with blackberries and pink mallow and resonant with the sleepy drone of bees. No one at first dares to match the distinguished bearded gentleman stride for stride or attempts to engage him in conversation, for he has been known to outrun the most persistent of tourists when pursued, and for stamina and familiarity with the steep ascent there is none to rival him. Even the very young among the party such as Beth find it hard going, and the convivial conversation, laughter and small talk among the crowd soon give way to an assortment of puffing, wheezing and gasping among the less agile members of the company as they strive to keep up.

Eventually they emerge from the top of a narrow tree-lined lane, to the open grassland and big skies of High Down, the sea to their left so near yet so far below, framed by the very edge of the cliffs on which they walk, and all the while the great man himself continuing to lead the way with all the confidence and familiarity of one who makes the climb most ever day. The group, assailed now by the blustery wind that invariably blows up here, begins to disperse – spreading out across the wide expanse of grass which undulates gently from east to west - a sward as smooth as a billiard table, cropped short by sheep and vast nocturnal populations of rabbits - until each settles to their own pace and personal route to the top. Eventually, though, everyone converges upon the Nodes Beacon - the highest point of the downs, almost five-hundred feet above the sea, a place marked by a sturdy black, buttressed pole of old timber with its empty cage for brushwood and pitch atop, an object so old that it - or else perhaps one of its predecessors - had once been part of a chain of beacons standing all along the southern coast of England and which when ignited one fateful afternoon long ago in the golden age of Queen Elizabeth had also once served to alert the nation to the approach of the Spanish Armada.

From here, together, they gaze out far and wide, absorbing the broad panoramic view, the high-sea horizon a vertical wall of blue water and foam-capped glancing waves in front; the occasional cloud-shadows cast upon the sea showing a luscious iridescent lilac and mauve as they move across their vision from west to east. Behind where they stand, meanwhile, the downland itself slopes back to the hidden lee of the hills from whence they began their walk – and then, back further still, to the winding ribbon of a river leading across low marshland to the tiny port of Yarmouth in the distance. Beyond that there is the turbulent stretch of sea that separates the island itself from the mainland; as busy a stretch of water as one would find anywhere in the world, populated by yachts with coloured sails, by paddle steamers with their tall black chimneys and plumes of rising smoke and which this afternoon shimmers and sparkles in the sunlight like a distant filament of diamonds. It is quite simply stunning, utterly exhilarating; and anyone whose spirit cannot be lifted by such a sight as this, they conclude, must surely be beyond redemption.

'Well done, me bonny boys and good fair ladies!' the poet cries. 'I hope you will agree with me that the air up here is worth sixpence a pint!' he adds, as the very last of the stragglers complete the ascent, plus one or two tourists having tagged along in the meantime, wide-eyed and totally agog at the spectacle – and upon which with a final flourish of the much celebrated broad-rimmed hat which has by this time become filled with as many sixpenny pieces or bank notes as it can contain, the celebrated poet thanks everyone for their contribution this day, before turning and, with the assistance of his steward, begins straight-away to retrace his steps, back downwards to the seclusion and privacy of his home.

Many in the group disperse now, choosing to go their separate ways, including the trio of Amos and the two ladies who have elected already to continue on westward towards the remote and ever-narrowing tip of the island where, they know, the headland finishes in the precipitous plunge down into Alum Bay and the famous white-chalk rocks and jutting pinnacles known as the Needles – a good forty minutes brisk walking still – but they are, all three, relishing the prospect.

'What do you reckon on our Poet Laureate, then, Beth?' Amos inquires, perceiving her excitement still over an experience that would no doubt last in all of their memories for many a day to come.

'I think he is a fine old gentleman, Sir,' she answers as she scurries along with Daphne at his side. 'I believe he has done much good service today for a needy widow by his charitable work, and that he loves his own dear wife more than anything in the world.'

Amos nods his agreement. He has never really thought of Tennyson in that way, as a husband, a father. Beth was perceiving the man behind the poetry, whereas he had experienced only the legend today, the magician and his powerful incantation.

'They say he and his wife have been together for twenty-seven years, Daphne remarks, pensive now all of a sudden. 'I cannot imagine what that must be like, can you - to be with the same person for so long?'

She is referring to her own marriage, of course, a union that really has little prospect of reaching much beyond its second anniversary.

As they continue on their long trek westwards, the pathway gives way to wild, unmarked expanses of downland, rolling and rising gently, untrodden and where the hot sun raises the scent of untouched wild flowers - vast seas of pink and purple vetch - and where the last of the blue-winged butterflies of the summer skit and flutter in the air above them. Beth, meanwhile, sensing perhaps the need to keep herself separate, holds back and remains some distance behind - wandering away further and further, ostensibly to gather wild flowers but really to allow him and Daphne a precious opportunity to talk together – for clearly there is something she wishes to tell him. But to his surprise she does not discuss the unwholesome outcome of their last meeting, does not even refer to the portrait. It is as if none of it had really occurred.

Instead there is, it seems, something far more important on her mind, and so he waits until she is ready.

'Oh, Amos,' she eventually begins without prompting, 'how am I to describe to you this latest outrage?'

'What do you mean?' he asks.

'I mean this: that my marriage is at the point of breaking,' she replies, 'and, as a matter of fact, so am I,' she adds as she takes her handkerchief and dabs beneath her veil at a little tear forming in the corner of her eye, making as if to remove a fly or some such irritant. But he can see how distressed she is.

'Tell me what you mean,' he urges her, gently as they continue to walk.

'Polly returned yesterday from his latest business trip,' she explains, 'as bloated and as repulsive as ever. Not even bothering much to bathe or tidy himself for me at home these days, he walks around in a dressing gown most of the time. Last night I was raped by him. Yes – that is the only way I can describe it. He will have none of this sleeping in separate rooms, he says. Even worse, he has informed me quite calmly – as I suspected – that he will have me put away in a lunatic asylum if I protest any further or fail to do his bidding.'

Amos is furious – though for her sake he tries to maintain some semblance of calm. 'That is – well, just terrible!' he says, trying to speak without venom, trying to exercise restraint. But as he walks he targets a nearby pebble of flint and kicks it far into the distance.

'Yes – it is terrible. It is disgusting and, to be frank, more than a little painful. So, Amos, what prospect do I have now? You tell me! I can either sit back and pretend that Polly is not debauching himself at every turn and submit to his demands, to be violated by him against my will whenever he chooses until we both rot from some ghastly venereal disease – or I can protest, keep him from me and so provide him with a perfect excuse to demonstrate my insanity and have me locked away – to live out my days in some institution among all the mad, despairing souls there that will surround me and eventually drag me down to be numbered among them. It may already be too late to choose the former option, and the chances have to be high that if I go to London to be assessed I shall not be allowed to return. Oh, he assures me it will not be difficult to arrange, my incarceration. He knows all the right people, he says, to make it happen. The actual truth of the matter, evidence of any kind, is immaterial. Such are the meagre rights of all women. Such are the times we live in.'

Amos grits his teeth, his anger coiled up inside of him, feeling so desperate - until a long, despairing sigh escapes his chest. What can he possibly do to prevent this? – knowing full well, moreover, that it is something that goes on far more often than should ever be countenanced in any civilised society. *Hysteria* is the term they give to it, the catch-all diagnosis. The physician's word is law. And now Daphne is to be judged and sentenced!

'I feel so very sorry for you' he says, trying to look into her eyes, but as she walks, her hair all loose and chaotic now from beneath her bonnet in the stiffening wind, she raises a hand to attend to it and thereby manages to shield her face from him - which leads him to the conclusion that she would be holding back her tears still. In time, she returns to link her arm under his again, and tries to become more settled, but it is not easy for her. He can feel her breast against his side, her heart pounding, her breath on his cheek until she even allows her head to rest upon his shoulder as they walk, allowing him to take her weight, as if drained of all care. He feels certain now, knowing, too, that the end of this idyllic moment in their lives might almost be upon them, that he has never loved her so much. And he feels so helpless, so desperately helpless.

'None of this must affect you,' she says. 'And when I am put away, I don't want you to even contemplate visiting me. Do you understand? I do not wish to be the object of your pity as you visit me in my cell - or whatever doleful place it is they put people like me – until my anger and bitterness become so intolerable that even you will eventually shun me. This must be the end of it, dear one, our wonderful time together.'

They continue on in silence for a while. Then eventually they spot Beth nearby, ready and waiting to be re-united with them in her own quiet way - so they call to her - Daphne holding out a welcoming arm, urging her to join them at last – and this she does, a freshly braided band of wild flowers woven into her bonnet. And so with Daphne in the middle, linking arms and putting on a brave face for everyone's benefit, they continue on their way, full of little gems of laughter and conversation that seem so precious to him now, as if every moment needs to be slowed down and savoured, and yet everything is racing on ahead of them, all so quickly, never to be regained.

After a time, and with the land and cliff's edge on either side narrowing all the while, the pathway becomes again more defined - eventually dropping them down into a lane by a farmstead where cottage-garden hollyhocks and old poppy-heads stand tall, nodding in the warm, dusty breeze. There is a moment of coolness and shade here – and then suddenly they emerge: thrust unexpectedly out before the vast hot sky and the wide expanse of cliff-tops high above Alum Bay - the faintest murmur of the sea hundreds of feet below. Breathtaking! But there is still further to go; and from here, availing themselves of a narrow pathway cut between the land to their left and the very edge of the cliffs themselves, plunging sheer and unforgiving to their right, they must continue to skirt the vast perimeter of the bay at dizzy and exhilarating heights, bringing them closer and closer all the while to their destination. Far below in the bay a little pier is visible, where the tops of pleasure boats can be seen and the occasional small paddle steamer weaving amid the rows of lobster pots to disgorge their cargo of tourists and day-trippers who picnic on the beach or else wander and gather for themselves, in little bottles or glass vials, samples of the famous coloured sands, all golden ochres and purple tints that spill and trickle down from a great wall of rugged colour above the bay itself.

Another twenty minutes along the white chalk pathway and, at last, they are upon the very western-most tip of the headland. Here to their side is an archway of brick, the entrance to a sunken fortress - the artillery battery where throughout so much of recent history sparsely manned weapons have been set in concrete, pointing out to sea towards French invaders whose ships have never yet dared sully the horizon - and probably never will. There is nothing much to see of it or to hear today as they scramble around the side of the flinty crenellations of the fortress walls, and behind which the cannon are lodged - for it is virtually a deserted place at present. So they proceed onwards just a little further over treacherously thin paths, so close to the edge that it is terrifying - until a corner is turned and suddenly there it is, the view they have come so far to see: the Needles, there beneath them, stretched out ahead in a perfectly straight line of sharp gigantic white pinnacles, the farmost of which is buttressed by a lighthouse – dwarfed in comparison to the stacks themselves, and even this so far below that it is as if they are standing on the clouds themselves and looking down from the heavens.

Here they remain, all three in mute distraction and admiration for some time before Daphne finally ventures to break the silence and in words that are so dreadful and unexpected that they strike Amos to the core.

'What a fine place this would be to end ones life!' she states, as if thinking aloud, her voice barely audible against the wind – and then, to Amos's dismay, she slowly and very deliberately takes a step from the chalk path out onto the narrow, sloping strip of grass that forms the very edge of the precipice itself. And then she laughs, a high-pitched crackle of laughter that scatters and carries in the wind like the crying of the gulls – as if her very mind has been taken by the elements and flung in all directions. 'My little neck would break soon enough on those rocks down there,' he hears her say, still as if speaking only to herself as she places one hand slowly to her throat, as if measuring its circumference with her fingers.

Amos is frozen in horror at the spectacle. It is no longer the Daphne he knows: it is a wild creature, standing on the very edge of oblivion, unfettered, impossible to anticipate or contain.

Beth, however, with merely a look of profound unease towards Amos at her side has already decided to take matters into her own hands. With a deep and audible breath of courage, she steps out - following with caution in Daphne's footsteps, slowly - so very slowly - towards where she is standing and there with amazing bravery links her arm beneath hers. The two women stand for what seems like an eternity looking into each other's eyes until, in a voice which is firm and calm, Beth simply says, 'Go not too near the edge, Ma'am, for we should not wish to lose you.'

Daphne, so tall, so powerful in comparison, looks down at the diminutive girl as if angry. Her eyes flash at her audacity - that she should instruct her on what to do - a look of madness for a moment as if for the hell of it she would fling her off with a flick of the shoulder or else haul her down with her to certain death. But she does not. Responding to the younger woman's gentle urging she does finally relent and, by slow degrees, she steps back with her onto the relative safety of the pathway where, for a moment, they all stand in silence, Beth still with her arm linked under Daphne's.

No longer rooted to the spot in horror, and feeling unable to resist, Amos takes it into his head that he too should perhaps venture forth - just to take a peep at what they would have seen. And this he does. As the two women walk past him, he steps, unnoticed, very cautiously out towards the edge himself, advancing for a moment to that very same spot. It makes his head spin - the vast drop down to the roaring ocean so far below and the jagged serrated edges of the cliffs that seem to him to be like enormous white teeth waiting to impale anyone who dares to throw themselves towards them. A pebble becomes dislodged at his feet and tumbles into an eternity of a fall that never seems to finish - so far does it have to plunge. The gulls cry and pass by so close that it seems they have almost flown under his feet. The wind pushes and tugs at him as if drawing him towards the infinity that is there. His head feels light ...

'Sir!' Beth calls softly - until he too realises he is going too far with his foolish bravado, too far upon the slippery grass. She is the only one with any common sense, he realises, as he returns to the path - a rather sheepish and embarrassed smile upon his face as he meets her disapproving eyes. Having, it seems, already adopted the role of overseeing their preservation - taking charge in a matriarchal way as would a woman of twice her age, Beth continues to regard him with a look of relief but also of disparagement as she continues to press her arm beneath Daphne's, still not wanting to set her free. Extraordinary, her presence of mind! However, as they retrace their steps around to the entrance of the fortress, and then further up and back in the direction of the beacon, she gradually relinquishes her guardianship and drifts away once again - while Daphne, her arm linked beneath his once more begins to step along in a curious jaunty fashion, almost skipping at his side - totally at variance with her demeanour just a few short moments ago, as if some kind of decision, some kind of pact that she has made with herself has relieved her of all her cares. And then suddenly she laughs again and takes both his hands and spins him this way and that - a little dance of madness upon the grass as they go.

'Oh Amos, how seductive life is,' she cries, 'that it makes us fall in love with its beauty only to take it away so soon, just as we become devoted to it.'

'Why do you say such a thing? What do you mean?' he demands, feeling quite panicked at her impossible changes of mood.

But Daphne merely juts out a defiant chin as they come to rest and in a voice of some frivolity asks: 'Now, tell me Amos: if Beth and I were hanging by our fingernails back there, and you could rescue only the one of us, which would you choose: she who feeds your body, or she who feeds your soul?'

Upon which, and before he can respond at all, she clears her throat and, holding forth her arm as if brandishing a knightly sword, launches into a spontaneous parody of Tennyson's poem, even matching his sonorous voice in her own fashion:

'*A lady and a maid so fair,*
With raven black and red their hair,
The knight must be so brave, and there
Must choose which one to rescue - not a pair,
From the steep plunging down to Camelot'

And she finishes her clever little piece of improvisation in another one of her wild and rapturous bouts of laughter as she skips at his side again and the wind roars and whistles about their ears, tugging at their clothing, dragging them along as would sails upon a ship as they go. There is no answer to any of this, he realises - and thus, weary from their long walk, intoxicated by all the fresh air, the excitement of the poetry at Farringford and their excursion to the dizzy heights of the chalk cliffs above the Needles, they return with hardly another word between them down to the village and their homes.

It is an uncomfortable evening for Amos. He dozes in the chair after dinner so deeply that he can hardly wake himself when he should. Then later, as darkness falls and he climbs the stairs to his bedroom, paradoxically he finds that he cannot sleep at all! The hours pass, and the lonely night finds him still thinking of Daphne – there at Parnassus just a short walk away down the leafy lane of elm and sycamore – the place where he would wish to be, but one which is so closed-off, so forbidden to him now that it might just as well be an impenetrable fortress. Never before has he felt so powerless, so ineffectual and embittered - yet wanting to protect her all at the same time – a volatile combination of cares and sensations that leaves him feeling utterly desperate. He imagines her anxiety, her loneliness, her tormented mind torn this way and that by so many bizarre and conflicting emotions. What did she mean earlier today - about choosing which one to rescue - she who feeds his body or she who feeds his soul? Was it really just so much nonsense, or was it a call to arms, a plea for him to take a leap out of his own comfortable domestic routine and do something decisive for once, something heroic? - because the cause and origin of all this pain and suffering is plain enough for anyone to discern. And it leads to a whole new set of questions for Amos, therefore. Why should a beast like Ramsey live in this world? What right does a reptile such as that have to life? And dark and unwholesome thoughts occupy his mind.

An hour passes, and then another. The air feels so warm, so hushed and stifling. He tries some tincture of cannabis to help him sleep, but to no avail. And not long after this he finds himself up, in his dressing gown and wandering down to the kitchen where, in the darkness, the scrubbed wood of all the benches and shelves stand as white as bleached bones in the moonlight. Here he pours himself a little left-over wine, lights a lamp and begins to examine all the various knives from the draws, laying them out one by one on the bench by the sink and wondering just how one of them might be used to kill a man. What are the options, he asks himself as he tries to remember all those reports and descriptions from the *Illustrated Police Weekly*, that most popular of magazines these days, on sale in London and packed with lots of lurid illustrations of murder scenes. As a student he had even contributed to some of the drawings himself based on police records. In the case of Ramsey, a thrust to the heart would be useless, of course; with so much blubber to get through it would only be by enormous luck that one could ever succeed that way. Rather, it would have to be a slitting of the throat. Yes, that's it, he thinks, while selecting a great heavy cleaver of a knife – the one Beth uses for chopping mutton - and holding it in his hand. The assailant usually strikes from behind, he seems to recollect. Ah yes, but then suddenly he sees the famous painting by Caravaggio before him, the one in which the biblical heroine Judith is dispatching the enemy of her people with a broadsword - clasping the hair of the supine and drunken Holofernes, drawing back the head and slicing through the sinews and bones of the throat in a carving motion, her squeamish face, full of disgust for the task, turned away, keeping everything at arm's length as she carves - and all the while twisting the head of Holofernes to one side, twisting it by the hair to allow the blood to spurt away from her.

Ah, Caravaggio! Now there was a painter! That seventeenth-century genius of dramatic narrative, that master of the darkest chiaroscuro - a man who knew intimately, at first-hand, all the bloody business of combat - he who dispatched the rival to his mistress's affections with a duelling sword, castrating him in the process, and then living out his remaining years on the run, fleeing from the vendetta, always moving from place to place, constantly looking over his shoulder in all the dark alleyways and taverns of Rome and Naples, waiting always for the arrival of his nemesis, yet producing some of the most astonishing and dramatic works of art along the way. Yes, painters were certainly different creatures in those days, he concludes, a little ruefully as he sips at the final dregs of his wine - artists of the highest calibre yet living almost every moment under the shadow of violence, rivalry and assassination. As for himself, if he could just gain entry to Ramsey's bedroom by some means - yes, then take him in his drunken stupor - that would be the answer. Probably a quick enough end for him, too. Naturally, there would be no hope of getting away with it. He realises that. He would be tried very quickly and hung no doubt. But Daphne at least would be saved. One great and heroic act on his part! And then suddenly as he sets his empty glass down and inspects the edge of the largest of the carving knives with one nervous finger's touch running along the length of the blade he is aware of another person in the room - behind.

Beth is standing there, also in her dressing gown, observing him from the doorway with an expression of puzzlement and trepidation on her young face.

'Ah, good evening, Beth,' he says in a tremulous voice, trying not to sound like a culprit caught in the act and, feigning nonchalance, placing the knife down swiftly on the bench.

'Is everything all right, Sir,' she inquires, a little apprehensively, he feels, brushing some wayward strands of sleepy hair from her brow.

'Oh yes. Yes, I was just wondering ... is everything here serviceable and sharp enough for you - for all the work you must do? I know it's not always easy, to find someone to put an edge on these things.'

'No, indeed not, Sir,' she says, speaking in an unfamiliar, clipped voice - tense and anxious, not like Beth at all, in fact. 'In London, as you recall, there was always the gentleman on the bicycle, the street grinder who would come every few weeks. Here on the Island, I have yet to meet with anyone like that.'

'Yes, quite, quite,' he responds. 'Well, we must still see to it that we keep everything up to standard,' he announces, picking up one of the largest of the carving knives again from the collection laid out on the bench and realising as he does so that he is probably a degree unsteady on his feet and sounding a little bit worse for drink, his voice slurred. 'I will take these into town tomorrow and have them done for you.'

'Thank you, Sir,' she says, watching him with continued concern as he passes her and leaves the room, still brandishing the carving knife in his hand. He stops on the stairs, realising how peculiar it must all look, going up to bed thus. And then, when he turns, he discovers her staring up at him, observing him with genuine alarm, and trembling a little, too, almost cowering in the doorway. Clearly, she wishes to speak. And so he gives her a little nod of encouragement.

'Sir ... am I safe? To be here in this house tonight?' she asks, biting her lip and now clearly terrified.

Seeing her anguish, cowering at the prospect of being under the same roof in the company of a madman with a knife, it makes him feel suddenly so ashamed, so embarrassed and so full of pity for her, this poor, tiny girl in her dressing gown, her hands clasped tightly together, staring up at him – she who had been so very brave earlier today out on the edge of the cliff. How frightened she must be feeling now; as if all of her courage were exhausted and used up. And all because of him. Because of him and his stupidity.

'Beth,' he says coming back into the kitchen and stowing the weapon away where it belongs in the draw before turning to meet her eyes. 'Beth, there is nowhere in this entire world where you are more safe or more valued than here. I promise you that with all my heart.'

She does not, however, seem to have become entirely pacified. So he continues to put away all the other knives, too; all back to where they belong in the draw.

'Have you also not been able to sleep, Beth?' he inquires, aware of her eyes still upon him from behind, 'after such a day as we have had, it is little wonder, wouldn't you say?'

'Indeed, Sir,' she replies, 'I have been disturbed by a dream, and then I could not sleep, and then I heard you here, downstairs and ...'

'Yes ... well, perhaps you should make a pot of tea, eh? And we shall sit together a while and you can tell me all about your dream. How would that be?'

Obeying straight away, she takes the kettle and coaxes the range into life with astonishing skill, finding an ember somewhere by which she might rekindle the stove, adding some wood, so that within minutes the tea is made and they are seated at the table. She remains pensive, however, and far from settled even now. For a moment he feels he should break the silence, but then seeing that her eyes have become moist all of a sudden he tarries, hoping she will unburden herself - but she does not. There is a look of desperation about her, as if fearing to speak – especially about any dream she might have been experiencing - and then he notices how awfully worn and old is her dressing gown: an old woollen thing with frayed sleeves and full of holes, so that he feels self-conscious in his own fine cashmere robe seated there with her. Oh, all these infernal divisions and social customs! That a serving girl is not supposed to speak to her employer unless spoken too first, never to unburden her soul, not for a moment because it is somehow not deemed to be *proper*. Damn it! And so he waits patiently, still, allowing her time; and when eventually she begins to speak, the words are prefaced with a deep sigh that seems to express a blend of relief and gratitude. That he has waited, after all.

'I was dreaming about a poor creature – one that you found outside in the garden, Sir,' she begins, as she pours the tea.

'What sort of creature?'

'A swan Sir, a lovely swan – but black. They are rare, aren't they? But this poor one was not well, either. She was damaged somehow, and when you tried to pick her up her wing came away in your hand and broke in two pieces. And I said to you, this is no good, she will not be able to fly now and will surely die. We were both so sad, and you held the wing and could do nothing. And then the swan began to walk away, very unsteady, as you can imagine - limping all lopsided, and so sorrowful to see, so pitiful, as we followed her, and then we were out on the downs and the swan climbed to the edge of the cliffs and threw herself off. You said to me you did not know whether she did it to try to fly or else to end her life of suffering. But when we went to the edge of the cliff and looked down we saw her at the bottom and she had turned into a white swan.'

'A white swan! And did she fly away?' he asks.

'I do not know Sir, for then I woke and heard you downstairs.'

'Well ...' he says getting to his feet, clutching his cup rather than holding it by the handle and sipping the last dregs gratefully as he somehow realises he is fighting back his tears, 'let us conclude your dream with a happy ending by imagining her flying away, and finding happiness. What do you say to that!'

Beth, rising also, nods her agreement, smiles, and a little tear forms in her eyes also. And he notices a difference in her appearance then - different to how he normally sees her. Her face once so round and even a little chubby, like a child's, has lengthened, her eyes have narrowed and become more almond shaped and lovely. She is changing, he realises; she is growing from a girl into a young woman. It has been happening under his very nose all this time and he has scarcely noticed at all until now. Unaware of his observations and of how he is still watching her, she gathers up the tea things, the cups and the spoons and takes them to the sink, and as he follows her with his eyes he notices the moon is in front of her, visible through the little lattice window there, and so he comes over to point it out to her. 'Look, Beth how high up it seems, and almost full by the look of it! There's surely no evil shall befall either of us tonight, not with such a fine old lady watching over us, don't you think?'

She looks up, too, her eyes so very large and black he notices, gazing at the silvery disc; and she seems at ease, at last - her eyes wandering alternately back and forth between the moon and his face, no longer frightened at all, reassured and with renewed confidence in him ... perhaps. He sincerely hopes so.

I must become worthy of this, he tells himself in thoughts that are vague and barely formed still. *Somehow, I must work to become worthy of this trust – and to be a better person because of it.*

He returns to his room. It is three in the morning, and for all his passionate fantasies and gallant resolutions of swift revenge on a wicked enemy, it is not long before he curls up under the sheets, back to reality, and where he falls into a deep and unbroken slumber. 'Ah, alas, you are no Caravaggio,' he tells himself just before he drops off. 'Thank the Lord for that!' And he remembers no more.

Chapter Twenty

A Window onto a Fabled World

It is a cool day, squally and dull. The wind outside rattles the shutters and trellises of the house. Grey sheets of swirling sea mist descend from time to time, rolling in and covering the trees and bushes outside in beads of moisture. There is the presentiment of early autumn in the russets and golds of the leaves in the gardens and in the crimson of the Virginia creeper that adorns the walls of the cottage. It is, to be sure, a decidedly gloomy prospect for anyone wishing to walk or take a turn upon the seashore or downs this afternoon, as he had half-hoped he might – for he feels restless, apprehensive. Having not heard from Daphne for a day or two, and at such a difficult time in her life, he cannot help wondering how she is, or whether he should send a message across to inquire.

Beth is busy about the place as always in her usual quiet and capable way while he sits at ease in his decorative smoking jacket, pours a little coffee for himself as he leafs through his book of appointments which at least provides some good cheer – because, he is pleased to see, his commitments really have grown steadily since his arrival here some months ago, full of commissions to paint for many of the well-to-do residents of the Island: more work than he could ever possibly complete this year, in fact, even should he stay until Christmas! Here he can make a living, and a good one - selling not only to those who want narrative or sacred paintings but also to those who simple enjoy representations of beautiful women, of which he remains an accomplished practitioner. Moreover, as his reputation grows, he finds himself climbing up the social scale - and even has hopes of fulfilling the ultimate ambition now of working in some humble capacity at Osborne. To this end, an interview with the Queen's private secretary is scheduled for the end of next week, even possibly including a word with John Brown, Her Majesty's closest aide and companion.

There is a ring at the door, which Beth responds to straight away. Having written to his solicitors in London in an effort to ascertain some kind of information on the rights of women in Daphne's plight, he is hoping this might be the postman with a return letter. In fact, it is a private delivery to Amos of a little package with Daphne's seal upon it, brought over, Beth says, by one of the staff from Parnassus.

'The steward said that it was not supposed to be delivered until later this afternoon, Sir,' says Beth, 'but because he has to go off to Yarmouth, he said he'd drop it in early, anyway.'

To his surprise it contains Daphne's book of verse. There is also a letter enclosed, and while Beth, at his request, waits nearby, thumbing through the book itself with her typical enthusiasm for the volume, he breaks the seal and reads:

'Dearest Amos,

'The doctor has called once more and Polly has informed me that we are to go to London tomorrow where I am to visit an eminent specialist who, as anticipated, is to finally assess me for insanity. I am so dreadfully appalled and frightened that I cannot think clearly. I am not, I believe, expected to return. That is all – but it is well and good, because the reality of the situation is that I shall not be going to London tomorrow. I have resolved to take charge of my own destiny in that respect. By the time you receive this letter, in fact, my remedy will already have been accomplished.

Do not be sad, dear one. There is no need. One day you will wake from your memories of our time together and regard it as no more than a dream, a fantasy, and you will discover others who are more real to you and who you will love in a different way. As one episode draws to and end, another is just beginning. Knowing that, I feel I can let go at last.

Daphne'

Troubled, mystified by what he has read, he hands Beth the letter, which she reads quickly. For a moment they continue to look into each other's eyes until the awful truth is suddenly there between them – a mutual understanding so terrible that it strikes them both at the same instant with utter horror. Without need to speak a further word, they run from the house, run as fast as they can - with coats hauled across their shoulders and flying in the wind as they struggle to fasten them and keep them in place – so violent is the weather - until within moments they are at the gates of Parnassus. Here, they hurry up the drive, straight into the hallway and with as much decorum as they can muster, which is not very much under the circumstances, insist on speaking with Lord and Lady Bowlend. Their urgency is met with the usual indifference of the staff here towards Amos, while the butler himself can only stare with some consternation at Amos's frantic visage and Beth, equally as alarming, clad in Amos's reefer jacket (like an overcoat on her) and which had been the nearest thing to hand as she came out. Lord Bowlend is busy, he states, at work in his study, not to be disturbed, and Lady Daphne has taken to long walks alone of late and is at present out of the house.

'Out of the house! What in this weather – unaccompanied!' Amos exclaims, only to be met with a shrug of the shoulders and an indifferent nod of confirmation from the butler himself as if to suggest that such eccentricities were surely only to be expected of someone who was already quite mad,

Amos and Beth exchange further glances of consternation. With chilling clarity and the utmost certainty they know there can be only one explanation: she has gone to the Needles.

'Do you have a horse available, anything that I can ride?' Amos demands, only to be met with a polite but curt apology, that both horses are in use at present, the stables empty.

Out of the house they go, and again they run – run along the lane, trying to calculate the direction and the steps she would have taken. Which way? They run until their breath has almost deserted them and they can only walk. They chafe themselves on briars; they bruise themselves on stones as they stumble and struggle along, ready to crawl if need be until they reach the top of the steep, wooded pathway leading up to the downs. Will they be able to find her, overtake her, save her from the terrible resolution she has surely already set her mind to? They know only that they must try; with every breath left to them they must not relent or slow their pace one bit more than human endurance will allow.

Here, at the top of the path, the glades of willow and the dark wedges of fir trees quickly give way to the vast open expanse of the downs themselves which, to their surprise are shrouded in a thick, swirling sea-mist, a cloying dampness and drizzle that shrouds everything in a fog so dense and impervious that it defies every breath of wind, and for a time they become disoriented and draw to a halt, not knowing which way to go. Disconcerting noises from vessels out at sea rise up from time to time; ships horns, doleful bells and the strange deep-throbbing of steam engines out on the water. Amos feels utterly confounded by the unfamiliarity of it all, his senses in turmoil - until, eventually, a little glow of milky sunshine illuminates a segment of space ahead, indicating the direction of the sea, far below them now, and the drop of the steep chalk cliffs upon which they stand and which, they know, must therefore be kept to their left as they set off once more. Amos is aware of his own breath, panting, gasping as they run. The worst of it is that even if Daphne were up here and walking westward towards the headland they would not be able to see her in the fog. There is just no way of knowing how far she has progressed.

'Look Sir - there!' Beth cries, and suddenly they discern a shape that looks vaguely like the form of a cloaked figure, a woman - but not where they would expect it to be. The figure, if indeed it is a human form, seems to be in a place that would be foolishly close to the cliff's edge. He runs towards it and the cry escapes his lungs despite himself, 'Daphne! Daphne!'

But Beth, behind, is tugging at his sleeve, holding him back. A further curious sound fills the air then, like whistling wind or - and they hardly wish to acknowledge it - like a woman's shrill laughter. And then, so abruptly as if from nowhere, vast swarms of swallows - all flocking together and preparing for their autumn departure - come darting and buzzing everywhere through the thick air, whizzing past them so recklessly close to their faces, like arrows in the thick of battle, their multitude of tiny voices adding to the utter horror of it all.

'Sir, do not go too far!' Beth cries, harried by the onslaught. 'I swear the edge is there. We will not see it until it is too late and then ...'

'No!' he screams as the shape vanishes. 'Oh God she's gone over!'

'No look – look there!' Beth cries again, turning him by his shoulders to where, in an entirely different place, the same dark shape appears again. No human, no living thing could have traversed that distance in so short a time – and they can only crouch and stare into the gloom, paralysed with fear and astonishment as the spectre creeps away, seeming not to be walking at all but rather as an insubstantial shadow drifting – until suddenly it vanishes, engulfed once more by the wall of grey fog.

'What in heaven's name was *that?*' he cries, as Beth squeezes herself against his side,

'We must surely have been mistaken, Sir,' she says, sobbing with fear, burying her face in his shoulder as the mad swallows continue to shoot past, diving, swirling in all directions in some kind of mass hysteria, their wing tips so close about them. 'It was only an illusion. We must not chase shadows.'

She is right - of course. They are simply wasting time. So they begin running again.

Beth, he quickly realises after only a few moments, is not only younger but much fitter, seasoned to the hardship of regular labour, and so covers the ground briskly - but for him his lungs soon start to burn with the unaccustomed effort. The wet grass slides and squeaks beneath their feet as they go - and then every once in a while they must leap to avoid the forms of isolated brambles that come upon them suddenly, all bejewelled with drops of moisture from the mist but treacherously sharp and upon which Beth's skirts have already become snagged several times. The way is long, they know, normally an hour on foot to the Needles themselves - but eventually the black timbers of the beacon loom into sight and they know they are at the top of High Down. But still this is only the halfway point – so they cannot pause, not for one moment. Keeping the hidden sea still far below to their side, they continue on towards the ever-narrowing headland of Alum Bay and the Needles. And still no sign of Daphne. Where can she be?

And then from out of nowhere there comes an almighty gust of wind and the mist at last gives way, driven off at its approach as if swept by the hand of some reckless giant so that all is clear and illuminated for one golden moment, the lowering sun breaking through the fog and strafing the land with a broad, piercing shaft of sunshine that races across the downs from one end to the other with astonishing rapidity, illuminating everything as it goes.

'Look – there!' Amos cries – and they see her at last – unmistakable this time, the diminutive figure of a woman far, far ahead of them in the sudden light - battered by the elements, her long, dark dress flowing, crescent-shaped from the relentless wind at her side, her hair loose, like a mad woman, walking briskly but staggering at times from the onslaught. But this precious moment of clarity is followed almost straight away by further sea-mist, and within seconds, just as quickly as it had dispersed, the dreadful swirling gloom rolls up and over them once again, and they lose sight of the woman in the distance completely.

The harsh truth, the appalling reality of the situation is upon them now and cannot be escaped: that even if Daphne were to stand still, it would take them at least ten minutes before they could possible cover the distance to reach her – while if, as seems likely, she continues on her way, then she will have reached the place and be broken on the rocks below long before they could ever possible save her. There is really no hope, no hope at all.

'She might not jump straight away, though' Beth suggests in a breathless gasp, reading his thoughts with perfect accuracy, clasping his hands in hers for a moment to offer encouragement. 'We might still get there in time.'

He takes hope from that as they set off again. But then

suddenly he remembers something – something vital: that there is in fact an alternative route – a lower pathway down to the right, through woods, and possibly, *just possibly*, shorter in distance. It is a gigantic gamble, but he knows it is one he must take.

'Keep going, Beth!' he cries, running off and down to the side and already at a distance from her before she has even time to consider what is happening or to protest. 'God pray that at least one of us will reach her in time!'

And a moment later, even as he turns again to glance back over his shoulder, he has already lost sight of Beth; she is already gone, vanished into the swirling mist leaving him feeling suddenly so very alone. Determined now to do what he can, he slides and almost tumbles down the bank until he locates the footpath - and from here he turns again to take the westward direction.

It becomes much darker now, any light at all remaining of the overcast afternoon being masked by tall woods of ash and hawthorn and waist-high bracken, too, all tinged with gold now, and through which he must thread his way. The path is rugged at this time of the year, overgrown and flanked by prickling gorse and not anywhere near as easy going as the smooth pastures of the downs above. Yet on he goes, trying to establish a rhythm to his walking, which breaks into a run whenever the terrain becomes flat enough to allow his breath to recover, but the ground is rising all the while, rising, rising – until at last he reaches Alum bay. And here, to his dismay, as the vast expanse opens up before him, he realises he has come upon it far too late. Beth has arrived here before him. He sees in the gloom the two distant figures already on the narrow path that is cut into the cliffs of the bay – high, so very high above the sea. Beth is closing the distance between herself and Daphne - he can hear her calling to her - but at this, Daphne, looking over her shoulder, seems to quicken her pace, clutching and gathering up at her skirts as she realises at last that she is being pursued.

It is already becoming dark – the early darkness of an overcast September afternoon – and the wind is so strong, so merciless in its intensity here on the exposed Western tip of the island, that what little fog might have remained is finally dispersed – and therefore, despite the fading light, the scene unfolds before him in terrible clarity, laid bare in all its horror as he runs towards it. He sees Daphne take the narrow path around the mound of the fort, sees her and Beth scrambling, almost on their knees as they go, one after the other, until he realises they have almost reached the very same spot where Daphne had stood yesterday. Beth is nearly upon her - but Daphne, perhaps realising she will be caught now, veers off and advances towards the nearest part of the precipice instead, determined to throw herself off anyway. For his own part, he is getting closer but his legs feel leaden now, hardly able to walk let alone run. Around the side of the fortress he goes; the tips of the great chalk stacks are already in sight, but it is useless, he knows. He must look upon it all now from a distance, watch helplessly even as he runs knowing there is no hope. Daphne has slid away, almost out of sight, only the top of her head visible now, her long hair loosened, flying in the wind. And then suddenly the horror becomes multiplied as Beth begins to stumble down as if on top of her, until the two have completely disappeared. Are they gone? Will he arrive in a few moments only to find them both broken to pieces on the cliffs so far below, the foaming sea mixed red with their blood?

A moment later, utterly breathless, his lungs burning, he comes to the spot and looks down. There is a narrow, sloping ledge, and it is upon this that the women have come to rest, caught for a moment, but Daphne is slipping, and Beth, holding on to her with both arms, embracing her, clutching at handfuls of her voluminous dress, is slipping also. 'Beth!' he cries as she turns her face up towards the sound of his voice, her eyes full of despair while everywhere, all around the bare cliffs are lit suddenly by a brilliant shaft of setting sun, all red, and so very severe in its intensity that he can hardly see. He climbs down a little and reaches out an arm so as to grab a handful of Daphne's clothing, too, but realises instantly that the combined weight of the two women will prove too much should Beth also slip away. He presses his body down into the soil, claws at the turf and sharp thistles with his other hand until, with all his might, bleeding, exhausted almost beyond endurance, he somehow succeeds in holding fast. But for how long? How long before he must call out to Beth and tell her to let go to save herself.

'Please Ma'am, he hears Beth gasp, all her breath spent, 'Do not leave us, Ma'am, I beg you, do not leave us.'

There is no way back from this he realises. He feels the last drop of vitality draining from him, his strength exhausted. Then suddenly he is aware of someone else - a shape looms above him, silhouetted against the sky. It is a soldier, surely, from the battery - he can see his red-coated uniform and cap, and the buttons shining on his tunic; he is reaching an arm down towards Amos and then he speaks: 'Hold on, Sir, all is well, hold on ... here!'

Amos, burning from heat and exhaustion clutches his hand which feels icy cold in comparison - and somehow, with his own face still pressed into the turf, the combined effort of them both is sufficient to haul the two women up from immediate danger - Beth quickly managing to manoeuvre herself into a position beneath Daphne so she is able to support her, until in a moment they are all up - and although still not back on the path, at least not sliding any longer - everyone flat upon the ground, prostrate with exhaustion, their lungs heaving, their voices groaning - and Beth, still with a hand clutching at Daphne's clothing, not letting go even now, not for one moment as she embraces the older woman more fully and more securely - waiting until Amos is recovered enough to lend his strength and to haul her into a seated position, where he too embraces her and holds her tightly in his arms.

'Let me go, both of you! It is all over for me, this life, don't you understand?' Daphne cries with such pain, still trying to wriggle free as, by slow degrees, they manage to get her to her feet and shepherd her yet further away from the precipice towards the path itself - and providing Amos at last with an opportunity to look around for the soldier, to thank him. But the soldier is gone.

'Come with us Ma'am,' Beth urges, still clinging. 'All is well. We are going to take you home.'

As if these words have stunned her into obedience, Daphne immediately becomes still and totally pacified. She stares into Beth's face and shakes her head in disbelief, as if her words themselves constitute some magical incantation that has complete power over her. And then her tears begin in earnest – hot, wet tears that seem as though they will never cease.

It is almost dark now, as Amos still puffing and trying to calm the beating of his heart continues to search about for the soldier. But there is no one; no one else at all. Much of the cloudy sky has dispersed by now and the moon is up, just rising to the East, and thereby indicating the direction in which they must go in order to commence upon the long walk back down to the village. It seems so calm, so peaceful everywhere, and not a living soul within miles.

'Did you notice the soldier, Beth?' Amos asks, much to her confusion it seems as they, all three, begin their walking.

'No Sir, what soldier?' she answers, looking for a moment as concerned for him as for the poor soul they have just hauled from the precipice and glancing over her shoulder rather unproductively, for there is no one else to be seen.

But Amos does not answer. He realises now that in the gloom he had not seen his face entirely, anyway. He had only felt his ice-cold hand.

―――――◇―――――

At the Villa Parnassus, where Daphne is taken by Beth to her room amid much consternation among the butler and maids over their mistress's dishevelled appearance, Amos – still in his top coat - strides through straight to the end of the hallway where, fortuitously, he encounters Ramsey standing in idleness by the door of the drawing room, cigar in hand. Although the same height as the big man, Amos feels as though he is at least a foot taller, looking down at him through a red mist as, with one firm and powerful palm upon his big barrel chest, he pushes him through into the room, slams the door shut, locks it behind him and pockets the key.

'How dare you!' Ramsey blusters, still stunned by the abruptness of what has just occurred. 'What is the meaning of this? What have you done with my wife?'

'What have I done! I have just prevented her from hurling

herself off the cliffs back there, that's what I've done. And I hold you responsible for it!'

'Ha! I knew it. Utter madness!' Ramsey cries with a look of exultation and triumph across his face.

'Oh yes, you'd like that, wouldn't you! Just the evidence you have been looking for. But you're out of luck, my friend. And I am going to tell you why ...'

'I'm not interested in anything you have to say. Kindly leave!' the big man declares, attempting to give out the orders even now.

But Amos is not to be deterred. 'No. I shall not leave!' he says, pointing an intimidating finger almost into the other man's face as he advances on him again. 'I have something to discuss with you. Listen closely - and you would do well not to doubt my sincerity. My next commission is to paint for the Queen. Yes, that's right. I am to meet with Her Majesty's private secretary in a few days time and perhaps even to have an audience with Victoria herself when she returns from Balmoral in order to discuss the possibility of portraits for some of the grandchildren. I will have ample opportunity, therefore, to relate in conversation the sordid history of your rise to power. I will be able to expose your penchant for visiting the brothels of London and Manchester. I will be able to explain how you have attempted to drive your wife insane and to have her placed in an asylum, and I will explain how you have constantly bullied and coerced your way into local society and into the homes of every person of merit here on the Island and where, it is widely known, you prey upon every man's wife and serving maid with the same salacious appetites with which you so very clearly indulge in matters of food and wine. You will be finished, Ramsey. Disgraced. And any prospect of political advancement or a successful marriage with the woman you currently have in mind will go up in smoke - it will be blasted to kingdom-come as surely as if I had shoved your fat arse down the barrel of one of your cannon and fired it myself.'

Ramsey, clearly disturbed by the dramatic metamorphosis occurring in the normally mild-mannered Amos, listens in stunned silence, his jaws working, his teeth grinding in fury -

but remaining silent, nevertheless: a most untypical condition in which to behold him.

Eventually, in exasperation, he lets forth a loud grunt, turns his back on Amos and marches over to the window, as if looking out – even though it is by now completely dark outside. Amos can discern his own reflection in the glass as he advances to stand closer behind the man, not letting him forget his presence, not for one moment, nor his determination to overcome him.

'Well?' Amos demands, boldly still as he approaches.

The silence in the large, dark room with its heavy curtains and lush velvety wallpaper seems to last an eternity. Only the casement clock, its pendulum swinging behind the glass, provides any sound at all, as the eyes of the two men meet in the reflected window.

'What do you want?' Ramsey finally murmurs at length, acquiescent at last as he draws on his cigar.

'This: that you do not take your wife to London tomorrow, or consider placing her in an institution of any kind – *ever*. That you do not allow her to become the subject of malicious gossip regarding her mental health – for you know it is all groundless and put about by yourself in order to be rid of her. Finally, if she so chooses, you will allow her the liberty to decline your disgusting claims upon her person.'

Ramsey does not respond straight away. And when he does it is in an attempt still to save himself by diverting the battle onto different ground:

'Supposing you take her from me? You could do that, couldn't you,' he suggests, still with his back turned and speaking to Amos's reflection in the window. 'That would be an arrangement that would suit us both. Why don't you?'

'She is not mine to take,' Amos argues, speaking through gritted teeth towards the malign reflection in the glass. 'Nor, actually, is she yours to give.'

'Fair enough, my friend,' Ramsey says, turning to confront him at last. 'You leave me no other choice. Many great men, even emperors and kings, have suffered from the arts of wicked women – it's nothing new, and people will forgive me, they will sympathise with me if I appear to be the wronged party in all this. I shall divorce her – and they will all understand when I name you as co-respondent. Then it will be you whose name becomes mud! What price your audience with the Queen then? I have all the evidence I need.'

But Amos is ready to call his bluff.

'Do you! Actually, I know you don't. But, tell you what, Oliver old boy, why don't you go ahead and try anyway? I expect to be speaking with the people at Osborne as early as next week. What I said still goes. Lift a finger against Daphne in any way, and you're done for.'

But Ramsey laughs, still as arrogant as ever. 'Ha! Fool - don't you realise that whatever you do, it will still just be your word against mine!'

'Yes, precisely,' Amos responds, 'and it is my word that will be victorious. I have the advantage over you, Oliver. You might not realise it yet, but I have!'

'What do you mean?'

'I mean that I have art and refinement on my side, whereas you have merely power and greed. People admire my work and the things I do. They love me because I inspire them and make them feel happy, but they will always hate you because you threaten them and make them feel miserable. In the end, they will trust what I say, therefore - and that is why you cannot win. Think about it, my friend. You are, in fact, already utterly defeated.'

At which Amos walks away, thrusts the key back into the door, unlocks it and with calm dignity saunters out from the room where, gathered outside in the hallway he encounters straight-away the steward and butler who can only watch in stunned silence and amazement as he shoulders his way between them.

Meeting with Daphne's chambermaid at the foot of the staircase he inquires of Lady Bowlend's welfare.

'She is well enough, thank you,' the woman replies brusquely. 'Only, would you mind taking your girl away with you now? She says she will not leave Lady Bowlend's side and that is simply not ...'

'Surely my maid can remain with her if that is what Lady Bowlend wishes,' Amos interrupts curtly. 'If you would just like to wait just a moment, I'll check if that is in order.'

To which, taking himself back to the open door of the drawing room he inquires loudly: 'I take it, Oliver, old boy, that you have no objection if my maid remains here this evening?'

And with the grudging nod from the noble lord, who is in the process of pouring himself a very large brandy, Amos returns to the chamber maid to relay the news, announcing with the utmost pleasure: 'Beth may remain with your mistress as long as is necessary – orders of Lord Bowlend.'

And so, with everyone present silenced into dumb amazement at the sound of authority in his voice, the battle-weary Amos – much of his clothing still hanging in shreds and covered in mud, leaves and returns to his own home.

By the light of a solitary candle in one of the substantial upstairs bedrooms of Parnassus, the two women, having cleaned their faces and changed into fresh clothing, talk together alone - with Daphne sprawled comfortably on the bed, propped up by cushions, and Beth in an armchair alongside and clothed most untypically in one of Daphne's finest linen dresses. Here she holds the other woman's hand from time to time until gradually she becomes calmer and more coherent. The minutes pass. Occasionally, they hear the sounds below of people arguing and then of voices that become hushed - a mark of respect for the poor woman upstairs, no doubt, and which after a while they both find quite amusing. It is this shared experience that eventually steers Daphne back towards some measure of stability, though there are still moments in which she remains confused and most distressed.

At one time there is a timid knock at the door - a maid inquiring, not for the first time, of Lady Bowlend and to which Beth, going to her with a commanding air, simply reiterates the fact that Lady Bowlend does not wish to speak to anyone until the morning and that there should be no further disturbance.

There is a sealed letter, however, that has arrived from Mr

Roselli, and this is duly handed over.

'Thank you Beth,' Daphne whispers as the younger woman closes the door and returns to her side. Declining to take the letter from her, and clearly not in any mood for it to be opened, either, she simply allows the younger woman to take custody of it. 'Oh, you must think me a terrible fool!' she continues, groaning in a voice of consternation over what she has done and the embarrassment it has caused – about the first time she has really broached the subject at all since their return. Only now is she ready, it seems, to acknowledge what has happened. 'If Polly ever needed proof that his good wife had gone insane, he certainly has it now! I have played right into his hands, haven't I. How stupid of me! You should have let me go, the pair of you. Really, you should.'

'No Ma'am, we could never allow that,' Beth declares, leaning over closely to place her palm over the other woman's hand once again. 'You are much loved and cherished by Mr Roselli. We would both of us be heartbroken to lose you.'

'Oh, but you will lose me anyway now, I'm afraid,' Daphne sighs, a grim smile of resignation upon her face. 'Tomorrow I shall be taken to London. There can be no question about that now. I will be taken to the living death of detention in a mental asylum from which I will most likely never be released. I will die tomorrow, Beth, just as surely as if you had allowed me to throw myself from the cliffs this afternoon. This is my final evening of comfort.'

'Do you want me to go, then, Ma'am?' Beth asks a little forlornly.

'Not unless you really must,' Daphne replies, and Beth's silence and attentive gaze, a gaze that does not for one moment waver in its steadfastness, informs her that she will certainly therefore stay. 'Really, Beth, you are so very kind,' Daphne murmurs, looking so intently into the younger woman's face, almost as if seeing it for the very first time. 'How fortunate Amos is to have one so loyal and so true!'

Beth bites her lip and turns away then, as if wanting to respond by asking something of importance but which she dares not put into words – and noticing this, Daphne places a friendly hand upon her arm and encourages her to turn her face back to her and to speak: 'What is it, Beth? Do ask! Who knows whenever we shall be able to converse again like this, with such liberty.'

'I don't feel I can ask, Ma'am. My curiosity is surely of no concern to you, especially at a time like this.'

'Dear little Beth, you saved my life a few hours ago. Your curiosity is more important to me than anything in the whole wide world.'

'It's just that I have always wanted to ask you, why did you never marry Mr Roselli. I know he loves you so very much, and I think that you love him. So why …'

'Amos? Oh heavens no!' Daphne interrupts with a little chuckle. 'My parents would never have approved. They always told me I was destined for a brilliant marriage, always expected the top prize for their daughter – insisted upon it, in fact - because of my looks, I suppose. And of course that is how it transpired. I wanted to make them happy and proud of me - and to be frank, I think I was afraid of being poor, anyway, which I most likely would have been with someone like Amos – cut off from his inheritance as he was at he time.'

'Did you think then that you would be happy with Lord Bowlend?'

'Yes, I thought I might be contented enough, and not just because of the wealth and prestige. He was younger and a little more presentable when I first encountered him, you know. Prior to his accident he was even quite gallant and courteous in his ways. And, in any case, a man like Polly is … well, how can I explain? You know what it's like when you encounter something very powerful, like when you stand by the sea and look out at the enormous waves and the infinite horizon? It becomes something so vast and strong, so indomitable that you find a kind of peace and resignation in the feeling – standing there before something so much mightier. That's what it is like being married to someone like Polly. But of course it isn't sufficient. It can never be sufficient. I've been a fool, really - because I was never brave enough to join myself to the man I admired the most.'

'Mr Roselli?'

'Yes. You see, Beth, Mister Roselli is different. He is an

artist, and a particularly brilliant one, as I'm sure you know – the kind of person who helps us to understand things, to question things and to wonder about ourselves in a special way: the complete opposite, in fact, to someone like my husband who can only give out orders and commands. We need people like Mister Roselli. They open up a window for us, a window onto a fabled world, a different and altogether more glorious kind of reality.'

'Do you believe such a world really exists, Ma'am?' Beth asks, as Daphne, more settled now reaches over to gather her hair brush from the dressing table and then begins to work through her own hair with long, lingering strokes, an occupation which seem to have a further calming effect on her.

'Oh yes, it does exist,' she answers, 'though most of the time I fear we only glimpse reflections of it – just shadows. 'But I know it is there when I am singing or listening to great music, or when I am intoxicated or in love. I have sensed it many times when I have been with Amos. I even had a glimpse of it, I think, when I stood there on the edge of that cliff the other day. Yes, it does exist. And when we are tired of shadows and tired of illusions we seek a different kind of reality in the world that shines through that window. We discover it there in the glorious realm of the spirit. It is a place where Amos lives much of his life – and that is why he is so precious to me. He is someone who can take me to that window, he allows me to see through. I suppose I understood this even as a young girl. I thought even then, if only I could help such a person, to assist him in his work, then I would have done something worthy with my life. I became his model, therefore. Later, I wanted to serve him by becoming influential and wealthy. And marrying Polly – well, that was really just another means to that end. Now, of course, it has all gone so dreadfully wrong. I can do nothing further to aid that dear man. He is like a lamb among wolves, an innocent amid all the treachery and filth, all the ignorance and greed of this world that will eventually be his undoing. How can it be otherwise! Isn't that the fate of every heroic soul? But it is no use trying to tell that to someone like Amos. He would never understand, never in a million years. He rides through the world as if on some golden chariot – a world that is filled only with beauty. He has never stopped to contemplate ugliness, not once, because it is invisible to him, and always will be. All the cruelty and squalor, all the horrid illnesses and suffering of the poor, all the greed and arrogance of the rich - none of it will ever divert him or turn his head for a single moment. That is why I love him so very much. And against that kind of love my marriage to a creature like Polly is nothing more than some dreadful curse, a curse entirely of my own making. The mirror cracked the day I first set eyes on Amos - my handsome and hopelessly improbable knight. And now ... well, all that's left for me now *is the journey from which no traveller returns,* as they say. And I rather suspect I may have almost reached that destination.'

Listening intently, Beth lowers her eyes for a moment, as if searching for some words of comfort. But there is really nothing further she can say. Instead, and as soon as Daphne has done with the brushing of her hair, she simply leans across and then very slowly and gently lowers her face onto her breast, embraces her, and remains there for quite some time. 'I still cannot bear that you should leave us, Ma'am,' she finally whispers, wondering whether it would mean anything at all to the other woman, wondering whether she has even heard. And then, abruptly, for one extraordinary moment her thoughts take her back to the past, back to a dusty noisy high street gazing with Mrs Edwards into a shop window at the beautiful dresses and wishing aloud that if only someone would lend her such a garment to wear 'if only for an hour' how happy she would be. Well ... that wish has come to fulfilment now, she realises, here this evening in one of those very dresses, lent to her for an hour by Lady Bowlend, a dress just like the one she had looked upon with such longing that day, with its beautiful hand-dyed colours and finest embroidery. How far away it all seemed – not only that place, but the person she had once been! Whoever could have imagined it would have happened like this! And she feels the tears running down her face as she wonders over it.

Placing her hand upon Beth's shoulders, Daphne responds as best she can, for it is almost too painful to speak. 'Look after him, Beth,' she whispers tenderly. 'If it is at all possible for you, keep him safe. I know you care for him and that you are wise enough, too. But for now you must be brave, little one. Be brave for me. You have all your life ahead of you. And you must not be sad on my account.'

After a while, Beth remembers the letter that was brought in earlier. She raises herself and eventually locates it at the back of her chair.

With more than a little reluctance, Daphne takes it, opens the seal and reads Amos's words. There does not appear to be much to it, after all, because within seconds she has put it down again in her lap. Yet when she raises her face there is a look of such elation in her eyes that it makes Beth gasp in astonishment. So Daphne immediately picks up the note again, and this time reads it aloud for her:

'Daphne, I have had a frank exchange of views with your husband this evening. There is a solution to this situation, which I trust will be lasting. You will not be sent away. A reprieve at the very least! Be of good cheer, therefore, and we shall speak soon. Amos.'

'Oh, Ma'am!' Beth cries and falls upon her again, this time sobbing tears of joy.

Chapter Twenty-One

Restoration

The light streaming in through the great south-facing windows of the Chapel illuminates the nave and dances in little pools of evening sunshine upon the perfectly re-laid flagstones of the floor. No one would be able to guess, had they not know, that just a few short months ago the place had been almost entirely laid bare to the soil. Now the renovation is finished. Everything as good as new – or as good as the day it was built so many hundreds of years ago in the age of the noble Tudors.

A modest group of assorted dignitaries, Tower staff and visitors are met here this evening, as has been the case for several evenings of late to admire the work and to mark the occasion with prayers and a little conversation as they congregate in pairs or small groups to inspect the results for themselves. Some of those present have been actively engaged in the restoration – others, such as Lord Bowlend, merely as benefactors from afar. It is a moment for reflection, therefore, for well-earned celebration now all the workmen have departed. And thus, after so many months of planning and effort, of discussions and endless committees meeting in smoke-filled rooms, the work stands complete – and it is the genteel hum of satisfaction now, the sounds of the long trains and flounces of ladies skirts that brush upon the surface of the stones, the gentle tapping of gentlemen's canes and elegant heels that fill the silence of aisle and nave – and all so sedately, so very right and proper, that among all those gathered here in their finery everything appears the perfect triumph of good taste. And indeed it is.

Meanwhile, the bones of the those unfortunate souls that were once discovered here, dispatched by the dull axe or gleaming sword, have all been stowed away with due ceremony in lead-lined caskets, placed under the floor beside the altar and marked discretely with armorial crests and special tiles of green and white marble at the places where they lie - thereby indicating that two Dukes of bygone times now appear to rest in good company between two former Queens - a peculiar and altogether amusing happenstance, everyone agrees, so that the mood at moments might even be said to extend to one of conviviality.

'I was under the impression old Bowlend was to be here this evening - or am I mistaken?' one of the gentlemen inquires of another, fixing a pair of pince-nez spectacles onto the bridge of his nose before introducing himself as Doctor Murry, part of the original archaeological team, he says, and present at the start of the renovation when the skeletal remains were first unearthed.

'Oh, I gather there's been a bit of a delay, actually,' answers the other man. He has a thin face, and sleek silvery-grey hair, liberally plastered with oil or some such agent that gives him a slightly rodent-like appearance. 'By the way, my name is Newman - Tommy Newman. Same regiment as old Bowlend, y'know. I suppose you could say the poor chap's had his fair share of misfortune lately, what! You've seen the papers, of course?'

'The story of his wife, you mean? Oh, hardly credible,' says Doctor Murry with a demonstrable wag of the chin. 'Yes, tragic, most tragic.'

'What happened, darling?' inquires a tall, elderly lady standing nearby, elegantly attired in a fashionable jacket-and-skirt costume and whom Doctor Murry introduces as his lady wife.

Newman takes her gloved hand limply and smiles a greeting before continuing - speaking with all the inappropriate yet inevitable enthusiasm of one who has a tale to tell concerning another's misfortune: 'Well, quite a rum sort of do, it was. You see, his wife was proving, how shall I put it, rather an embarrassment to him. And the noble lord – never a man to be trifled with at the best of times, you understand – elected to send Lady Bowlend abroad, therefore. It was for her own good he said: health matters, if you get my drift. He insisted that she take an extended holiday, in other words, and go to France – to the museums and art galleries of Paris. Even more peculiar, though, he insisted that she take her friend along – a gentleman-friend, mind you, the painter Amos Roselli. I've met him once or twice. Bit of a bounder, if you ask me. Anyway, I gather his sister went with them, too - most likely to lend an air of respectability – though all still dashed peculiar, what!'

'Roselli? The name seems familiar,' Doctor Murry declares rather gruffly pressing an habitual, nervous index finger again onto the bridge of his nose to prevent any slippage of the pince-nez stationed there.

'Yes, dear, of course!' the doctor's wife interrupts, a hand lightly upon his sleeve. 'Wasn't that the young man we met here that evening, the one you brought in to record the remains? I hear he's a jolly fine artist, actually. He has shown at the Academy. And there was an exhibition recently, too. Such delicate brush work. Watts speaks highly of him, they say.'

'Oh yes, of course, that's right, my dear. Can't imagine what possessed me to ask for those drawings – we never did use them. I suppose it just seemed like a good idea at the time. Funny sort of chap. I think our society's obsession with opiates has a lot to answer for, don't you, Newman?'

The other man laughs and nods his concordance with this latest observation before continuing with his story. 'Yes, well anyway, off they went - Lady Bowlend and this Roselli chap on the steamer to Boulogne – though of course she never did reach France or the museums of Paris, did she, poor thing! Whether she slipped or was pushed or whether she simply threw herself over the side we'll never know. They do say she had emotional problems. Highly strung and all that. But, of course, never a good idea to go overboard at sea on a paddle steamer. Took her head clean off of her shoulders, they say - almost instantly. Nasty business.'

'Oh how awful!' Mrs Murry declares, clearly horrified but also, by the look of intense curiosity on her face, also keen to learn of all the lurid details. 'Lord Bowlend must have been devastated – I mean, how did he take it?'

'Old Bowlend – why, he took it all astonishingly well, I'd say,' Newman replies. 'Even went to identify the body, or what was left of it, some weeks later when it was washed ashore. But the Roselli chap was distraught. They detained him at first, on suspicion, but there was no motive of course, and no witnesses to the event, either. In the end even the French police realised he was probably not responsible - though of course that's not how Roselli would have felt about it. Returned to London a broken man, apparently. Said he would never pick up a brush again. So that exhibition of his must have been pretty old stuff, eh?'

'I believe so,' Mrs Murry replies. 'That would make sense, because they did tell me he was not taking on any new commissions. Well, well - what a tragedy!'

'So they did find the body - eventually?' the doctor inquires with morbid curiosity.

'The body, yes, some weeks later – but never the head.'

'Oh!' cries Mrs Murry, clutching a hand to her chest, breathless with horror, and several further renditions of 'how terrible!' or 'how ghastly!' are to be heard among the trio until all eyes turn towards the entrance and to a party of very loud and uncouth sounding guests arriving, led by none other than the right honourable Lord Bowlend himself, just stepping over the threshold.

'Missed the service? Oh well, bad luck!' Ramsey is heard to remark with a wink to one of his colleagues. He has an attractive and opulent-looking young woman on his arm who, though not small herself, seems diminutive against the prodigious bulk of the big man as he waddles from place to place, inspecting for himself with swift cursory glances the achievements of the renovation team. At length he spots Newman, greets him and, setting aside his lady for a moment, steers him away into a more discrete area of the Chapel, into the solitary and gloomy north isle that everyone else tends to avoid.

'Ramsey old boy. Sympathies. Dreadful business!' Newman declares, rather being carried along by the much bigger man still.

'Yes, most unfortunate. But there you are: life goes on, eh! You must come to the estate some time, Newman – some shooting perhaps, even from the upstairs windows again if you like, eh!'

Newman chuckles a little and nods his approval. He has only rarely been to Bowlend Court since that incident when Lady Daphne had ordered him from the house. He seems pleased – and his eyes also light with approval on the buxom young woman Ramsey has bought with him this evening, at just that moment inspecting the various memorial plaques in the Chancel.

'Nice little filly!' he observes, as if on a day at the races.

'The future Lady Bowlend,' the noble lord responds with an almost imperceptible licking of the lips. 'I'll introduce you in a moment – though you would have seen her on the Island that time.'

'Oh yes, that's right. That party you had. Yes, I remember. And she's a good girl is she?'

'She is,' Bowlend observes, his voice low. 'I've already done a spot of – er - reconnaissance, if you catch my meaning. And I can confidently report, therefore, that we have high hopes for the future – an heir, at last.'

'And the business of the firm - going from strength to strength, I hear, what! How's that purge in the boardroom progressing?'

'Splendid. All this unfortunate business has at least presented us with an opportunity to cull a few of the less productive members of the team – her bloody awful brother, for example. We got shot of him soon enough, and one or two of the others that we managed to fire by virtue of association with him. We can advance now, move forward unencumbered.'

But at this, Ramsey takes Newman by the arm once again, the same vice-like grip as before, and motions him still further aside and, eventually, with a firm palm on the small of his back, out of the Chapel altogether, guiding him. well away from the building; for there is, in fact, as Newman well-knows, something even more important to discuss and which this time requires the utmost privacy. The air outside is cool and already quite gloomy.

'So, Newman, you have been a good man,' Ramsey begins again – though this time in what for him is an untypically hushed voice as they stroll together past the execution sight with its wrought-iron railings and little memorial plaque there to the victims of the past. 'Even though your services were not required, after all, you won't be forgotten, don't worry, and you'll be rewarded just the same. The Swiss bank – I have arranged it all. Enough to keep you in Burgundy and cigars for a few more years.'

Newman nods his gratitude and, as if to emphasise his achievements, awards himself an extravagant intake of fresh air, puffing out his little thin chest in the process – but only succeeding in spluttering on the city fog which is as thick and caustic as ever this evening. 'Funny how it all worked out, though,' he remarks once his coughing has subsided, his voice uncommonly hushed. 'You're a lucky bugger, Ramsey. Always have been. Oh, don't worry, we were ready to do the deed. We were going to see to it that she never came back – nor Roselli if we could manage it. But on the steamer - it was all rather busy. There was no opportunity to dispatch her there, or so we thought. We decided to bide our time, therefore, to wait until everyone reached Paris, then make it happen in the hotel, like a burglary gone wrong – you know the sort of thing. But there you are, we didn't need to worry about any of it, did we! Fate intervened.'

'Right enough!' Ramsey agrees with a little snort and a chuckle under his breath. 'Even I didn't expect *that!*'

'What was it like, by the way, when you saw the body?' Newman inquires with a macabre turn.

'What do you mean – how did I feel? Well, there wasn't' much left of it, to be frank, not after its encounter with the paddle wheels and nearly a week in the English Channel.'

Newman nods bleakly at the vision. No, it would not have been nice. There would have been little there amid the hideous remains to remind anyone of the smart, vivacious creature that had once been Lady Bowlend - the beautiful woman that even he, like most of the other men in Ramsey's circle, had been just a little in awe of - and actually rather admired.

In silence, the twilight falling, the gentlemen in their top hats, figures of such absurdly differing heights and builds, one so thin and inconsequential, the other so gross and enormous, continue to walk for a while on the pavements around the edge of the green, their heels echoing off the walls of the ancient buildings, their senses choosing not to be filled with the fragrant greenery of spring, the new leaves on the plane trees, the occasional desperate melody of the songbirds, but instead with the intoxicating resonance of the city, the ever-present grumbling of the traffic; the busy sounds of the river and the commerce of the docks nearby - with all the ships, colliers, barges and tugs, the voices and cries of warehouse workers, stevedores, carpenters, and engineers - all serving to move the goods of the nation, including Ramsey's own manufactured weapons of course, to the furthest reaches and outposts of the empire. Britain – the workshop of the world! Even in the darkness of the early evening, the whole area has about it a clamour of industriousness and blind purpose hard to ignore: music to his ears.

'We're going to make this country great, aren't we, Tommy!' Ramsey observes warmly as he raises his eyes to survey the silhouetted skyline of spires and belching chimneys across the river. 'People like you and me – we're going to make it so great that people will be in awe of us for centuries to come.'

To which Tommy nods his total and unequivocal approval, receiving a hearty, celebratory slap on the back from his companion, the reasons for which are promptly revealed with: 'Anyway Newman, it's a honeymoon in Berlin for me this summer. An important day for the firm, too, what! You will be coming to the wedding, I take it?'

'Oh yes, of course,' Tommy replies with suitable enthusiasm. He has been to the two previous ones, he reminds his friend. Why not this one, as well! To which, in the manner of two rather over-grown schoolboys, accompanied by further slaps on the back and nudging of ribs, they return side by side to the hallowed walls and welcoming hubbub of the Tudor Chapel.

Chapter Twenty-Two

Wild Garlic

'You must miss her terribly, Sir?' Beth ventures to suggest as she comes out to collect the morning tea tray, half questioning, half commenting almost as if to herself on his wretched state of indolence – one in which he scarcely seems to move from his rocking chair for hours on end, a much used piece of furniture now which either she or the butler must manoeuvre into place on the veranda for him almost every day after lunch so he might catch the welcome rays of the sun as it breaks around the corner of the East Wing. The family home here is a substantial building – a place now under his stewardship entirely since the death of his father last year - yet one which he does not seem to relish living in at all as yet. And she can understand well-enough the reasons for it. For he, just like her, is still mourning. Still in a state of shock.

Shielding his eyes against the brightness, Amos regards her for a moment with surprise. He should, as master of such a substantial estate as this, really disapprove of any servant, even Beth, his housekeeper, talking in such a familiar manner, but he does not. Instead, and noticing her hesitancy over whether she should remain, he motions with a little movement of his hand for her to take a seat nearby; something that she does often of late, in fact, sitting with him for an hour perhaps after lunch, without a word, providing some company in his solitude. For his part, he regards her, more than ever now, as someone he can rely on, even confide in occasionally; and it pleases him in a strange kind of way that after so many weeks since his return from France, it should be she who has finally broken the silence and spoken of it, that one dreadful issue that has dominated his existence for half an eternity, it seems, and yet over which he has hardly been able to say a word to anyone.

'How long have you been with me now Beth?' he asks with a note of surprise in his voice, as if the question had only just occurred to him.

'Over two years now, Sir,' she replies taking her seat close by with some diffidence and sitting bolt upright as if at any moment she would be dismissed and told to get on with her duties.

Amos casts his vision outwards to the wide expanse of lawns, already well-lit by spring sunshine and which extends way down towards the river, taking in the beautiful vista of winding woods and well-tended shrubberies which he remembers from his childhood and youth and which now belong to him in their entirety, of course, the owner of all he surveys. Then his eyes return again towards the diminutive young woman seated next to him in the little mop cap. And suddenly he smiles – the first time she has seen him smile in weeks. And she notices, too, how very blue his eyes are, reflecting the blue sky, no doubt - so brightly blue they are almost overpowering in their intensity. She notices some silver-grey hair at the sides of his temples, too, in the otherwise still-almost black wavy locks. He is the most handsome, of men, she concludes, and surely this self-imposed solitude and despondency is a terrible waste on one so gifted – for he has not painted at all now, not one brush stroke since his return.

'Two years. What a lot you have been through with me in that time,' he says. 'You have suffered as much as any of us, I should think, and have born it all with dignity. Well Beth, I am glad you have broken your silence today and have asked me that question. And in response to it, I am going to relate to you something very important. I am going to tell you because I must tell somebody – and of all the people I know, be it the most humble of servants or the most eminent of landed gentry, you are one of the few I feel I can really trust. In fact, I am coming to realise that you are probably the most trustworthy person I have ever known in my life, and certainly one of the most loyal and selfless. And yes, you are correct, I will certainly miss my lovely Daphne, as I am sure you will too. But I have to tell you that the impression you have of how our loss has come about is not entirely based on reality. Ah, I can see you are puzzled. Let me explain - and please Beth, do make yourself comfortable. Sit back into your chair and be at ease, because it is going to be quite a long story. And please relinquish your cap, too. Let me look at your lovely red hair in the sunshine.'

She does his bidding, unfastening the little ribbon at the back of her cap and gently removing it, though she finds it difficult to sit back, despite his instructions - and when she finally does succeed, she can only stare ahead into space at first, unblinking, her fingers tightly interlaced, not entirely at one with this unusual tone of intimacy.

'Firstly, I have some good and also some bad news for you Beth - and for you in particular.'

'For me, Sir?'

'Yes, that's right. There is the matter of that small allowance that you receive in the post each week - yes, don't worry, I do know all about it, and I do not mind in the least. It's nothing to do with me, either, by the way - I can tell you that. But I can also solve the mystery for you concerning its source. It has been sent to you via a solicitor in New Eltham, as you know, a Mister Parker. He has in fact been acting on the behalf of Lady Bowlend. It is she who has been your benefactor. Don't be anxious. She made arrangements in her will for it be continued in perpetuity, or rather it will continue until you marry - a minor detail, that perhaps you are not aware of. That was the only condition - the bad-news part, I suppose, of my message: that it must all come to an end then, whenever that might be.'

'Oh how kind of her, Sir!' Beth exclaims, almost tearful by this time.

'Indeed it is,' he agrees, and then adds with a rueful smile: 'I hope it will not discourage you from walking down the isle one day if you ever encounter *Mister Right*.'

'Oh no, that would never be a hindrance, Sir,' Beth asserts, her voice somewhat breathless by now and dabbing at the corner of her eyes with a little lace handkerchief. 'Should I ever be so fortunate, Sir, I would only ever marry for happiness - for love. And that would be something far more important than any sum of money.'

He nods his understanding. 'Well put, Beth,' he murmurs with approval and almost a note of admiration, she feels, which makes her blush. 'I am glad we have gotten that out of the way, because I want to get on now and impart to you just exactly what it was that occurred that day, that terrible fateful day when we lost our dear Lady Bowlend. There is, in fact, quite a lot more to it than you realise, and I rather suspect that you will find what I have to say of particular interest. It is widely reported in the press both here and abroad, that Daphne Lady Bowlend met her end on the Folkestone to Boulogne steamer, perhaps due to the taking of her own life, or perhaps even by foul play. No one has really ever been able to determine with total confidence the cause. You and I both know only too well how much she feared for her life towards the end and of the extreme emotional strain she was under at the time. Her husband, Lord Bowlend, was especially keen on the idea of me accompanying her to France, and he knew full well that I would not refuse - because to do so would have left her terribly exposed. He had us both where he wanted us, therefore, out of the country, alone and vulnerable. Clever. That is why Daphne insisted on inviting her friend, my sister Margaret, as well, for the Paris journey. Safety in numbers, you see. But of course none of us ever reached our intended destination.

'Indeed no, Sir,' says Beth and looks at him in an almost pitying way.

'The body, once it was located, was formally identified as hers - and Lord Bowlend buried her with all due honours not long afterwards in the family vault at Kensal Green. But Beth, I can tell you now - trusting that you will treat this with your usual utmost discretion - that the body buried there in the sepulchre is not that of Lady Daphne. I can tell you that with the utmost certainty.'

'Sir? How? I do not understand.'

'I mean it is not her body because of a curious and ingenious plan that she and I hatched up shortly before we departed for France. We knew that her life was in danger, and perhaps mine also - and that sooner or later the powerful enemies that were being marshalled by her husband would overtake us. We even suspected there were people onboard the steamer with us that day who were of sinister intent and were watching our movements. I even recognised one of them as a friend of her husband, a cur of a man I had met briefly one weekend while staying at Bowlend Court.

'On board, Daphne, my sister and I had been given one of the few cabins available thanks to the largesse of the noble lord, and it was from here that we put into operation our plan for her escape - a kind of stowaway-in-reverse exercise. Instead of smuggling someone onboard, in other words, we resolved instead to smuggle someone off - and that someone was Daphne. We had our luggage with us, and so we used some of my clothing to disguise her - a nice pair of tweed trousers and a topcoat - all of which managed to cover and to flesh out her slender figure - to render her appearance quite masculine, in fact. A dear-stalker hat was used to cover up her hair, which was pinned tightly into place - until, that is, we quickly realised that any head of hair thus arranged still tended to look a tad long and feminine, with wispy bits hanging down - and so we took the drastic step of cutting away almost all of her beautiful hair. She was given what the barbers refer to as *a short back and sides,* in other words, much to her consternation and, to be truthful, a little to our amusement as well. With a tiny piece of that same hair we then fashioned a handsome moustache; glued it into place - and the result was a very personable young man of about twenty odd years standing there before us. Her own clothes, meanwhile, we stowed away in my elm chest, the one containing my painting equipment and which always contains lots of props and bits of clothing, anyway, of course - so even if it was searched, no one would be any the wiser.

'Anyway, with the old Daphne safely put away in the elm chest, this gallant young fellow of ours that we had created was one of the first to disembark when we arrived at Boulogne.

Amid the first chaos of docking, what with all the porters and the paper boys jumping on board, and the seamen and bookies' runners jumping off, she joined the throng.'

'But what about her documents, Sir?' Beth asks, almost mesmerised by the bizarre tale. 'Did she not need to show a passport or ...?'

'No, the French have ceased demanding to see documents of that kind at their ports or borders. And there was no passenger-list, of course, for such a short journey. They probably didn't even ask for her ticket at Boulogne. We were pretty certain she would get through, therefore. Once we were satisfied that she was ashore, and long before the bulk of the first class passengers had begun to disembark, we raised the alarm and informed the captain that one among our number had gone missing. The ship was searched, but of course no trace of Lady Bowlend was found, nor could the people ashore report seeing anybody answering her description having left the ship - and so the suspicion that she must have gone overboard was fostered in the minds of those responsible. The gendarmerie were called, and I was questioned at length and, as you know, even taken into custody for some hours. Once it was learned that Daphne had been under some considerable emotional strain at the time, however, and that she had already attempted to take her own life on at least one occasion – a fact confirmed by none other than Lord Bowlend himself via telegraph and who also came over the very next day to assist the police - they released me.'

'But what about the body?' Beth inquires, her voice breathless with astonishment and confusion. 'They found her, Sir, did they not?'

'Yes, and until then the whole thing would have remained an open case, of course, with no certainty either way regarding what had occurred. But then something remarkable happened, more extraordinary than any of us could ever have envisaged. As providence would have it, a few days after Daphne's disappearance news came of the discovery of a woman's body– washed up on the coast of Brittany. It was not the body of Daphne, however, who was by that time at liberty somewhere in France, but that of some other poor soul who had met a tragic end at sea - perhaps even by her own doing, who knows – but at any rate someone who, most significantly, was minus her head. Not only was this discovery a stroke of good fortune for us, but it was also an opportunity too good to pass up for Lord Bowlend, who promptly went over again and identified the body as that of Daphne's - with as much certainty, he said, as was possible under the circumstances. Whether he really believed it was his late wife's corpse or not when they rolled back the sheet in the mortuary that day and revealed the grizzly spectre we shall never know, for the body was badly damaged and decomposed. But with a new lady, a fresh amour in his sights and the wish to marry again as soon as possible it must have seemed like a heaven-sent opportunity for him to confirm his wife's demise and thus put the whole matter to rest. The body was returned to England and then came the funeral which you and I both attended at Kensal Green.'

'And Lady Bowlend herself? What has happened to her?'

Amos averts his eyes, appearing to her now, for the first time since he commenced his story, to be somewhat distressed. 'I honestly don't know,' he replies. 'Daphne, Lady Bowlend – as we agreed that afternoon on board the steamer – was to die, at least metaphorically: heralding a complete break with her past, her family, her commitments, *everything*. She realised only too well that this was the only remedy, the only thing that could guarantee her survival. She will never return, therefore, never disclose her whereabouts – for that would be to expose my perjury, of course - but has instead, I believe, established a new life overseas, possibly in America. So in a sense, yes, she would appreciate more than anyone that her *death* must remain permanent ... for all of our sakes. And no matter what her husband might have thought of the whole thing, no matter what he might have suspected, he would have come to the same conclusion – if only to serve his own interests.

'Anyway, it was such a hurried and spontaneous parting that day on the boat, that there was no time for elaborate farewells, no time for tears. We shall not see her again, Beth. May God bless her and keep her safe! She has plenty of friends and associates overseas, I know that, particularly in France and America who will help her re-arrange her future. But it will not be a future shared with any of us any longer. And perhaps that is just as well. I loved her dearly - you know that - but the pain of being together was almost too much to bear at times, so that now we are parted forever it is almost a relief – and I can look at that final picture, look at her tragic likeness on that wall back there in the house, with her standing on the headland and all those laurel leaves tearing around her like arrow heads, and not feel so hurt or desolate any longer, knowing that she has gone and gone forever.'

Beth continues to stare in amazement at her employer and for quite some time, too, before venturing to voice her acknowledgement and her understanding of what he has told her - shedding a further tear as well, though perhaps more of happiness this time. Knowing that the woman she had come to admire so much and has mourned so deeply these past few weeks is in fact still among the living, is a joy almost too much to comprehend. She dabs at her moist cheek with her sleeve - a little scowl of self-reproach upon her face - before meeting his eyes again with a renewed smile which makes her look quite beautiful.

And then with the strengthening sun – just at that moment emerging from some cloud - the fragrances of hawthorn blossom mixed with rosemary and the astonishing and evocative aroma of wild garlic, comes wafting through from the garden, born on a warming breeze. It is a revelation to him, bringing back a thousand memories and sweet recollections of the past, his childhood, his youth, all at once. He feels almost overwhelmed by that special blend of fragrances, the scent of May and the sensations that accompany it.

'Beth, I am suddenly feeling much better,' he announces. 'Look - the sun is shining! Will you come with me for a stroll in the garden, and I will continue to impart the details of my story to you there.

And together they step down from the veranda and begin to walk from the shadows, he making sure she remains at his side and not lagging behind - as it is her instinct still to do. He'll have none of that this afternoon, he says, and makes it plain as they go that she should keep up with him. They walk, side by side, therefore - together towards the source of the fragrance and then right through it, allowing it to brush upon their clothing, immersing themselves in all the magical, intoxicating odours of springtime. And he realises that the scent of spring flowers is something eternal, something that will come each year with its message of renewal, unending and perfect in its disregard for all the trivial sorrows that people allow to mar their lives. And although it will no longer be Daphne at his side to share in it, there will be other young souls who will embrace and hold hands and walk through gardens and meadows, experiencing just these very same fragrances. It will continue forever. And why should he, still so young and full of vitality, shut himself away from this wonderful flow and tide of life?

'Oh Sir, how will she fare - alone in a foreign country?' Beth says, gaining confidence now to speak her mind. 'Alone and with no property, no husband to aid her?'

'Oh, I wouldn't be too anxious, Beth,' he answers with a rueful smile. 'The quantity of jewels she had upon her person that day, alone, would have been sufficient to make for a comfortable new start for anyone in this world. Her husband was also, if nothing else, always generous - excessively so, I understand. She would only ever spend the half of whatever he gave her. The remainder was always squirreled away somewhere. She'll be fine.'

'You could go overseas yourself, though, Sir, could you not?' Beth suggests, lifting her head towards him as if delivered of a moment's inspiration. 'Perhaps there is a way you could locate her, and then you too could begin a new life together. A happy ending to a sad story.'

'No, I do not think so, Beth. Why should I do that! I am young enough to start over. And, anyway, I want a life without pain now. Oh, of course, I won't forget her; and probably every time I pick up a brush and paint a face - as I shall do again, have no fear - there will always be a part of her in it, always present in what I do. But I can move on now. We can all of us move on. Things will be better for us now, Beth, I am convinced of that - and more settled. We will increase our staff here, too, take on a new head maid and housekeeper - someone to do the duties that you have to do now.'

'Another housekeeper? But then what shall I do, Sir?'

'Well ... you can look after it all. What do you say? I will be busy, after all. I only have to give the word, let it be known that I am available, and the work will flood in. And no more allegorical painting. I shan't be doing that kind of thing too often anymore. After all, we are all of us here now - alive now in the nineteenth century, aren't we - not living in the dark ages! I am going to paint the people of today - in all their splendour, in all their amazing self-confidence and elegance.'

With a little gasp of pleasure, Beth nods her acquiescence, happy for him and excited, too, by this latest turn in her fortunes, while Amos for his part begins to realise that he is, after all, quite possibly rather a lucky man, to have come through it all unscathed like this, to have such a lovely and resourceful young woman walking here at his side, the afternoon sun shining on her red hair and making her glow with its fine, gentle radiance - she, the most humble of all people and yet one who has somehow humbled him - and done so without even being aware of it herself, as if by some invisible, magical process. It is a good feeling - something, he reflects, closely resembling what most other people in their simple and unsophisticated ways have always called *happiness* - an unfamiliar sensation for him and, he has to admit, for the time being at least, a seductively interesting one as well.

'You know what, Beth, he says turning to face her for a moment, 'perhaps it is time I did a portrait of *you*. That would be a good way to start back, don't you think?'

She fumbles for a moment with her spectacles in her hands, considering his proposal before raising herself up to her full height and looking directly up into his eyes, for the first time ever considering him as an equal - for she understands now the purpose he has asked her to fulfil. 'Yes ... as good a challenge as any, Mister Roselli, I should think,' she replies with a confidence that pleases him greatly.

They do not notice much more of the afternoon as it passes. Together, arm in arm, they walk in their garden, look at the swans on the river, stroll around the whole of the building several times, then down to the big iron gates at the bottom of the drive with their elaborate spiral bars and scrolls, their tall stone pillars that denote a great house within, and then back up again, where he takes her hand in his – speaking all the while of the future that they plan. They do not notice the time as it flies, and they do not notice the weather's changing or the mist that moistens the air and hangs in tiny drops of dew upon the fragrant branches of the juniper and pine trees as the afternoon draws on. They do not notice the lamp that is lit in the porch of the house welcoming them in whenever they should choose. Nor do they notice the lovely dark-haired woman who is walking nearby along the road her face veiled, and who pauses for just one moment, hardly visible, at the foot of the drive. For a moment she lifts her veil as she glances their way, quite hidden behind the tracery of the gates, before continuing on to the end of the lane where a horse and carriage are waiting. There is a further cloud of mist rolling in, dissolving everything it touches, like a fog now. And in a moment the woman is gone, vanished silently, like a ghost of someone who once lived but has become no more than a passing memory.